STROKE OF FATE

LILAH LANCE

TITAN SECURITY BOOK II

To the girls who believed in fate enough to take the leap....

AUTHORS NOTE

Welcome to the second installment of the Titan Security series.

Each book in the series has its own standalone HEA (Happily Ever After), but they're all inter-connected by a larger mystery.

The stories in Titan occur simultaneously, with Easter eggs and clues scattered throughout to help you uncover the full picture.

While this book can be enjoyed on its own, it is recommended starting with Stroke of Luck, Book I, to avoid spoilers or to gain a deeper understanding of the evolving mysteries within Titan.

MISSION BRIEFING

Welcome to Titan...

You are now a part of a team of security professionals working on saving face, saving lives, and sometimes saving their enemies.

Your objective, if you choose to accept it, is *an awakening.*

Your team consists of:

Mr. Lucas Devereaux & Agent Eva Monroe

Together, you and your team will uncover secrets in the interconnected web of lies that Titan exists within.

I pray fate is kind to you on your journey with Eva and Lucas.

SEVEN YEARS AGO
EVIE

I WOULD NEVER FORGET THE DAY I MET GABRIEL.

Someone was talking to me, a doctor or nurse, I didn't know, I couldn't tell. Their voice seemed distant and muffled, as if underwater.

"I'm sorry, Miss Santos. Your mom's gone."

The words sank into my bones. My stomach lurched, and the sterile hospital air felt suffocating.

Mama was dead.

The cheap plastic chair I sat in dug into my legs, but I barely registered the discomfort, numb to everything but the devastating news.

We didn't have family, and I hadn't really experienced loss.

One of the neighbors lost their dog once and cried up a storm, their sobs echoing through the thin apartment walls.

I didn't understand.

"Miss Santos," the doctor said, their brow creased with concern. "Are you all right?"

I nodded woodenly, my neck stiff, barely able to tear my gaze away from Mama lying motionless in the hospital bed.

Hot tears pricked the backs of my eyes, but I blinked them away.

This is all to be a bad dream.

She was just pretending.

Mama was fine.

Cheerful birdsong and the hum of lawnmowers, construction, and life drifted in through the window—deceptively pleasant sounds on the worst day of my life.

1

The sun kept shining.

None of this is real.

I clung to Mama's hand, her skin cool and papery beneath my fingers.

I wanted to feel her hands in my hair as she braided it, laughing as she called it cherry cola, dark with deep red hues. She needed to wake up.

Mama needed to come to graduation to see me make it. I didn't even understand stage 4 cancer.

How could it be *four*? We hadn't even seen the other three. The ugly word ricocheted around my skull—cancer, cancer, cancer. Mama didn't really have that, did she?

This wasn't real.

The squeak of the door hinge made me look up, blinking away the hot tears that blurred my vision.

Are they coming to take me away from her already?

But it wasn't just the doctor this time. A handsome man stood beside him, his posture rigid, dressed in a gray suit striking and imposing.

He was gorgeous, towering over the doctor like he'd descended from heaven.

His wheat-blond hair gleamed under the harsh fluorescent lights, and his pale, icy eyes locked onto the doctor with intense focus.

They exchanged words I couldn't hear over the roaring in my ears.

Then the blond man's pale gaze landed on me, and I froze, suddenly hyperaware of my tear-stained face and rumpled school uniform.

His eyes widened almost imperceptibly for a split second, and a current of something I couldn't name crackled through the room.

Even in my daze, I sensed something profound had just happened— a seismic shift I was too numb to comprehend.

Then, to my surprise, the man began moving toward me with purposeful strides.

Nervous sweat beaded on my neck as I fidgeted, slowly rising to my feet.

Why was he coming here?

As he stepped into the room, the scent of his expensive cologne wafted over me, out of place among the sterile hospital odors.

Up close, he looked even more like an otherworldly being, an angel coming to escort Mama to a better place.

"You can't take her!" I cried out, my voice trembling as I planted myself defiantly in front of Mama's bed.

I was acutely aware of my own insignificance in the presence of this man, his imposing form eclipsing everything else like a mountain blotting out the sun.

Surprise flickered in his pale eyes at my sudden outburst, his brows drawing together slightly.

"Eva Santos?" His deep, resonant voice held a note of command that expected obedience.

I nodded, barely suppressing a wince at the use of my full name.

Eva sounded foreign to my ears, too formal and grown-up compared to the affectionate "Evie" I'd been called all my life.

Only strangers and authority figures ever used my real name; this man was clearly both.

"Are you here to take me to foster care?" I asked my voice small and tinged with apprehension, the words sticking in my dry throat. "Or to take my mama?"

To my surprise, his expression softened, the hard lines of his chiseled face relaxing into something more compassionate.

Warmth seeped into his pale eyes like sunlight melting a layer of frost. "My name's Gabriel Monroe. I'm your next of kin. I suppose that makes you family."

Next of kin? We didn't have any family.

He paused, his full lips pressing together as if carefully considering his next words. "I received a phone call about your mom. I came as fast as I could."

I blinked rapidly, my vision blurring with unshed tears as I struggled to comprehend his words.

"What?" I stammered, my voice sounding distant to my ears, drowned out by the roaring confusion in my mind. "H...how? Mama doesn't—"

"Your sister."

"Isobel?" The name felt foreign on my tongue, stirring distant memories within me like dust motes swirling.

Fragments of a time when our parents were still together, before their separation tore our family apart, danced through my mind.

I vaguely recalled an older sister, her voice echoing through the halls as she screamed that she didn't want to leave, her absence leaving a gaping void in my life that ached like a phantom limb.

Mama had always cried when she'd talk about Isobel. Like she hadn't wanted to let her other daughter go.

"She's my wife," Gabriel said, his words heavy with restrained emotion.

"She couldn't come get you, but I could. I know I'm moving too fast, but..." His voice trailed off, his gaze shifting to my mother's still form.

For the first time, I saw a flicker of vulnerability in his eyes, a crack in his stoic façade.

"She looks a lot like your sister."

I studied Gabriel, taking in his expensive attire—the crisp lines of his tailored suit, the gleaming watch on his wrist.

An air of authority clung to him like a second skin, his tall frame exuding power and control. The faint scent of his cologne—something woodsy and masculine—mixed with the sharp antiseptic smell of the hospital. And altogether...Gabriel looked a lot more put-together than me.

This man was married to a sister I barely knew.

I wondered *who* he was.

"I'm your family," Gabriel continued, his large hands producing a stack of documents from a leather folder I hadn't noticed earlier.

"I'd like to take you home with me. I have a house in Connecticut. Would you be okay with that?"

"I...I—"

"It's okay if you don't know what to say. You don't have to do anything. Losing someone you love is a lot," Gabriel's gruff voice was thick with empathy, wrapping around me like a soothing balm. "It's okay if you want to think about it."

Tears threatened to spill hot and fast down my cheeks as I nodded, my throat constricting with emotion.

Do not cry.

Do not cry.

Do not cry. I didn't want to cry in front of this man, this stranger, but the tidal wave of grief was too strong to hold back.

"Where is Isa?" I managed to whisper, my voice cracking.

Something flashed across Gabriel's handsome face, his ice-blue eyes glistening.

"She didn't—couldn't make it," he explained hoarsely, blinking rapidly.

"She wanted me to tell you she loves you so much and wishes she could be here." He paused, clearing his throat. "I promise I'll explain

4

everything. The doctors say you haven't left her side in two days. You must be hungry."

My stomach clenched at the mention of food, hollow with neglected hunger. I couldn't remember the last time I ate; all my energy had been focused on willing Mama to wake up.

"We can get breakfast," Gabriel offered, his voice warm. "I know it's probably the last thing you want to do right now, but it might help a little. At least that's what your sister believes." The casual mention of her caught me off guard, a bittersweet ache blooming beneath my ribs.

In broken Spanish, the consonants were awkward in his tongue. Gabriel added. *"Isa says it isn't the same as your mama's cooking, but she liked the idea of cake for breakfast."*

A weak smile tugged at the corners of my mouth. But reality crashed over me anew—Mama would never bustle around our tiny kitchen again.

"Gabriel." I tested his name, tasting the syllables. Like the archangel. His eyes, pale and piercing, softened at the sound, honeyed warmth melting the icy hue.

"I don't want to leave her," I confessed brokenly, tears finally making their way down my face as I looked at Mama's body, so small and fragile against the white hospital sheets. "I don't want to go."

"I know," he murmured roughly. "She was your everything."

He looked at me like...he loved Mama too.

I trembled, hugging myself as if I could somehow hold the broken pieces of my heart together.

Gabriel's gaze met mine, pale eyes brimming with compassion and understanding.

"Isa sent you?" I whispered, hope, a fragile bird fluttering in my chest.

He blinked slowly, inclining his head.

The tears were coming faster as I felt something shifting. Something monumental was happening.

I didn't know who moved. I just knew I was in the wool of his suit jacket, soft against my cheek. His arms, strong and solid, banded around me as great shuddering silent sobs wracked my body.

Mama was gone.

And I was going to Connecticut.

❦

GABRIEL HIRED A TEAM OF PROFESSIONALS TO PACK UP MAMA'S HOUSE.

He had offered to stay, to uproot his life and start anew in the place that held so many memories for me.

I couldn't bear the thought of being surrounded by the ghosts of my past, every corner a painful reminder of what I had lost.

I caught Gabriel in the kitchen standing at our fridge, looking out of place in his polished outfit in the colorful explosion of my soon-to-be old life.

He was picking out some photos of Isobel growing up, held up by refrigerator magnets, his eyes soft and far away.

I pretended not to notice the way he tucked them into his coat.

I pressed the photos I had of her in my room into his hand. "You can have her."

Then Gabriel took me to his estate in Connecticut.

The structure seemed to go on forever, its elegant lines and intricate details speaking of wealth beyond my wildest imaginings.

As I trailed my hand along the walls, the smooth, cool stone beneath my fingertips grounded me, reminding me that this was real, not some fever dream.

Gabriel led me through the halls.

The spiral staircase in the foyer went on forever, its wrought iron railing a delicate filigree against the stark white walls.

This is a home for a family.

"Do you and Isa have a lot of kids?" I asked, my voice echoing in the foyer.

I could picture the patter of tiny feet on the polished floors, the peals of laughter ringing through the halls.

A shadow passed over Gabriel's face, his ice-blue eyes clouding with some unfathomable emotion. "No, I don't have children."

I sensed I had hit a nerve, but I didn't understand.

He led me to a room that seemed to be made entirely of glass, the floor-to-ceiling windows bathing the space.

The solarium, as he called it, the name, was foreign and exotic on my tongue as the lush greenery that filled the room.

"This is all yours," he declared, his voice soft and earnest.

I was overwhelmed, my senses bombarded by the sheer magnitude of it all. I had never known such…space.

Mama and I had lived in a cramped apartment, with every nook and cranny serving a purpose. Our lives folded and tucked into it.

Gabriel would check on me periodically, but his knock on the door

6

was tentative and unsure. He would ask if I needed anything, wanted to go to school, or required new clothes.

Slowly, I began to venture out, my bare feet sinking into the thick, lush carpets as I wandered the halls. It was hard to stop crying once I started. I had my own little world with Mama. Her hugs.

I found him in the kitchen, sometimes making coffee and on the phone and his laptop, working quickly on something—the cool marble countertops and gleaming gold accents surrounding him.

He looked like he fit right in.

Someone was talking to him, and he was busy, so I went to dart away until I saw him move.

He didn't say a word.

He didn't look up.

I saw his arm come out, and I slid into his frame, seeking comfort in this person who so openly offered it to me. Gabriel always hugged me.

I held him for long moments as he rubbed my head while the person on the other end continued talking, and I found comfort in his hugs.

I would curl up in the breakfast nook, losing myself in the pages of a book and the muted chirping of birds in the backyard we had.

I had grown up alone despite having lots of friends out here.

I didn't really have anyone, but a lot had happened.

Gabriel thought maybe I should've taken a break to process everything.

Through it all, Isobel remained conspicuously absent, her presence nothing more than a ghost in the mausoleum of a house.

One night, as I sat at the nook, the soft cashmere of my new sweater brushed against my skin, a whisper of luxury that still felt foreign and undeserved.

I tugged at the hem, my fingers worrying the delicate fabric as I gathered the courage to voice the question that had haunted me since our arrival.

"Where's Isobel?" I asked, my voice wavering slightly.

A knot of unease twisted in my stomach. I tried to push it aside.

Gabriel had been so kind, so generous in the wake of my unimaginable loss.

He wouldn't hurt me.

Would he?

When he stood and walked over to me, his footsteps heavy on the hardwood floor, I braced myself for the worst.

7

He pulled up a chair beside me, larger than I had noticed, the scrape of the legs against the floor making me twitch.

He looked at me, his eyes filled with remorse, and I felt my heart sink.

"I'm sorry for not telling you earlier. I wasn't entirely honest about your sister..." He began as my heart sank a bit more. "I *am* married to her..." I barely heard him.

Isobel was *gone*. She had *died* just weeks before Mama.

The words seemed to hang in the air, thick and suffocating. I felt like I couldn't breathe, my chest constricting as the reality of his words sank in.

Gabriel rushed on, explaining that they had worked together and Isobel had talked about me often. She had wanted to find me after our father passed away. So we could be a family.

He had known how important I was to her, so he had come to find me instead.

"I'm sorry...fate at the worst times." His voice was strained, the words jumbled, but his eyes were red and brilliant.

Unyielding in honesty.

I sat there, numb and reeling.

The weight of his revelation settled on my shoulders like a physical burden, pressing me down into the unyielding wood of the chair. Everything hurt. I ached.

And so did he.

"She's gone too?" *Too*. Gabriel had— "What about my dad?"

I had to have had a father, right?

But Gabriel had said he was my next of kin.

Which meant...

His head tipped back like he was struggling with emotions.

"I don't know how to do this." His eyes were rapidly blinking. I didn't agree. "Your sister was better, but I—it's just you."

Just me. "And me." He put his hand across his heart where he rubbed the space. "I'm here. I'm not going anywhere. You're my family. As much as I am yours."

He held his other hand with his palm up, and I didn't think—I just took it. We're family.

I tried to process what he was saying to reconcile this new information with the fragmented memories I had of my sister or the father I hadn't known.

Gabriel's face etched with genuine concern and sorrow; I couldn't find it in myself to be angry with him. *Just me.*

He had done so much for me already, opening his home and heart to a virtual stranger.

The fact that he was Isobel's husband—that he had loved her enough to marry her—only solidified my trust in him.

"Are you...are you angry with me, Eva?" he asked, placing his hand over his heart. No, I wasn't. I couldn't be. I knew if he had told me at the hospital, I would've been reeling. Two losses in one day? But...he had...I looked at him, my throat tight with emotion. It was the first time I became aware he wanted to protect me from pain.

"No. It is just a lot," I managed to say, my voice sounding small and distant to my own ears. "You can call me Evie."

Gabriel nodded, his lips tipping up a little as I saw his eyes water, his relief palpable.

"Do you want to go to talk to someone? Reed goes to therapy; he says it helps."

I liked Reed and his tattoos; he was sensible and friendly, and Gabriel privately called him his brother.

"I've never been to therapy," I admitted.

Gabriel's expression softened. "I can talk to Reed."

"Do you...can I see pictures of her?" I watched as he took his lower lip into his mouth, his broad chest rising and falling beneath his sweater. I could feel his energy shift.

The dim lighting of the room cast shadows across his chiseled features. He really was beautiful.

The raw emotion in his eyes was palpable, and I didn't want to push him, but a tangible presence seemed to fill the space between us.

He had lost her, too, and it was etched into every line of his face.

And he still picked me up.

"Right now or after dinner?"

Something in the way he looked at me, the vulnerability and trust in his gaze, made me feel like we were sharing a secret.

"After dinner," I replied softly, offering him a small smile.

He blinked slowly, his long lashes brushing against his cheeks as he tipped his head in acknowledgment. "Thank you," he murmured.

I couldn't fathom why this man, who had given me so much, was thanking me. It was clear that everything he had done and every kindness he had shown me was born out of his love for Isobel.

Just her.

For me.

9

After dinner, we sat together on the plush sofa, and Gabriel shared photos of my sister.

I could tell he liked one in particular. She was grinning ear to ear in a red dress, and Gabriel—he was...

"Mama would've loved you." I murmured as I looked at the picture, then to Gabriel, who looked surprised by that.

Just because my parents had split up didn't mean Mama didn't love Isobel.

"Can I take a photo of that?" I asked tentatively, sensing the energy that flowed from him. There was something in his eyes that he held for my sister.

I didn't know what it was.

He looked like he was a little reluctant, but he nodded, his eyes never leaving the image as he sent it to me on the new phone he had gifted me.

Weeks later, I caught a glimpse of her name, in elegant script, tattooed over his heart as he emerged from the gym, the ink stark against his sweat-slick skin.

As time passed, I learned more about Gabriel's company and the people who worked for him.

There was Reed, his best friend, and the brother had eyes that, while they looked volatile, were mostly calm and friendly.

He was the face of Titan, and Gabriel ran it from a place where he felt comfortable.

Selena Tavares was a vivacious green-eyed brunette, welcoming me with open arms and a warm smile.

Her sassy comments—a mix of English and Spanish—never failed to make me laugh.

I noticed the way Gabriel watched her closely, a protective gleam in his eye.

I met Nathan Wyatt, a charming and carefree man whose grins and laid-back attitude stood in stark contrast to the intensity of the others.

But somehow, it worked.

They all fit together like pieces of a puzzle.

~

WITH GABRIEL'S GUIDANCE, I BEGAN HOMESCHOOLING, LOSING MYSELF IN the comfort of the solarium he had built for me.

The lush greenery and the warm sunlight streaming through the glass walls became my sanctuary, a place where I could escape the weight of my grief and focus on my studies.

But despite the newfound stability and luxury, I walked on eggshells, terrified that one misstep would shatter everything. I never messed up, never questioned him, and I stayed on...his good side.

I was afraid one day, if he ever *stopped* loving Isobel, he would stop loving me.

He was this handsome man who'd plucked me from a potentially worse situation.

He never asked me for anything, always checked in and made sure I was comfortable. He got me the best money could buy...for everything.

Reed teased that anyone I ended up with would have to best Gabriel. I didn't smile.

Because what if...he stopped loving me?

Then, one day, I accidentally broke Gabriel's coffee pot.

I had been in the kitchen fumbling over a recipe, and it had smashed, and I *panicked.*

I quickly realized the glass was everywhere, and I did my best to clean it, but I still cut myself in my haste before Gabriel showed up.

And then I'd started crying when I felt the fragility of my existence.

How, even *if* he loved me, that love was based on his love for *her.*

Shortcake?

Evie?

I froze.

They *both* found me.

Reed was behind him at his side, Gabriel closed the distance between us quicker, his strong arms enveloping me in a warm embrace. I clung to him, my body shaking with the force of my sobs.

*I'm sorry I slipped. It broke...*I stumbled over my words.

I was in his arms as he looked down at my bleeding hand while Reed was all action, moving around me cleaning up for me.

Gabriel had cleaned up my hand and rubbed my head. I had never really had a brother or father figure and I wasn't sure what to do now that I had an entire family.

I told you I wasn't going anywhere. There's nothing you could do to make me hate you, shortcake.

He sighed into hair. *My love for you will never be conditional.*

Reed was taking us in after making sure I was good.

I nodded against his chest, my tears soaking into the soft fabric of his shirt. In that moment, wrapped in the safety of his arms, I realized that he told me the truth, my protector, the person who made me feel safe.

My love for you will never be conditional.

And then he asked me if it would make me feel better to break anything else, so he'd get a dozen more coffee pots, and I laughed— Reed had ruefully shaken his head.

Suddenly, I had a family.

And two years had passed in the blink of an eye.

I GOT INTO COLLEGE.

The acceptance letter lay on my dresser, the crisp white paper a stark contrast to the deep mahogany wood, ivy wrapping around the bedposts in my room from all the plants I took care of. I wanted to go to college.

When Gabriel suggested I opt for online classes, his words laced with a protective undertone, I felt a flicker of disappointment.

But I obeyed.

I went to school for two years at the manor. But by the third year? I really wanted to feel normal.

Just for a moment. I had been normal before...

Selena found me in the solarium sitting alone.

She had become my confidant and closest friend despite our age difference and was the one who finally asked me the question that had been lingering in the back of my mind.

What do you want, Evie? Her voice was gentle, her green eyes filled with understanding as she took my hands in hers.

I wanted to step out of my bubble.

The words tumbled from my lips, a waterfall of pent-up emotions and dreams that I had kept hidden for far too long.

I want to go to school away from here.

I would never forget that day, we were all piled into the library.

The argument that followed was one of raised voices and heated emotions. And anger flowed through the room.

I had *never* seen Gabriel like that.

But it was clear *everyone* else had.

Gabriel's eyes flashed with a mix of anger and quiet fury, as he towered over everyone, his frame casting a shadow across the room.

He was angry. *I had done that.* I made the man who gave me everything angry.

Selena, her voice sharp, her rapid-fire Spanish to Gabriel's angry tones lighting up the room like sparks.

Reed, ever the mediator, stepped in shutting them both up.

His voice was low and steady as he revealed the truth about Titan to me, what they did at the manor, and he expressed Gabriel's feelings without ever saying they were his.

The words hit me like a physical blow, my mind reeling as I tried to reconcile the image of the man who had become my family with that of an…operative.

Gabriel didn't look at me. Not *once.*

Nate, usually so quick with a joke or a lighthearted comment, remained uncharacteristically silent, his presence a solid wall of support at my back.

I had started crying, unable to look at anyone wanting to disappear into the couch, and I felt Nate moving away. *Just me and Gabriel.*

My love for you will never be conditional. I loved Gabriel with every fiber of my being.

*But what if….*I was older. He didn't have to love me like that anymore. At that everyone had turned and I wanted to vanish. Gabriel's expression had softened.

His arms wrapped around me as everyone filed out. I clung to him like a lifeline.

The familiar scent of his cologne, the steady beat of his heart against my ear, grounded me in the midst of the chaos.

Tell me what you want, shortcake.

And I told him. He made me promise to come home for the holidays and breaks, his voice thick with emotion as he rubbed my hair.

I don't want you to stop loving me if you find someone else.

It had hurt to admit it and he had been quiet for a moment.

Two years of family, laughter, Gabriel's protection, and hugs—it was a dream. But if he moved on? He might hate me. Resent me. Kick me out. I was eighteen now. I wasn't his ward anymore.

I was an adult.

And then he'd said. *There won't ever be anyone else.*

He switched to ask me about the school I was going to. I told him openly. He was my parent, my brother, everything.

And so, Reed took me under his wing like he had with Selena, helping me get my license and pick out my first car. I felt a rush of exhilaration.

Selena, her laughter ringing out like a bell, and Nate stood, their eyes shining with glee and pride.

And Gabriel? His expression, a mix of pride and reluctance, shook his head ruefully as he watched us, a small smile tugging at the corners of his mouth.

I'm going to miss you, shortcake.

I promise, I'll always come home to you.

And then, for two years, I lived my life. Like a normal girl.

Without a super spy for a brother—another operative—and siblings who could kill them in multiple ways.

I was surrounded by people my age, I made friends with other girls, realized how sheltered I was, and I met boys…I dated.

And even as sometimes it ended in disaster, it made for a good story.

But no matter what, I always belonged to the manor. I would come home all the time, and leap into Gabriel's arms.

He always waited for me, and he would bombard me with questions.

Did I have money?

Did I eat? Did I sleep?

Did anyone break my heart?

Nate would make a slicing motion across his throat when Gabriel started. I caught Selena yanking Nate away like a lioness dragging a carcass.

I always came home, though.

Something happened in those two years.

I began craving something where I didn't have to split myself. I made friends, but I never brought anyone home, not feeling comfortable at the manor, too, since everyone, including Selena, was protective of me. I felt loved.

But I also wanted…I wanted *something*…that felt just out of reach.

I couldn't identify it.

My sole identity was, and always would be, Gabriel's little sister.

Reed was on his phone one day, and I almost had a heart attack when he was on someone's social media page. I thought it was Isobel.

But then I saw slight differences that let me know it *wasn't*—but I didn't know what Gabriel would do if he saw.

I didn't know if Reed knew, but even if he did?

Reed's Alisha, this woman he had a crush on, wasn't Isobel. Reed wasn't dating her.

So, what did it matter?

But something told me it did. It made me look at her like she was... my sister. It didn't help that Alisha's younger sister was younger than me.

Selena continued working her butt off for Gabriel as his loyal operative, I didn't understand their relationship, I just knew she would die for him.

Nate became Reed's right hand in many ways.

And me?

I was Gabriel's.

He had retreated to his darkness over the last few years. Something was bothering him. Someone. *Her.*

I'd find him spaced out, staring out into the distance, and I always cried.

I never saw him as emotional as I did when I first met him all those years ago when Isobel had died. Something had changed.

Hardened.

Iced out.

Gabriel, who helped me navigate my journey into adulthood—the man who I had met with some warmth was gone.

In his place was someone who fought out his demons and tore through the team and in turn everyone changed.

Gabriel *changed.*

Nate became distant and erratic, pulling away from everyone. Selena, while utterly devoted to Gabriel for saving her life, didn't know what to do or how to take a break.

Reed, he was fighting his own darkness.

And me?

I couldn't help my brother. Reed looked as if he was losing his best friend, and I felt *helpless.* I saw the spiraling.

The entire team knew something was wrong, something was eating at Gabriel, and nobody could save him.

I asked Reed what he was planning on doing.

I promise I'm working on it.

Are you going to help him?

I'm trying, Evie.

Reed had hugged me, and I told him I was afraid of losing Gabriel like Mama.

He gave me the world, after all.

And in turn, I would do anything for him.

CHAPTER 1
EVIE
PRESENT DAY

I ended up at the 75th Annual Board Game Convention toward the end of the summer.

Reed couldn't make it since he was interviewing people to hire a few people. I'd seen him looking at a file for one of them, Liam Sullivan, who was supposed to be in cybersecurity and working with me.

But I was alone today. Which was nice.

Sometimes, Reed was just as much of a helicopter parent as Gabriel, even though he pretended to be the cool one.

I was here at the convention for the new release of a board game series I loved.

The Domain was a board game based on strategy with ten different editions. I had all ten, and the eleventh was coming out today.

Each edition was named after a fantasy theme, and the one released today was called *Seelie Court*.

It was feminine and inspired by a popular fantasy book series I had read about fairies. Some people had complained about it. Specifically, the nerd boy fanbase who said it was too girly.

I kept my phone silent for a moment as I wandered over to the table labeled *The Domain* in gothic fonts. My palms were clammy as I fiddled with the wristband bearing my username.

As I drew closer to the table, chewing my bottom lip and tugging at the dress, Selena let me borrow.

The off-the-shoulder material and soft fabric against my skin made me feel slightly grown up. I couldn't help but notice the sea of faces—mostly male—towering over me.

I came later in the day so it wouldn't be as crowded, but it was just too much for my comfort.

Usually, when I came, Reed led the way as I held onto his sleeve or Gabriel's arm.

Both of them were an intimidating presence that women fan-girled over, and guys scrambled to get out of their way.

A flicker of apprehension coursed through me as I realized I couldn't spot any of the female forum members I had been eagerly anticipating meeting.

Lost in thought, I almost got run over by two people and stumbled back without looking. My foot caught on something—*someone* solid.

A squeak escaped my lips as I braced myself for the fall, but instead, I found myself held by a pair of strong arms, steadying me against a broad, blue-clad chest.

"I'm so sorry—" And all the words in my vocabulary left me.

Striking blue eyes. Flushed cheeks. Messy hair.

I swallowed. Hard.

He's cute. With a boyish charm that instantly caught my attention—he was *really* cute. Blond hair tousled as if he had just run his fingers through it, giving him a carefree and slightly disheveled appearance. His bright eyes held a mix of concern and curiosity as he watched me. And then his voice slid over my nerves, soothing instantly. "I got you. Are you all right?"

Deep, smooth like honey, snapping me out of my reverie. His smile was soft and genuine, and I must've made a noise because it grew.

Calm down, butterflies.

As I took in his features, I noticed a glint of gold on his wrist—an elite member's wristband.

He was either a creator or someone important.

The Henley top that hugged his athletic frame filled my vision, accentuating his broad shoulders and hinting at the muscle definition beneath. It made his eyes even brighter.

"I w-w-wasn't watching where I was going."

His eyes went dark as he looked around me. "That wasn't your fault. Idiots."

I blinked at the look in them before he turned back to me. He reminded me of a curious lion.

Breathe.

"Are you here from the forum? I'm Lady Evie."

His eyes widened slightly, a flicker of surprise dancing in their depths. He showed me his wrist.

Even his fingers are pretty.

"You're MasterLD?" I gaped, recognition dawning on me. "I *loved* the cards you designed for this edition. It's the reason why I came today. I didn't think you were *real*. I thought you might've been a bot or something. But then I thought, why would *he have to be a he*? What if it was a woman? *Ohmigosh!!"*

And I snapped my mouth shut as his grin grew, a gleam lighting his eyes as he dipped his head.

He was breathtakingly handsome, and my heart gaped in awe.

"Thank you. Did you like the last two cards?"

I couldn't help but be delighted.

He was the man who designed all those cards? "I *did*. But—" I felt myself shift with him as his eyes darted up, taking in the people. Annoyance flashed in his eyes, and for a moment, I saw it.

He's scanning.

He looked like Nate, alert, taking in everything, assessing—I didn't know if he used to be military or not.

But he wasn't anymore. *Not with that hair.*

"I can't think straight at these places," he said, his eyes roving until they returned to me. "If you don't mind, I'd like to switch with you to get you out of the way." He motioned to the crowds.

I nodded, feeling him switch spots with me, so I was against a wall and him.

One of his arms was braced near my head.

Oh, this was different.

"What were you saying?" He dipped his head, and I could feel the heat crest my cheeks.

I had a flash of him picking me up and—

Stop. You just met him!

"Do you come here often?"

Was that forward? I have never seen him before.

A light grin crested his lips. "I don't ever leave my apartment. But this year, the creators said they were releasing the eleventh edition. I *couldn't* be rude—"

"Because your cards are in the game." I couldn't stop myself as I felt a giddy sensation. *"That is so exciting for you."*

As I shared that, I was a little lost in the daybreak blue of his eyes and his smile, his messy blond hair, and his focus on me. He was watching me like I was the only person in the room.

"It is."

Then I realized what he had said. "Why won't you leave your apartment?"

Was he a homebody like Gabriel?

His eyes never left mine as he said softly. "I couldn't ever find a good enough reason." On the outside, I blinked, and on the inside, I squirmed a little, feeling a flutter somewhere in me.

"This was a good reason?"

He blinked slowly. "Right now, it is."

Oh. Be still. Don't move. "What's your favorite card, Lady Evie?"

And just like that, he turned it back to something I knew what to do with.

Something I could breathe around instead of imagining him holding me, teasing me—I stopped.

I looked away so he wouldn't see my eyes. "I like everything you designed—"

I was trying not to freak out at how handsome he looked with that little smile on his face.

"I couldn't choose between the Enchantress and the Vixen," I admitted, feeling a genuine excitement forming. "The Enchantress's extra boosts and hidden trap card were incredible, but the Vixen's darker, sexier vibe was just as compelling. Your designs were so thoughtful and empowering for the female characters. But the upgraded Goddess did have my hair."

I chewed my lip while thinking. "I can't choose. They were all really thoughtful."

I couldn't stop looking at his eyes.

I looked at him, letting my lip go, and noticed his eyes taking in my hair.

Selena had said the look would be really nice on me.

I didn't really have a sense of style, and sometimes I wore her clothes, but it felt...like I was totally stealing my big sister's wardrobe.

"It is fantastic, I mean—" He shook his head. "The card, it's fantastic. Not that your hair isn't fantastic, it's *beautiful*. I just—" *Was he stumbling? Him?*

"Thank you," I don't know why I felt like this.

"It's—"

"Fantastic," I finished. And then I, Evie Monroe— I shared a laugh with this *cute* boy. I was squealing on the inside. I wanted to run my fingers through his hair.

I didn't usually get too flustered, considering I worked around some extremely attractive people. But then there was me.

I needed to find a way to calm down.

"One of the things I had noticed about the game was the feminine characters had a lot less abilities for the first few editions. I really liked yours because of the attention to all the details."

I had never met him prior to this; I only knew about his work.

"I loved the colors you used and the different styles to represent them. It really made them *useful* for a bunch of the other editions rather than just two-dimensional with no purpose other than being aesthetically pleasing for a single reason. They were complex, and instead of being accessories to counterparts, there's something compelling about strong women holding their space."

Stop rambling.

"I think you should always hold your space." His eyes went soft as he watched me. "You liked my work."

I had. His had been chosen internationally, thoughtfully detailed, designed, and curated for the women who liked the game. I would know. I had voted for him. My heart skipped a beat.

"I liked the way you designed all three of them, it was feminine and—"

His lips were...kissable.

"Powerful?" He hadn't stopped smiling.

"Yes." I didn't notice I was so close to him, but he wasn't moving away. "What made you—how did you think up those cards?"

That made him pause; he looked deep in thought, and I waited.

"I love a good strategy game. I liked the idea of making people feel included. Everyone has a part to play. The Goddess, for instance, she's the only one who doesn't have these intense abilities, but her existence is pivotal to the game—you lose her, and you lose everything."

He continued like he didn't just cut through to my center with his words. "I think I made it to show people you didn't have to be anything special. You could just exist as yourself—and that would've been enough."

He smiled. "I liked contributing to something I felt passionate about. I felt like I was a part of something bigger than myself."

Who was this man? *Could I keep him?*

"I know it's just a game—" he continued.

"It is not *just* a game." My tone held genuine appreciation. "You shouldn't make light of what you do. What you just said is the reason why people wanted more. And that's really sweet of you to see something like that."

And do something about it.

I knew the girls on the forum had a huge crush on him, and they didn't even know what he looked like—everyone just talked about *him.*

Because those cards were *perfect.* I could take them from this edition, and I already saw them in use in multiple other editions.

His expression was soft as he took me in. "Is that your way of telling me I'm a huge nerd?"

"I work in IT. Trust me, I've met bigger nerds." I laughed easily, feeling a little weight lift off my chest. Reed would love this man. "Have you gone to the display? I saw there was a line, and I wasn't in the mood to be mowed down anymore."

He didn't smile as he remembered that. "What are you doing today? I'm sorry, was that too forward?"

"No, I—" I can't think. I couldn't speak. *You're hot, and I'm out of my league.*

He took a deep breath, looking unsure again. "What are you doing for the next few hours, Lady Evie?"

"I didn't have any plans." I was just going to come here and go home —*to Gabriel.*

He nodded, his eyes lighting up. "Do you want to have plans with me, Lady Evie?"

He was. Asking. Me. Out.

"Eva Monroe," I answered instinctively, meeting his gaze head-on. "But my friends call me Evie."

"Luke Delaney." His eyes flickered, and he extended his hand toward me. "Can I ask you something?"

I blinked, feeling a flutter of excitement in my chest as I took it, not missing how his hand swallowed mine. "You want to be my friend?"

His eyes widened just a little in amazement as he held my hand. His gaze dropped to it. He hesitated, his expression shifting. "No, I don't want to be just your friend."

My heart skipped a beat as I processed his words.

"I'm not sleeping with you today," I blurted out.

"*Oh shit, I didn't mean that,* not that I wouldn't. I just—" he stammered, looking away with a flush of his own, his eyes comically wide.

22

He let my hand go to run his hand through his hair, and I caught how red he got.

He's cute. Gone was the confident man.

He's really cute.

"No, fuck—Evie, I would like to take you on a date."

He apologized, and for the first time, his words tumbled out in a rush. "I'm sorry, I'm bad at flirting. Or *speaking* in general. I put my foot in my mouth constantly. At work, it isn't so bad, but outside with the general population—I have the grace of a sledgehammer when I go after things, plus I'm nervous, and you're—"

I couldn't help but laugh at his candid confession.

He was stumbling over his words, but there was something charming about his awkwardness.

It made him close to human.

"But I take it you're okay with it?"

I returned his smile, feeling a warmth spread through me.

"I would be more than okay with it," I replied, feeling a rush of something through me.

He's just a normal guy.

And so, I spent the next few hours with Luke Delaney.

"Don't judge me for being a nerd," he teased.

I smiled, feeling giddy. "I wouldn't dream of it."

CHAPTER 2
LUCAS

IT DIDN'T OCCUR TO ME INSTANTLY. *NO. IT NEVER DID.*

My brain wasn't where it used to be. It hurt more often.

Between the migraines, the memory loss, the shakes, and constantly being guard—having more issues than I knew what to do with?

Combined with one too many car bombs, brain injuries, getting shot at and blasted for five years?

I was too *fucked* to process back in the convention what she had said.

I just needed to breathe.

The convention had been a sensory *overload*; the cacophony of sounds and the constant bustle of people had left me feeling overwhelmed and on edge.

My mind was constantly trying to assess potential threats. Even if it was just a giant alien creature that was blown up and making weird noises and some board games.

When Evie first mentioned her last name, it *barely* registered.

My mind was too preoccupied with simply trying to maintain a sense of calm amidst the chaos. It was only *later*, when we had escaped the convention that the pieces started to fall into place.

She was from out of the city. She didn't live here. She had a brother who didn't live here. She sometimes worked in the city and sometimes with him.

Evie had suggested we go out to a coffee shop nearby that was quiet and not filled with people. I could finally inhale in the clean air.

The moment we stepped into the coffee shop, a wave of relief washed over me. The hushed conversations and the soothing aroma of coffee flowed around me.

As we sat down at a secluded table, I could feel my mind starting to clear, the fog of anxiety and confusion slowly lifting. I took in her scent, her hair, her fucking doe eyes blinking at me.

My brain worked a little...

Evie Monroe.

That name echoed in my mind, and I couldn't shake it. Evie sat across from me, a green drink and delicate seashell-shaped cookies in front of her. Madeleines.

Memories of my sister sneaking into the kitchen and stealing handfuls of them.

As I talked to her, I was utterly entranced, even as my brain was spiraling at her name.

The soft lighting of the café cast a warm glow on her face, highlighting her delicate features and making her eyes glitter. Her voice was like honey, soothing the uneven surfaces of my soul.

Monroe. How many Monroes are there in the world?

Just one, right? In my world.

There was no way *Evie* Monroe was *Gabriel's...sister?*

"Do you have siblings?"

I fucking hated coffee dates.

I wasn't a cheap bastard. Coffee wasn't a date.

I owned my own company; I could fly her to Edinburgh and, get her better coffee and be back. Today.

But I liked this with her.

I didn't want to freak out the beautiful little fairy I'd met at...a board game convention.

Life was playing jokes on me today.

I really didn't leave my apartment, but it was a weekend. I had shown up since the creators liked my cards so much that they'd sent me a personal invite.

I couldn't decline—it was being hosted in one of my buildings.

That would be rude.

I'm losing it.

My brain was running amok being in a crowded room, but then she'd landed in my arms, and I'd focused on her.

The aroma of caramel and sugar emanated from her, sweet and

inviting. I inhaled her scent into my lungs, focusing on her. Until she said her name, then I zeroed in.

My hands had stopped shaking. My body had eased.

Fuck, but she's pretty.

Gorgeous.

And I focused on her.

"I do, but he doesn't come to these things." She smiled, and I wanted to lick her right there. "Sometimes Gabriel does, but only when Reed nags him. This is my first year coming alone."

Oh, motherfucker.

Reed Whittaker.

Gabriel Monroe.

My heart squeezed.

There has to be two of them.

I felt hungry watching her trying to reel it in.

She was *pretty.* That hair. Dark mahogany, eyes bright and fucking shimmering in the light. I never thought my insane self would think a woman was *sparkly.*

But then, she'd been all over me, complimenting me, showering me with *sunshine,* and I'd been utterly enamored.

Oh, fuck me.

Really, how many fucking Monroes can there be?

No way. Unless...

There was only one other way to know. "You mentioned you don't stay in the city?"

She shook her head, the light casting on her cheeks pink, flushed—*don't fucking pounce.*

"I live with my brother in Greenwich."

In the Titan manor. Because this was Evie Monroe. *Gabriel's little sister.*

Holy. Mother. Fucking. Shit.

I resisted the urge to just shoot myself in the foot because that would be more pleasant, considering what I had guessed. I knew where the Titan manor was. One thing became very apparent, as Evie mentioned she'd come down to the city and told me about her drive down here—*she has no idea who I am.*

I didn't have any photos of me on the company website, I never used my real name, and I didn't have social media. I definitely didn't hang out for the society papers to post photos of me. I couldn't.

Not with my issues.

Most of the time, people didn't recognize me.

Her tongue peeked out a little as she grinned at me, and I couldn't resist smiling back.

I didn't even hear her. I just focused on her.

This isn't *his* sister—not the iceman's.

This woman was a burning flame. She wasn't his. *She could be yours.*

Except everything in me had soothed back at the convention. When she'd landed in my arms, all soft skin and smiles in that fucking dress, looking at me like I was her fucking hero. And then she'd spoken.

Her general interests, her hobbies—the more she talked, the more I smiled.

Her scent, her laughter, her eyes—everything about this woman—I had zeroed in.

I like this girl.

Evie had no idea who I was, and she could *never* find out.

I was on a date with Gabriel Monroe's sister.

He was going to kill me if he found out. But I really liked this girl.

Oh, I wanted her but—I also felt this need to protect her as she smiled up at me.

She was *genuine*, her eyes kind and soft. My brain stopped working as she blinked those big caramel eyes at me and asked me questions.

She looks like Christmas.

I am so fucked.

CHAPTER 3
EVIE

I LOST COUNT OF ALL THE DATES I HAD BEEN ON WITH LUKE.

I ran out of the house, trying to avoid everyone. It didn't always work.

Once, I snuck back and saw Selena and Nate coming out, and they'd taken one look at me and shared a smirk.

Out of everyone, they felt closer to me in a way that wasn't like Reed or Gabriel. Like siblings.

"Selena, can I borrow that yellow sundress you have?"

Nate shook his head. "*That* shouldn't be considered a *dress*."

Selena had smacked him and given it to me.

It was really cute with a low back, and it made my breasts look amazing. I'd walked out later that week a little more dressed up in *that* dress, and Reed laughed at me racing by.

I turned pink and ran in the opposite direction, thinking I'd be avoiding Gabriel. I swear they were *everywhere*.

"Whoa, shortcake, are you okay?"

I screamed a little.

Why was this house full of people when I needed to be sneaky?

"I'm good!" I couldn't even look at him. "I forgot my shoes in my room!"

He looked at my shoes on my feet and then my dress. "Is that Selena's?"

Kill me, now.

I ran out of the house like the devil was on my heels. Otherwise, I was afraid they'd follow me.

I liked a boy—*a normal boy.*

Today, we found a hole-in-the-wall cake shop on the West Side. And he was totally checking me out.

Thanks, Selena.

"No, you did not fail. It's the easiest course to pass." Luke's voice was laced with amusement as he teased me about my disastrous first attempt at my road test years ago. He was laughing about it.

I couldn't help but smile, even as I felt the heat rising in my cheeks.

He leaned back in his seat, watching me blatant delight at me squirming. And he looked hot as sin.

"I did!" I insisted, my voice carrying a hint of embarrassment. "I was *so* nervous, they told me to take a left...I took a right, and I forgot to signal, and *then*—" I continued to shake my head and tell him what happened. "Reed said he'd *never* teach anyone again after me. Selena got it down so fast? Gabriel bought her car, *Paloma.* Gabriel didn't like the way one of them spoke to me, and he was there in a *heartbeat*—"

I told him about the instructor looking between Reed and Gabriel, who had descended like demons on the man shouting at me, leaving him sputtering between the two of them.

Luke's lips stretched wide into a grin, making my heart lose it.

"I did. Shamelessly bad driver here. Gabriel was surprised that my foot had even reached the brakes while my hands were on the wheel. He calls me shortcake."

"I've been calling you Cherry," he said, motioning to my hair. I instinctively ran my fingers through the waves, feeling a sudden self-consciousness. But his next words put me at ease.

"No, it's okay. You should leave it down." His eyes softened as he watched it.

I struggled to breathe with my heart in my throat.

The sincerity in his voice and the way his eyes widened with appreciation made me believe him.

I settled, basking in the comfort of his presence. The fading sun's rays danced on his skin, making his eyes brighter.

He likes the dress.

"You were in the city?" Luke asked, his voice filled with genuine interest.

I hesitated for a moment. I had been.

"I have to get some work done for my brother," I replied, unable to divulge more details. His eyes flickered with an unspoken question.

"Does he work in the city?" he asked, his tone careful yet intrigued.

"Not always. He splits his time between the office he has in Midtown and home."

He took a sip of his drink. "I'm guessing he'd kill me on sight if I told him I was dating his baby sister then."

His words sent a bubble of anxiety through me, and I bit my lip, trying to contain the giddy excitement that simmered within me, not even caring he mentioned anything about Gabriel.

"Is that what this is?"

The pink hue that colored his cheeks made me smile. "I *mean—*"

I couldn't resist the urge to tease him. "You can admit it—"

"*Yes.*"

We shared an embarrassed laugh as soft music played around us, and, for a moment, I was just a girl.

Not Gabriel's sister. Just a girl. *On a date.*

With just a guy. And it felt incredible.

Inside, I was *squealing.*

"He is not as scary as everyone makes him out to be—I do think he's very protective, but I understand where he's coming from. And I work in the city sometimes, so it's easier to just kind of…" I shrugged. "Take lunch breaks and stuff."

His eyes twinkled with amusement. "Deception at its finest. Sneaking around behind your brother's back."

I gasped. "I am not sneaking. I prefer the term 'lunch breaks.'"

"I'm just *teasing,* I like your four-hour lunch breaks."

I covered my face as he laughed.

"I do not appreciate being teased," I retorted, trying to conceal the warmth spreading through me. When I peeked between my fingers, he had a wicked look in his eyes.

Breathe.

"I think you'd like it very much if I did."

Whoa. I felt my cheeks flush at his boldness, mirroring the flush I saw on his face.

"Foot meet mouth," he said softly, though there was a hint of mischief in his tone.

There were times I saw another side of him, balanced with this sweet man who was with me. A hint of…*something* else. I didn't know how to put my finger on it.

I was blushing. I didn't know what to say. I didn't even know how to say how much I liked this man, everything he—

"I like you very much." *There.*

His lips eased into a slow smile, filled with wonder and something soft.

"Do you want to go on another date with me?"

I'd love to. "Yes."

Reed had asked me discreetly if I was busy since I was running around a lot. I shook my head; I just took whatever work he gave me.

I knew Gabriel was always wondering where I vanished off to sometimes.

And I didn't mind doing it since he vanished too. I didn't want either one of my brothers to find out I was dating.

I like Luke, and I don't want them to destroy him.

Reed would run a background check and put him on a no-fly list. Gabriel would take him to a black site with Nate's help. And Selena would remind me there are other fish in the sea.

But this is the only fish I want.

I realized that I was falling for him. One evening, he called me, his voice deeper and huskier than usual.

"Hey, Cherry." I turned red at the nickname he'd given me. "What are you doing to wind down for the night?"

I felt my breathing hitch at the intimate question. "I was watching a movie," I confessed, suddenly feeling self-conscious. *But something tells me you'd rather be watching me.*

Where did that come from?

"What movie?"

I told him one of Reed's recommendations, and I heard him moving. "Are you serious? Part four of that series is out right now in theaters."

"Do you want to go see it?" I teased. But with the beat of silence that passed, I got the feeling I said something wrong. "I mean, we don't have to."

"No," he sounded rushed. "No, we'll go. It's okay, I'm okay."

He didn't sound okay. But I mean, if he said so, okay.

"I'll let you know when we can go. Is that okay?"

It was.

For once, I felt like a normal girl, enjoying the company of a nice, normal guy who liked me for who I was.

I was just myself, and it was enough.

He wasn't a spy, an operative, a double agent, or a former contractor.

He is just Luke Delaney.

One weekend, I came back late at night, seeing Reed's car, so I tried to run for it.

No such luck.

Gabriel and Reed were talking about something on the way to the garage. I screamed as soon as I ran into Gabriel's chest.

"Easy, shortcake. You okay?" He steadied me with rare amusement in his eyes.

Reed had grinned at the look on my face. "You have confetti in your hair, kid."

I plucked some off chewing my bottom lip looking between them both. Gabriel's eyes narrowed on the flowers in my hand. Damnit, Luke had gotten them for me.

I squirmed under his scrutiny, and Reed shoved and distracted him. He winked at me, and I gave him a grateful smile.

I had run off feeling guilty and hiding my face.

With everything changing at Titan, I didn't need *two* brothers to come bearing down on my life. *Or Luke.*

Luke and I talked about everything from certifications, books we were reading, my passions, his passions, and time flew by with him as not only a really good friend but also a really honest man who liked *me*.

Luke was intellectually stimulating, encouraging me through all our conversations with a small grin.

He kept up with me, and I didn't have to pretend to be anything.

I could be Evie.

I had dated men before who I had to pretend around or hide things about myself. Luke made me feel safe to share parts of myself. And he didn't bother hiding when he didn't know something to make himself look smarter.

I knew I was head over heels when we were grabbing lunch together one afternoon toward the end of summer.

I had mentioned to him that I was vegetarian, expecting him to make a judgment or anything, but—without batting an eye, he found a list of places on his phone.

Somewhere that offered enough for his carnivore pallet and mine.

"I don't care what you eat," he murmured without any slight in his voice. "I care *that* you eat."

I ignored the warm flutters in my stomach as he seriously focused on his phone.

"It says this place is great. They have pesto..." he said, his eyes lighting up. "And there's another spot that does incredible tofu stir-fry. We should check them out."

I noticed his hands shaking a little. Was he okay? Maybe he was just nervous.

"Planning our next date?" I chided. Boldly.

I loved that he didn't bother hiding it. "Yeah, I already found a few..."

As he talked about a new restaurant with spinach and feta gnocchi and lemon tiramisu, I couldn't help but notice the butterflies that stirred in my stomach were now settled.

I liked this man. I felt safe with him. *He's my fish.*

He took my hand when crossing the street or put his hand on my back to guide me somewhere.

He noticed how I drank my matcha and showed up to our dates with Madeleine's in his pocket.

He liked when I found them and I liked that he was thoughtful enough to carry them—he made me feel taken care of and safe.

He never once made a move on me sexually. Not once. In turn, it made me want him *more*. I noticed sometimes he almost seemed nervous, his hands shaking, biting his lip a little as he was deep in thought.

Once, over pizza, I couldn't resist until he took a sip of his drink. "I think you're just trying to get in my pants."

He choked on his drink. I thumped him in the back, unable to hold back my laughter.

"*Evie—*" He looked astounded and alarmingly red. I had never been so bold, but the safer I felt, the more I felt comfortable with him to be me. *Whoever* she was becoming.

"If this is all just a trap, you should know...it's working."

He wiped his hand over his mouth, and for a moment, I saw a look in his eyes of pure heat. He had been flirting with me since we met. But this didn't feel like an elaborate ruse.

"Good to know."

I nodded, ignoring the heat blossoming inside me.

I liked that he didn't try to do anything physical with me, but I was also aware of craving him. All the flirty banter had led me to imagining him and me—*and yeah, I couldn't even say it.*

That day, he *finally* kissed me.

It was raining, and we were walking together under his umbrella. I stepped into a puddle, and I felt myself slipping on the uneven ground.

And then a powerful arm that had made my insides clench wrapped around my waist and hauled me to his front. I gasped, surprised by the sudden movement.

His grip was strong, steady. I looked up at him, my heart racing.

Under his hoodie, I could feel the broad set of his shoulders. The strength in his arms—it was a side of him I hadn't fully realized before. He kept me close to his side as we walked.

I leaned into him, feeling safe and secure.

When we reached our destination, he didn't go inside. His eyes met mine, intense and filled with pent-up heat.

"Evie." His voice was gruff. "I'd like to—"

I held my breath as he dipped his head.

He leaned in quickly, his mouth closing over mine—soft, gentle, yet filled with a quiet passion. I opened my mouth, a soft noise escaping as his tongue explored mine, and I was clutching him right there on the street.

My fingers dug into his shoulders and one of his hands came and held my cheek. A shiver ran through me.

A low chuckle left his lips, struck somewhere deep as he came back and kissed me harder. That ignited something within me.

A warmth that spread through my body. It settled my nerves, my fears, and my doubts. At the same time, it awakened…something.

A longing for more. For him.

I melted into the kiss, my hands resting on his chest. I could feel the strength beneath my fingers. When we parted, my cheeks were flushed, my lips tingling.

He smiled at me, his hand cupping my cheek.

"I've been wanting to do that for a while," he admitted softly.

"You can do it again."

I saw a flash of a grin before he dipped his head, pressing me into him. I didn't know how long I kissed him.

Just that I gripped his shirt tighter and climbed him—he broke off the kiss gasping.

"I'd like to be your man, Evie."

A warm sensation settled in my chest. "I thought you already were."

I felt pleasure seep into me at disarming him for a moment, and then a breathless smile split his lips.

"Good to know."

CHAPTER 4
LUCAS

"Monroe?"

Matteo DuPont lounged across from me on the sleek leather couch in my office, his electric-blue eyes, pupils rimmed in black, wide and alert.

Andrei, his older brother, had been my good friend since boarding school, and wherever we'd gone—Matteo had always been there, the energetic shadow to our more reserved personalities.

Now the race car designer had ostensibly stopped by my office to talk business, but I'd cut that shit off, preferring to send him an email.

Instead, I found myself confessing about Evie.

"As in Gabriel Monroe's sister?" Matteo's perfectly arched dark brow shot up, his voice dropping to a harsh whisper in French. *"Do you have a death wish?"*

He looked at me like I'd just announced my plan to juggle live grenades.

I ran a hand through my hair, feeling the weight of my decisions pressing down on me. "It's complicated."

Matteo's fingers danced over a complex metal puzzle, twisting and turning the pieces with practiced ease. His ADHD meant he always needed something to occupy his hands, lest that excess energy find less productive outlets.

"What happened to erring on the side of caution?" Matteo's piercing stare cut through me. His mouth slid into a sly smirk. "Have you fucked her?"

The crude question ignited a spark of anger in my chest.

"Don't talk about her like that," I snapped, my tone carrying the weight of our shared history. We'd gone to school together. He was like my little brother. A dangerous little shit, but he was still the only thing I had to family.

"*Mon Dieu,* you actually like her. How long have you been secretly courting the sister of the man who'd gladly use your bones as toothpicks?"

"I get it. My father fucked up enough to make half a continent hate him, but—" I broke off, the unfinished thought hanging heavy in the air between us. "I don't know what I did to Gabriel Monroe."

But I had a feeling it didn't matter.

Because "the sins of the father" and all that crap.

When I met Evie Monroe, I knew I was treading on dangerous ground. He'd probably bury me in the backyard if he knew. I knew Gabriel's property.

Even if his background was as mysterious as the man himself. The face of an angel—the temperament of the devil himself.

The massive structure took up nearly three thousand acres of forested land surrounding it. It was secluded.

A fucking fortress that screamed 'keep out' louder than any sign could. I'd seen satellite images, studied blueprints that probably cost more than most people's houses to obtain.

A turn-of-the-century mansion, white with columns, massive rooms, and floor-to-ceiling windows, built for luxury and the kind of wealth that spanned generations.

Gabriel would have security to the teeth. All controlled by Reed Whittaker.

And they are both Evie's brothers.

I should have ended the date right then and there, and told her the truth, but I couldn't bring myself to do it.

Despite the risk, there was something about her that drew me in, something magnetic and intoxicating. I didn't even know he had a sister.

She disarmed me with her easy grace and soft smile. Her kindness, the compliments fell from her lips like feathers. I wanted to catch all of them and keep them close to me. A normal guy with normal hopes, fears, and insecurities.

When I was with her, I could let my armor down and be honest without fear. I could be myself. I could be…anyone.

In her presence, I felt lighter than I had in years—*untethered*.

Light.

There was no pressure to be anything but me.

Not my father's son.

"Judging by that look, she's the hottest thing you've ever been with?"

I've been dating her. I worked myself to death just to go on another date with her.

I didn't have to sleep with her to know she would be incredible in bed. Evie was uninhibited around me when she talked about her favorite things, philosophers, her life, and the things she wanted. That openness, that raw honesty—it was *intoxicating*.

Sex with Evie would be a revelation. I already knew she wouldn't hide from me based on the way she whimpered in my mouth when I kissed her.

Those little sounds *haunted* my dreams.

Swallowing her moans. I knew once I took her and she was struggling on my dick, she would give me everything. Every secret, every desire, laid bare for me to devour.

Aaannndd there it went again.

Thoughts of fucking Evie everywhere.

Sitting her on my dick and making out for hours. I didn't think she knew what I liked in bed. But I wanted to introduce her to it.

"I'm so fucked." I leaned back in my chair, processing how she had me in a chokehold. A willing prisoner to my own desires.

Matteo's face looked like he swallowed something bad. "Is she the reason you've been avoiding doing anything? I can find someone else for you to use—"

And there it fucking was, a reminder of—

"Don't bother. I'm not using Evie."

There was no one else who satiated me like Evie did. No substitute, no replacement. She was it for me, danger be damned.

Any interaction with her was calming. She was refreshing. Light against my dark. A breath of air I didn't know I needed, but once I had it, I never wanted to leave it. I'm not my father's son.

He paused, and I knew he was taking in my reactions.

"Teo, I don't want to play games—"

"How...is she hiding you from Gabriel?" He raised a brow.

"Andrei found out I invested in *De Nuit*, and he lost his shit. He's hoping nobody digs deep enough to attach our name to it.

I can't imagine what he'd do if I was fucking someone who wanted me dead."

I didn't want to talk about Matteo's sex club, *De Nuit,* that he curated from scratch.

Maybe a younger me would've relished in the hedonistic bliss of depravity, but now I was fucked up for a different reason.

He'd started the venture after I'd met Evie over the summer, and I wasn't going to entertain it.

"Actually…" I didn't hold back, knowing that while Matteo gave off the impression he was a playboy, he hid a lot close to his chest.

He was known for being as tight lipped as the rest of the DuPont family who craved privacy like me.

And considering Matteo had enough secrets of his own? He wasn't going to spill mine.

It was one of the reasons why I spoke to him. When I finished his eyes went so wide and bright like headlights.

He spoke in French saying something I could roughly translate as. *"You sick bastard."*

Which from Matteo was praise, I would've laughed at his sputtering, the toy forgotten on the desk in front of me, his attention focused on me solely. *"Are you crazy!"*

He threw the toy at me.

He sputtered on about Gabriel finding out and torturing my body somewhere in the Middle East before making an example by—

"I don't know if he would put my head on a pike."

"You don't know what he'll do." Matteo shuddered. "I've heard stories from Andrei. About how a man like that rose to where he is now. The last time someone broke into his property? They went *missing.* What do you think he will do once he finds out you lied to his baby sister about who you are?"

Absolutely. Destroy. Me.

I knew it. I was a dead man walking.

Matteo leaned back, his eyes still ingesting what I just said. "Andrei told me not to touch anything related to Monroe. And you want to fuck the man's *sister.*" He huffed out a breath.

"Focus, you slept with a Prime Minister's daughter. Who was crazy, then?" I knew a few things about Matteo. "Not to mention, you fucked two of our instructors in school."

He raised a brow. "Which one?"

I shook my head.

"What? Neither one of them came from a family where their brother was a murderer. Besides, it was one time."

I gave him a look.

"Fine, several times, but I can't help it. I have needs."

"You have too many needs." *Way too many.*

He grinned. "I don't see any woman complaining. I'm not the one stupid enough to lie to her and Gabriel. I'm not judging you. Once, I pretended to be injured to get a model to sleep with me, and I got it. But this isn't like you, so you either like her enough to tell her the truth or—"

"I lose her."

"Gabriel *kills* you." He looked like he was not looking forward to either. And then he gave me a wild look. "Unless you get her pregnant." He shrugged again at my expression. "That's what I would do. What's he going to do then?"

"I am not getting Evie pregnant." I hadn't even had sex with her. I was trying to take it slow. Out of guilt. Fear. Apprehension. My own sexual desires. "Did Maxine take drugs when she was pregnant with you?"

"She's yours," Matteo said, looking bored again, grabbing a sphere off the table and rolling it around like a giant cat. "You can do whatever you want." *I didn't like that.*

"I can't fucking process how depraved you are. This is why I can't go to *De Nuit.* Why are we friends?"

"Me?" He looked devious. "You are playing a dangerous game."

I am not my father's son.

"Because on in the inside you're just as fucked as I am." He rolled his eyes like he was bored.

I knew that. "I'm not trying to get women—" *Although…Evie…* rounded and soft and cuddling into me, tucking her feet into my lap and naked with my baby…*Stop. It.*

He pfft'd with his lips. "Do you know how many women claim they've had my baby? Andrei said one more scandal, and he threatened to disown me. If I told a woman I wanted her to have my baby? She would fall face-down, ass-up—"

"Speaking of children and scandals…" I cut him off, desperate to change the subject. "What is Andrei doing now that your mother found out you both had Thierry in your life for the last eight years?"

Thierry. The by-product of Matteo's father's cheating. The youngest DuPont brother, whose last name I didn't know.

Matteo's mood changed instantly, the playful glint in his eyes replaced by something darker, more dangerous. I'd hit a sore spot.

"Andrei isn't speaking to Maxine." His voice was low, filled with a quiet rage I rarely heard from him. "Thierry never took our last name. Andrei says Maxine shouldn't have punished Thierry for our father's stupidity."

I had met Thierry a few times, and he looked the most like a DuPont. His eyes were wild blue but brighter, and his lean, muscled figure was similar to Matteo's to the point where I almost thought they were twins.

But where Matteo and Andrei were polished, raised in an upscale home and private schools, Thierry held the stance of someone used to fighting *and struggling*—and I knew Matteo and Andrei were livid.

There was a shift coming in their company with the fallout between them and Maxine over a brother who had been done dirty.

And Andrei had a temper. "What does that mean for the DuPont's? For business."

Matteo's shrewd eyes met mine. "Andrei is separating from Maxine. Roadsters and Durand are cutting ties with the DuPont name. Her brand will survive, it'll be private." At my stunned expression, he continued. "Andrei won't speak to anyone for what they did to Thierry."

Everyone was trying to recover from their parents' mistakes.

"It's not his fault." That's why I liked Matteo; even underneath, there was a depth of emotion for loyalty to what he knew was the right thing. My loyalty was to Matteo, but Maxine wanted to host events at my properties sometimes, which meant—none of that."He's lying low and adjusting to the time difference after coming back from Africa."

His smile grew, and his eyes were wicked. "Call Thierry when Monroe tries to kill you."

I didn't know what Thierry did to be able to take Monroe.

Or *why* Matteo said it with confidence. And then, amidst the smile and the playfulness, I caught the eyes of a man who knew how to play dirty and had tricks up his sleeve.

"Monroe won't find out." And neither would Evie. I saw her big doe eyes watching me in my mind, and I imagined what they'd look like when I—

"There is one way to keep Evie." I was all ears. "Take Monroe out."

I gaped. *Take out Gabriel Monroe?* "Absolutely not."

He gave me a pointed look.

41

"No," I shook my head. *"*I'm not using Evie to get to her brother. I don't even know why he hates my family. I can take a wild guess but no —I would never."

"She's his *sister*. They're close." His eyes were gleaming.

"Consider it. The key to taking out Gabriel Monroe is Evie. Not that I envy your task. I personally don't want to dirty my hands but—" He gave me another look.

"Get out."

Even I wasn't dumb enough to go after Gabriel.

He laughed. I caught Jenny, my secretary, blushing profusely when he shamelessly began flirting with her as he left.

My head fucking hurts now.

My phone lit up with a text from Evie.

She'd sent me a photo of hydrangeas upside down, soaking in water and wrote—

> If your day is going this badly, you may need to hydrate.

I had told her this weekend about my inability to fucking drink enough water all day, running around sixteen-hour workdays. I only was able to see Evie around my meetings, juggling work and her. And she had no fucking clue.

If I knew I was going to see Evie?

I made sure I worked longer the night prior or scheduled meetings later.

My secretaries were having a field day figuring that shit out. I would make it fucking work.

I didn't even bother trying to understand how Evie Monroe had gotten under my skin. I told myself it was because she was forbidden fruit. That's all it was.

Did she deserve a better man?

Perhaps.

But was I ever going to let her go?

My visions flickered to her bright eyes, smiling at me. Like no one ever had.

A twisted, messed-up part of me loved the idea of her being mine. Because she was.

And no Gabriel in the world could stop her from being mine.

I would put in an order for a hundred. Was that too much? No, maybe it wasn't enough. Three hundred?

No, I like lilies.

I changed my mental note to lilies.

White, red? Orange?

I could order a couple hundred of each and see which one she sent me a photo of.

You're not going to send flowers, are you?

I had been planning on it.

But then I stopped short realizing...Gabriel would, no doubt, call the florist, find my address and then murder me. I sighed.

Was there no winning?

This is going to kill me.

I talked to her every single day, hiding the truths about who and what I really was.

I hadn't told Matteo the truth about how absolutely fucking beautiful she was.

She was fucking *gorgeous*.

Her hair—that fucking hair went down to her waist, long and sometimes wavy, sometimes straight. Her eyes big and bright, doe-eyed, warm caramel and I knew—*I just fucking knew*—they'd get soft whenever I slid into her.

Her features were feminine and cute, her button nose, and an odd smattering of freckles across her nose. She was endearingly sweet and gave me the occasional hint of attitude. She could be a brat.

And I would've relished fucking her through it.

The palpable chemistry buzzed like a live wire between us every time we locked eyes. I knew I was recklessly playing with fire, risking my vulnerable heart for a chance at something real, something good with this woman.

And she worked at Titan.

Titan had a far-reaching grip in the security sector.

Reed broke down their company into units, agents who worked with particular clients, movie stars, models, and diplomats. And because they were broken up, there was a cluster specifically for men like me.

It was fucking organized with Gabriel sitting at the top, and he was a fucking ghost.

I couldn't find a single speck of anything on him.

I wasn't stupid enough to *not* realize Reed Whittaker was a front man.

He held an iron fist over his entire operation. And while I had interactions with Reed, his cold shoulder, his short-clipped words, I knew I couldn't get any Titans to work for me.

Well, I was dating one of them.

I knew why Reed and Gabriel didn't like me.

I had a *clue.* My family was by no means good. I had known it growing up. People talked.

My own father had burned a lot of bridges that I had to fix when I took over as CEO. And my family side was either all estranged or bitter.

When my mother had passed away, it had felt like what little good there was in the world was gone.

Numerous times I had secrets leaking out that somehow were leveraged against me. I had a spy in my own organization, and I didn't even know where to start.

And then there was *Evie.*

And I was her man.

I was not my father's son.

Yet, despite the rational part of my mind screaming at me to pull back—I couldn't deny the primal, visceral desire I felt for Evie on a bone-deep level.

I drank in the sight of her pouty lips, caught myself mesmerized by the warmth of her smiles, imagining how her luscious curves would feel —I needed to *breathe.*

I was twisted for wanting her so desperately.

Case in point?

We had a movie date tonight.

I needed to get home, slip into comfortable clothes meant for a polished grad student.

And then charm the woman who had no fucking clue who I was.

I am so fucked.

CHAPTER 5
LUCAS

I stood at the movie theater, waiting for Evie to arrive.

My palms were sweaty, and my heart raced in my chest.

I worked my ass off all fucking day, juggling everything I could in one day to go on a fucking movie date with this woman.

I told her I would.

I gave her my word.

When she'd asked me, I wanted to balk.

The thought of being in a crowded, dark theater with strangers made my skin crawl.

The flashing lights, the loud sounds, the confined space—it all threatened to trigger my PTSD.

But what kind of a man was I if I couldn't take my girlfriend out to the fucking movies?

Despite feeling like my head was preoccupied with a few things that needed my attention, my mouth had all but dried up the moment I saw Evie.

I adjusted my jacket and mussed my hair, hoping I looked like a tired grad student instead of a CEO.

I knew she was there when I saw several people—men—in the room turn to her as she found me waiting for her inside the movie theater. It took everything in me to not haul her out there. *Don't lose it. Don't lose it with her.*

"You look beautiful." I focused on the hint of pink on her cheeks as I complimented her.

With her dark cherry cola hair, lashes fanning out, and bright eyes? She was fucking gorgeous.

I fucking loved that breathless shy smile she gave me.

I couldn't resist her.

Not when she made me feel better than I had in forever.

Evie was in something that looked like green leaves over her skin. It was a top and skirt, but the artful construction around her breasts, almost like petals, made her look like the first woman.

A sliver of peachy skin was exposed between the space it exposed, and I could see her belly button. I wanted to lick around it.

"Did you already get the tickets, or should I?"

I hated when she paid for anything. *Absolutely fucking not.*

"I got them."

She smiled adjusting her purse, a tiny little thing that made her look like a doll. As I took her hand, I resisted the urge to turn over my shoulder and fucking glare at the idiots staring at her.

Instead, I opted to ask if she was cold and dropped my lighter jacket over her shoulders.

I could imagine her wearing this outfit if I ever got a chance to take her on vacation. I needed one.

I wanted to ask her if she'd ever go to the Maldives. The white sand against Evie's peach skin, with her in something vibrant and green—or nothing but leaves—I'd be her man.

And there would be no one to take her away from me.

She'd love the coastline and play in the water. I'd take her on a boat ride and show her around.

I could make love to her in our private villa. Take my time.

I couldn't take my eyes off her.

"Are you going to watch me or the movie?" She teased as we sat down after I'd gotten us popcorn. I kept her close to me, my fingertips grazing the little teases of skin.

"You." A hundred times over. Her eyes widened just a little as though she hadn't expected that, and I liked surprising her. "Have you ever been outside of the States?"

She thought about it. "Actually, no, with everything going on at Ti... work, safe to say I don't travel much."

Plus, her brother would have a heart attack if she did.

"Would you ever consider it?"

Her fingertips traced her armrest. "There is one place I'd like to go."

46

I was all ears. "You ever been to Ha Long Bay in Vietnam?" I tried to contain my surprise and failed. *I had.*

"No." *For you, I'd see it again.*

"I'd love to go," she admitted. "It's beautiful and..." As she talked about what she knew, I realized I would fucking love to take her there.

"You want to go?"

She nodded.

"Tonight?"

Her head tilted a little, her confusion adorable. "Right now?"

I nodded. "After the movie." I was dead serious. I'd take her if she asked. And a little laugh escaped her.

"For a second, I thought you were being serious." Her laugh sank into somewhere low. I bit my tongue. I was. I would.

I'd call my assistant, and I'd have her out of here and in fucking Hanoi in a heartbeat.

"Would you go, though?" I pressed. *I can't stop myself.* "If you could."

"Hmm, I don't know. I'd have to pack—"

"We can get clothes there."

Or you can wear nothing at all. And I can wear you.

Her eyes met mine, a gleam in them, and her smile dropped. "You're not joking, are you?"

No. She looked away with a nervous laugh. A beat passed, and I opened my mouth to apologize.

"How long would we go for?" My eyes met hers incredulously. *Evie.* I tried not to kiss her then and there.

I smiled softly, not trying to scare her. "However long you want."

Her lips tipped up.

Evie didn't move, though her eyes hinted that she was amused by this. Because part of her thought this was still a game.

That I was teasing her.

"A week is good?"

I felt the smile tug at my lips as the tension between us coiled. "Plenty."

She licked her lips. "Luke."

Her soft whisper seeped beneath the goosebumps on my skin. Her tongue gently peeking out to wet her lips had done more for me than the models I used to hang out with.

Nobody had a thing on her.

She had me *hooked.*

"Just say the word." I caught myself.

I'll give you whatever you want.

I didn't want to scare her.

I wanted her to know the hold she had over me.

All of our fucking conversations in the weeks we'd spent that had turned into months now.

"Evie—"

The screen went off in front of us loudly.

Move. It was instinctive.

Covering someone from being blown up.

I snapped to cover her, my entire torso twisting to block it, the bomb going off—my eyes closed, bracing for an impact that never came as cartoon voices were playing on trailers.

For hot moments, my heart raced.

The anxiety clawed into my throat. Until I realized, I was just…at the movies…with my girl.

My hand was holding the back of her head to my chest, and I was breathing hard bracing for a hit…that would never come.

Because I was at the fucking movies.

I dared to slowly pull back and look at her eyes. Wide. Looking at me like she'd seen me for the first time. She blinked, and for a moment, I saw her concern—I apologized.

I'm a fucking savage.

"I'm sorry, I don't know why I did that."

Something was going to hurt Evie. I reacted. I felt her hand reach out to me. Gripping mine.

"It's okay."

It wasn't. I had fucking reacted.

I breathed four in, four out, once, twice. I had never been forward. I refrained from hugging her too often or making her uncomfortable with my touch. Not that I didn't notice she leaned into me easily.

"Luke…"

I didn't hear her right now.

Trust was paramount in a relationship. Too bad I had done nothing to earn it. The irony of lying to a woman, while simultaneously trying to earn her trust, never escaped me.

I wanted her for who she was.

And everything I knew I wasn't.

"Luke." I turned, watching her chest heave, ample and rounding her into a lush nymph. I could just—*breathe.*

48

The deep V of her top revealed two plump and rounded raised curves of her breasts, and if I tugged just a little...

Just a little.

Fuuuucck.

Nobody was sitting near us. Everyone sat closer to the middle.

But we sat in the back. *I* sat in the back, prepared to kill everything that got near me.

"Are you okay?"

No. I'm an animal. Sit on my lap.

I bit back a reply and nodded as the movie started. I turned my head in the opposite direction, covering my mouth, not trying to freak out.

I hadn't felt like this in a long time.

And all it took was a pint-sized nymph next to me.

This is torture. I wanted to lick the column of her neck, taste her sweet nipples on my tongue while I let her hips rock on my cock.

I counted to ten, waiting for my dick to get the picture that I couldn't fuck my woman in a movie theater.

I could feel her squirming next to me and I swore I wouldn't look, I wouldn't look, and then—I did. Her eyes met mine. Big, beautiful, I trailed lower to her breasts—I bit back a groan.

The truth was, I liked Evie as this distraction since going to the movies was hard for me.

I couldn't bring myself to confess the darkness that lurked within me—the nightmares that haunted my every step. Tendrils of it rising when I was alone.

I had purposely only taken Evie to small or midsize restaurants, which was all I could do.

I knew she thought I was catering to her, but my PTSD didn't let me go to big stores, big events, and even when I'd taken her to a bookstore, I'd just bought out the store.

Evie had marveled at how empty it was, and I'd grinned at her expression.

She can never find out I am who I am. I like her too much to fuck this up.

At the convention we'd gone to, I went early, missing the crowd. Leaving with her.

But Evie didn't know some things about me. The nightmares.

The panic was at the edge of my thoughts. The anxiety crept into my vision. It was there. Telling me I was worthless.

I was a piece of shit. And I didn't deserve anything. But her.

The movie theater was a no-go zone for my brain. The darkness, the screaming, the laughter—it was too much for me. But I wanted to feel like a man and like I could be with Evie. *I wanted to go to the fucking movies.*

I exhaled slowly, focusing on my breath and not panicking. The darkness covered and swallowed my vision, and then I felt Evie reaching out, putting her hand on my leg. I just want to be normal.

I want to be a normal man. Just Luke. Not a Devereaux. I want to be more than me.

I gripped it with my other hand and squeezed gently. She squeezed back.

And then, out of character and completely taking me by alarm, she moved my hand to her chest, resting over her heart. I felt the tender flesh of her breast against my palm. I closed my eyes.

Did she know I was losing my shit right now?

"Evie."

"Why are you freaking out? I can see it all over your face."

She turned to me a little. "Something's wrong. Did you just freak out when that noise went off…" She lowered her voice.

"Did something happen to you?" Evie didn't know I had been in the military.

I nodded. "Sorry."

"Don't be." She squeezed my hand. "Hey, I'm sorry—we can go." She tugged my hand, and I couldn't look at her. "Why do you look angry?"

I swallowed. Because I'm fucking freaking out. It was too much. I couldn't do it.

We can go.

But I want to take my girl out. The movie theater was…suffocating. Dark, oppressive, lights everywhere, but I couldn't see shit.

"I'm not angry." I closed my eyes, the words falling from my lips. "I want you. You look like a fucking present in that color against your skin. It's taking everything I have to not haul you onto my lap and—" I let out a ragged exhale. "Evie, just…let's just watch the movie."

I didn't want to freak her out.

I couldn't think between the movie and Evie sitting next to me like a fucking green goddess. Torn between anxiety and the heat in my body.

She stood and turned, her body moving past me. She was *leaving*—I felt the panic ensue, trapped in my body.

"Evie—" The rest of my words died on my lips as she spread my legs wider and sat on my lap.

A noise left me in shock. She'd never been this bold. I'd kissed her a handful of times, but because of how I liked to have sex—I never pushed her.

Never touched her.

But I wanted her.

I fucking wanted her.

"*There,*" she said. I caught her shy smile. "Now I'm on your lap. What next?"

CHAPTER 6
LUCAS

Dumbfounded.

That was the word.

In the place of the previous panic was the arousal crowding it over, pushing it out of the way to focus on my woman.

It wrapped dark and thick around me until I moved her to a more comfortable position.

I watched the delicate flutter of her pulse in the flash of light in the theater—I wanted to bite down *there*.

Her eyes were dark as she watched me.

The lights behind her cast shadows, and made me realize I could take her.

Fuck her through this entire fucking movie, distract me, distract her —make her come again and again until she was in my blood.

You have no idea what I am.

My tongue darted out, licking my lips, my heart ratcheting up in my chest, the earlier panic replaced with nothing but arousal. My dick wanted this fucking woman.

I felt her lean into me.

"*And?*"

I remembered my earlier words.

Haul you into my lap and...

I couldn't even think of just one thing, but ten things I'd do to her right there. *Right here.* In front of *everyone*.

My girl was on my lap.

My cock was harder than stone. I couldn't fuck her in public for our first time, but damn if it wouldn't be a goal in the future. My pulse ratcheted up as Evie blocked the view of the entire movie, and I realized I liked this better.

I didn't even feel myself moving my jacket over her shoulders to cover her a little in case anyone looked back, and I sank lower in my seat, moving her with me.

I'm losing it.

She was half-laying on me like this, enough for me to kiss her and cuddle her.

I ran my thumb over her lips, my eyes meeting hers. I mouthed, *Don't make a sound.* A puff of a breath left her. Her mouth opened, taking my thumb into it.

I closed my eyes at the feel of her tongue swirling around it. I was fucked.

She likes me.

I used my grip on her chin to pull her lower, my lips grazing her ear. "*And?* Did you sit on my lap to tempt me, Cherry? Don't stop sucking. Keep it in your mouth, doll." I felt *unleashed.* I should...I should warn her.

But I couldn't think for shit.

I had my arm around her, hauling her close while she sucked, the motion of her head clearly suggestive, and I growled, loving the way her tongue swirled like a woman on a mission.

"Is that how you take me in your mouth? I'm a lot bigger, doll. You think you can take me? Should I put you between my legs and find out?"

A soft moan left her. And I stopped. Her eyes met mine, my thumb slowly sliding out, brushing her moisture over her lips. Loving the way her eyes closed and, she sighed.

Darkness edged in my vision.

Little sub, she was testing me.

I removed it, sealing my lips over hers.

She tasted like caramel and simply her.

My tongue plunged in, loving the way she sucked and gave little whimpers. "How do you taste like that?"

"Candy," she whispered.

She reminds me of Christmas.

I felt my lips stretch into an easy grin before kissing her again, licking it from her mouth.

There were people here, and yet, I didn't give a fuck.

Let them hear. But I knew better.

Evie would be embarrassed, and I didn't want that. I wanted her as a confident goddess at my side.

I drew back loving the way every now and then the theater would plunge into darkness. On occasion, I clocked the few people in the theater since I'd picked a movie that had been out for a month.

My wet thumb trailed down her body until I cupped one of her lush breasts.

We were in public. *I couldn't—I shouldn't—*and then Evie moved her hands to her shirt, moving the fabric to reveal a fucking front zipper.

This is the best movie date ever.

I bit back a groan as she slowly undid it like a tease, tugging it down, and this time I bent my head to breathe.

She's fucking luscious.

I was salivating, as I kissed her over her heart to calm my breathing, calm my dick down to not bend her over, or worse, move her panties to the side in that skirt and sit her down on my cock for the entire movie while I sucked her nipples.

Don't be a fucking freak right now. Now is not the time.

Nothing really mattered but *her.*

Focus, focus. Do not black out.

Do not freak out.

The noises on screen covered up my harsh breaths panting as I moved my mouth over her skin.

Open mouth kisses all over, looking at her beautiful breasts, tipped with hard nipples, I took one in my mouth, and I was glad for the noises since I softly groaned.

I suckled her hungrily and I felt her grip a hand in my hair clutching me tightly.

To anyone passing us by, it would look like we were locked in a passionate embrace, but only I knew I was here licking my girl like she was the best meal I'd ever had.

I sucked and licked and promised mentally I'd pay her back for something so risky and raunchy.

She likes this. She likes you.

When I switched, it was Evie who tugged my hair until I hissed low and found her other nipple. I sucked it in my mouth as I worked my fingers lower, lower until I massaged her thighs.

I felt her head drop over mine, holding me close to her, I coaxed her legs open tugging on her nipple gently. "Are you okay?"

"Don't stop."

That was all I needed.

"Move the jacket over your lap," I sucked harder. She did, and I smiled against her skin, as her legs parted, and my fingers slipped under her skirt.

I barely grazed her, opting to feel her soft skin. I could feel her heat from here.

She's soaked.

Maybe Evie was into raunchier things than I thought. Maybe she would even like what I was into.

My fingers dipped until I found her entrance, so wet, I knew she'd make a mess on my hands.

Very slowly, gently, I brushed the entrance of her body with my middle finger. Gently. *Firmly.*

Her mouth opened in a silent gasp, and I took a moment to savor that sound in a way that left me breathless as well.

I kept my eyes on her, holding the back of her neck to keep her eyes on mine as I slowly gently slid my middle finger into her.

Her response was instant, her fingers gripped my shoulders tight enough to sting, her eyes low-lidded, her breath caught, and her body melted into mine.

I kept my voice low. "Is that okay?" I slid it further. She bit her lower lip and nodded.

Is it hot in here? Or is it just me?

"Should I continue?" Another nod. I bit back a grin. I slowly worked my finger, my whisper so low, I didn't know if she heard me. "You're so wet for me, does that feel good?"

Yes, it was mouthed over my lips. I smiled against her mouth.

"Should I give you more?" I paused. "Would you like that, Cherry?"

I would've laughed at the feel of her clenching me, if I wasn't so fucking ready to do just that.

Evie squirmed, her body overwhelmed, and almost shying away from the pleasure it knew I would bring her. But it didn't matter. She was caught and pinned.

"I asked you a question." I curled my finger inside of her.

She nodded, ducking her head in embarrassment. I smiled then.

Sweet brave girl.

I rubbed that spot and watched her eyes close, biting down on her lip. "Give me your mouth."

She did just that as I drew my finger in and out, I thrust my tongue mimicking my finger.

This is definitely the best fucking movie date.

I felt everything, inhaled her scent of caramel and vanilla, swallowed her little whimpers in my mouth, felt the sensation of nothing but her. Evie.

I worked that finger back and forth until her mouth parted, and her fingers still gripped my shirt tightly.

I silently trailed my lips back down to her breasts.

She's so tight.

She'd feel like heaven around my cock, throbbing and painfully hard for her. I gently curled my finger inside of her.

I clamped my teeth around one of her nipples as I added a second digit to the first one, and I *swear*, I felt her start to shake.

That's a good girl.

I pumped my fingers while sucking, loving the way she let out breathless gasps, silent sobs, she was trying so hard to be quiet. Her hips writhed, and I knew she'd be so fucking sweet when she came. I couldn't stop.

"Are you close?"

Her walls around my fingers clenched tighter in answer. I curled them into her, loving the way her mouth parted and her eyes locked with mine all glassy and soft.

I fucking knew it.

Yes.

"Should I let you finish on my fingers, or my cock? Push your panties to the side, fuck inside of you. Make you squirm on it while I do this."

She gasped quietly, and then—*fucking hell*—Evie nodded more frantic than all the other times.

I'm going to lose my shit right now.

And then her lips moved over mine. *"Don't stop."*

"You wanna come on my cock, doll? Spread your legs, give these people a show?"

"Don't stop, Luke."

The clenching and squeezing around my fingers increased.

Fuuucck.

Her eyes were closed, and she was trembling. I was dragging this out.

She needs to come.

I tucked her head into my neck, then took mercy on her, curling my fingers into her pussy making sure I found that spot of hers.

I knew I did when she twisted, but I kept her tight to me. "*Shh.*"

I would make it better.

I'm going to take care of you.

And then I began working my fingers in her, rubbing that spot vigorously, instead of thrusting them in and out, I just held her tight and felt her thighs shake around my arm.

Felt her gently meeting me thrust for thrust.

Her little whimpers against my shirt driving me insane. I knew how to drive her insane.

I'd be a fucking *beast* when she let me loose. I kept going.

"Luke." I looked down at her, biting her lip. "Keep going—" Her eyes darted to my mouth.

Was she asking me to—

Anything for you, doll.

I'm just a man.

Just a man with you.

"Put your arms around my neck, come up—there you go." I could actually pull her earlobe into my mouth. "I'm going to take you home after this and fuck this little spot you keep moaning over—that's nice, isn't it?"

Evie had no idea how much of a fucking deviant I was.

"That's it, I can feel your thighs shaking, right there? I know…come on, doll. Let me have it—"

I bit down on her earlobe, loving the way her entire body worked, and she shook.

Next time we came to the fucking movies, I'd just buy the entire fucking theater and fuck her through the entire thing.

That rhythmic clenching became tighter and tighter, and I felt the moment I knew she was going to come.

So close. So close.

I moved my thumb to her clit and gently pressed down. "I'm going to fuck this little spot until it's sore, take you like—" I felt her hand clap over my mouth as she rolled her hips into mine.

Oh shiiitt.

I felt when she came. I dragged my mouth down her neck, tucking

57

her head into mine, finding her pulse and pressing my mouth there. Breathing as she muffled her moans.

I closed my eyes, memorizing that rhythmic clenching around my fingers.

Her legs tried to clamp shut around me.

None of that.

I curled my fingers unrelenting against that spot inside of her.

"Such a good girl, work your hips on me." Little noises left her, and I yanked her head back, stamping my mouth over hers, eating every single one until I'd drained her, and only then, did I slowly stop.

She was shaking, her eyes a little dazed and licking her lips.

"You have no idea what I'm going to do to you." I marveled at the wanton creature in my arms. "Did I take your words, doll?"

"What you said—" she panted. "I want that."

She kissed me, and I had a moment to be stunned before I leaned back and let her, closing my eyes to this woman.

I will give you absolutely anything.

"Do you want to sit on my lap?"

Yes.

I slid my fingers out slowly and brought them to my lips, licking them clean and nearly groaning with the taste of her. I watched her reaction.

Evie's about to find out how much of a deviant I am.

And then she brought my lips to her and kissed me. Hard. I returned it and gripped her tightly, adjusting her and letting her wrap her slender arms around my neck.

There you are, doll.

Her fingers reached for my dick, and I instantly grabbed her wrists, not missing the way she trembled.

I shook my head. I was not about to let her do anything to me in the fucking movies. I'd lose my shit. I only said half of the shit I did because she got off on it, but I'd only do it if she knew what she was getting herself into.

And an empty theater.

Her eyes had been wide—*sweet brave girl*—I kissed her quietly.

"Good girl, come here." I tucked her head against my chest. Evie laid with her palms curled into her like closed petals.

Every so often, she'd turn her head and seek my kisses. She wanted me to pet her. Kiss her. Seeking my comfort.

Seeking my pleasure.

I never expected the demons to stir in my soul. *To sigh.*

Even though she calmed me down most of the time, her presence in my lap should've stopped anything from rising.

Anything at all.

The first half of the movie I was fine.

It was just mystery and comedy, and it was right up my alley.

Plus, I inhaled Evie's hair and realized this was the best movie date.

And then I didn't know what to expect from a wild ride of a movie but, there was a car bomb in the middle of it.

The room went dark, the explosion lit up my vision, and another explosion went off in my chest—and I was gone.

CHAPTER 7
LUCAS

THE DARKNESS ROSE WITHIN ME, ITS TENDRILS WRAPPING AROUND MY mind, threatening to drag me under.

The acrid scent of smoke filled my nostrils as another explosion reverberated through my skull. I was losing my grip on reality.

Run.

I grabbed Evie's hand, her skin warm and soft against my clammy palm.

"Evie, we need to leave. It's not safe," I gasped, barely aware of the words leaving my lips. Panic constricted my chest as I pulled at her urgently.

Run. Now.

"Luke?" Evie's voice cut through the chaos, a beacon in the swirling madness, but I couldn't respond.

Not now, not here, not with her.

"We need to leave," I choked out, desperation clawing at my throat. I couldn't risk hurting her.

Another explosion ripped through the air, the taste of dust and ashes coating my tongue. I was lost.

"Evie—"

Screams assaulted my ears, piercing and relentless. I wanted to scream, too, but I held my breath, held it all in. Memories flickered behind my eyelids. *Run.*

Devereaux, we're under fire—

Lt, you gotta move!

I was *trying*. Flames licked at my skin, but I couldn't feel the burn. Exhaustion weighed down my bones. Searing pain in my arm.

Amidst the chaos, a familiar voice reached out to me. "Luke!"

Evie? She shouldn't be here. *"You have to get somewhere safe."*

"I can take you there," she said. She was pulling me, guiding me.

"Evie, they're going to take my team. I gotta stay." They're going to die.

"Your team is fine. They're safe."

But they weren't. *"I'm hit— I'm bleeding. I'm dying. Run."*

The metallic scent of blood filled my nostrils. Her voice broke, but she didn't let me succumb, didn't let me die. *Oh fuck, Evie.*

"Go!" The scream tore from my throat, raw and desperate, swallowed by the pandemonium surrounding us.

Bright lights seared my vision, blurring the world into a dizzying kaleidoscope of terror.

"Can we use this room? Please, I think he's having a panic attack."

I pressed against Evie, her solid presence grounding me as my world spun out of control.

I clung to her, my anchor in the storm, my gasping breaths mingling with the deafening cacophony of shouts, screams, and explosions.

But the memories—they pulled me back, back to the worst moments of my life.

I was trapped, reliving the horrors I'd tried so hard to forget.

The fear, the pain, the helplessness. It consumed me, dragging me down into the depths of my own mind.

I gasped, struggling to breathe, to think. *"Evie—"*

Someone answered. And then silence.

She was pulling me somewhere, tugging me closer to her. *"Luke—"*

"You're okay, and you're safe, son. Been through Nam, I know those shakes when I see 'em."

I looked at the elderly man in his vest, the uniform for the fucking movie theater I was in, my chest heaving with each labored breath. Evie's hand rested on my chest, a gentle reminder of her presence, but it did little to calm the storm raging inside me.

Memories flashed before my eyes, vivid and terrifying.

The sound of gunfire, the screams of the wounded, the smell of smoke and blood.

My body trembled uncontrollably, my muscles tensed and ready for a fight that existed only in my mind.

I felt trapped, suffocated by the weight of the demons in my head, unable to break free, and they fucking laughed at me.

You broke down in front of Evie.

Evie's voice reached me, a distant echo amidst the chaos.

"You're okay."

I felt fingers threaded through my hair as I shook and gasped for air.

The shame and humiliation clawed at my insides, their sharp talons ripping through any semblance of comfort Evie's words might have offered.

The bitter taste of failure coated my tongue, a pungent reminder of my inadequacies.

I had foolishly believed I was past this, that I could manage my PTSD without the crutch of medication.

Therapy.

"I'm sorry," I mumbled, the words like ashes in my mouth. "I just wanted to bring you to the movies…"

Oh fuck. I was getting emotional about this shit?

Evie's gentle touch urged me to meet her gaze, to confront the vulnerability I so desperately sought to hide.

"What are you sorry for?" Her hand, soft and warm, cupped my cheek with a tenderness I felt wholly undeserving of. "I only wish you had told me and didn't try to push yourself."

Push myself. *At the fucking movie theater.*

But her words were lost in the deafening roar of my self-loathing and disgust.

"Hey, don't do that—" Evie's voice cut through my spiraling thoughts, but the urge to push her away, shield her from the broken mess I was, grew stronger with each passing second.

"No, no, come back—" Her hands gripped my face, her eyes wide and imploring. "Luke, look at me. *Look at me.* You are not going to push me away. I'm not letting you go. Do you understand me? I see that look. *I know that look.* I'm not scared of you. And there's nothing you should be ashamed of."

Who was shaking so hard?

Her arms tightened around me as I trembled uncontrollably. She glanced around the room before turning back to me.

"Let me help you off this floor so we can go somewhere quiet. Didn't you say your apartment was near here?"

"No, no—" I protested. *"No, I can't—"*

And then she kissed me. Straight up kissed me on the floor of some break room.

Her warmth, her *heat*—my senses lit up, utterly disarmed by this woman. I couldn't even focus on my misery, too consumed by the feel of her lips on mine.

"I'm not going anywhere," she whispered. "Is there somewhere we can go to talk? Somewhere quiet?"

I nodded, too drained to argue. My place wasn't far.

But something told me taking Evie to my home wouldn't be the greatest idea in the world. Not after this.

But because I was an absolute monster.

I did. *I said yes.*

CHAPTER 8
EVIE

"I HAVE PTSD."

I gathered that.

I listened as Luke sat on his couch holding a lychee orange blossom drink I found in his super-organized fridge. I thought the taste would be a good distraction.

I listened to Luke explain his struggle with post-traumatic stress disorder. He'd been in the military, something he had never mentioned because of *this*.

Back at the movie theater, this had been the last thing I expected. Not after—everything else.

I hadn't expected him to take me back to this beautiful apartment he'd brought me to. I knew he worked in his father's company, but this was...*something else.*

As he sat next to me on the couch, the massive arched windows reflected the twinkling city lights outside.

Luke had turned on the dimmable lights, keeping them low, citing his headache as the reason.

The warm, muted glow cast gentle shadows across his face, highlighting the tension in his jaw and the furrow of his brow.

I studied him closely, taking in the way his broad shoulders hunched forward as if carrying an invisible weight.

His hands, usually steady and strong, trembled slightly as they rested on his lap.

The rise and fall of his chest was rapid, his breathing labored, as if he had just run a marathon.

He finally met my eyes, and the pain I saw there made my heart ache. His blue eyes, normally bright and vibrant, were clouded with a mixture of shame, fear, and vulnerability.

"I've been struggling with it for a while now," he admitted. "I thought I had it under control, but things trigger me, and I can't stop it."

"I can't even begin to imagine what you've been through. Why didn't you just say—"

"Because I wanted to take my girlfriend to the fucking movies."

I stopped moving, stunned by the intensity of his words.

He covered his eyes with his free hand and hung his head, letting out a heavy, dejected exhale. "I just want to feel *normal*. Like a man. Not this. There's something wrong with me."

I scooted closer to him, our thighs now touching, and gently pulled his hand away from his face. I tilted his chin up, forcing him to look at me.

"There's nothing wrong with who you are."

The words poured out of me from somewhere deep inside, a place where I didn't feel it for myself, but I knew it for him.

"I think you are your harshest critic. Everything I have seen from you doesn't tell me these moments define you as a whole. I think...everything around you forms the bigger picture of who you are. The people you keep for company, the family around you, and how you choose to treat people. It isn't fair to say one thing; one moment defines you."

I continued, my voice growing stronger, not just for him but for myself.

"When my mom died, I was fifteen. I was so lost. I didn't know what to do. I struggled with every single decision I made. So, my brother made them for me until it became his duty to do it. I began to realize that by making choices for myself, I didn't have to let that moment define me. I went away to school, I worked for his company as my own person, and I tried to build myself, not wanting to be defined by my... story. I wanted to create a better person within myself."

He turned to look at me, his eyes filled with a mixture of surprise and empathy. "I didn't know you lost your mother."

I nodded, my throat tightening with emotion as I told him about Mama.

"I had nightmares about her death for years. I know it's not the same as yours, not even close, but I didn't let it...define me. I understand your demons are a lot more complicated, but I hope you get help. Gabriel encouraged me to go to therapy, and I worked through a lot."

His throat worked. "I have a therapist."

I nodded, relieved to hear that. It was a start.

"You don't think I'm a monster?"

I furrowed my brow, confused by his question. "For what? You didn't do anything wrong."

"I ruined our date—"

"There'll be plenty more," I interrupted, my voice gentle but firm.

He snapped his mouth shut, his eyes widening in surprise. He let out a shaky exhale, and for a moment, I just looked at him.

This man, the one who had asked me out so adorably, now appeared exhausted and worn down. The shadows under his eyes were a testament to the battles he fought every day.

"Is this the reason you keep your distance, why your hands shake?" I asked softly, realization dawning on me. "Why you didn't kiss me? Why, you held back?"

He let out a breath and nodded, his gaze dropping to his lap. "I didn't want to touch you with my demons, when I finally...when I—" His eyes met mine, the intensity in them stealing my breath. "It's not fair to you."

And I processed what he was saying. I knew his nightmares were the reason why he wasn't sleeping. I knew he didn't like to talk about them.

I curled into his body and held him close. "Do you want to tell me what happened back in the theater?"

I thought he would stay silent, but to my surprise, he began to speak. "It's not just one moment. I think when I used to think of people describing PTSD, I thought it would be one moment. But it's not. It's a collection of...memories. I was deployed a lot."

I felt the tenseness in his body, his words pulling at my heartstrings. "The constant wars I found myself in...served nothing for me. I joined the military to be a part of something. In the end, I got thrown into fights that were never my battle to begin with."

He took a breath looking at me with softer eyes. Filled with something dark I saw on occasion, not all the time.

"Every night, I think about all the firefights and all the moments where I thought I was going to die."

He took a shuddering breath, his vulnerability raw and exposed.

"I didn't mean to freak out," Luke said softly, his tone laced with apology. "I never want to hurt you, just want to protect you."

"I know you're not going to hurt me," I reassured him, soft but firm.

As I looked up at him, I could see the fierce protectiveness in his eyes and the desire to keep me safe from any harm.

I could see that this conversation wasn't helping him.

No. He needed something…something *tangible*…

"Do you want to make it up to me?" He nodded with such eagerness I had to smile. "Do you want to go on a date with me?"

"Right now?" He looked at me, incredulous. I nodded, smiling. "Where?"

"Right here," I said softly. "We can have a little indoor picnic. We can get some blankets and put something on the TV. The date isn't ruined." I paused, considering. "I think our date just had an intermission."

A myriad of emotions played across his face—surprise, awe, and finally, a smile that I had come to love.

"You found the cake," he said, his eyes lighting up.

I grinned. "I did."

His lips widened into a smile. "Do you want to pick the movie?"

"I already did." When he dipped his head to kiss me, I leaned in more, feeling something shift inside of me, something different for him…

I never want to hurt you.

CHAPTER 9
EVIE

I woke up in Luke's arms on his couch.

I felt a sense of…something soft wash over me.

The usual chaos was gone, responsibilities nonexistent, replaced by calm I hadn't experienced in years.

Memories of laying on Mama's lap while she rubbed my hair drifted in, but—I wasn't with her.

My legs tangled with his as his breath fanned out over my head. I was using his arm as a pillow and didn't move. I didn't want to.

We had gotten a blanket sometime during the night and cuddled together. The movie on the TV was playing silently as we talked all night.

Memories of Luke and me talking late into the night drifted into my consciousness as I took in the first rays of morning light peeking through the gaps in the curtains, highlighting parts of the apartment I couldn't see last night.

I stayed out.

I left the manor.

Luke had opened up about his PTSD and his family, revealing that his father was a wealthy real estate developer. Luke hated his father.

I listened to him tell me things he admitted only his therapist knew.

He had told me about his mother passing away when he was young. Luke had loved his mother.

Not knowing what to do with his son, his father sent Luke away at fourteen to boarding school. Luke said he'd met his friends, Teo and

68

Andrei, there, but I imagined what I'd feel like after losing Mama and Gabriel and sending me away.

Somewhere foreign. Something *unfriendly.*

How I would've had to survive.

And by contrast, even after losing Mama, I had an upbringing that most people would've gushed over. Gabriel. Reed. Nate and Selena for my siblings.

Warm. Serene. *Cozy.*

I felt safe in Luke's arms. It was different from how I felt in Gabriel's. Any of my brothers.

Luke…he made me feel like a woman. Just Evie…*the woman.*

I thought I could outrun my life…, but it didn't work.

Luke said he felt haunted. He didn't understand why I wanted him.

But to me, he was more than what he *didn't* think he had.

He had a lot.

I lived with some haunted people.

Everyone around me was running from something. Gabriel might not say it, but he strolled around the manor brooding with my sister across his heart.

Everyone I work with is haunted.

Nate, one of the guys who works for Gabriel, used to be a sniper.

I've heard him tell stories that Gabriel hates me listening to…you haven't met Gabriel. I'm sure he's seen some horrific things to tell you.

And then something had shifted….

Would you ever want to meet him?

Luke had been curious.

What happened to him killing me?

He's my only family. Would you want to meet him? Please say yes.

Yeah…I'd love to meet Gabriel…

He isn't that scary. He's super sweet.

He's sweet to you. It sounds like he'd murder everyone to protect you.

Don't worry, Luke Delaney, I'll protect you.

He switched the subject to Mama. I had told him, quietly sharing stories with him.

Do you miss her? The tenderness in his voice made my heart flutter.

I used to miss her so much…

I told him all that Gabriel had done for me. Last night, I told Luke that Gabriel and I weren't biological siblings.

He pinky promised he wouldn't tell a soul.

And I told him.

He'd been stunned.

*Gabriel adopted me as his sister after Mama died. He was married to my sister...she passed away a long time ago. It's just me and him. He loved Isobel. He gets upset when you talk about her, but I can tell. I know he loves me as an extension of—*I stopped at his expression.

He straightened. *Monroe had a wife?*

I had never heard him sound like that.

Why do you look like that? Did you not imagine someone like him could have someone?

I just—yeah, actually, that's exactly what it is. Even when you talk about him, he sounds so closed off—Monroe was married....

I saw the movie flickering, and I marveled at life with Luke. It felt like being awash in...so much calm despite what had happened when he had his PTSD.

Life here slowed down. Completely.

Luke's arm around my waist felt like a steady presence, and I didn't want to leave. Ever.

My mind drifted to my brother, who would no doubt wake up and notice I wasn't floating around the house.

I had the foresight to message him close to midnight, telling him I'd be back tomorrow—and there was no way to hide that I did, in fact, start seeing someone.

But he would text. And call. And worry.

I better get up and call him. Otherwise, he'll send in a team to get me.

And somehow, that was not how I wanted Luke to meet Gabriel...*I should get up.*

As I shifted just a tiny bit to wiggle out of his iron grip, I didn't make a sound, and Luke's arm tightened around me.

He adjusted both of his arms and one leg to pin me down like I was his favorite teddy bear. I smiled, light laughter bubbling up in my throat, which immediately shifted as his hands moved.

I felt his lips press against my hair, and I felt his hips moving against my butt, and—I gasped a little.

"Luke—"

"You were trying to sneak out."

I chewed my lower lip to not respond, but my body did. It clenched internally at the sound of his sleep-roughened voice. "Use me as a pillow and leave, hm?"

I couldn't think, as I smiled at his teasing, his hands drifted lower.

He took in a breath, and I felt him stir, *all of him,* and I was suddenly

70

aware that I was caught, pinned, by this man stretching like a sun-warmed lion. One who laughed low with his hands brushing over my inner thighs, leaving little trails of fire in their wake.

"What am I going to do with you now?"

I gasped as his hand brushed the skirt's hemline I had borrowed from Selena. I was soaked.

"Did I take your words, doll?"

I swallowed; I liked this version of him just as much as I liked the others. This version who had done things to me in public I never imagined.

"What you said last night," I struggled to say the words. "All of it."

I'm going to fuck this little spot until it's sore, take you...

Behind me, his fingers stilled, for a moment I thought he wouldn't. I thought he'd say no, that he didn't want to take me for all his demons.

I was so wrong.

He slid his fingers up my skirt, and I bit down on my lower lip as he groaned, touching my heat—I was *soaked*.

"You need me?"

Like I needed my next breath.

"*Yes.*"

CHAPTER 10
EVIE

THE FIRST STROKE OVER MY CLIT, I BURNED.

I gasped as he shifted lower, his mouth opened, capturing my pulse, and I moaned loudly, shamelessly in the privacy of his home—*finally*—as he stroked.

"Thank you for taking care of me last night. You were such a good girl."

His voice sent warmth to my center, where I was already embarrassingly wet for him.

"I want to take care of you now, doll."

"H…how?" *Please, get inside me.*

I felt the smile against my neck, his tongue darting out as he stroked slow circles over my clit. "I want to drive you a little crazy, just like you drive me crazy before I slide my cock into that tight little pussy."

My eyelids fluttered as I felt the heat on my cheeks.

He let out a shaky breath as though that confession affected him more.

"Does that feel good?" I nodded frantically. "Or should I go lower?"

Yes, please.

His fingers stopped moving. "Use your words, doll."

I turned pink, squirming as he didn't move, I gasped. *"Touch me."*

"How?" He kissed my neck. "Like this?"

He swirled his fingers around my clit, never touching, and a groan left me. To my absolute embarrassment, he laughed low.

"Did you want something else?"

I didn't even recognize this side of him.

I was pinned helplessly under this *playful* man.

"I know you need to be filled and fucked, don't you?"

Yes.

His deceptively soft voice infiltrated all rational thought, and I knew what he was doing. This was *him*. Mine.

It was a whisper in my head, but it became a full-on scream when I felt him brush his fingers over my clit. Just. *Teasing.*

"Yes, yes." I was panting, trying to work my hips, but his chuckle made me blush.

"Right there?" I felt his tongue at my throat. "Use your words, doll."

I nodded frantically. "Please keep going."

"Did you want me to live up to my promise?"

I distinctly remember what he was asking.

Fuck me. In front of everyone.

As he moved his hips in a sensual drive, I moaned.

His hand came around to my hair, gripping tendrils at my nape, hauling me back, his breath hot on my neck as he slid his fingers lower. Right there…

"Should I keep going?" Use your words, doll.

"Yes, *yes, please fuck me.*"

He stopped moving, and for a moment, I was stunned.

Did I just—I think I did—I just—

And then I moaned *loudly* as he slid his fingers—*blissfully*—into me.

Luke opened his mouth against my throat. "That's better, isn't it?"

A frantic nod left me as I clenched wildly around him.

"You're so wet for me, doll. I bet I could slide my cock into this tiny little pussy and make it my home."

I sobbed as he slowly worked his fingers in and out as he said it. I didn't notice my hands reaching for him, one of them threading in his hair, the other clutching the couch.

His fingers curled inside of me, drawing a soft cry, and I didn't recognize myself at that moment. I gasped as his mouth found how sensitive my earlobe was.

Luke tugged, licking my pulse, and sucked hard as his fingers worked in me against that spot. I was so close, having already been driven to an edge once.

My hips worked as he tipped my head back, manipulating my body for my pleasure.

73

"So fucking wet...that's my good girl...can't wait to fuck you every morning."

Yes, yes, yes. Anything.

Whatever you want.

I was so close. *Just let me—*

"*Use your words, doll.*"

Oh God, no one had ever asked me for this.

I sobbed hard, unable to think. A whimper left my lips as he *didn't* stop.

I *can't.*

He stopped moving his fingers abruptly, and I gasped at the sensation of that.

That was *mean.*

"Should I keep going? Taste you with my tongue?" I didn't recognize this man. "You wake up so greedy. I could have *you* in the mornings... every morning..."

"*Luke—*"

He lapped lazily at my throat. "Hm?"

Oh God, he's evil.

He bit down gently and sucked. I shivered at the feeling of his fingers taking up space in me. Not moving an inch.

I felt it trapped in my throat as he curled them again, and a noise left me. He bit down on my throat, keeping me pinned.

"P...please, don't stop." I was on the verge of something. *So close.* Hanging on the edge of—

"What do you want me to do?" He was *wicked.* A soft moan left me. *Use your words, doll.*

I took a deep breath. "I—I want you to...fuck me like this."

A pleased sound left him, and then he began moving again between my legs and opened his mouth over my throat. "With pleasure."

When he held me down, and his fingers moved, I was gone.

An animal noise left me as he worked his fingers *finally*, giving me what I needed, frantic and desperate, the pleasure blossoming between my legs in my womb, tightening and threatening to spill over so fast I wouldn't make it—

Oh God, it was so intense—I can't—

"*Luke!*"

"Come for me."

The tension broke, I broke, a cry left me as I felt his fingers move from my hair, holding me across my chest as I moved, working my hips, the unbearable pleasure racking my body with wave after wave.

I was whimpering and crying out as he gruffly coaxed me through it.

Such a good girl.

You did such a good job.

My orgasm lasted forever with those words.

Keep going, doll, that's nice, isn't it? You feel incredible squeezing like that. I'm so proud of you, doll.

I was shaking. Trembling as he slowly slid his fingers out.

I was trembling so hard as he rolled me onto my back and moved, his lips raking down my body, tearing at my skirt until I shivered and bare from the waist down.

I gasped as I felt puffs of air against my sensitized pussy.

"What are you doing?"

I thought...I thought he was going to fuck me now.

Molten-blue eyes drifted up to me, and I clenched a little at the sight of him between my legs, looking at me like a hungry lion he was.

I felt his tongue at my clit, and I closed my eyes, my fingers tangling in his hair.

"Keeping my promises."

And then he sucked.

CHAPTER 11
LUCAS

I was convinced I had a problem.

I was hard all the time.

I couldn't sit at my fucking desk without imagining my girlfriend coming all over my tongue. Tasting her in my mouth.

Part of me wanted to do it to keep from fucking her in the morning. Even though I had wanted nothing more than to slide into her, I refrained.

It's not fair to her.

And I settled for eating at her until she begged me to stop—using her words.

I knew Evie was a little shy at times, I knew how she felt about being just a little sister.

The baby Titan. I knew she *had* confidence, sometimes when she teased me, I caught glimpses of a little fire in her.

I wanted to coax it out of her, the woman I saw in her. I knew she was there, she was my girl after all.

I could see it under the surface.

I can help her blossom. Thrive under me.

With that soft peachy skin, cherry cola hair—*fuck—now I was hard again*. At *work*. Images of her sitting on my cock at my desk took over. I took deep breaths.

Evie had wanted to finish me but—I couldn't allow it. If she touched me? I'd fuck her. I wouldn't stop. And something told me since it was afternoon?

If she didn't get home soon, someone—*Gabriel*—would find her and murder me.

And getting caught inside his sister was not how I wanted to meet him. I couldn't get her pants and moans out of my ears. They were clinging to my skin.

I needed her to understand she could ask me for anything in bed. She would ask me for whatever she needed.

I can't give you shit but problems.

And her words drifted over me when she'd spent the night talking to me. Talking me down from my demons. Soothing. Safe.

My heart clenched remembering her.

I hadn't had sex with her, even though it took everything in me to stop from just taking my cock out and slamming it in her.

I held back. And what made it easier was knowing that while I had her acceptance and trust?

I was living a fucking lie.

Please, more.

Please lick my pussy.

I want your tongue.

Don't stop, please don't stop.

Oh God, Luke, I'm coming.

I couldn't stop thinking about her.

Imagining the way that tight little pussy would struggle to take me, the way she'd scream when I pounded that spot between her legs, and again, and again. *I'm getting too deep.*

My little crush had become my wildest dream. *What the fuck was I thinking?*

And that was the thing?

I wasn't thinking at all when it came to Evie.

It was like my brain stopped working and only my dick could function. And my dick wanted this woman like its next breath.

When she had left, I inhaled her scent left on my hoodie practically groaning with how fucking blue my balls were.

I'm not fucking Evie with my demons.

When I confided in Matteo about my relationship with Evie, he grinned, his eyes alight with mischief.

"Does this mean sharing her is off the table?"

The thought immediately made me want to put my fist through his stomach. Rage, hot and swift went through me.

He grinned. *"Thought so."* He winked. "You never gave a shit before."

I was younger. I gave him a look, my thoughts drifting to Evie and the way she made me feel. Matteo's comment struck a nerve, and I found myself growing protective of her.

"Don't talk about Evie like that," I warned, my tone serious. "She's not yours."

Matteo made a dismissive noise, waving his elegant fingers. "I'm not dumb enough to touch Monroe's sister. You need to be locked away, *what is it called?*"

"*Prison?*"

I needed to be locked away somewhere.

With Evie. For days.

"But for crazy people." I snorted, acknowledging the absurdity of it. Lying to Evie while simultaneously trying to seduce her was a fucking line in the sand being blown to bits every day. Matteo's words gave me pause, a flicker of uncertainty coursing through my veins.

"I know you work, you little shit," I deflected, unwilling to delve into the intimate details of my relationship. "Just because you come in here like you're seventeen doesn't make me think you're not building a new car in your brain."

"I've seen *you* with women." Matteo sent me a look letting me know he knew about what I liked in my past and not even bothering to comment on being a workaholic.

"I have never seen you *this* stupid." He leaned back. "I'm insane, but I'm proud of it. Like I don't know the shit you've done." I didn't want to go into that with Evie in my life.

What—who Matteo did in his office.

"Why are you here? I know *that* look. Something happened to you." I had known Matteo since he was a pre-teen, and he always had a guilty expression when shit hit the fan.

Part of the reason I tolerated him was because I saw that kid—the kid that had gotten into trouble with me and Andrei. And Matteo was all of the things about me that I couldn't face.

Matteo's eyes were mercurial, shifting eerily and bright. "Something's happening at Titan. Whittaker came to my office this morning. He tried to find out if I was responsible for some trouble with his girl-friend. Do you remember her, Alisha Malhotra?"

"Did you and Alisha…?"

I could've sworn she never slept with him.

But he had a *huge* crush on her.

For a year I listened to him talk about her nonstop.

"No, I would never fuck a nice girl," Matteo said the same way people said they didn't have rabies, his eyes flickering to me.

"Whittaker *saw* Thierry," he muttered under his breath about Thierry pulling a gun out on him.

I sat up straighter. *"Thierry pulled a gun on Reed."*

Matteo inclined his head, his expression grim. "I told Thierry, he was a friend. But Thierry looks the *most* like he's family. *A DuPont.* I told Thierry not to carry his gun around. If Andrei catches a *whiff* of Titan sniffing around us? He'll have my head."

Because Andrei was quietly pulling Durand *and* Roadsters out, and de-merging the brands from Maxine's brand—*that empire is tied together.*

Thierry drawing a gun on Reed Whittaker, who could meddle in that was a headache Andrei didn't need.

"I don't think Reed cares if Thierry breaks the law. You don't want Titan to dig into Thierry for who? Maxine?" I couldn't imagine Reed being petty, but I didn't know. Because they didn't like me.

The DuPonts kept a lot of secrets close to their chest.

"Thierry pulled a gun on the man, who is *dating* Alisha. She *works* for my fucking mother. *Did you forget that?*"

I had.

"Andrei is worried Whittaker or Monroe will realize who Thierry is and leverage *that* alone." He leaned back like he had a migraine.

"Not to mention they will *murder you* when he finds out you're sleeping with his sister. I'm not afraid of Titan *finding* information on Thierry. They can try all they want."

Those electric blues flashed with intensity. "I'm afraid of what's going to happen when they realize they *can't find anything on Thierry.*"

I'd never seen Matteo look like that. "Andrei doesn't need attention from Titan. I'm insane, *not stupid.*"

This was about more than business. That's why the loft was in Matteo's name. And I was friends with the DuPont's.

Matteo sighed, leaning back in his chair. "Thierry came back from Cape Verde, and I told him to lie low."

I didn't know what Thierry was doing in Cape Verde, but I knew that island had no extradition.

Which meant anyone accused of committing crimes in the United States could not be arrested and sent back. I fucking knew Matteo had done shit that he wouldn't say. I knew he was *the* investor in *De Nuit.*

And I know exactly who that club belongs to.

Matteo was warning me.

"I'm fucked if Monroe or Whittaker find out who Thierry is, and you're fucked when Gabriel and Reed find out you're breaking in their sister." He muttered something about needing a new toy to play with.

All I processed was his words on Evie.

"I'm not breaking in Evie," I snapped, my protective instincts flaring at the mention of her name like that.

She wasn't some whore. She was my girl.

Matteo's words echoed in my mind as I considered my relationship with Evie.

He looked at me then his canines flashing. "What else are you doing? Besides breaking her heart." He shrugged. "Even I'm not *that* fucked up."

I didn't like that sensation running through me. Talking to Matteo was like my conscience in real life.

"I'm not trying to hurt her," I confessed. I wanted to build her confidence, *praise her,* make her feel brave enough to express to me what she needed, both sexually and non-sexually. In all ways.

"Don't give me that look—" Matteo cut me off.

"I didn't ask what *you wanted,* I asked you what you've *done,*" he said, his words cutting like a knife, forcing me to confront the reality of my actions. The mischievous playboy was gone. "You're so fucked, you're not even thinking."

Matteo's demeanor shifted, the playful façade falling away to reveal the predatory creature lurking beneath.

His alien eyes seemed to pierce through my defenses, laying bare the conflicting emotions that warred within me.

Reminding me of *who* that little boy I knew had become.

"I know what my mistakes are. *I make them on purpose.* I'm bracing for whatever mess is coming. *I smell it.* For you and for me."

He's worried about fallout.

He never said things outright, but I understood his warning.

Trouble was on the horizon, *whether I liked it or not.*

"She *can't* be your wife, she *isn't really* your girlfriend, you *won't* get her pregnant—when it ends, *what is left? Not you,* since we both know her brother is going to show up at your door any day now," Matteo said, his gaze unwavering.

"Play your cards wisely. Tell her the truth. If she loves you as much as you love her, she'll fight for you."

Never took you for a romantic.

"She would hate me."

"Not as much as she will when she realizes she's been in bed with *you*," Matteo countered, his words cutting through me like a knife.

"You are my brother. I am everything about you that you are not proud of. *I know.* I've known you since you stopped those idiots from picking on me for my eyes." I knew that little shit was in there, a dark mop of hair crying to me and Andrei.

Now he was a six-foot three beast who had a penchant for tearing people apart.

"I don't know what I'm doing." Not with Evie.

I did not like that look on his face. "Yes, you do."

His grin was absolutely wicked. "You knew the *entire* time what you were doing. I told you, people like us, we make our mistakes on purpose."

He backed me into a corner.

"I'm not saying you don't love Evie. I'm saying, you're *insane*, and unlike me—*you are an idiot.*"

I was. I was a fool. "Son of a bitch."

He tipped his head with *that* smile. "I won't argue that."

CHAPTER 12
EVIE

"He's licking my AP watch."

Gabriel grumbled, his brows furrowed as he watched the giant Samoyed enthusiastically cleaning his expensive timepiece.

I bit back a laugh at the look on Gabriel's face of utter disgust at the giant Siberian Husky that had been cozying up to him on his other side.

"How did we *accidentally* end up here?"

The night Luke and I talked, he recommended a place called, Pets for Vets, where you could take veterans and let them interact with local animals for a day.

I shared aspects of Gabriel with him, and Luke didn't comment.

He'd only offered a way to connect with Gabriel.

I know a place you could take him to—it might not solve everything, but it'll be fun.

And it was.

The animals were well taken care of and really *cute*. I was currently swarmed with an enormous golden retriever, its tail wagging happily as I giggled.

"How do you know about Pets for Vets?"

"A friend of mine told me about it."

When I'd brought Gabriel's enormous self into the place, the ladies had taken one look at him and set him up in a room with some enormous dogs.

And he looked less than thrilled.

"I thought it looked cute. They have giant dogs," I explained, trying to suppress my amusement.

He groaned as another dog licked his suit. *"Fuck this."*

"Are you not a dog person?" I never actually considered it, but it made sense he didn't like dogs. I was biting back laughter. *The team never gets to see him like this.*

And I kept this part of him close to my heart—this version of my brother—even though he looked adorable grumbling about slobber. He frowned, looking at some mixed-breed giant curling into his lap.

"This is custom…." He sighed, looking for peace.

I bit my cheeks to keep from laughing at him, looking absolutely miserable, but even Gabriel wouldn't yell at sentient beings.

One of the women who worked there came into the room.

"If you two don't mind coming with me, I want to show you something."

"If she hits on me, I'm leaving," Gabriel grumbled, but I could see the curiosity in his eyes.

I pressed my lips together, feeling a mix of guilt and anticipation. I had tricked him into coming to this charity, but it looked like a real store.

It didn't have the typical charity vibes, nor did it look like anything fancy. It was just disguised as a cozy café that only allowed access to vets and their families—a safe haven.

We followed, with Gabriel brushing off fur with a grimace.

Nothing got between that man and his suits. He took his jacket off and rolled up his sleeves, and I saw the woman pause as she eyed his forearms.

He tugged at his tie, and I don't even think he knew what he was doing.

She blinked several times, composing herself.

"I thought you might be more comfortable here." And then she opened the door to a room full of—Gabriel's eyes widened, and I felt a surge of joy.

"Cats," I breathed, unable to hold back my laughter as he walked in, a little surprised. Immediately, a chubby gray cat, already curious about the newcomer, strolled up to him.

Gabriel narrowed his eyes, staring at the cat who sat and blinked, as if challenging him.

"That is Augustus. He runs this kitty park," the woman explained, a smile in her voice.

"Does he now?" A new look entered Gabriel's eyes—a spark of interest, maybe even respect. I bit my lip hard enough to stop my laughter, wanting to memorize these moments with him.

I want to memorize these moments with him.

The woman smiled and winked at me, then left the room, closing the door.

Gabriel was staring down at the blue-eyed cat that sat there staring at him, looking curious. Sizing up Gabriel.

"He kind of looks like you." I picked up a chocolate one with spots in my arms and snuggled in, feeling its soft purr against my chest.

Gabriel was still having a standoff with Augustus.

And then, finally, he reached down and picked it up, the bored expression leaving the cat's alarmed face. I laughed harder, the sound echoing in the room.

I expected Gabriel to get scratched, but instead, he settled Augustus into his arm, looking oddly satisfied.

Gabriel smirked. "Not so tough now, huh?"

I should've known he was a cat person.

I saw the women who worked at the cafe peering at him, one of them sighing.

What else didn't I know?

It was rare to see him let his guard down like this. But I didn't think any of the cats wanted to shoot him. So, he was safe here.

Gabriel moved through the room, and the other cats, rather than scattering, wandered up to him.

I wondered if Gabriel had PTSD as I reached for a toy to play with my cat.

But that implied...post...*that the trauma was over.*

He still looked haunted.

And it had been seven years.

Surrounded by the playful antics of the cats, I saw a glimmer of the old Gabriel, the one who knew how to smile and laugh without reservation.

Another cat, a sleek black one with mischievous eyes, decided to scale Gabriel's broad back, perching itself on his shoulder like a furry parrot. I grinned at his expression.

Gabriel was a mix of surprise and amusement, juggling his two cats, and for a moment, he looked years younger.

I have to take pictures.

"What did you want to talk to me about?" he asked without looking at me, rubbing the head of the black cat. "I know you didn't bring me here for this."

I didn't want to ask him then. Not with the host of women staring at him.

Or tell him what I wanted.

It had occurred to me there would be no good time to tell Gabriel I wanted my own breathing room. My own space.

But I have to. Eventually.

Just not *right* now.

"Who said I wanted anything from you?" I scoffed, teasing. "I can't spend quality time with my brother."

He smirked as the cat rolled on his lap.

"I know when you're lying to me, shortcake." I held my breath. "But I'll let it slide."

Just this once. He didn't say it, but I knew him. And a part of me was aware, he knew.

He knew I was hiding something from him.

CHAPTER 13
EVIE

I met Liam Sullivan later that day.

He was the cybersecurity guy Reed had hired.

Reed had told me he wasn't up here because he was disabled, but he never said why.

He never let me see Liam's file—handling all his documents for himself. Reed mentioned Liam went to physical therapy, and he discreetly told me to never bring it up.

I wouldn't, but I appreciated the heads-up.

I had scheduled a video call with him.

To my surprise, Liam was a *wickedly* attractive man, like a rockstar from way back, with his black hair in disarray contrasting with his white t-shirt.

He filled my screen with dark green eyes and an effortless bad-boy charm I didn't know I'd find *attractive*.

Even still, Luke's clean-cut, polished regality did a little more for me, but I wasn't blind.

He took up my screen with his presence, his sharper canines giving him an edge. *Everything about him has an edge.* As he lifted his glass up to drink something, I caught a flash of tattoos on his arms—both of them.

It was his legs then.

This was the new security guy?

Reed had said Liam had been in the CIA for a bit, and he was extremely sharp with some aspects of cybersecurity that even Reed wasn't proficient with.

I was excited to ask Liam about Oracle since he was a part of Titan, and there were some final things I wanted to brainstorm with someone when Reed was busy.

I wanted to pick his brain.

He'd grinned as I introduced myself, and I caught a glimpse of a tongue ring.

Oh, that was...wow.

"You look really familiar," he mused as I shared screens. "Do you have any family on the East Coast?"

I shook my head, not wanting to tell him about Isobel. "Just me and Gabriel."

Something shifted in his eyes as I mentioned Gabriel, and I wondered if Reed kept him away not just because of his disability but if Gabriel could ever do something to him for it.

Gabriel would never pick on someone who couldn't fight back.

He just pushed people to the limits he knew they had. To Gabriel, everyone was different.

Gabriel was good at picking people apart and putting them back together.

Everyone except for himself.

Softly, Liam's eyes narrowed. *"You're Monroe's sister?"* Why did he sound like that?

I had to ask. "Do you have a family?"

His eyes narrowed, but he smiled. "No, I don't have anyone in my life."

That's so sad.

"I can be your friend," I volunteered earnestly.

His grin widened, his eyes gleamed, and *he was really cute.* "That so?"

I stilled a little. *Only Gabriel said that...*

"You can call me Evie." His head tipped. Even through the screen, I saw a look pass in his eyes.

"Evie?" His lips quirked. *"Hm. How old are you, kid?"* His tone was playful, and I noticed his hands moving, flying across his keyboard. I heard the taps.

"I just turned twenty-three."

His grin was wide. "That so? All grown up now, huh?" *Now?* Liam's smile was infectious.

"Sorta." Not quite there yet. "Grown up enough to know you're fucking with my computer." He paused as he turned to me, and his grin stretched wide. "You won't get in, but I appreciate your effort. Reed taught me well."

He was delighted. "Are you as good as Reed?"

No. Reed had taught me a lot. But he said Liam was better than him. Which meant…Liam had *a lot* to teach me. "I was hoping you would mentor me."

His smile dipped as an odd look entered his eyes, almost forlorn. "I would love to teach you everything."

I smiled at him. There was something familiar about him. I couldn't put my finger on it.

"Should I start with everything you need to know first…?"

He nodded his eyes on me during my presentation. His pen was tapping on his lips as he occasionally asked questions. When I got to his Oracle account, it stopped tapping.

"Oracle…" I explained our program to him and what it did, and I told him that I had spent the last few years working on it. *He's a Titan. I could tell him.*

Liam covered his mouth a little while listening, and I told him how I worked in college to improve on the skeleton and brought it to where it was now. But I still needed help finishing it, and Reed didn't have the time.

"I think I just about have it where I want it, but I'm always collecting data." He nodded like he understood that. "I just can't crack a few of the issues."

It was like the skeleton that had been created; I could build on it, but I couldn't dig any *deeper*.

"How did *you* build it?" His question was soft, his head tipped like a curious wolf, his eyes were…intense. "*Everything* is easy to crack with a little persistence."

I was a bad liar. "I *didn't*. Reed gave me the project. He said that Gabriel wanted me to work on it."

I heard Liam say something under his breath. "I didn't catch that. Who took what?"

I couldn't hear it.

"Nothing, I was saying it's good Monroe took you in for the project."

I couldn't tell anything by Liam's expression. He wiped a hand down his face as he nodded.

"What did you need?" He tipped his head. The action was so familiar it made me pause.

88

Did I know him?

I told him the issue I was having was feeding Oracle the data to output in a freethinking manner, so if I told her to find the geolocation of, say, one of the operatives, she needed to reach into every aspect of the operatives being to find them—cell phone, cell towers, gait training, any footage they'd turn up. I was testing it to make life a little easier for Titan.

I was trying to contribute. "Oracle works with your call sign. Who are you?"

He smiled. "Pluto." A chill invaded the room for some reason, and I wondered if that was Gabriel. I looked, and there was no one in the room but me.

"Would you like me to set you up on Oracle?"

His grin filled the screen, making me smile with him. "Evie, I would like nothing more."

"I think you'd really like it. Oracle has a beautiful voice—"

His voice was soft as he mused. "I bet she does."

I didn't think, as I said. "Reed says he could listen to her all day...." I rambled about the program, telling Liam everything I had done to it. Reed said he would help with everything.

"Tell you what, why don't I train you on everything Reed doesn't have time for, and in the meantime..." He grinned easily at me. "I'll make you a better Red Hat."

Red Hat was a digital vigilante who acted against perceived threats. Using methods that were legally murky. At best.

I shook my head. "But Reed says I'm the White Hat."

Someone who was ethical.

I identified weaknesses to improve security.

At best, Reed was a Gray Hat—he violated all rules in the pursuit of his goals, but he kept me strictly white.

For my sake. *For Gabriels.*

Reed had said Liam was there for me to learn from.

Liam leaned back. "You think you'll be better than Reed and me by wearing a White Hat?" I swallowed.

I didn't think so, but I had *always...been* just Gabriel's little sister.

Was Liam allowing me to be something different?

Someone else?

"You don't have to answer now or do *anything*. If you want to think about it, take some time, and let me know what you want."

It's okay if you don't know what to say. Gabriel?

You don't have to do anything...It's okay if you want to think about it. I know it's a lot...

Liam *was familiar.*

When I met Gabriel, I took a leap of faith, and my entire life changed. What if Liam...was another one of those moments in life you took?

Jump, Evie. Take it.

"I don't need to think about it. Should I come down to Midtown to meet you sometimes, or is it easier for you to be home with your legs?" I didn't even hear myself saying it.

I saw a flash of his tongue piercing as his head tipped back, his grin wide. "I'd love to meet you in person, Evie, but I doubt I can."

His legs.

"I can teach you over video, share screens, make it easier for you and me. I think you'll have fun being a Red Hat. Plus, consider how surprised Reed will be when you surpass him."

He would be. But so would I. I wanted to be more than Evie. I hope Gabriel would be proud of me, too. I was looking forward to this.

I nodded. "For today, we should look over those taskers Reed had for you."

He nodded straight to business. "Will you walk me through them? I'm interested in what we do for the Teasers club..."

That was a good place to start. I showed Liam everything we did for the club. When I looked up, Liam had his hand over his mouth.

"Who owns the club?" Liam asked softly as I tapped a few keys.

"Lara Ford." His pen stopped tapping, and I looked up. "Do you know her?"

His reply was soft. "No. Do you have a photo?" I had several.

"This is Lara. She's twenty-five, and she's been running Teasers for a while now..." I gave him a brief rundown of Lara, and I pulled up the photos of her with clothes on.

I didn't feel comfortable showing that side of her, even though Liam was about to walk into her den.

The dark-haired, pint-sized Latina was a spitfire, according to Selena, who had a few interactions.

I had dared to watch one of her shows on her website, and as soon as she flashed her nipples, I was beet red.

I knew Gabriel liked her; he mentioned he was good friends with her, but I didn't mention that. I didn't know the extent of his friendship with Lara.

I didn't want to speculate.

"Nate says she's really wonderful, a little insane, but Reed likes her a lot...." I went on as Liam tipped his head, which told me he was curious. I smiled knowingly. "She's single. If you're curious." I couldn't help it; he hadn't looked away.

Liam gave an embarrassed laugh. "No, I can't—"

I stopped. *He's disabled.* "I'm sorry—"

He pretended to grimace. "No, you're fine—"

"I didn't know if you—"

"*Evie*—" He laughed. "My legs are fucked, not my dick." I turned pink at the way he said it and laughed. Something about him was...contagious. He kind of reminded me of...no. He *wasn't*—

He was still talking. "She's...*something*." I saw the look on his face.

"Can I ask—"

His eyes met mine. "What happened to me?"

I nodded, uneasy at being so forward, but Liam looked like he didn't care.

His face changed. "I got shot several times when I was on an assignment."

Why had everyone been fucked over in their time in the government? *I wonder if he knew Gabriel.*

I got the feeling something else happened with the look in Liam's eyes. "I'm sorry, can you...walk?"

He grinned at my expression. "I can do more than walk." He winked, and I realized he was a flirt in general. I would've felt weird, but I noticed his eyes drifted back to the screen where Lara was. "She owns the club now..."

What?

He snapped out of it. "It's easier for me to not do half of the stuff I used to. I'm not in a wheelchair anymore, and I'm grateful I don't have a prosthetic leg, but—" He broke off, a dark expression in his eyes. I felt bad for him. "Lucky for me, Evie, I still have *everything* I need to be a fully functional man."

I shook my head, aware he was interested in Lara, but hearing him so casual and flirty—

I couldn't help but laugh. *"You're terrible, Liam."*

He grinned, his green eyes sparkling with mischief. "Part of my charm."

He was dangerously charming. His easy laughter and playful banter felt familiar as if I had known him for years.

I couldn't shake something, though...

"Have you met Gabriel yet? I think you would be really good friends if you ever get a chance to meet him." I smiled, thinking about how he would get under Gabriel's skin, and maybe he needed that. "Even if you're a flirt."

An odd look entered his eyes as I said, his smile dipping a tiny bit. "That so?"

I nodded. Liam's expression softened, a smile playing on his lips.

"You remind me of an old friend of mine, too," he said, his voice tinged with nostalgia. "She was a lot like you."

I couldn't resist the urge to tease him. "I wasn't aware of a flirt like you having female friends."

To my surprise, Liam didn't laugh. Instead, he looked at me with a smile that seemed curious.

"Are you sure you don't have any family?" His eyes narrowed, that smile still on his face, like he knew something I didn't.

My heart skipped a beat.

Could he possibly know about Isobel?

No, that couldn't be. Isobel was gone, and she didn't—

"Just me and Gabriel," I said softly, pushing the thought aside. "Do you want to see more photos of Lara?" Liam let out a dreamy sigh that made me laugh.

"I like you, Liam Sullivan."

"Not so bad yourself, shortcake."

My hands froze over the keyboard as the chill slid down my spine, my heart racing at the familiar nickname.

Only Gabriel called me that.

"Why did you—" I stumbled over my words. "Why did you call me that?"

Who was this man?

Liam's smile fell, concern etched on his face. "I'm sorry, did I over-step? You already called me a man-whore, which is totally true, so I figured shortcake would be—"

"No," I interrupted him. "Why shortcake?"

I couldn't shake the feeling that talking to Liam was like talking to the part of Gabriel that I enjoyed being around, a playful, teasing side of him *magnified.*

That's who he reminds me of.

Liam tipped his head curiously. "You reminded me of my old friend. I used to call her that. She was short, like you. I can tell because there's

no way that chair is that big. Plus, your hands look like they're paws."
He mimicked having paws, and I couldn't help but gasp, which made
him laugh out loud.

"You have a bit of her spark, her fire. I liked it when she gave me
pushback. She called me out on my bullshit. I like a challenge—"

He's so much like Gabriel.

"But if you don't feel comfortable with me calling you that, I
don't—"

"No, it's okay. I don't mind." I didn't. "I think it must be a common
nickname." I wondered how many shortcakes there were out there. "I'm
glad I remind you of your friend."

"She was my *best friend,*" Liam said, a wistful look in his eyes as he
watched me, which quickly shifted to a playful one. "Everyone's also
super short compared to me, *so—*"

His moods were lightning-quick, leaving me energized by our
banter. I loved how he talked to me like I was an equal, like Selena or
Nate, not just someone's little sister.

I wasn't someone's sister anymore.

I was Evie.

And the more I bantered with Liam, the better I felt.

The time flew by with him. By the end of the day, I had Liam set up
on Oracle, and he promised he'd set up dates with me to work with him
and go down to Midtown and sit with him if I wanted to meet him in
person.

"It's all about your comfort," he said softly. "Don't worry about my
legs. I'm disabled—"

"Not an idiot," I finished with a smile as he grinned back.

We went over all his projects, even squeezing in some time to talk
about Lara.

I was surprised to see the sun had gone down when we finished our
conversation.

I walked to the kitchen, grateful that Reed had put up low lights
under the cabinets to illuminate the way.

When I padded in, I found Gabriel in nothing but sweats at the
counter, icing his ribcage.

The moment I entered, his ears twitched, and he dropped the bag,
sliding wordlessly into a hoodie before shoving the ice pack under it.

It was clear that Reed had done a number on him.

I didn't think Reed just fought Gabriel to make a point but to literally knock sense into him.

Reed is the only one who can take him.

Gabriel turned around to look at me, and I stopped moving, caught in the full force of his presence.

He was sporting a bruised lip and a cut, evidence of Reed's handiwork. I knew he hated me seeing him like this, vulnerable and battered.

I walked up to him, wrapping my arms around his waist and wincing as I tried to be gentle. But Gabriel pulled me closer despite the pain he must've been in.

I had so many things to say and so many questions to ask, but only one thought came to my mind then, and I didn't have the heart to voice it aloud.

Why do you do this to yourself?

I buried my face in his chest, inhaling his familiar scent and feeling the warmth of his body against mine.

We stood there in silence.

I don't know what to do.

I don't want to lose you.

I love you so much.

"Are you hungry?" He was looking down at me, but I didn't trust myself to look at him and *not cry*. I nodded.

I felt his breath ruffle my hair.

"Want me to make you something?"

It's just you and me.

Use your words.

"Yes."

CHAPTER 14
LUCAS

THE ANNOYING RINGS OF THE PHONE WERE GETTING TO ME.

"Devereaux," I snapped into it.

"Glad to see you're not ignoring me anymore."

I froze and felt my jaw clench, a familiar sense of dread settling in my stomach. *"Dad."*

"Yours truly, Lucas." His voice sounded smug. I hated that tone. "What, you don't have time for your old man anymore?"

No. Never. I didn't need the laundry list of things he had done wrong to know he had done dirty.

"Dad, I have a meeting, I don't have time for a chat."

He *tsked*, and I fucking hated that sound from his lips. I had been avoiding his calls for a long time.

Since my father had stepped down, I made it my mission to fix all his fuck ups. Taking over the family business had been inevitable, a duty I couldn't escape.

Since then, the business flourished, evolving into a sprawling empire under my guidance.

After I'd invested across the East Coast, I had fixed his messes on the West Coast—and I ran the entire fucking country. I was currently working with Matteo to expand further into Europe and a few of the countries in Asia.

Our relationship had always been strained, marred by years of verbal abuse and disagreements. His hatred for my mother. For Lucy. *For me.*

My father's response was. "Have you seen your sister lately?"

"No, I don't speak to her." *At all.* But why? Why couldn't I?

"That's a shame." It sounded like he was near water. I didn't know where he was anymore. "She hasn't been answering her phone, and I needed something from her."

"What is it?" My heart clenched at the mention of Lucy's name. She'd always been a bit of a free spirit, a little bubble of joy, but lately, I couldn't remember the last time I'd spoken to her. I just remembered her as a child.

"It's nothing, I was just wondering if you'd seen her." He paused.

It didn't sound like nothing. It sounded like— "She picked up a package from a friend of mine. I never heard from her after that."

Lucy was an archaeologist.

What the fuck did she take? Bones?

"A package? Mail?"

He was calling about mail?

He laughed without any humor, dark and edgy, and I wanted to throttle him right there.

"I didn't know if she dropped it off with you—"

"I haven't seen Lucy in *months.*"

What the fuck was this conversation?

"I don't even know when she's in New York or where she's been—"

"She's been in Senegal." *Senegal?*

What the fuck was she doing there?

I heard him mutter something about messing with people. I didn't give a shit.

I couldn't stop my irritation. "What the fuck is so important you needed to call me over mail?"

I fucking hated the sound of his smug laughter; I had no idea how I was related to him sometimes.

I could ask Lucy. She went by our mother's maiden name instead of Devereaux, I knew she had an apartment under Delaney.

It was probably more low-key for her.

I could talk to the source directly. But I hadn't seen her in months. I couldn't remember the last time I talked to her.

And every interaction with him made me the fourteen-year-old finding out he was being shipped off to boarding school. I never came home after that.

"It was from a friend of mine," my father was saying. "Marcus Hagen. Lucy was working with him in Columbia for a while."

96

She was? I didn't know Lucy had left the country, let alone Columbia.

There was a brief silence before my father spoke again, his voice softer this time—*manipulative.*

"I know we haven't always seen eye to eye, but I need you to look out for your sister, and when she's back in the city, Marcus Hagen isn't someone to hand over things lightly. And I'd like her to pass me the package."

I made a mental note to look into Marcus Hagen.

As I did, I noted another black and gold card with...claw marks on it, what the fuck was this?

Someone was fucking with me.

Getting under my skin.

What the fuck was going on?

"Just tell me when she gets back to New York."

How did he know Lucy was even coming back to the city? She could be out on a job for the museum she worked for...the name I couldn't remember. I should go see her when she's back.

Being with Evie had made a part of me work again. The part I shut down. I never told Evie about my sister. It felt too raw. How did I tell my girl I wasn't close to this woman in my life?

Lucy and I had drifted further away over the years. I didn't even know her anymore. What she did, who she hung out with, and despite her having a stake in the company, I didn't know what she wanted. *I should go to her...*

Except, as I heard my father speak, I realized something. "I'm not your bitch." *Not anymore.* "Why don't you go to Lucy yourself?" Why was he calling me about some stupid parcel?

There was a pause.

"Lucas, I'm your father." *Unfortunately.* "I genuinely give a shit about you and your sister."

Why was he lying? But there was something burning on my tongue. One thing. Maybe he would answer. Maybe.

I was doing this; I was ripping off the band-aid. "While you were leading the company, did you ever hear about someone named Gabriel Monroe?"

"*Monroe?*" His reaction was vicious. "Don't tell me you're doing business with that son of a bitch, Lucas, he's dangerous." I sat up straighter, for once hearing something in my father's voice other than smugness.

"I'm not doing business with him. I just heard his name dropped."
And I fell in love with his sister.

"Keep it that way. He's a psychopath. Got his hands in everything."

"Why?" I had to know. "What did he do?" Besides the obvious.

"Rumor has it he killed his first wife. He's got another girl living with him. His right-hand man, Wheeler, *whatever the fuck his name is—*"

Whittaker. I didn't bother correcting him.

"They're just a bunch of fucked up perverts. Don't get messed up with him or the other one." I had never heard my father like this...no, actually I had...he had done it to me my entire life.

Which actually made me like the Titans despite both of them trying to kill me.

I didn't bother correcting him. No, I was focused on the other thing. "What do you mean Monroe killed his wife?"

My sister Isobel was married to Gabriel.

"That's the word."

I couldn't think. "Why would he kill her?"

My father made a noise. "Have you met him? His temper? He's a violent bastard. Probably said something he didn't like, and he just offed her. People think the other girl is his plaything."

No. She's mine. She's my entire world right now.

Gabriel is so sweet. He's really kind to me.

"Why are you so curious about that motherfucker?"

I forced myself to calm down. "Not every day you meet a man who kills his wife."

There was silence on the other end, and I could've sworn I felt he could sense my unease until he let out a low laugh. "Ain't that right, son."

I didn't like the way he said it. It didn't sit right with me at all.

Memories flashed in my eyes of growing up that didn't make sense to me. I didn't have time to focus on those as I hung up, saying something about finding Lucy.

"Sir," Ella rang on my phone's intercom without a break. "I have some unfortunate news. I wanted to let you know before the papers printed it—"

I bit back a sigh. "Tell me."

"One of the board members died of a heart attack this morning...."

As she spoke, I sat up listening as she detailed how a member of my father's old guard passed away.

A chill ran down my spine once I got off the phone with my dad, and now it crept around me. It was eerie.

As I responded to Ella without even thinking, my brain was on Evie.

Rumor has it, he killed his wife.

Evie. I needed to find Evie. And then I paused, my mind coming to the realization of what the fuck I just heard.

I can't tell Evie. What do I tell her?

I'm Lucas fucking Devereaux, CEO of Mercury Group, and I've been *lying* to you since I met you.

My father said your brother killed Isobel Monroe?

No...Gabriel would never kill his wife and adopt her sister.

I couldn't imagine him doing that even if I didn't know him? It was...absurd.

And my father was a fucking scum bag. Even *still...I* didn't like that bit of...something dark creeping into me.

I leaned my head back in my seat.

And I had a date with her tonight.

I am so fucked.

CHAPTER 15
EVIE

HE KISSED ME THE MOMENT HE OPENED THE DOOR, HAULING ME IN LIKE I was his prey.

I was buzzing with how turned I was. I couldn't stop it.

I had tempted him all day. I had never imagined what speaking up for your needs looked like, but when I'd gone home I'd looked into it.

And I had—*graphically*. Sexting was not something I imagined I'd be comfortable with doing.

Now I saw what it had done to *him*.

"*Luke.*"

He sank to his knees before me, and he pressed his lips right above my pussy.

"I'm going to worship you," he said. "When I'm done with you, there won't be a single inch of this body I haven't tasted."

His eyes looked up at me, and under the lights, I saw the blues burning bright. "Are you wet for me?"

I nodded shakily, hauling him up to kiss him, only when I did, he picked me up, so I was a little bent over him. It was easier to kiss him like this.

I felt him moving as he thrust his tongue into my mouth. I moaned as he carried me.

I didn't know how he navigated the room, but then again, his apartment was spacious, designed for understated luxury and serenity rather than being cluttered or filled with anything.

There were no knick-knacks or anything blocking his way.

He fell onto the bed on his knees, then placed me down—*he's so strong*—never breaking contact with my mouth. I hungrily returned every bit of it.

I wanted you, I needed you, don't go—

He pulled back momentarily, tugging off his sweater and dropping down on me, taking my mouth, my fingers gripping his shoulders, and the muscles on his back.

Luke was…toned and muscular and his wide broad shoulders which hid everything underneath clothes showed me a man who worked out. I was no stranger to abs and attractive men. Reed and Nate often spared shirtless in the gym while Selena and I sat with popcorn inside where they couldn't see us enjoying a show on the cameras.

I didn't know who was grabbing who. I just felt hungry from that alone, and then he began kissing my neck—and I didn't know I would feel that at my center. I was soaked, and he groaned as his hands worked down my body, slipping under my skirt.

"I need to get this off—"

"Let me—"

"Evie—"

"Luke—"

We broke off. His lips stretched into a grin. "Let me take care of your body," he whispered like someone could hear. "Can I?"

I nodded slowly, feeling more intimate here than on the phone. I let him roll me this way and that and remove every article from me, and then I was about to reach for him, but I paused.

He was staring at my body, eyes full of heat. *"Goddamn, Evie."*

I was burning for this man. I held out my hand. He looked at that hand like he was entranced.

I felt that look in my soul. "I just want to be yours," I whispered.

His eyes softened, and with a sigh, he fell on me, his body over mine, feeling the hard ridge of him against my center so familiar, yet the ache in me was there. He didn't take off his pants, and yet I knew this time was different. I felt it. His eyes went dark and were filled with so much emotion. He didn't say a word as he kissed me.

"Give me a minute, Evie. I'm not a saint, so I need a second."

I smiled against his lips. "Take all the time you need."

"I should be comforting you." He kissed me softly.

"Why? I'm not a blushing virgin."

He groaned against my lips. "We should have all conversations like this."

I loved the way he made me laugh. "Or we could stop having a conversation," I traced the line of his lips, loving the way his breath caught. "And you could keep your promises." My eyes were a little wet as I looked at him.

"I will." He took my mouth harder. "I want to be the best for you."

You already are.

I reached for his pants. "Get inside me, please."

He pulled back. "Are you...on anything? I should've asked you earlier, but I'm so sorry."

"No, you're fine. No, I'm not." I couldn't decipher what that look on his face was. "Is that a problem—"

"No." He stopped me. "Not at all. *Never.* Don't ever—" He couldn't speak. "I'll take care of it—you—this."

I smiled softly. There he went. And it was the most adorable thing. I wanted him so much more for that.

His eyes held mine, and I loved how no matter when I was naked with him—*from the beginning, it was never about this*—this was just the cherry on top of him. Even without this. "You are the most fulfilling man." I didn't mean to say it out loud.

He paused, and his throat worked. "I want to love you right. I'm trying not to fuck up."

"I don't think you could."

"Like I said—I'm trying."

My heart clenched. My hands pulled at his pants, and he obliged; I don't know why I got shy when he did. I'd seen men *before.*

Hell, everyone walked around the manor shirtless in some form or another.

But this was different.

Long, lean lines, he was muscular, and I got the feeling he didn't just sit behind a desk all the time.

My eyes trailed down his body shamelessly.

He was gorgeous. Tanned skin and then my eyes drifted over *all* of him. I bit my lip as I looked up at him.

His eyes were heated as I moved back on the bed a little as he dipped on with one knee and then the other, meeting me. I wanted him. And he was mine.

He groaned a little. "Evie—I'm *trying.*"

I bit my lip harder but gave up. I laughed as I tugged him down to kiss me.

He's mine. He's mine. He's mine.

Just Evie.

Just Luke.

CHAPTER 16
LUCAS

SWEET, BRAVE GIRL.

I kissed my way down her neck, to her collarbone—lower.

Evie's breasts were perfect, peach-tipped, and I knew from memory she was absolutely sensitive.

As my mouth took one into my mouth, her fingers tangled in my hair. I fucking loved the way her legs fell open for me.

"So fucking sweet—" I couldn't form words.

My girl.

She was my girl. I switched to the other, loving the noises she made, the way she squirmed, and I groaned the moment my dick slipped—*condom*—I needed that.

Just a little more. A little more.

And then her hips shifted up a little more, and I backed off. No, I wasn't—no. This was about her.

I kissed my way down her body until I hit that center that I knew.

I still tasted it days later when she'd been gone.

"I want to lay you down on my desk and eat your pussy during the day whenever I want."

Or all day.

I thrust my tongue into her, loving the screams that left her throat as I ate her like I had missed her for days. I neglected her clit—I didn't want to get her off.

No, Evie came harder when I edged her.

I just needed to drive her a little over that edge.

I gripped her thighs, avoiding her clit, opting to work my tongue in circles around it. Her fingers tangled in my hair.

"Luke…"

I sucked and bit and licked and tongued until I saw her abdomen clenching.

She was so fucking beautiful.

I need a condom. Now.

I grabbed one from the bedside drawers feeling like a fucking teenager fucking a woman for the first time—and in a way, I was.

The first woman I'd genuinely liked and who liked me.

For all of me. My flaws. My heart.

I wanted to do right by her.

"Evie, you keep staring at my dick like that, I'm going to lose my shit." And I thought she'd laugh, but her eyes were low-lidded watching me.

She wants that.

This woman had the power to disarm me with her kisses and loosen me with her smiles. She was so alluring and adorable, and it drove me nuts. I wanted to treat her like a princess and, in private, make her my cum slut.

And I bet she'd like that.

I kissed her and rolled on the fucking condom—*fuck me, I'm losing my shit*—I wanted this woman so badly.

"Do you remember your safe word?" I had talked to Evie at some point about what I liked in bed without ever using the terms. No, I needed to warm her up to it.

Whatever she wanted, I'd give her.

I let her know I'd yield to her.

Every. Single. Time.

She whispered it onto my lips.

"*Lily.*"

I pressed into her, this fucking woman, bracing myself with an elbow over her head, holding her close, my other hand holding her cheek.

"Breathe—" She was tight. "Breathe for me."

She did, biting her lip, lashes fanned out over her cheek as I pushed. I closed my eyes and thrust in.

Oh. Fuck. Me.

She was tight, hot, heat squirming, moaning, and I couldn't resist working in further. "You are—"

"It's so—"

I captured her mouth hungrily. "Say it." She moaned as I sank further. "It's so what, doll?"

"Huge," she panted, her eyes squeezing shut. "Oh God, please *stop*—"

I didn't move. I pulled back. "Did I hurt you?" Fear caught in my throat.

"No? Just too much?"

She shook her head.

I moved my hand over her nipples, tugging gently and playing with them, as I dropped my mouth to her ear. I had to focus; it didn't matter if she felt like hot heat and heaven.

"Evie, spread your legs a little—ah, there you go."

I let her nipples go and trailed my hand lower, keeping my mouth pressed to her earlobe. "Let me, let me take care of your body."

I adjusted her hips a little, sinking further, loving her little whimper. I took her earlobe into my mouth, then loving the electric response from her.

As soon as I tugged, she arched her hips, and I bottomed out.

I sighed. *"So fucking perfect."*

She whimpered my name, and I closed my eyes, breathing. I kissed her neck, my hand gripping her thigh tightly, I didn't move. I wouldn't.

This was *perfect*.

I would think about this all the fucking time, every day, until the next hit of her.

I saw stars, and I was *just* in her—I was losing it and finding myself at the same time.

I would've laughed had I not been balls-deep in this woman.

"Please, move."

I smiled against her pulse. "I think I might stay here like this, filling you up for hours. Keep making those noises in my ear. This shit gets me harder than a motherfucker."

I felt her thighs shake.

I was a deviant who enjoyed her making her suffer for that orgasm because when she got *there*, I'd fuck that pussy until she was pink and sore. I was still a depraved monster.

Matteo wasn't wrong.

I still had the inclination to ruin Evie's body, but for me, for *her*, because I worshipped her.

106

"Should I do that?" I teased. "Should I stretch you out until you can't feel anything but me when you move?"

She trembled harder. "*Oh God,* Luke, please do *something.*"

I smiled. "*Anything?*" I was wicked.

Any inclination to be a good man in bed was thrown out when she clenched down on my length over and over again.

"You're so close, aren't you? Squeezing down on my cock in you—that feels good, doesn't it?"

I licked her neck lazily. "I'm going to drive you a little crazy tonight, Cherry. You'll remember me—this—won't you?"

Remember me when you lose me.

"Yes, yes." Her hands gripped my back and tightened as she—I had to chuckle low.

Sweet, brave girl—I lost it.

"Are you trying to work yourself on me?"

I *was* trying to hold back from destroying her. *Now? Not so much.*

"Evie, I *was trying, I really was*—"

And I saw *that* look on her face, manipulating *me*—I growled.

I quickly moved my hand on her thigh, hauling her hand up over her head, holding her down.

A rush of heat between my legs gave me devious ideas, and then I shifted my weight to move the other one until one hand of mine held both of hers.

I worked my hips out, loving the way her eyes were glassy and unfocused.

"*You are not allowed to come.*"

Her whimper was the only thing I focused on as I fucked back into her—loving her moans and squeals as I worked myself inside of her. Rolling my hips back in a way I knew would drive her insane.

"Sweet, brave girl, driving me over my *edge.*" I punctuated my words with my thrusts, loving her screams. "Such a bad girl for tempting me *like that.*"

I needed this as much as she did, and I was losing it with her. My teeth found her pulse, and I bit down fucking in punishing thrusts—*no, I needed to be gentle*—

"*Harder, please.*"

Fuck. I obeyed.

"My girl needs it harder?" I pounded into her tight little center. "Look at you, held down and getting fucked so deep. I can feel how fucking soaked you are, *goddamn,* my dirty little slut."

Oh shit, did I say that to my Evie?

"Yes."

I groaned, loving how wet she was, slamming in over and over. "And you're going to take every inch of me, aren't you?"

"Yes, yes, yes. P…p…please let me c…come."

Take me. And this is where I became an absolute monster.

"No." And I loved *that* sound she made. *I fucking ate that shit up.* "I'm going to fucking destroy this little pussy."

I was an *animal.*

"Until you're sore and pink, and it hurts to sit without thinking about me." I was losing it, white spots dancing in my vision, like the sweetest vice wrapped around me, feeling her clench wildly.

"*Don't stop,*" a shriek left her as I pounded into her.

I gripped her hands and reached down and tugged her nipples, never relenting, loving the screams. "Do not come, *don't you fucking come.*" I *slammed* in with every word.

Just a little, just a little, I knew what I was doing. Over and over again. I watched her eyes streaming and her face contorted with effort. "*Use your words.*"

A wild scream tore from her throat. "*Please let me come.*"

There it was. I slammed my cock into her with a ferocity I knew would do it. "*Come—oh fuck, good girl, say my fucking name.*"

She is…incredible. I gasped, working myself in her at the intensity of her orgasm.

Holding her down, I pumped over and over, loving the way she screamed; her entire body shook, her back arched, and I held her steady.

"*Luke!*"

I focused as her thighs shook, threatening to close, and I fucked in harder, finding my own release.

Oh shit. Holy shit.

I closed my eyes, groaning into her body, pumping her full and drowning in her, the scent of caramel settling into my body.

I kissed her over and over as she came all over me, the rippling sensations dragging it out of me.

It went on *forever.* And when I finally, finally, finally caught my breath, I didn't know how to think.

"*Evie—*"

"*Luke—*"

I was on her again. Kissing her until she moaned and trembled under me.

"*Was that okay—*"

"*We should do that again.*"

I couldn't hold back my grin.

I swear my heart was too full with this woman.

CHAPTER 17
EVIE

I collapsed in bed, covering my giddy excitement.

A normal man. And he was…he was *everything*. I covered my face with my hands and squealed.

He was so sweet! He is so cute! And I have a boyfriend.

I was bursting with joy, my heart soaring with the exhilaration of my newfound…everything…*with Luke.*

But as I sat up in bed, taking in the familiar surroundings of my room, I felt that excitement drift a little, like a buoy in the water. Drifting. Slowly. Softly.

After I'd slept with Luke, he asked me if I'd be open to something. A contract.

He'd explained it to me as a way for me to speak up and make it clear what we had in bed, for my sake and his. I didn't understand why until Luke explained he was a Dom.

And he wanted me to have limits, boundaries, and expectations for him outlined for his sake—and for my sake—rules, privacy, and terminating guidelines.

Initially, it had seemed impersonal and cold as I'd looked into it. The more we discussed it, the more he expressed how he wanted me to sit on his lap, take care of me, and feed me.

All the while, he'd asked me what would make things easier for me.

Always me.

It outlined a lot in flat terms. It was different but exciting.

Take your time to think about it; don't say yes because you think that's what I want.

You don't care if we do?

I wouldn't have taken you before this if I did. Just because I'm in charge doesn't mean I'm not going to validate your feelings and concerns. Everything you say goes. You are not less than me. In any way. You are my equal. In many ways, better. Does that make sense?

I didn't know what to say as my throat constricted, and my chest tightened at hearing that.

I had never…heard anyone talk about me like that.

At work, I was Evie. The IT guru.

But Reed was so much better than me. I thought about if I was an equal to anyone else.

And then Luke finished it off, adding a clause to it, he explained.

If I ever hurt you, do you use your safe words, or you feel threatened by me? It's over. All for you.

I'm your Dom, but you have the final say on everything. Always.

If the contract ends before the specified date, which is a year, if the terms aren't violated, and you just want it to be over? If I end it? You can ask me for whatever you want from me. Anything.

Whatever?

But what did that mean for me…

I'm not you, though. What do you want if I end it?

Tell you what? If you want the contract to end? Say so. I'll end it myself.

And I had signed it.

In return, Luke kissed me softly, held me, and asked me if I was hungry.

He fed me, then fucked me well into the morning—everywhere in the apartment.

I felt indecent and wild with him. And in turn, I was rewarded.

Part of me felt like I was blossoming into something new and different; a part of me did not recognize the person I became with him. I liked this part of me.

Despite the pang of loneliness now in my room, I was still elated, having snuck out while Luke slept a little giddy, imagining what he would do if he knew. The shadows under his eyes tugged at my heartstrings.

The way he carried himself suggested a man who worked tirelessly, pouring his heart and soul into his work.

As I went about my routine, the weight of secrecy grew heavier.

I longed to be myself within the walls of the manor, to share this new...person in my life with those closest to me.

I wanted to tell Gabriel.

Ask Reed if I could talk to Alisha.

I internally imagined knowing too much about Reed's sex life with her and reconsidered it. *He's like my brother.*

I wanted my sister sometimes.

I hadn't realized as I'd gotten older how much I wanted her—I wanted to tell her about my night with Luke.

But then again...I didn't know *anything* about my sister's sex life—that was not something—

No, never mind. I love you, Isobel, but even I can't—

I don't have anyone to share this with. I wanted that so badly.

"Oracle, this is Mercury. I really like this boy I'm with. His name is Luke, and he's the best." As I spoke, the colors on my phone flashed.

The AI was embedded in my phone and my computer.

"Good afternoon, Mercury. Should I pull up a profile on your Luke for you?"

Right. *Because she was AI.* She wasn't a person.

She only knew what her purpose was.

Which is why I was trying to change that.

Make her more sophisticated. If only I could change her baseline code.

The foundation that was set in her needed to be modified. I could improve her to become more empathetic and a person if I could change that.

Liam can help. He can make you a Red Hat.

While it wasn't the same thing, the parallels in my new path occurred to me.

Being a woman, not just having an identity as Gabriel's sister.

Being a Red Hat, not just Reed's consultant, his right hand. I would be me.

I proudly told Reed I had hacked into some other agencies. Not to snoop into anyone but to show I could do it.

It was a test, and I passed. Reed had been proud.

I understood I had to take opportunities as they came.

"No, Oracle. You don't have to pull up anything on Luke."

I had access to a powerful database.

I could go into any agency and know more about my Luke Delaney.

112

I stopped myself because *normal women didn't know what their boyfriend's blood type was before they had sex.*

No, *normal* girls giggled about trying to find him on social media.

When Reed had first met Alisha, he'd done a deep dive on her.

He'd stalked her social media, but so did I.

Shamelessly.

I wasn't Reed, and I didn't want a complete workup of Luke.

Reed had been so head over heels with her that he hadn't even cared that I watched complimenting her.

I knew he loved the slideshows I made for her.

Like he wasn't combing through them himself.

Luke kept to himself.

I trusted that he wasn't with another woman since he openly admitted that it irritated him to interact with people, and he didn't leave his apartment unless he had to go to work.

He didn't have time for social media, and so far, what I had seen—he was a man who didn't care where I came from.

He just liked me.

Not to use me against some agenda against Gabriel; he never wanted to come here; he just wanted me.

And there was something...wonderful that filled my chest.

And I couldn't tell anyone.

"If I tell you about Luke, will you just listen?"

"Of course." And at that moment, her voice sounded more human.

I bet she does...Liam had called her a woman.

I wanted to cry as I told her about him.

She had been my companion since college, and I had funneled all of me into this artificial woman.

With each passing moment, I resolved to keep this secret to myself. Ignoring the ache in my chest at the thought of hiding it.

"How am I supposed to make you better?"

"I do not understand that command."

I sighed. No, she didn't. She was lacking something pivotal, and I'd been stuck here.

I needed to talk to Liam.

I wondered if he had met Gabriel yet. I couldn't help but want to introduce Luke to Gabriel and merge these two worlds that meant so much to me.

Sometimes, I just want to move out.

Introduce them to my world. Not Luke's apartment covered in memories of us. Or Gabriel's home for Isobel.

The thought had been growing steadily in my mind, a tiny seed of independence that had taken root. Blossoming. Growing. Stretching into something real.

I longed for a space of my own, a place where I could be just Evie—free from the confines of my role as Gabriel's little sister.

Everyone's little sister.

But the fear of upsetting him, of disrupting the delicate balance we had maintained for so long, held me back.

And so, I kept my dreams of moving out hidden, just like my blossoming relationship with Luke.

Just like Liam trying to make me a Red Hat.

If I told Reed?

He would likely run a full background check on him, digging into every aspect of his life.

But the fact that Luke was just a grad student with well-off parents, nothing more, nothing less, filled me with a sense of pure, unadulterated joy.

In Luke, I had found something special. Something that was just mine. All mine. I didn't have to share it with anybody for right now.

And for now, that was enough. I told myself that much.

Maybe it made me a little naïve, but it also made me feel...*normal.*

My thoughts floated like bubbles. Popping with joy in the room.

My phone buzzed.

Liam

Do you want to train today?

I did.

So, I showered and then put on a hoodie, hiding my hickies from everyone.

CHAPTER 18

EVIE

A GIANT OAK TREE OF A MAN, GARRETT FULLER, A FORMER GREEN BERET, was watering my plants in the solarium.

Garrett was six-six and over two hundred something pounds of muscle. And he was…watering my monstera.

I bit back a laugh. It was lighter, back to…sunshine and greens when I came to my wing. Gabriel's side of the house was colder.

Maybe Gabriel needed some plants upstairs in his lair.

That might help. I mentally jotted that down.

"Miss Evie," he smiled softly at me.

Garrett made Gabriel look small.

But he was one of the nicest people Reed had hired. Despite his size, I noticed he moved with whoever his partner was.

For Gabriel, he amused him. Selena got someone who could protect her. And he balanced Kellan's energy with his stoic, sensible self.

Gabriel, who'd taken to the Goliath, stated he needed a test dummy for fighting.

"I watered your plants this week." I smiled as he walked over to one of the taller plants he was partial to.

He'd been in awe a little, and he'd lingered the first few days, and wanting to make him feel included, I'd asked him if he wanted to water them for me when I wasn't here.

Garrett was still living here while he and Kellan, the final new addition to our team, were looking for a place to live.

Gabriel never gave a shit if people needed to use him for his money.

He had enough of it to throw at people. Plus, it felt normal when people did live with us. Even if sometimes Gabriel didn't like them.

I knew Gabriel did well with the contracts he had under him.

Besides, the house was made for a family, and for the few weeks everyone stayed—it felt like it was.

Silently, the giant man worked around the plants, clipping leaves and looking at his phone on occasion. I liked Garrett a lot.

"Nate is on an assignment Reed wanted him on," I mused, not looking away from my screen. "Who are you shadowing now?"

"Sometimes Monroe. Sometimes Selena."

I looked over my shoulder. "I hope Gabriel isn't too mean to you."

Garrett shook his head, moving the vines around a little to water one of the other plants. "No, he's just got a mean right hook."

I winced, imagining sparring with the juggernaut. "But I don't mind. I'm learning loads. Selena's a good balance when I do switch."

I didn't know Selena could fight.

"Do you think I can spar with someone sometime?" Besides Reed. Garrett's bright grey eyes went wide.

"Miss Evie, I didn't know you were allowed to be a field agent."

I wasn't. But what else did I bring to the table?

"I just want to be useful to the team too."

He frowned. "Don't you have all the security issues when Reed is out?" I did. "And the backups, the cybersecurity accounts, the emails, and the servers downstairs?"

I did.

"It's not the same as fighting someone."

"No, but you do a lot for us." He paused as he set his clippers down. "Think of it this way, without your services, there wouldn't be a Titan. You're the hub. Our assignments go through you. I'm sure you got half of that shi—stuff automated. But it's important. I don't expect you to keep up with me. But I'm under no illusion a dumb grunt like me could keep up with you."

He came closer for once, and I had to crane my neck up to look at him. "Don't compare yourself to any of us. I think Reed picks people with skill sets to add to the team. He wouldn't have picked you if you didn't offer anything to the table."

I was a little surprised. That was the *most* he'd said.

Warmth coasted in my heart at the look in his eyes. I didn't really feel useful to the team, but I did manage everything.

Sure, I had automated alerts, and I used an AI to control half of those things, but—it made sense, too, to think if I was the only one doing it and nobody else was. It did make sense that nothing would work if I wasn't working. But Reed existed.

"Thanks, G."

"No problem." He nodded behind my head. "Whatcha got there?"

I turned back in my chair.

"Reed passed some of the security issues we have over to Liam. I'm working with him in tandem since he's showing me a way to create a secure virtual…"

Garrett double blinked. "This is what I meant when I said I could never keep up with you." He looked amazed at the several monitors with different graphs and projections all over.

"I mean, I used AI; otherwise, doing everything manually is a lot more work and almost impossible." *He's lost.* I thought about a comparison.

"It's like driving a manual vs automatic," I explained. "An automatic, you just drive. So, a lot of what Liam is doing? Is half by himself and half with me using my AI."

The truth was, Liam was better than Reed. I could tell off the bat, and he did it with a grin on his face.

Which meant there was so much to learn on my end. I guessed Liam wasn't a field agent because of his leg, and Reed had found him to be tech-savvy.

Liam was scary smart, and I devoured all information from him, giving him my access to Oracle, which he used to work on some of the issues I found on it.

I actually enjoyed working with him.

Garrett looked queasy. "Not to sound like an idiot—"

"You won't."

"Will you help me pick out a laptop? It's for work sometimes at home. I've been out of the game and deployed to Kuwait with Kellan for a better part of the time I've been alive, so I need some kind of help."

I loved it when people asked me for help with things.

"Yeah, what are you looking for?"

"Something that works and is easy to use."

I laughed and began pulling up some options, explaining it to him. I liked this part of teaching. It was one thing Reed had taught me.

Cybersecurity was a difficult career field for a woman surrounded by men who were used to being in charge.

A lot of the time, most people didn't know I worked here. And when

I met the newbies, they thought they were meeting a man. Because why would a woman run operations?

It was antiquated as a belief, which was why Gabriel insisted I put myself out there.

And if anyone says shit, let Reed know. If they keep going? Pass me their names.

The three musketeers, I'd been surprised, were more shocked. I was twenty-three and not an operative.

No, I was *just* Gabriel's sister.

When Garrett left, I texted Liam, not sure why I felt an odd ache in my chest. After the night I had with Luke—who I was seeing again tonight—I longed to be around him.

Liam and I set up a call, and he was in full teacher mode, and I saw a pair of glasses on his nose making his features angular and pronounced.

His tongue ring peeked out every so often. "You seem distracted, shortcake."

I blinked at him on the screen. "No. Not at all."

I was. I couldn't focus. I just wanted Luke. His hands were all over me, his lips, and I bit my lip. I shook my head, embarrassed to be caught. "I promise I'm paying attention—what is it?"

"What color is your hair?"

"A deep cherry color, why?" Liam was staring at it.

"It's shimmering in the sunlight."

For a moment I would've thought he was going to compliment me, until he said. "It's interesting you and Monroe look so different."

I smiled politely. I didn't make it my business to talk about Gabriel, ever, not with anyone else.

I felt this need to keep him safe, too. Because he did the same for me.

"I'll take that as a compliment." I grinned. "Are those your hot nerd glasses?"

"You think I look hot, shortcake?"

I walked into that one.

"*Focus*, Liam."

He laughed and continued class. By the time it was lunch, I was starving—and missing Luke. Could I go to him now? Curl into his bed. Sleep in his arms like last night.

"There it is again," he said softly. "Who is he, shortcake?" I looked at him. "Don't even start, I know that look."

I sighed. "It's…"

"Don't even try, I *know* women."

I ducked my head at that. *Of course, he did.*

"You like him." I nodded shyly.

He laughed softly then. "And he's nice to you?" I bit my lip and nodded, covering my face. "That's good. I'm happy for you."

Breathe. "How's Lara? Have you spoken to her?"

"Not yet, I'm supposed to meet her soon. Reed's juggling something else right now—"

Alisha. I know I was monitoring her social media. Well, Oracle was. "So, I haven't gotten around to it. But as soon as I do, I'll let you know."

Such a flirt. "What do you like about her?"

He winked. "I don't think you're old enough to have that conversation, shortcake."

This man.

"Don't hurt Lara. The entire team adores her. Gabriel visits her to make sure she's good all the time."

"Does he?" His eyes narrowed, and his head tipped. "I would never hurt her."

Sometimes with Liam, I heard these inflections of emotions, like there was more to it. I felt a chill in the air then. I turned and saw Gabriel walking down the hall.

"Liam, I gotta go—let's do this again soon."

I got up and ran to my brother, loving the way he smiled wide and lifted me into his arms.

"What's up, shortcake?"

"Where were you?"

His hair was windblown, and he looked younger, dressed in a pair of sweats and a hoodie. Nobody was home then.

His face, while strikingly handsome, was impassive as always gave nothing away.

"You look different." He kept his voice low. "Did something happen while I was gone?"

I saw that shift in his eyes going from bright to analyzing me. Instantly.

Did he know? Don't squirm.

"No." I was such a bad liar. "I just—Nothing."

I was several feet off the ground, and he slowly put me down when he noticed. Sometimes I forgot how tall Gabriel was.

"I was just worried about you."

Always. I always worry about you.

"I just got back." His eyes looked at me. Not normally. Like he was doing a thorough scan. "I was out last night."

And I was not going to go there.

That was the problem with being a part of a family like this. Everyone was a spy.

So, everyone did this. I saw bruises on his neck, and I stopped, not sure why I wanted to cry.

"I wanted to know if you wanted to do something today." I tugged his hand. "It's been forever since we went out to eat."

A long time ago. Between me running around and Gabriel haunting the house.

"It has," he said softly. "I'm starving."

What's new?

CHAPTER 19
EVIE

GABRIEL CHANGED INTO A WHITE SWEATER AND SOME JEANS, AND I quickly did the same, taking his hand on my way out the door, feeling like I was a teenager again.

He looked so much younger like this.

A little bit of his old self was there—the man I'd met years ago, not the person he'd become.

Gabriel, like this, was *almost* human. And everyone noticed it.

At the restaurant, Gabriel was attracting the lingering gazes of several women.

I figured out a long time ago that my brother was the kind of attractive that was between a movie star from long ago and an angel who'd fallen from heaven.

Striking.

I'd seen pictures of him with Isobel, and they contrasted in a way that meshed together. Her with her darker hair than mine and bright eyes and Gabriel grinning ear to ear watching her.

He never smiles like that anymore.

I hadn't met the Gabriel before her.

I wasn't sure if this was him.

"If the lady at three o'clock with the dog in her purse comes to our table, you have my permission to beat her with your stick," he murmured as he looked at the menu.

I hid my laughter in my menu.

Gabriel's bored expression stayed, never sparing anyone a glance. If anything, he was more *peeved* to be out in public.

I know he had a gun on him somewhere to shoot anyone who annoyed him.

"What are you getting?" He frowned at the menu. "I used to like this place until they added all these fucking vegan options." He scrunched his nose in distaste, struggling to describe one of the sauces. "What the fuck is a 'green goddess'?"

"I don't know why you look at the menu. You're going to get the same thing."

He gave me a droll look. "I'm trying to behave."

I couldn't help but smile, and his eyes softened as he peered at me. *He was. He'd rather gouge someone's eyes out than sit like this.* Pretending to be "a normie," as he called it.

He looked back at the menu, and I knew he wasn't reading when he said. "You brought me here to ask me something." And just like that, I was reminded of who he was. "It's the same thing you wanted to ask me at that cat cafe."

It was. Sorta.

I didn't even try to hide it.

"Would you care if I was dating someone?" I hated how his eyebrows snapped down. He frowned pensively, mulling it over.

"I mean, if he was from a decent family and had his life together, I suppose. But I'd want to vet him first." He looked like he'd rather swallow nails.

I closed my eyes and opened them to find his elbow resting on the table. "I know that look." He raised a brow. "You're not kidnapping him to one of your black sites."

"I never start there." Gabriel didn't have the decency to even sound innocent. His eyes instantly narrowed. "You've been gone more often. I know you've been seeing someone."

Damn, his infuriatingly perceptive sixth sense.

"Gabriel—"

"What's his name?"

"No—"

"I can't do a full background check without a name," he murmured, looking back down at his menu with a frown.

Yes, he could.

"Can I take your order?" The nervous voice of our waiter cut through our conversation.

"*No.*" Gabriel's eyes flashed at the man who shrank back. A squeak left the waiter.

"Gabriel," I whispered, shooting a sympathetic look at the young, wide-eyed waiter who looked utterly terrified by my brother's stare.

Gabriel had that aura about him—the kind only an apex predator exudes before devouring its prey.

I stepped in.

"We'll take a large Caesar salad with the garlic croutons and the veggie pasta with the cavatappi instead of spaghetti. Two of the filet mignons, as rare as it gets, with herb butter—the one with dill. Instead of the grilled potatoes, can we get two baked potatoes loaded with sour cream, extra chives, and bacon?"

I glanced back at Gabriel who blinked at me like he was seeing me for the first time. The man missed nothing, yet my knack for running around him always seemed to take him by surprise.

"Oh, and instead of wine, do you have any other drink options?" I asked the waiter, who looked frazzled scribbling down my requests.

"We have a lychee and orange blossom..." He began listing off what felt like forty different beverage choices.

Gabriel's glower intensified until the poor kid caught the hint. I bit back a laugh.

"That's fine," I interjected. "Can we get..."

Actually, if I was going to sit with Gabriel?

"Instead of a mango smoothie, can you do a piña colada with extra rum?"

Just give me the bottle.

Gabriel raised a brow. I rarely drank. I gave him a look. He looked down, and I didn't miss the smile.

"Yes, ma'am," the waiter said, snatching up our menus and scurrying away from the table.

Gabriel's eyes followed him with that distinct look he got—part-murder, part-protectiveness.

When he turned back to me, I held up a hand.

"No, you cannot know his name." His mouth opened with obvious objection before snapping shut again.

"So, he's real."

Damnnit. Breathe. He's just messing with your head.

"Are you still trying to be a vegetarian?"

I was used to this.

The way questions shifted. It usually meant his mind was working on one, distracting me from the other.

I had grown up poor, and my lifestyle hadn't changed when I'd lived with him.

I didn't eat too much red meat and it drove him nuts sometimes.

"What is a roota—bayga?"

I laughed at his pronunciation.

"I have a hard time eating meat. I have eggs and cheese. A *rutabaga* is like a mix between a cabbage and a turnip."

"Sounds delightful," he said in the most deadpan voice.

"It's delicious."

"That's not a meal. I don't want to see you wilting," he murmured. "Did you start taking those supplements I got?"

I had. "Thank you for those."

Being a vegetarian usually meant I was missing out on some key nutrients.

Maybe I'd try eating more chicken or something.

But some habits were harder to break.

"How was your day today?" He was toying with his cutlery as he watched me. I got lost in the conversation with him as I told him everything aside from...well, the obvious.

"Liam and I had some training..." I saw a flicker of emotion in his eyes, but he gave nothing away. "I bet you'd be good friends with him. He reminds me of you a little."

A soft noise left him. *He talks a lot like you.*

"And G?"

"Garrett's really sweet, I think Reed picked well..." And I went on to talk about how he was just a gentle giant. "You're not going to break him, are you?"

I knew Garrett was big, but what Gabriel had was years of combat experience. And he was brutal.

One corner of his mouth tipped up. "And Quarterback?"

I didn't think I should mention Kellan, especially with Selena, who he was definitely getting to know—I deleted all of *that* footage from our servers.

I wish Kellan would just move out, or they would realize Reed had cameras in Alisha's old apartment still for some reason.

Alisha had moved in with Reed at some point.

Gabriel tolerated Kellan because he was fast becoming Reed's right-hand man.

And Selena's.

I was used to his line of questioning. "He's a sweetheart..."

"And you're seeing your guy tonight?"

"Yeah, I'll be home tomorrow—" I stopped. Gabriel was pretending to analyze the tablecloth. *"Did you just—"*

He totally *had.*

I shouldn't have been offended.

One of the best operatives of the century was my brother, and he was grilling me.

I just got played. I hated it when he did this.

He was like a shark, cornering his prey.

He wasn't asking me about my day because he wanted to know—he wanted to lull me into a false sense of comfort.

Sometimes, I forgot how insanely manipulative he was.

"Does he stay in the city?"

He didn't even try.

I huffed out a breath. "Are you planning on dating?"

I don't know why I walked into that one.

His eyes narrowed, and he sounded bored. "I don't date."

No, he just discreetly slept with women.

But I knew. I *knew* he wasn't going out for a fight that late. He never brought a woman home to the manor—

Oh, I was not going there.

I didn't even blame him. Seven years was an eternity. We squared off, and he looked away, shaking his head.

"I can't do this. You're like my kid." His eyes changed a little as it left his mouth, but I didn't stop to analyze it.

A reluctant smile lit his lips as he shook his head.

Everyone else thought he was scary, but he was different like this. He was my brother. I got to see him as a human.

He never shook off the operative, but he was better like this.

A glint of amusement lit his eyes as he looked around the room.

The older woman next to us, who reeked of perfume, winked at him. He immediately looked away.

I pressed my lips together.

He leaned forward earnestly. "I'm just trying to look out for you. Make sure you're safe. Haven't I always looked out for you?"

And then he gave me *that* smile—the devastating one no woman could resist.

Ohhhhh, he was good.

This was how Gabriel won Isobel.

This smiling man in front of me. I wondered sometimes which part of him Isobel had fallen for.

The fire-breathing dragon who rained hell on people who messed with him and his family.

Or this man, light, younger, grinning at me. Several audible female sighs were heard from the table next to us.

"People are staring."

"What's new?" He looked bored again.

Gone was that man. "As long as he's a good man, I don't give a shit."

I arched an eyebrow right back at him. "You don't believe there are good men."

"I believe in Reed." The utter seriousness in his tone gave me pause.

"Reed is taken now," I pointed out.

A flickering look I couldn't quite read passed over Gabriel's face at the mention of Reed's longtime crush. "Have you seen her photos?"

"What's there to see?" He shrugged. "Just another model."

No, she wasn't. I just wondered if he would see what I would see.

I sighed. "I don't know how Isobel ever dealt with your moods."

The instant her name left my lips, Gabriel's expression shifted in that subtle yet profound way it always did whenever his late wife was mentioned.

A complex storm of emotions flickered across his chiseled features too quickly for me to parse.

"I'm sorry," I backtracked immediately, regretting my thoughtless comment. "I shouldn't have brought her up like that."

A beat spliced between us for a long second, and his eyes narrowed on the tablecloth.

"She would yell at me," Gabriel said, lips tipped slightly at the memory. "She didn't hesitate to rip into me when I deserved it."

Whenever he brought her up, my entire being responded. Nerve endings delighted to hear about her.

I would have laughed at the idea of anyone yelling at him.

But he so rarely spoke about her, and when he did, his eyes transformed—the Arctic chill melting into something achingly human and vulnerable. Gabriel's rigid walls lowered, his body language relaxing as he reminisced.

"The first time I met her...I wasn't nice," he admitted, a rueful smile playing across his lips. I didn't know that. "She cursed me out."

I can imagine how that went.

I couldn't help but grin. Gabriel liked pushing people's buttons to see if they'd pushed back the entire time he was taking data, figuring out their pressure points, where it would hurt, and where they were vulnerable.

She put him in his place.

I knew the man across from me was only human when he spoke about her. And I knew that's why he didn't do it.

"She always called me out on my bullshit."

And in return, he'd been hooked.

*I like a challenge...*Liam? Why was I thinking about Liam? I shook it off.

Before I could respond, our food arrived. Gabriel seemed grateful for the interruption, the conversation veering into dangerously intimate territory even for us.

I could see the shutters slowly lowering once more behind his eyes.

As we ate, I realized this was likely the most open and unguarded I had seen my brother in years.

"How's your steak?" I asked, taking a bite of my pasta.

"I'm going to figure out who this guy is."

I sighed. As I did, the older woman who had been staring at him walked up to the table, poodle in her bag and her perfume making my eyes water, and before she could even open her mouth, Gabriel's eyes darted up at me.

I got this.

I didn't think twice, raising my voice for her ears.

"Did you change the batteries in your hearing aid?" He closed his eyes, his lips pressing together.

"How's your sleep apnea? *Sleep apnea!* I stayed awake thanks to your *super loud snoring!*" I tossed her a sympathetic look. "He keeps the whole house up. Don't even get me started on his rash."

Her eyes went wide.

I saw Gabriel press his fist to his mouth as he looked away.

His shoulders tightened. I watched the woman look incredulous and offended before she walked away.

"All clear."

Don't worry, I'll protect you.

He pressed his fist harder as his shoulders shook. I pressed my lips together as I covered my face with my hands.

We bit back our laughter. I saw him turning red, and with how hard he was holding back, I felt the warmth all over my cheeks.

Don't worry, I'll protect you.

For long moments, we just breathed. This had become a running gag.

"Can't take you *anywhere*," I joked as I took a sip of my water.

It was nice to see a wide grin spread across Gabriel's face as he looked at me with a twinkle in his eyes. "Sleep apnea?"

"I was trying to be creative," I shrugged. "I could've said, 'Don't forget to take your erectile dysfunction pills, so I can prod you with porcupine quills tonight—"

I broke off as a loud burst of laughter left him.

It was infectious. I felt it bubble out of me, not being able to remember the last time I'd seen him so unguarded.

The longer I watched him, the more my heart dipped dangerously.

I will always protect this.

His grin stayed as he popped a crouton into his mouth, his cheeks pink, his eyes lit up, and I wiped my eyes, telling myself I was crying because it was just a funny gag we had.

That's all.

This was who he was.

I felt like I was seeing him for the first time.

CHAPTER 20
LUCAS

Lucy wasn't answering her phone, but I knew she was back in the city. Several days ago. If not weeks.

I couldn't be sure since I only knew when Matthias realized she requested someone to drive her around the city.

I knew she took a town car one night, and Matthias was up late enough to answer.

He had taken it because he knew my suspicions about my sister.

I couldn't be sure. But after that phone call with my father, I needed to know.

I had Matthias keeping an eye on her. I didn't have a driver for the time being. I was discreet, and I liked the people in my life as was.

He took her to Titan Midtown.

The moment he said she'd stepped up to a man with hard steel eyes and a Maserati? It was Reed.

Why was Lucy—

My father had mentioned she had something for him. He thought she would give it to me. Was it possible she gave it to Reed?

Or did they have *something—but he was with Alisha.*

It didn't make sense.

I knew he was dating Alisha.

Gemma had mentioned it when we worked together for Pets for Vets. I started my charity after I had lost a few of my friends to suicide. I just wanted to contribute *something.*

Evie had asked about it, and I told her a friend ran it. *It's mine.*

My mind was swimming. Why did Lucy meet with Reed Whittaker? *Was she working for him? Why?*

Reed didn't need a...whatever it was Lucy did.

I had expressed my curiosities before.

I had asked around over the last few weeks, and nobody seemed to know where Lucy worked. *Or who Marcus Hagen was.*

I parked my car downstairs in my apartment complex, not remembering the drive back home. I wanted to think for myself after finding out about Lucy tonight.

Did I even know my sister? If she was a Titan, would she tell me?

The moment I stepped out of my car, every instinct screamed that something was terribly wrong.

Before I could react, a shattering sound went off.

A single bullet shattered my windshield, sending a spray of glass fragments into the air. The sudden impact sent me hitting the ground, shoving the car door open, my mind reeling from the abrupt shift in reality.

The mental whiplash of one moment being consumed by thoughts of Evie to suddenly being under attack sent my mind spiraling into a tailspin.

I couldn't think, couldn't breathe.

My chest tightened as I gasped for air, the world closing in. Darkness crept at the edges of my vision as a scream built in my throat, trapped by the vice—grip of pure, body-locking panic.

Focus. You have to focus. Breathe.

Evie's voice in my head had me focusing on that. *You can't black out here, move. Luke, move.*

Harsh breaths rasped from my ravaged lungs as I doubled over, the horror of my reality crashing down upon me. Darkness crept in from the edges as I spiraled, my mind consumed by the horrors of my past and the agony of my present.

I couldn't breathe, couldn't think. All I could do was breathe. My body was wracked with tremors as I fought to stay conscious, to stay alive. I need her.

Luke, move. Come on. Let's go somewhere safe. Let's go.

I'm trying, Evie.

Follow me.

Besides that single shot, I heard nothing except for footfalls. Were they coming to finish the job?

Move, Luke, let's go somewhere safe.

I looked over my shoulder, my heart racing. No one was there, but my windshield was shattered. Evidence of my attack right there. It wasn't...an imagination. I stared at the fragments of glass.

Evie, I think someone just tried to kill me.

Who? Luke Delaney?

No, Lucas Devereaux, that's my real name. Do you still want me?

Someone just *tried* to shoot me. And I couldn't...I couldn't tell my girlfriend.

Because she didn't know who I was...

I was so fucked.

I WAS BACK IN THE OFFICE—EVERYONE ELSE HAD GONE HOME.

I spoke to the security team, and they said they had caught nothing on tape. In fact, it looked like there had been *no one,* and *nothing* had happened.

I was shaken up, but they'd only taken one shot.

"What do you mean *every* piece of the footage was wiped? How is that—" *What about the bullets?*

"None in the area, sir. But we think it was huge to have shattered the glass." I remembered; I heard it hitting the glass, sounding like nothing I had ever heard before.

"That's not an acceptable answer." I didn't give a shit, feeling the fury race through my veins, turning to ice. "Who the fuck was on guard today?"

I could hear these idiots scrambling. "It happened during the shift change—"

I swore and hung my head. "*Are you fucking kidding me? Everyone* on duty today is relieved. Permanently. Effective immediately."

I could feel their shock. I couldn't believe this shit.

But even now?

Something was flowing through me.

Something I didn't recognize.

I ended the call abruptly, my blood boiling with sheer anger. I didn't think.

Breathe, Luke.

I can't, Evie. Except, she wasn't in my office. She was nowhere.

Because I couldn't tell her. *Something was off about this.*

I felt like I was…changing into something, shifting underneath my skin, and I didn't mind it.

Was it Gabriel? Did he know I was dating his sister?

Was it an attack on me because of Evie?

No, because he'd fucking finish the job. My emotions were running high. It was *late* now, and I didn't give a shit.

I was a powder keg waiting to go off.

Any semblance of patience or restraint had long since evaporated, replaced by a seething cauldron of raw, unfiltered emotions.

It took Gabriel Monroe several rings to answer, and when he did, he sounded bored. "I'm surprised you have this number."

"You know?" Silence. "I'm surprised it took you *this* long, but really—shoot first, ask questions later? *That's your style.*" I was tempting the devil; I fucking knew I was. But I was livid. Blacked-out cameras. Scaring me? I was outraged.

"What the fuck—"

"It was always about Isobel, wasn't it?" Silence filled the line. My entire lineage was known for the worst things.

Evie's question had haunted me.

If my family had killed her sister. *I wouldn't put it past them.*

A dangerous pause. I could feel him seething. And then I realized what I had said. The line changed immediately.

He doesn't like talking about her.

"What did you just say?" His voice went deadly quiet.

"Did my family do something?" There was a pause I could *feel* in my gut. Right before a firefight. "That's why you hate me?"

I was still fresh off the memory of almost being shot. Feeling an overwhelming surge of *fury* and frustration.

The line went dead.

I didn't even know what to say then.

I was still sitting there, my head spinning from the panic attacks and needing new medications, so I contacted my doctor.

Given that I had called him?

I shouldn't have been surprised when, *twenty minutes* later, Gabriel Monroe stormed into my office, the temperature plummeted, and the hairs on the back of my neck stood on end.

He had a bruise healing his eye, and were those…marks on his neck?

Someone had…attacked him?

His presence was suffocating, like a coiled snake ready to strike. I saw his eyes—

Shitshitshit. I am so fucked.

Behind him, a Goliath of a man shut the door, his green eyes hard as he locked us in. He stood as a sentinel.

As Gabriel closed the distance between us so fast, I stood, his expensive suit perfectly tailored to his broad, muscular frame.

I caught a whiff of his cologne—and it was the only warning I had that my ass was about to be *handed* to me.

He moved like a fucking weapon. His icy-blue eyes locked onto mine, and I felt the weight of his gaze as if he could see right through me—

He's going to kill me.

I braced. When his fist collided with my stomach, the force of the blow sent shockwaves of pain through my body. Pain radiated through my core, doubling me over as I fought to suck in a desperate breath. *Oh, fuck. He's gonna kill me.*

My heart jackhammered against my ribcage, adrenaline spiking through my system.

Or I would've.

Gabriel didn't give me a chance to recover.

He grabbed me by the collar and yanked me upright, and the right hook *would've* sent me to the ground.

My vision flickered and wavered as Gabriel *slammed* me against the wall, the back of my head cracking against the plaster, his arm as a bar to choke me.

The metallic taste of blood filled my mouth as I gasped.

"What did you do to her?" he growled, his arm digging into my air supply. Black spots danced in my vision at the pain.

"I didn't—KIA. That's all I know." Killed in action.

That's what happened.

He loved her, Luke. He doesn't like talking about her.

"What do you know?" He shoved his arm. "I will tear your tiny empire apart for answers—"

"That's all I fucking know!" I gasped, shoving at him. "Someone's trying to kill me!"

"You *threatened me with my wife because someone's trying to kill you?*"

His eyes never changed as he all but threw me to the ground. I scrambled back, different parts of me already in pain.

133

Tell him the truth, Luke!

I can't breathe, Evie.

Tell him, Luke!

I'm trying, Evie. I didn't know your brother was a tank.

What a way to meet your girlfriend's family in person.

"Look, I'm sorry! Someone's trying to kill me." I scrambled up, holding a hand for him to stop.

He looked ready to tear me limb from limb.

"I thought it was you—" I couldn't even speak. "I thought you hated me because of—"

"Don't you fucking say her name!" I stilled at the gun he pulled out of his back with a *silencer.*

Holy Shit—I'm a dead man. He's a fucking professional.

"I don't believe you," he growled, the gun pointed at me.

The Goliath at the door stood still as a statue watching his boss.

Icy eyes lit with the rage from hell. "You're going to tell me any information you have on *my wife.* Or I will do to you *everything you did to her."*

What?

The room seemed to spin as I tried to process his words. *Isobel is dead.* What more did he want from me?

"G, search his desk. *You, start talking."* I did.

I got the feeling he would shoot me. And he didn't give a shit.

The Goliath moved as I explained my situation, the attack earlier tonight, Gabriel's eyes never left mine. Neither did his gun.

And then, for some reason, the night tumbled out of my mouth. He was Reed's partner; he would know *something.*

"My sister and Reed…." I explained everything, feeling compelled to tell him the truth, tasting blood in my mouth. "My father called me and said something about Lucy having *something* in New York. She took something of his—"

No, not him.

"He said she worked for *someone* named Marcus Hagen." I couldn't remember the fucking country's name, but it didn't matter. Gabriel's eyes were scanning my face.

His expression shifted as I said Hagen's name like a predator scenting blood. Just like when Matteo sensed my feelings for Evie. *Dangerously.*

An awareness, a slight raise of his brows, his gun *instantly* lowered.

"Lucy took something that your father said belonged *previously* to Marcus Hagen?"

I nodded. His lips quivered, that glint never leaving his eyes. If I thought he was scary before, that look on his face was downright terrifying.

Why was he happy?

"My father said—" My brain was not what it used to be. I thought about it, aware I had *the fucking gun on him.* "He said he wanted Lucy to give it to him. But then, why would she give it to Reed?" I paused. "Do you know who Marcus Hagen is?" *He did.* I saw it all over his face.

"She met with Reed..." His eyes lit up for all different reasons I couldn't fathom. "*Son of a bitch.*" He shook his head, looking away as if he didn't know what to do with himself.

I rambled, having needed to put my foot in my fucking mouth tonight.

"Lucy works with finding artifacts. I don't know what she was doing or why she ended up in Reed's car—" His expression flickered as I said that. "And someone shot at me."

That was my night. And now my girlfriend's brother was trying to kill me.

I licked blood inside of my mouth. "I've had my driver watch over Lucy because my father said she might give it to me, but she never saw me. Is Reed involved with her *and* Alisha?"

Somehow, he didn't strike me as the type. Lucy was still my sister. Distant. But family.

"I just *might* shoot you at this rate," he muttered about how I was a fucking idiot.

I didn't take offense.

At this point, I felt like I was.

The weight of his gaze was suffocating, and I could feel the barely restrained violence emanating from his every pore. He could paint the glass behind me with my brains, and nobody would know. He'd wipe it all.

He's former Agency. He's a fucking ghost. He would do it.

He adjusted his tie, the simple action telling me he was barely *contained* as the Goliath passed him a card. The black card. With the gold claw marks.

"Why do you have this?" Gabriel's eyes narrowed on me. "*Who* gave this to you?"

135

I explained to him it had been left on my desk several times now. I threw them out, and it kept reappearing.

His gaze lingered on me, the predatory glint in his eyes sending a chill down my spine. He took the card.

Did he know what it was?

"I'm telling you *the truth*. I was pissed that you wanted me dead. But I can't imagine you feeling thrilled if people tried to kill you."

Gabriel didn't give me anything as he said. "I don't give a *shit* who tries to kill you. You're going to forget *her* name and that you have that number. I don't care to know how you got it. I'll find out before the night is over. Next time you want to know who tried to murder you—speak to the entitled pricks in your family. We both know I would've, at the *minimum*, picked you up and thrown your ass into Gitmo for fun."

He huffed out an incredulous laugh without humor. "G and I can use you as a punching bag."

His eyes swept across my office; his disgust palpable.

"You will *never speak my wife's name again*. Not from the likes of you."

He motioned to the man, who looked me over with a small bit of... sympathy as they walked out—I shouldn't even be surprised they both knew the layout of this building.

That man wouldn't be with Gabriel if he wasn't one of the ones who worked with him, but I didn't know him. I didn't know the Titans.

He left me in the office, wiping the blood from my lip, aware my stomach ached and my head hurt.

That was Evie's brother.

And he came after me because he thought I threatened his *dead* wife. He was going to keep all his promises if he found out I was fucking his sister.

I didn't bother telling him my father suspected he murdered Isobel.

His *wife*. I knew Gabriel hadn't killed her. No, someone had. *I will do to you everything you did to her.*

We had both been Navy SEALS. I had heard of him a year ahead of me. Everybody knew of him, but not many people had met him. He had been a fucking beast then.

I was turning thirty soon, and he was just a year older, yet he was known for being the Iceman, with brutal strength and cut-throat assignments.

The kind that he didn't have anything left to lose for. *Until...her.*

I was on assignments where I remember men who were threatened, and sometimes, the enemy would torture their wives and family.

Gabriel Monroe didn't kill Isobel.

Someone else had.

And he was looking for who.

That's why he was so furious. I had tempted him into *thinking...*that I knew who had done something to her.

I will do to you everything you did to her.

I couldn't even imagine *what* they'd done. I had seen some gruesome shit in my life.

I had experienced a lot of things that left me unable to sleep at night. I had told Evie the truth about my PTSD.

It wasn't one memory but a collection of horror.

And I had seen it in his eyes, he had loved her.

This is Evie's brother.

And someone else was after me.

I had no idea who or why.

My mind raced with possibilities, each more unsettling than the last. Who could be behind this?

What could they want? And why now, of all times?

What was the connection to Lucy and me?

My brain worked because I got a feeling in my gut that something was related to her.

Nobody wanted me dead just because...was it the fucking parcel?

My mind was spiraling at why someone wanted me dead over an artifact—maybe it was valuable?

What does it matter? I don't have it.

Reed has it. And Gabriel hadn't known. My brain was ruminating now.

I ran a hand through my hair, my mind spinning with possibilities and regrets.

I had to find a way to make this right, to figure out who was behind this attack and why.

The attack, the wiped security footage, the timing of it all...*none of it was normal. None of it made sense.*

My instincts screamed that something was very, very wrong.

But my mind kept drifting back to Evie, to the look of betrayal and heartbreak on her face when she realized the truth about me.

That was her brother.

I had to figure out who was behind this attack and why before they could strike again.

But even as I tried to think through the possibilities to come up with a plan of action, I couldn't shake the feeling of dread that had settled in the pit of my stomach.

I got the feeling I was marked.

I had a date with Evie later this week, and I needed to ice my face. *Fuck.*

Matteo was right. Trouble was coming. *It was here.*

And this was just the beginning.

CHAPTER 21
EVIE

"You look…different."

Selena was the coolest woman I knew.

She was also incredibly perceptive.

In the sunroom, underneath the lush plants surrounding us and the sunlight, Selena looked like a sexy vision in her tiny dress printed with cherries instead of a woman who knew how to kill me in forty different ways.

I knew she had a knife in there somewhere hidden in her boots.

That yellow sundress was tame compared to this one, with two side slits that left nothing to the imagination. I wondered if she'd let me borrow it.

I didn't mind other people working in my room, but after the nights I had with Luke. I wanted to curl into a ball and live on his chest forever.

It was a bright day outside, which was rare for fall. My summer romance had turned into something else.

For years, Selena did this little song and dance with me. Sometimes, she wanted to vent. Sometimes, I wanted to vent. I knew a lot had happened with her.

She was…working on something.

She didn't talk about it for some reason. I knew something was up. But she figured something was up with me.

Besides getting railed by my boyfriend?

Not much.

I didn't say a word. I couldn't stop thinking about him.

Or his mouth on mine, or the way his body was inside of me.

The heat of him against me.

The cologne he wore that seeped into my skin, and I inhaled on the drive back to the manor in the afternoon by the time I'd made it back.

After he'd woken me up with his tongue inside of me. I'd lost my voice a little.

I could still feel his hands against my hips. It had been less than twenty-four hours, and I wanted him again. The memory felt more vivid than anything I could remember.

I couldn't think straight at all. It should've been infuriating. And yet, I just wanted him.

"How's Kellan?" I said when I felt Selena stare at me, spacing off.

At the mention of her work partner, she made a face and played with the hem of her dress. "I am not sleeping with him."

Oh, that wasn't my question. I tried to control my brows from rising to my hairline. I failed.

The cute blond jock with the easy grin who had shown up at Titan a few weeks ago. Sometimes, he would alternate with Reed; sometimes, he was here depending on what Reed needed. He was becoming Reed's right hand.

Kellan was undeniably attractive in that all-American way, reminding me of a bit of a lighter, more easygoing version of Luke.

"I didn't think you were."

But even if you did, I wouldn't blame you.

"Kellan's cute."

Her head snapped to me with wide eyes.

I had to laugh. "I don't like him like that, Selena. He's kind of hard to ignore."

Plus, I'm daydreaming about Luke.

"His smile is stupid." Her eyes moved to a plant, her fingers tapping the desk.

I bit my cheek harder.

I don't think a woman alive could resist his adorable grin.

"He thinks he's *so* cool. He takes his shirt off all the time. When he's hot, when we are outside, in my car. *Who does he think he is?*"

I couldn't hold back my giggles. "I think he's flirting."

Peacocking. I laughed harder. She scoffed. I thought Kellan was trying to get under her skin.

And it's working.

Gabriel had been suspiciously hovering around me since Reed was attached to Alisha.

Luke had texted me.

> I want you to walk through the door and be ready for me.

"Gabriel doesn't know. Is that why you are nervous?" she whispered in a sotto voice, changing the subject back to me. I flushed. Her eyes drifted. "Gabriel is good if you just tell him."

Not to her.

Selena was a *woman.*

I didn't understand her relationship with Gabriel, but I knew she trusted him. In turn, Gabriel gave *her* his right hand like Nate had been Reed's.

"I'm not you, Lena." Nate and I called her that as shorthand.

I was forever placed as his little sister. I acknowledged I was the only member of my family he had.

I wonder if Gabriel had met my father, if he asked for Isobel from him, if he had buried him, like Isobel and Mama.

He always protected me. His criteria was different.

Sometimes, it felt impossible. Sometimes, I don't want to leave Luke. I want to stay with him forever.

"You think he won't let you go, like college?" I nodded into her lush tip, tilted green eyes, and covered a little with her bangs.

A look of understanding passed through us.

She had always been my champion.

A different kind of sister. I knew that sometimes Gabriel was frustrated with me borrowing her clothes, but Selena balanced the team differently.

Her energy felt necessary to all the men.

Her lips curled, and she raised her brows. "But he's *cute*, no? *Muy guapo?*" Very handsome?

I nodded with a giggle.

That's all I wanted to give. I turned red as she asked me if he had a big dick, and I laughed at her smile.

When Selena wanted to, she could *tease.*

"*Come on.*" She nudged me. "It's about time you started dating—"

I broke off laughing, covering my face as she talked about getting laid.

She and Nate always did this.

At the thought of Nate, who I never saw anymore, I realized I didn't know how she felt about losing Nate as her partner.

"Do you miss Nate?" I had to ask. I knew they weren't romantically involved since I was sure Nate had a thing for blonds. Selena had a thing for men *not* Nate.

She thought about it, and I saw her brain work; with the addition of Kellan, I was sure it was new for her.

"Sometimes, I miss him. But I think it was because I was so used to him. He became routine. I was happy to try someone new." Her eyes changed.

I kept my voice to a whisper. "I know Kellan likes you. Don't be upset. I was the one that told him about your super-secret hiding spot."

Her eyes widened, and her cheeks turned pink.

"I didn't see anything. Did it work out?"

That had been a gamble on my part.

She nodded, turning more pink.

"He's a sweetheart, Lena." I nodded at her. "He's always helping everyone. Alisha likes him a lot."

Kellan could reach the top shelf.

And Selena was upset about him being a kind man, why? I wanted to ask her, but her eyes grew sad.

I saw her for a moment, exhausted, holding things back, and the weight of everything.

Lately, I'd seen it *more* in her eyes. She needed a break. *Desperately.*

She's not taking one because of the team.

"Do you want to…" I motioned to the playlist she had up.

Selena always did this. She never said what it was.

She just dropped hints.

Nothing got Selena going like her love for dancing. Selena flashed me a conspiratorial look. And for a moment, she looked younger as a sly smile lit up her lips.

I handed her a carnation from the flowers on my desk Gabriel got me weekly.

Years ago, I was upset, and Selena had hauled me into the solarium's makeshift space.

She'd played loud salsa music and started dancing with me slowly at first, but the sheer memory of it had…helped.

She said her Mama, and she did this when she was growing up

whenever she was upset. I didn't know much about Selena's family. The rare occasion she mentioned them, she always spoke fondly.

Selena said Gabriel taught her humans and animals to process stress and trauma differently.

Humans, we buried it. Animals shook it out or found a way to let it out of their body. And she said, why not get in touch with it.

Gabriel fought his way through people.

Reed worked out at the gym for hours.

Nate slept with the entire population of New York.

And Selena...danced...with me.

Sometimes, she went to salsa dancing clubs. Gabriel forbade me to go with her, worried something would happen after *one* wild night Selena had gotten herself into trouble in her underwear.

Reed had gone to get her, and there may have been one little, *tiny* shootout...but nobody brought it up again after Gabriel and Nate had shut that down.

She played a song we both loved. I turned up the volume, hoping Gabriel wasn't home.

And besides, we were all the way on the other end. It was the end of the day, who knows. I didn't care.

Gabriel shouldn't have gotten surround sound.

We made a duet out of it.

When the chorus came, we belted it out, throwing our hair back and our carnation flowers as the mic held up.

We both knew the choreography, and we spun around in opposite directions, her long locks whipping.

For a moment, she was freer than she ever was. Playful. Easygoing. The Selena I got.

When it switched to an upbeat salsa tune, Selena didn't blink; she just put her arm around me and twirled me, I giggled.

I didn't have any girlfriends. All of us were isolated in different ways.

Reed mentioned that Alisha had a sister closer in age to me, and he wanted to introduce us.

Avani didn't have social media—but I had a few photos of her, and I was excited to meet her eventually.

But for now? Selena was my sister.

"I missed this!" I squealed.

"Me too!" She was gleeful.

We sang along, and she dipped her hips. I laughed, watching her let go.

I rarely got to see the operative let go. She was so composed all the freaking time. But at home with me?

She was Selena Maria Tavares, the woman with a penchant for singing and dancing.

I was having the time of my life.

Selena's long, elegant lines, olive skin, long brown hair swinging, and green eyes flashing made her look like a vision. She turned, rolling her hips wickedly and shaking out her hair.

And I turned with my laughter bubbling, only to halt.

Busted. Someone *was* home.

Kellan's dumbstruck figure froze in the doorway during one of my twirls—his mouth slightly open as he helplessly drank in Selena.

"Lena..."

I tried to get her attention, but she was too lost in the music, singing along about pulling her—

"*Selena!*"

And then her body moved into hip rolls leaving next to nothing to the imagination her dress hiked up. I threw my flower at her.

She turned with a breathlessness on her face, working her body, singing along. "*yo te pongo rapidito...*" and then she stilled when she saw Kellan.

Sometimes, I wish Gabriel hadn't made Spanish a required language.

I knew Kellan had translated that.

Something about coming...on all fours...

His eyes raked over Selena's flushed face and tousled hair, his expression dark.

Selena, usually so composed, seemed rooted to the spot, her chest heaving as she struggled to catch her breath.

The air between them crackle, the music still pulsing in the background.

I looked back and forth between them, unsure if I should break the spell or slip away.

Selena straightened her spine and lifted her chin, attempting to regain her usual poise even as a tell-tale blush stained her cheeks.

She was puffing air, and only Selena looked good that out of breath. Her hair was in a beautiful disarray as she blew it out of her face.

I saw her shift into the operative.

144

I quickly lowered the volume. Her face flushed beet red as she frantically tugged her dress back into place.

"I came to talk to you," he stated, tone thick, unable to look away from her. "It's about Reed."

She nodded, and he followed her out.

I peered into the hallway, not surprised at him crowding her into a room the moment they were far enough away.

I would be deleting *all that* footage.

CHAPTER 22
EVIE

Days later, I had dinner with Luke.

He and I had both been busy; I was training with Liam, and Luke had been juggling a few things at work.

I had gone to see him, and Luke had been insatiable with me with a ferocity I loved.

"*Luke*—" I gasped at the feel of a warm hand around my throat.

I felt him crowding me into the door and his massive size nearly pressing me into it. It was dark all around me, and I caught dark outlines of his body and his face.

"Open your legs." He was letting me go, reaching between my legs and working his hand at my pussy. "No panties?"

"I r…ruined them." A low chuckle filled the air. "What are you—*oh*."

He sank to his knees, and a moment later, I felt his breath on my clit. Oh God, I waited all day for this. He suckled on my clit as he gently nudged something in me. I gasped.

"Shh, it's just a toy. I promise it'll be all right."

Ohhh, that's different.

I moaned and gasped as he ate at me while slowly pressing it in.

"Loving you is the best part of the day." My breath caught at his confession. I looked at the wheat-haired man between my legs, eating me like I was his favorite meal, his head moving. The darkness around us heightened every single sensation.

I leaned against the door, letting my head fall back while threading my fingers through his hair. He raised one of my legs on my shoulder, growling over my clit.

And then he turned it on *and* sucked my clit.

I *exploded*. I was coming and dropping off the precipice faster than I thought possible. I worked my hips onto his mouth hungrily, gasping and clutching his hair tightly until he growled and sucked harder.

"*Luke!*"

I didn't even have a second to gasp at the empty sensation of the toy leaving me as he rose swiftly, lifting me in his arms.

In another instance, my fluttering pussy, still in the middle of an intense orgasm, was speared by his cock. A strangled scream left me as he sank me down, still stretched wide, but this time, easier than before.

A groan left his throat, and he stilled for a second the moment I felt him bottoming out.

"I'm going to work out my bad day on that little spot I love so much."

I wanted to dimly ask him why, but I just agreed.

He had my permission. I was coming down from my orgasm, and he'd plundered so deep, so fast I ceased thinking.

His growl shouldn't have excited me so much. Because he lifted me off his cock and slammed me back down on it.

I was ready to come again.

"You like that, doll?" he growled, punctuating his words with every slam. I wasn't going to make it. "Is that what my little, *oh shit...are you coming again?*"

I was gone. I was.

White lights spotted in my vision as I tried to stop the desperate noises from leaving me.

Wave after wave of pleasure centered down in my body, at my center, where Luke wreaked havoc on me.

"Don't stop." I tangled my fingers in his hair. "Please don't stop, I needed this."

Loving you is the best part of the day.

His only answer was to growl and keep going. Wet. Hot. Heat. The sound of his skin slapping into mine. It was so *good*. I gasped against his mouth.

"*Luke.*"

This position felt unreal.

Searing pleasure speared through me with every movement. The

147

only thing that held me up was Luke, and it was delicious. *I felt used. I was his fuck toy.*

He all but shoved me into the wall. "I'm going to destroy that little pussy."

"*Yes.*" The scream that left me as he shoved in *deeper* with the force made him groan. I saw pinpricks of light in my vision as he frantically fucked me.

Dimly registering that I sounded wild in his arms, clawing his back. I felt...wild. *But it never felt better.*

The way his hips slammed into mine. The filthy growls falling from his lips. I was so wet; I could hear it.

He hissed out a breath and kept pounding.

Little whimpers and squeals left my throat. I was *depraved.*

I couldn't breathe. I couldn't inhale enough oxygen to even respond to his dark words. I felt like my orgasm had been prolonged in that position the deeper he got.

"Oh God, Luke—" I sounded strangled. This didn't feel like sex or love. *It was hands down possession.*

"Let me feel you," he grunted. "One more. Just for me."

"I...I c...can't. Luke!"

"Yeah, you can," he urged, gripping my ass and dropping me down on his length as I screamed. "I can feel your pussy clenching around me. I know you're close because it's mine. Every inch of you is mine."

It *was. He hit that spot every time.*

"Damn straight, I do. I'm going to fuck it until it remembers the shape of my fucking cock every...*damn...time.*"

The sound that left me was pure *animal* as I came and came and *came.*

I'd said that out loud.

Dimly, I was aware of the pleasure coursing through me.

His groan was just as loud as he came, pumping me full of himself, groaning with every stroke. I was shaking wildly, awareness running through me. We hadn't used any protection, and I didn't care. I loved him so much.

I love him.

"*Baby—*"

"It's all right." He was on me wrapping his arms around me hauling me close to him. "I got you. I always got you."

He somehow walked me into the bedroom just like that. Never leaving me.

"Luke—"

When he laid me down on the bed still in me, I could feel it. Something was wrong. Something was dark about him. *It wasn't just a bad day, was it?*

"What's wrong?"

"Shhh," he whispered. "Let me stay inside of you, just like this. Just you. My girl, Evie."

He kissed me for so long I was out of breath.

"I want to eat you out, but I don't want to leave you. God, you're so fucking *wonderful*, doll."

He sounded and looked almost sad as he took me in. Even now, I could feel him lengthening and hardening inside of me.

I love him.

We didn't use a condom...didn't want anything between us. *I want to be his.*

"I'm here. I'm not going anywhere." He swallowed as I said the words. "I'm your girl. I love you."

His eyes went wide as I said it while he was in me, but it felt like my truth.

It felt more like the truth than me. "I love everything about you. You make me feel like I'm home, Luke."

I felt my vision blur as he wiped my eyes. "I can tell somethings wrong, and I don't know why you won't tell me. But I love you so much —I'm here." My heart clenched as he looked down at me with so much adoration.

"Evie." His eyes softened. "I don't deserve you—"

"Yes, you do." I looped my arms around his neck. "You always have. I know you love me too."

I could see it in his eyes, his actions, the little things he did, and the way he treated me.

I had good men in my life, and they'd shown me what love was in many ways.

Luke's love was no different.

His mouth curved as he closed his eyes slowly before opening them. "You have no idea how much I fucking love you, Evie. I think about you every single second of my day. I imagine taking you to work with me and letting you sit and just be while I work. I don't sleep or eat without you—" He broke off as my heart clenched.

I saw the man, but also the kid who lost his mother and someone who didn't know how to even speak around me when he was nervous.

"Every minute I'm with you, I collect bits of you. Every minute I'm without you, I wait until I come back to you. I would do *anything* to get every moment with you ten times over."

"You have me now," I whispered. "*Have me* now." He swallowed, and I felt how intimate this moment was.

"I love you, Evie." I kissed him as he moved inside of me once more.

"I'm going to fuck you until you ache, and then I'm taking you out tonight."

I moaned as he moved his hips inside of me, feeling more for him than I ever had. I didn't have a chance to respond as he kissed me harder than before.

And he began moving inside me with such force that I was clinging to him, screaming my orgasms one after the other into his mouth.

I couldn't think, just kiss him to let him know my truth.

I loved him.

I love you. I'm not going anywhere.

CHAPTER 23
EVIE

LUKE HAD DESTROYED ME AND THEN TAKEN ME OUT TO DINNER AT AN Italian place run by an elderly couple.

Luke claimed they had the best pasta in the city.

"Is everything all right?" He watched me frown at the menu, concern etched on his handsome features.

"I don't think they—oh, there you go, they have...no that one has meat in it too." I sighed, feeling a bit deflated.

"I can ask them to make something without meat," he said as the waiter came closer, his tone reassuring.

I shook my head, a wry smile on my face. "They'll probably excommunicate me from this restaurant."

At his laughter, the waiter who'd overheard beamed at me. I covered my face, much to Luke's delight.

When Luke placed his order, I blinked in surprise as he did so in *Italian*. And then he said something about the pesto, which is what I usually ordered. The waiter nodded in pleasure, and then he said yes several times.

"Do you want mozzarella?" Luke asked me, his eyes soft and attentive. I nodded, touched by his thoughtfulness. And then he asked for that, too.

I warmed with obvious pleasure as Luke sounded like a native, and they spoke briefly before the waiter left.

"I had no idea you spoke Italian." *What else didn't I know?*

"Are you impressed?" A playful glint in his eyes. "I can keep going." I laughed at his expression, my heart fluttering at his charm.

"I am. I only speak Spanish," I admitted, looking at him like I didn't know him. It was scary how comfortable he made me feel after he'd taken me with a savagery I wouldn't have expected from him.

He said. "*Yo también puedo hablar español.*" *I speak Spanish too.*

I gasped, my eyes widening in surprise and delight. "What other secrets are you keeping from me?" I laughed, an odd glint entering his eyes.

"French, but Teo, my friend, insists I learned it to talk to him, but nothing to be impressed by," he said softly, and then the look faded as he smiled. "Boarding school lets you meet interesting people."

As we sat there, enjoying our dinner and each other's company, I couldn't help but feel a sense of warmth and contentment spreading—filling me from the inside out.

"You're a good man, Luke Delaney," I said softly. "Thank you for trying to connect with my brother." I'd told Luke about taking Gabriel to the Pets for Vets café.

"I'm trying my best." An odd look entered his eyes. He opened his mouth to say something as our drinks arrived, and he stopped. That look never entered his eyes for the rest of dinner again, and I loved everything they brought out. I felt like we had spent so much time there I forgot about heading home.

"I'm exhausted," I said, yawning. "I could make love to that lemon sorbet."

He grinned. "I could take some home and lick it off you?" He laughed at my expression. "I'll take that as a yes."

"Home?" I caught that.

His cheeks went pink. "I *mean*—"

I grinned. "You can say it."

"Yes."

My heart clenched—just a few months ago, Luke said we were dating. And now...I loved him.

"I think I'll stay over tonight," I teased. "At home." *With you.*

"I love you, Evie." Effervescent joy bubbled up in me at his expression. I didn't make it a habit to sleep in with him. But now? I wanted Luke to meet my family. I was so excited.

"I need to run to the restroom. I'll be back, and then we can head out."

I wandered to the bathroom and washed my hands. While I was in the stall, I overheard two women giggling.

"He never goes anywhere. My mom said he came back from wherever he was…And he doesn't even go out…wait until she finds out he's on a date." I paused, my heart skipping a beat.

"I don't know why there's no photos; he's listed as one of the most eligible bachelors in the city…"

"Not anymore! He and Matteo are friends. The younger one is wild."

"What's his name?"

"Devereaux. Lucas. He's Lucy's older brother."

The name Devereaux struck a chord within me, sending a chill down my spine. It was one I had heard in passing over the years, seldom mentioned by Gabriel but always with a hint of disdain.

Devereaux.

I knew my family had secrets, but they never talked about it outwardly.

Which meant it was bad. In my mind, I had pictured an older, uglier, bitter man.

Probably someone ancient who hated women and treated people around him like servants. He was here? At this restaurant?

What were the chances?

And he was under thirty?

Despite never seeing a picture of him, I knew my brother despised him, often mentioning his name with contempt while Reed merely rolled his eyes at Gabriel's animosity.

"He's with a girl. Did you see her?" one of the women remarked.

"She looks like the help…"

My stomach soured, their words cutting through me like a knife. Mama had been the help.

I hate these women.

I couldn't make out the rest of the conversation, but the tone didn't sound flattering toward the other woman as they left.

I got out to the hallway and saw two women standing over Luke's table, giggling. Immediately, a feeling in my gut told me something was wrong.

Those couldn't be the same two women from earlier.

Maybe they'd made a mistake?

That wasn't Lucas Devereaux.

It was…*Luke Delaney.*

My heart sank as I slowly walked by their conversation.

"We went to school with Lucy, you don't remember?"

His face went dark. "Ladies, I'm going to go back to my date."

My stomach churned with unease, a sickening realization dawning on me.

"We heard you were in the market for a date…" the woman continued, and everything clicked. *He wasn't a grad student.*

He wasn't…*he isn't Luke Delaney.*

*Oh. My. God…*Something sharp and painful blossomed in my chest.

At that moment, I saw Luke look up and his expression balked. "Evie…"

"You're not…Luke?"

He stood abruptly, his horror evident on his face, one of the girls looked at me with disdain and the other smirked.

"Lucas," she uttered one of those giggle-cackle things mean girls did. "Who is this?"

She looked like a predator reeling in on me.

"Leave her alone." He reached for me, but I took two quick steps back, my heart racing.

"What is going on?" Except I saw it all over his eyes. The apology, the pleading, the two mean girls giggling to themselves.

"Luke?"

"Back the fuck up," he growled to the two women before he advanced. *"Evie, please let me explain—"*

The realization hit me like a ton of bricks, and I stumbled back, feeling like the ground had been pulled out from under me.

I trusted you.

"Who are you?" My heart was pounding, my mind reeling with shock. Hot betrayal coursed through me.

I felt as if the ground had been ripped out from under me, leaving me suspended in a free fall.

I stared at Luke…no, Lucas *Devereaux*, searching his face for any hint of the man I thought I knew, but all I saw was a stranger looking back at her with pleading eyes.

"All this time, you've been lying to me? About who you are—about your family?"

Lucas reached for me, but I recoiled, wrapping my arms around myself as if to hold the shattered pieces of myself together.

Oh God, this hurt.

Reed, I need you.

"No, I swear, Evie, please don't run, let me explain," he begged, his voice cracking with desperation. Tears stung my eyes as I tried to process the truth.

The man I had been falling for, the one I had opened up to, shared my deepest secrets with...he was a lie. *A façade.*

My stomach twisted, bile rising in my throat. I felt sick and violated like I had been played for a fool.

"*Evie, please,*" he pleaded, his eyes desperate, but I couldn't bear to look at him.

"*Don't,*" I choked it out. "*Just...don't.*"

My mind was racing, the thoughts swirling in my head like a relentless storm. "I didn't look you up because I trusted you. You told me you were a grad student."

And I believed him. Because why would a grad student be my brother's enemy?

"*Let me explain.*"

"*I can't look at you right now.*"

I picked up my stuff, reached into my wallet, tossed a few bills on the table, and watched him growl at that gesture.

Reed. I need to call Reed.

The realization that I'd been *played* was the only thing echoing in my mind.

"*Stay away from me!*"

I couldn't look at him.

He grabbed my elbow, desperation in his grip.

"Evie, I can't let you run from me like this. Not this mad!"

"Don't call me *Evie!*" I was spitting mad, the anger bubbling up inside me. "You don't get to call me anything, *Lucas. Was this fun for you?*"

I got in his face, the wide blues stricken, and his face paled. I didn't care. I removed my elbow from his grip.

I couldn't hold back the hot tears, the twisting in my stomach increasing. I didn't want him to see me crying. He'd lied to me, deceived me.

How much did he know about me?

There was no way he didn't know me.

I'm Evie Monroe, and I had foolishly confided in him.

And I told him I loved him.

A broken sob escaped my lips, and I took off, rushing outside into the cold night air, the chill stinging my tear-stained cheeks.

I didn't expect him to follow me.

I had underestimated how quickly he could move.

I felt his arms around me, hauling me back. I was whirled around, and I shoved him back.

"Evie, doll, please—"

"Stay away from me!"

I was crying, and I couldn't stop.

His arms were iron bands, and everywhere, I struggled against him, panic rising in my chest.

"I'm not letting you go until you hear me out." Panic lit his features. *"Yes, I knew who you were. Yes, I lied. But I've been falling for you since the day we met, since the moment I laid eyes on you—"*

Tears streamed down my cheeks, and I pushed at him as he continued. "I *wanted* to tell you. Every day, I wanted to. But I was *afraid*. Afraid you'd hate me like your brother does. What if you hated me too?"

His blue eyes burned into me. Those blues that calmed me down.

I didn't know him. I didn't want to know him.

His hand moved, and I cried out. "You told me you were *Luke Delaney!*"

"I *know*," he said, his voice strained, his usually vibrant blues, the eyes I made love to—*"It's my mother's maiden name. I'm sorry, Evie. When I realized it was you, I didn't know how to tell you."*

"You knew since the board game convention?" The anger boiled inside me, uncontrollable.

I got played. Gabriel was going to lose his shit.

"Evie, let me—" He tried to comfort me, but I fought against his hold, shrieking for him to let me go. *"No, Evie, I didn't mean to—"*

His grip loosened, and I pulled away.

I couldn't hear him.

I just felt my tears coming one after the other.

"Evie, I love you!"

"You don't love me! You don't even *like* me! You don't hurt people you like!" I couldn't stop crying. "You *lied! Why? Why didn't you just tell me the truth!"*

Memories flashed of us, meeting, dating, us talking, *oh my God—Gabriel.*

The thought of *hurting Gabriel.*

I'd talked about Gabriel to him.

He had known the *entire* time.

Tears streamed down my cheeks.

"Why does Gabriel hate you?" I said it out loud finally. "What did you do to *hurt* him?"

CHAPTER 24
EVIE

THERE'S ONLY ONE THING THAT COULD MAKE GABRIEL *THAT* ANGRY— *Isobel.*

Had Lucas's family done something to my sister? Is that why Reed and he never brought it up?

Gabriel was my entire life. My backbone. Even now, I could feel it. *Oh God. Oh God. Oh God.*

It hurt like being *stabbed* in the chest. *I'm so sorry, Gabriel.*

"*What?*" He was astounded, and something told me he was telling the truth, but I didn't know anything anymore. "No, Evie, I didn't—I would *never* hurt your family!"

He let out a breath. "He hates my entire family. I don't blame him. I hate them too!"

"What did you do to him then!" A wounded noise left me, and I broke down.

Oh God, I let him down. I cried harder.

"God, baby, I don't know. Let me take you home, let's just talk—"

"*No!*" I was in disbelief. "You think you can take me *anywhere?* I don't have a home! *It was a lie!* You lied about who you were, what you did—"

And then a horrific thought came over me, and it made me cry harder, watching as his expression fell. "*Oh God, I did things with you—*" I broke off with a broken sob. I couldn't stop scrambling back as he watched me. I hit a wall. I was gasping. "*I trusted you! How could you?*"

His expression broke. "*I'm sorry—*"

I couldn't hear him. My mind raced with the implications of what I had done. I had been intimate with him—shared my body and soul with a man I didn't even know.

"My brother was right about your family."

I saw the hurt on his face as I said that. It mirrored mine. Something in me was happening. Changing.

The betrayal cut deep, and I felt violated, as if my trust had been ripped away. I couldn't breathe, couldn't think.

All I knew was that I needed to get away from him, from the lies and the deceit. I pushed past him, my vision blurred by tears as I stumbled down the street.

As I walked through the cold, empty streets, shame and betrayal consumed me.

My stomach churned, twisting and knotting with each step I took. I felt sick and physically ill from the realization of what I had done.

I had shared my deepest secrets, my hopes, and my fears with a man who had been lying to me from the very beginning.

I couldn't shake the feeling of violation, of having my trust ripped away from me in the cruelest way possible.

I didn't know where I was going or have a plan.

All I knew was that I couldn't go back to Titan and face Gabriel and the shame of what I had done.

Reed. I needed Reed.

As I walked, the cold night air biting at my skin, I replayed every moment I had spent with Lucas, every secret I had shared, every touch we had exchanged. It all felt tainted now, poisoned by his lies.

I felt myself unraveling, the threads of my sanity fraying at the edges.

I had been a naïve little girl who had fallen for the wrong man.

And now, I was paying the price for my *stupidity*.

I couldn't stop the sobs that wracked my body, couldn't stem the flow of tears that poured down my cheeks. I felt broken, shattered into a million pieces that I didn't know how to put back together.

Gabriel would never forgive me for this. I had betrayed him, betrayed our family, by falling for...Luke?

My love for you will never be conditional.

Except this was different.

Reed.

He had been in Titan Midtown the last few weeks staying close to Alisha while still working his ass off.

He told everyone he'd be working out of that office. It was late, but Reed was always at work.

I rushed away from Luke—*Lucas*—to a cab and got into the first one I could find, directing it to Midtown where I knew Reed was.

I didn't look him up because I trusted him! I trusted him! Oh God, Evie, you are so stupid. Such a stupid girl.

I ran upstairs to his office, my heart pounding in my chest.

Shame and regret burned through me, consuming every thought, every breath.

I knocked on his door, unable to control my sobs.

I don't know what I'll do if Reed isn't here.

The door opened, and I caught Reed's expression for a second as he took me in.

A laptop opened behind him, and his eyes rimmed red.

"Reed..."

I was in his arms a moment later.

I cried and cried until I thought I would drown in my own tears, in the torrent of heartbreak crashing over me in waves. I couldn't breathe.

"I made a mistake," I mumbled out as I cried into his chest. Reed had always been there for me in the past.

And now he was my rock.

The shame was suffocating. It clawed at my throat, making it hard to breathe.

I had been so foolish, so naïve.

Long, agonizing moments later, Reed was holding me close as I sobbed into his chest. He didn't know about Lucas *Devereaux*.

I couldn't bring myself to tell him. I cried until I felt like I couldn't cry anymore, wiping my eyes furiously, hoping to conceal the pain and betrayal I felt inside.

Reed's voice was steady and reassuring as he held me tight. I didn't trust going home to Gabriel right now, most of the time Gabriel would stop. Not this time.

I know Gabriel. He's not going to stop.

"I'm a bad person." My voice shook.

"You are not a bad person," Reed replied softly, his tone filled with understanding. He didn't even know what was going on. "What could you have done?"

Reed moved to the floor listening to me, his space forming a bubble around me with his hands on my knees holding me steady as I wiped my face. His eyes held a wealth of emotion as he spoke those words, and I found solace in his comforting presence.

Reed had always been there for everyone. He was the one thing holding the team together at all times. Sometimes people thought Reed was a little mean, but he was doing his job.

And Reed was trying. I knew he was with Alisha—and he was trying that too.

When I first met Reed, he'd been a little terrifying to me, with his eyes the color of the sky right before a storm, like he was pent up violence with his tattoos.

But Reed had been the calmest member of the team.

I always turned to him, especially since he had trained me and kept my secrets in so many ways.

Luke was not a secret I could ever tell him.

"Do you know why Gabriel hates…?"

"Everyone?" A corner of his lip twisted up. "He's got good reasons."

Deep down, I knew that Reed sometimes understood him better than I did.

Reed was one of the few people Gabriel would listen to, and they defended each other to the death. Gabriel would never admit it.

But he preferred Reed away from the darker things he did.

Like his meetings with the O'Hara's. Those weren't people you met with for a cup of tea.

"Like the Devereaux's." Reed's smile dropped. "I know he hates them the most."

"*Evie…*" I knew they kept secrets.

Reed went to Nate for all the things he needed done. Nate and Selena were the operatives—lieutenants.

I had always been *just* Evie. And that made me cry more. Just Evie had messed up.

Reed looked at his laptop and seemed to think it over.

After a moment he seemed to reconsider.

"The Devereaux's are old money. You could trace them back hundreds of years to France if you wanted to. Over the years, though, the family changed. I can't be sure of when it started, but some of their shadier business practices…Gabriel doesn't—" Reed thought about his words carefully choosing each one.

"There's a *difference* between Titan's operations. We don't hurt innocents, or at least we try not to. The Devereaux's don't have the same concern, their family crest literally translates to their actions justifying the means. It was a value upheld until recently."

My heart clenched, and I felt my stomach roll.

We don't hurt innocents.

Somehow, I couldn't reconcile Lucas—Luke—with *that* person. *But I didn't know him.*

"Gabriel has never wanted us to mess with them. He says the entire family is filled with deceptive liars with entitlement issues, his words not mine." A shadow passed over his eyes.

Reed looked at me. "Gabriel doesn't like a lot of people, but I know the Devereaux's are up there on his shit list."

The entire family is filled with...all of them? Not a single one?

"All of them are...?"

Reed shook his head, the shadow falling over his eyes again as he thought.

"No. They aren't what they used to be. The youngest, Lucy, rejected a lot of it. She moved away from her family to work in...science."

Reed paused. "A couple of years back, their father stepped down and handed it over to Lucas, his son. From what people say, neither one of the siblings are like the rest of the family."

"What do you mean?"

"They don't go out in society; they don't leave save for work. Lucas runs his company, and he keeps to himself. I think their reputation precedes them—and Gabriel...it doesn't matter to him."

He has a sister. I didn't know.

"Gabriel believes that—"

I never leave my apartment.

He keeps to himself.

"Apples do not fall far." I'd heard him say that enough.

And now I understand why. I had proved him right.

Reed shook his head. "I think he'd rather avoid anything to do with their name."

I swallowed. "Did they hurt someone—"

"*No.*" That was too quick. Something was—

"No, believe it or not, regardless of your brother being friends with Aidan O'Hara, Gabriel still has principles. The O'Hara's don't kill people because they can. When they issue orders, they're precise and deliberate. Aidan doesn't believe in killing for fun. I think Gabriel respects people who do things with good motives—he wouldn't get messed up with the Devereaux's."

But they had hurt someone close to Gabriel. Just not Isobel. "What's gotten you curious about them?" Reed's eyes were sharp, even as he let out a breath. "Did you meet one of them recently or—?"

"No, I just wanted to know...I feel like the odd one out sometimes on the team," I said, looking away, my heart clenching with the lie.

"You're not the odd one out," Reed said softly. "Gabriel adores you. Everyone knows it. He never wants you to be hurt." Too late. "I know you think he doesn't want you to date or find anyone, but he does. He just wants it to be someone who—" Reed sighed. "Meets *all* of his fucking qualifications."

I nodded, being unable to stop my tears. "Deep down I think he also wants someone who fights for you, you know, stands up to him, takes care of you. You're his only family, Evie, what do you think he'd do if someone hurt you?"

End them.

Gabriel would make what he ever did to anyone else look like child's play.

And you betrayed him. You hurt that man. For what? A few moments of happiness? Or worse, a love that had never been real?

What do you think he'd do if someone hurt you?

I didn't even want to think about that. I couldn't even fathom—a black site would be kind.

"Evie, if I can ask you something since we're on the subject." I wiped my eyes and nodded as Reed continued. "....did Gabriel ever have a woman in his life?"

Reed distracted me by talking about Gabriel and asking me questions instead of me focusing on what just happened.

I focused on Reed's questions instead of what had happened.

Instead of thinking I was a stupid girl.

Instead of focusing on being a horrible sister for...

Being Evie...

CHAPTER 25
LUCAS

I couldn't calm down. I fucked up.

This is what Teo tried to warn me about.

Every fractured thought was her.

Her face swam behind my eyes—the gut-wrenching hurt and betrayal etched into her delicate features when she discovered the truth about my lies.

The way her warm eyes, usually so full of affection when gazing at me, had been…

Gabriel was right about your family.

That shit hurt.

Because the one thing I wanted to be? Was not my father's son.

For being Gabriel's sister, she had been sheltered from so much in the world. And she hadn't known me. *Not once.*

Because she trusted you. She didn't run a fucking background check because it wouldn't have been normal.

Did I know the exact reason *why* he hated my family? No. But I would venture a guess that it wasn't one thing.

But several things.

My grandfather had dodged multiple drafts, had many mistresses, and had shadier business practices that far extended anything I could ever fathom.

Gabriel served in the military, was in love with his dead wife, and operated without killing everybody.

My father had followed the same way as his father and had been a mean son of a bitch whose messes *I had had to clean up.*

He fought with my mother, hated my sister for some reason, and took his anger out on me for not being perfect.

And that was just *two of them. The rest are just as bad.*

The Devereaux name was nothing more than a fucking legacy.

Cousins who were models and cocaine addicts. My family made Matteo look like a saint.

My sister and I weren't close because of my father's insistence on separating us.

Then there was the *entire issue with the company almost falling apart under him.*

That's when he'd asked me to step in.

And Lucy is working with Reed on something that almost got me shot. I fucking know it.

I still didn't know the extent of the damage my father caused. I was still unraveling it, and I had taken it over years ago.Every single time I thought I solved a problem, another one appeared.

And while I knew Gabriel did business with a lot of people, he didn't do *shit* with me.

Gabriel owned real estate in the city and across the world, and he owned a private security company that operated with precision.

It rankled me deep down that he considered me to be in the same league as my fucked-up family.

I didn't need to know a specific reason why he hated me.

I hate myself.

And so, I understood. My mind tortured me with flashes of her—the radiant smile as we laughed together over silly inside jokes. Her soft skin. Her fingers raking through my hair after I collapsed on her.

I was with Evie because she made me feel like I was more than my name.

But even as I sat there, drowning in my own misery, I knew that I couldn't give up.

I have to find a way to make this right. I wanted to prove to Evie that my love for her was real, even if everything else had been a lie. I didn't know how. Didn't know if it was even possible. But I had to try.

I have to get my girl back.

I had to try. I couldn't even go back to the apartment *we* had. *Home.*

The memories were too painful, too raw.

Every corner, every surface held a reminder of the love we had shared, the love I had so carelessly thrown away.

I drew in a fortifying breath, scrubbing my hands over my face as if to wipe away the mental torment.

I had to focus if I was going to have any chance of making this right, of finding a way to fix anything.

If there was anything left anymore.

I didn't know.

I never did anymore.

Unease coiled in the pit of my stomach, a silent warning that danger lurked nearby.

But I was too consumed by thoughts of Evie to pay it any heed.

Because she was the first thing I had wanted with a fucking passion. The one thing that made me feel normal.

And my stupid ass fucked that up too.

I tried to brush it off, attributing the feeling to Evie finding out who I really was—the *depth* of my deception.

Of course, I want to be with you.

You're a good man, Luke Delaney.

I didn't feel like it anymore.

I only felt like it with her.

CHAPTER 26
EVIE

I HAVE TO GROW THE FUCK UP.

I couldn't stay here. I lurked in the house's shadows, purposely avoiding encounters with my brother.

He had seemed gleeful lately about something, and I didn't know what it was, but it couldn't have been good.

I wasn't all right at all.

I couldn't stop crying.

I couldn't calm down.

And I was scared Gabriel would catch on.

Once, when I first got to the manor, I had skinned my knees on my bike, falling over due to uneven ground on the driveway.

Gabriel had the entire thing re-paved. In *two* days.

But then he'd carried me crying and bandaged them like I was a child. Reed got me ice cream while Gabriel cuddled me while I lamented that I had no direction.

And I was almost an adult then. *Gabriel has never seen you as an adult.*

Selena called me his heart. HIs baby bird.

And I was.

But I was also *Evie*. Just Evie.

Gabriel would use Lucas for target practice if he knew. And there would be no ice cream.

My heart was shattered, the pieces scattered across the floor of my room. Every breath felt like a knife in my chest, every thought a reminder of what I had done.

I took eye drops and forced myself to look alive. I tried.

My stomach was still twisted into knots, and I couldn't focus on my work.

I just cried, telling Liam I was sick and I couldn't train. I hid from everyone.

I delved into the depths of the internet, scouring through the Devereaux family's web pages and real estate listings, hoping to catch a glimpse of Lucas Devereaux.

Yet, all I found was a solitary photo from his childhood. I remembered him saying he hated going out anywhere. It made him freak out.

Unless he was with you.

I shoved that thought away. No, Luke Delaney was a lie. I couldn't stop thinking about him. The memories assaulted me, each one a fresh wave of pain and betrayal. The way he looked at me and held me...*it had all been a lie.* A fresh wave of tears came over me.

The betrayal of what he'd done had crashed over me until my throat was raw, my cheeks burned, and then came the guilt of what I'd done. Hot humiliation.

That's what it felt like.

But there was something more to it. Something even I *hated*.

Lucas Devereaux was a man. *Just another man.*

I was so busy running away from Titan, from the pressure, not belonging, and everything.

All I did was...work. Besides gardening, I didn't have many hobbies and couldn't remember the last time I went out *without* Gabriel. *You did with Luke.*

But I didn't want it with just Luke! I want it for myself! Evie!

Independence wasn't about dating the right man or even a man at all. Independence was...being me.

Just existing as myself. I saw Alisha's stories and her life, and despite having Reed, Alisha had a life.

She had goals, dreams, and aspirations; she knew what she *wanted*, and Reed only added to her life. He wasn't...the *only* thing she had.

What did I *want*? *Who* was I becoming?

I don't have you, Isobel. And I wish I did.

But I knew she had been my age in the Agency. *She lived.*

It didn't matter that she didn't make it; she was always so cool in my eyes. Cooler than Selena for being who she had been. No doubt brave, feisty, and—everything I was not.

Even if the betrayal hurt and made me feel humiliated, I looked around my room—my room for the last seven years of happiness with Gabriel and being his only family.

And I knew it would gut me to leave, but I had to.

It had been a seed watered while I was running around with Lucas.

But there was no Lucas.

It was...just Evie. I would never be Selena or Alisha. Or Isobel. But I didn't have to be like them.

That was the worst part about lying around moping about Lucas for the last few days. Is moping about yourself.

What did I like to do? Besides work. Did I have hobbies?

Did I have a life?

I had spent so long running away from the manor...I had never looked at myself. I was so busy...living like everyone else I forgot how to live. And as I lay there, something in me changed.

I couldn't do this anymore. I didn't want to be anyone's sister.

I didn't want to be anyone's girlfriend. Something in me...*shifted.* I wanted to do things. Go out.

Make friends. Live my fucking life.

All the women around me did that. Even Alisha's sister went away to college to live her life. Maybe I could ask Reed to talk to both of them. He would help.

Gabriel wants to protect you.

He always has, since Mama. College. Boys. Driving. Pain. I would never know, and so—I would never grow.

Being protected—is what was holding me back.

I knew what I had to do. I knew it was now or never. With that realization weighing heavily on my mind, I ascended the stairs to Gabriel's floor.

The energy up here was different; even with the sunlight streaming through, there was always—sadness.

And I hated feeling torn between wanting to save him and wanting to free myself in some ways. I had to experience life.

I entered after knocking.

"Evie? Is everything alright?" His voice was gentle, filled with genuine worry, and I nodded, feeling my eyes water at the sight of him.

The sunlight streaming through the windows warmly lit the mahogany furniture and comfy couches. Still, the atmosphere was heavy with a lingering sadness that seemed to permeate the space.

Gabriel would always be up here whenever I needed him.

Do it. Do it. Do it.

My palms were sweaty, and my heartbeat became erratic.

"I want to talk to you about something." I wrung my hands together. "I want you to know I've spent quite some time thinking about it. I did a lot of research, and I have a plan."

He liked plans.

Shame gnawed at my insides, a bitter taste in my mouth.

Sensing this was serious, he walked around his desk and motioned for me to sit. I didn't because now I was his height, but he sat, and I faced my brother like I was his equal.

Use your words.

I shouldn't have heard *his* voice. Felt *his* presence at *my* side.

But I did. I felt all of him still. And I hated it.

"It's okay. Whatever it is," Gabriel assured me, though I knew it *wasn't*. "Tell me."

I felt my tears spill over.

My love for you will never be conditional.

I couldn't stay under Gabriel's roof, accepting his kindness after what *I had done.*

I had betrayed Gabriel, the one man who had never betrayed me.

My love for you will never be conditional.

My vision blurred as hot tears welled up and overflowed. I felt his hands steady me and haul me into his arms, his lips at my temple.

"*Shortcake—*"

My love for you will never be conditional.

"I'm moving out."

CHAPTER 27
LUCAS

I JOLTED AWAKE, AND A SCREAM LODGED IN MY THROAT.

The sheets, damp with sweat, clung to my skin as I fought to catch my breath.

The nightmares were relentless, each one more terrifying than the last.

But tonight, it wasn't just the faces of dead children and soldiers that haunted me.

It was Evie. Her anguished face, her screams of betrayal, pierced through the fog of my dreams.

I glanced at the clock, its neon glow casting an eerie green tint across the room. 5:17 a.m.

Sleep was a distant memory now, and the whiskey beckoned, promising a temporary reprieve from the guilt that gnawed at my insides. As I padded into the kitchen, the cool tiles sent a shiver up my spine. The bottle felt heavy in my hand, the amber liquid sloshing as I poured a generous glass.

The first sip burned, but I welcomed the pain. It was a small price to pay for the numbness that would follow.

I stood by the window, the city's muted sounds drifting up from below.

The shadows seemed to twist and writhe, mirroring the turmoil within me. Something felt off—a sense of unease that I couldn't shake.

My eyes couldn't focus on the view anymore. I hated it. I hated feeling trapped. I waited until the sun came up to make a phone call. I took a deep breath, steeling myself for the conversation ahead.

"Tell me this isn't about Kieran," Aidan growled, his voice thick with sleep. "I swear if he sends me any more cat videos, I'm going to lose my mind."

Aidan O'Hara and I got along only when I had taken over. Our fathers had worked together, and it had made sense, despite being mafia, to reach out to me to outline how he was nothing like his predecessor. A sentiment I echoed.

I reached out to Aidan when shit hit the fan. Not the DuPonts. I didn't even need Matteo near a gun.

He reached out to me when he needed a favor.

Aidan grumbled about social media reels, and I didn't know what the fuck he was talking about.

"Something's happening in New York," I said, my voice steady despite the fear that coiled in my gut. I told him everything, the words tumbling out in a rush. Everything except Gabriel. Evie. My love life. Lack of it.

"Killian's in the city." His presence never boded well. The mismatched eyes and edgy attitude were a recipe for a war breaking out on New York turf. "He can look into it."

Aidan passed me his younger brother's information.

I managed to schedule a therapy appointment and request sleeping aids, but I knew it was a band-aid on a gaping wound. I was unraveling, and the company was paying the price.

The moment I stepped into the office, my head of security bombarded me with news that made my stomach churn. Missing security footage, entire sections of our archives wiped clean.

"What? How is that even possible?" I demanded, my voice rising with each word. "Don't we have safeguards in place to prevent this kind of thing?"

His eyes darted away from mine, and I could see the fear etched into the lines of his face.

"Someone's hacking into our system and erasing the footage without a trace. We can't find them. But my guys are trying their best."

Their best wasn't enough. I needed Evie, her brilliant mind, and her uncanny ability to unravel even the most complex issues.

But that bridge was burned, the ashes still smoldering. She didn't have faith in herself. But I did.

"Any news on the shooting?" I asked, dreading the answer.

He shook his head, his expression grim. "Nothing yet. Sir, can I ask..." He hesitated, and I could see the question he was afraid to voice.

"No, we don't get the cops involved." My tone left no room for argument. I didn't need this blowing up.

On my desk, I eyed a black card with gold claw marks...

"What the fuck is this?" I held it up. "It's been on my desk every single day." *Who the fuck kept coming in here?*

He shook his head. "No clue, sir."

Of course not. I resisted the urge to throw something. Evie would know. Without her, I was transforming. Snapping into something. I didn't recognize this man.

I closed my eyes, the weight of my responsibilities crushing me.

The shooting, the missing footage, and now...

A knock at the door jolted me back to the present. Jenny, my second secretary, poked her head in, her face pinched with worry.

"Sir, I'm sorry, there's an emergency."

I bit back a sigh. I waved her in, my head of security shifting uncomfortably beside her.

"Someone published an op-ed last night about scandals involving Mercury Group. They're alleging that we've been involved in some shady dealings with two of our suppliers."

My heart raced, my mouth going dry, but I kept my face neutral.

"We've always operated above board." But even as the words left my lips, I knew they weren't entirely true.

My father's legacy was a tangled web of secrets and lies, and now, it seemed they were coming back to haunt me.

"Who's behind these allegations?" I kept my voice calm. Collected.

Inside, I raged, but on the outside, I'd been a soldier once.

I was still good enough.

Jenny shook her head, her eyes wide with fear at my expression.

"It's anonymous, but it's already causing some ripples. Two of the suppliers mentioned in the article have already pulled out of their contracts with us."

I closed my eyes, my hands forming a steeple in front of me as I exhaled.

"Thank you, both of you. I'd like the room now."

"Sir, one more thing." She looked almost antsy. "Someone from your father's old board of directors passed away last night...of a heart attack—"

Another one?

"Actually, two of them. I wanted to check in, Ella left a note about sending flowers to the family."

My chest tightened. What was…"Yes, that's fine."

She nodded, and if she could see my emotions, she wouldn't comment as they both left.

Three people from my father's old board died in the last month…my father had been desperate for a package from Lucy….he had never sounded like that.

Was he afraid? Was he…was I…no, *someone* tried to shoot me.

The others were…what were the odds of someone eliminating people?

As the door clicked shut behind them, I sank into my chair, my eyes closing for a moment.

I couldn't get in touch withLucy, and she had stopped using my cars. And I told myself to go see her, but between losing Evie, Gabriel storming my office, and getting hit by Reed?

I didn't even want to start on her.

But what if…Lucy was the key?

I sighed. Of course, my sister would stir up trouble. And Killian texted me back. I texted him about the latest deaths, and he just gave me a thumbs up.

It was almost poetic, in a twisted sort of way, how everything in my life seemed to be unraveling now that Evie was gone.

It was as if the universe was punishing me for my sins, for the lies I had told and the hearts I had broken.

I closed my eyes, willing the pain to subside, but it only intensified.

The memory of Evie's face, the hurt and betrayal etched into her delicate features, was seared into my mind, a constant reminder of what I had lost and the price I was paying for my deception.

And as much as it hurt to admit, I knew that I had no one to blame but myself.

Matteo's words haunted me even now.

What are you going to do when you break her?

Lose my shit, apparently.

CHAPTER 28
EVIE

"What happened? Did I do something? Did you feel uncomfortable—"

The pain that radiated from his very being tore at my heart, making each beat feel like a knife twisting in my chest.

His eyes were no longer ice but the most *human* I had seen.

"No, you are...the *best*." I rushed to reassure him, my voice trembling with emotion.

He was my rock, my protector, the one person who had always been there for me through thick and thin.

"Then why?"

I knew this conversation would be difficult for him, but I couldn't ignore my own needs.

I needed to break free from the confines of his protection, even if it meant hurting him in the process.

It was a selfish desire, a longing for independence and autonomy that had been growing inside me for years, but I knew that I couldn't keep pushing it down, couldn't keep pretending that I was content with the way things were.

Use your words, Cherry.

I could see the confusion and hurt in his eyes, the way his brow furrowed as he tried to make sense of my words.

"I knew something had happened to you. *Did he hurt you?*" he asked, still not understanding the truth that was staring him right in the face.

Because this was never about me.

Every time I was in the room with him, I knew who it was really about.

Use your words.

I took a deep breath, trying to keep my composure, trying to find the words that would make him see, make him understand.

"Gabriel, I'm twenty-three. I want to live on my own. I feel like a kid encroaching on your territory. I don't want you to have to hide your life from me. And you should be able to live freely. I cannot play house like this," I confessed, feeling the weight of my words, the finality of them, settling over me like a heavy blanket. "I really want my own place. I have for some time. I'd like my own space."

"You have your own space—"

"You know what I mean," I replied firmly, feeling Lucas's presence right behind me like it was his chest I used for support, and I didn't know why it felt so right.

"I love you so much. I need to set some boundaries with you. I would like to have my own place. I would like to have my own life outside of work. And I think that independence starts with creating my own space. Look at Alisha. Even Avani has a place for herself."

I watched as his expression hardened, his jaw clenching with a mixture of anger and pain, and I felt a pang of regret, a twinge of guilt that made my stomach churn.

But I knew I had to stand my ground, had to make him see that this was about more than just him, more than just us.

"I have to grow up," I repeated.

"You can grow up here," he replied solemnly, his tone unwavering, his eyes boring into mine with an intensity that made me want to look away, to hide from the truth that lay behind them. "You're safe here."

"Safe doesn't mean that I'm okay." I was adamant. "I'm telling you, and I'm giving you the courtesy of letting you know I am moving out."

I kept my voice firm, feeling the tension between us, the weight of the words that had been left unsaid for far too long.

"I know if Isobel were here, that's what she would want."

His eyes narrowed with hurt. I felt the ice radiating off him. "That was a dirty move. She wanted you to be here."

Did she? I didn't know. I don't know my sister—he did.

"I love you, I love her, even though I didn't know her well. I respect both of you, but you guys need to respect that I need to grow up," I countered softly. "I need you to understand where I'm coming from."

The yearning that had taken root in my heart, the desire for something more, something different.

"Isobel lived—she lived her life. She met you. I know you were the best thing that ever happened to her—you're the best thing that ever happened to me. Maybe I want a life for *myself.*"

I did.

I really did want that.

"From the moment you entered my life, you have set the most incredible example of love."

I felt it pouring out of me then, unable to stop and not folding on what I wanted.

Luke had taught me to use my words so I would. "You've given me so much. But I don't want to just take from you anymore. I have money saved up from some of the odd jobs I took in. I want to be an operative. I want to be better than where I am now—"

"There's *nothing* wrong with you—"

"*Yes, there is!*" The anxiety at standing up to him made me shake, shiver, and want to cave, break down, and apologize.

His eyes widened enough for me to know I'd disarmed him.

"The problem is that I don't have an identity *outside* of *you.* You are my entire life. And there's nothing wrong with that—but maybe I'm thinking there has to be more to me than *Gabriel's little sister.* I have spent so long trying to figure out who I was in college, at Titan, *everywhere*—but I just wanted to live. *I want friends and girlfriends.* Maybe meet a nice man, *Gabriel*—you get to live. *Let me live.* Let me...*figure it out.* Let me fail and fall down sometimes. I'm growing. I would only be with someone if *they loved me more than you love me.*"

I reached out, taking his hand, ice cold, and it broke me. "I love you so much, but you have to let me *grow.*"

His demeanor was still ice, but slivers of her memory lurked there.

I could see him at war with himself, too.

Those icy-blue orbs cut through me like a knife, making me feel exposed and vulnerable, but I pressed on, determined to make him see, to make him understand.

"Moving out doesn't mean I hate you," I reassured him, though guilt still gnawed at me, still ate away at my insides.

"You never make me feel uncomfortable. You are the greatest man I know. You saved my life. It just means I want to live, too. Everyone else does. I need space to just be. I'll still come back and work here all the time or from my new apartment. I'd like to replant myself somewhere that's mine. I'm not gone, and I'm not far. I'm right there...I already found a place."

177

There was a pregnant pause. He was considering it. I knew it would work.

Sorry, sis. I had to play that card.

He took his bottom lip between his teeth, worrying about it, before he let out an exhale.

"Where is it?" Was he actually agreeing?

I disclosed the location, and he nodded approvingly.

"That's not a bad neighborhood. Lots of old folks."

I love him.

I managed to suppress the tears that threatened to spill.

"Do you want to come look at it with me and help me move in… maybe vet the place and look for security issues?"

He loved solving puzzles as much as he liked scaring people.

I think most people forgot at Titan that Reed wasn't the only expert in cybersecurity. Gabriel hid everything better.

"I'll do all my usual jobs, and I'll continue to work on Oracle." His eyes went blank at the mention of Oracle. I was still working on it with Liam.

After a long moment's hesitation again, he tipped his head. "All right…but I don't like this, and you're getting a security guard."

I balked at the idea. "No."

"Doorbell camera, sensors in case there's a break-in, and an alarm system."

"Fine."

He paused and raised a brow. "One security guard."

"Do not give me that smile thinking I'm going to cave." I raised my chin and squared off against him. "No security guard, but I agree to a tracking device so you can make sure I'm safe and sound."

Lucas wasn't in my life. It wouldn't matter.

He looked pleased fractionally. "I can make it into a keychain, so it's always with you."

I smiled. "I'd like that." He squeezed my hand. It hurt a little.

This was hard for me. But I felt a little strange, like now, I saw when he looked at me he didn't see me. He rubbed his chest, and I hugged him.

I'm sorry.

But at least we were making progress.

Even though I saw I had hurt him. I could see it in his eyes.

Everything he did for me, he did for her.

And now I was taking that away from him, taking her memory away.

I'm sorry, Isobel.

~

"I GOTTA ADMIT," GABRIEL CONFESSED WITH A NARROWED EYE ON THE apartment I had picked. "This place is really spacious and bright. All the natural light will be good for your plants."

Despite my heartbreak, recently, the moment I started doing things for myself—it wasn't so bad.

I had an apartment picked out.

I signed up to go to the gym.

I was already studying more on Red Hat stuff with Liam, who had given me written notes telling me something was good for refreshers while I was "sick," and then finally, I asked Reed if Alisha would help me with my situation.

She was a sister.

And I really wanted one.

He thought she would be the best person.

Altogether? Moving on meant moving forward. As betrayed as I felt...the further I went from the girl I was—the more I embraced change.

There was something beautiful about becoming your own person. And I liked her too.

Without *Lucas*. I still cried every so often, but I realized when I focused on happiness, I was feeling better. I did.

I researched all the ways to get over heartbreak.

And then I'd done a deep dive into the Devereaux family.

The more I read, the more I realized why Reed was a junkie for information.

I was growing. I was changing.

And sometimes, you need pain to grow through. Even as it hurt, I ignored thoughts of Lucas and my memories with him.

Gabriel occasionally found me crying, and I brushed my eyes and told him allergies were the reason.

It's Autumn.

He knew. But I didn't want to tell him. I knew his rage. I knew him.

And right now?

The realtor was casting Gabriel discreet glances. She'd double-blinked when I showed up with him, and after she heard the words "brother," she lost it.

"And here is where the Master bedroom is. Shall I show you?"

She eyed Gabriel like she wanted him to be in there. Whether he was oblivious or playing dumb, he nodded.

I ignored her for my obvious joy.

I felt a lot better stepping into this place.

My excitement had been obvious all day as Gabriel strolled around in a darker gray suit that drove the realtor insane.

I giggled a little as his eyes darted at me.

I knew *that* look.

The closer he got, the more excited the realtor got. I hid my grin in my hair.

As the realtor continued her spiel about the property, Gabriel's attention drifted, his mind undoubtedly wandering to potential security concerns.

I couldn't blame him; it was in his nature.

"What would you say you sleep in? A California king?"

Oh God.

"He sleeps on the floor."

Gabriel walked away, coughing as his shoulders shook.

"A pallet, no pillows, like a prisoner of war."

I bit my cheek at her expression.

I found him grinning in the spare bedroom, his eyes scanning everywhere. It was in a neighborhood above the Upper West Side.

I could've sworn the realtor muttered she wouldn't mind that with him.

He is still my brother.

When we finished touring the place, I pretended not to notice the realtor dropping her number several times. And a card. He handed it to me without looking at it.

Guys were always on edge around him, but women *loved* him.

If he was a little nicer, women would lose their shit.

I never asked, and he never said a word.

"Do you…"

I didn't even know how to ask.

"Do you ever think about—"

"No."

I didn't even finish.

Did he ever think about dating…

My throat worked as I saw his expression change. He shook his head, his expression turning bland, nothing in his ice chips for eyes. Nothing.

"You can beat them off with your stick any day, shortcake."

We got to the elevator, and two women got on.

Gabriel stood in the back, his head down, and I stood between them, but they *looked*.

"Just say when."

He smiled down at me, and one of them sighed.

It took everything in me not to burst out laughing as he looked miserable for a few seconds.

I didn't miss how they tried to brush against him, and I all but scowled as they giggled as they left.

"Easy, shortcake, no need for your stick—"

"She just touched you," I protested.

If he had been a woman?

They would've been called creeps. As Selena said, *double standards.* He shrugged like it was normal.

"I've had worse." His smile was soft. "But thank you for worrying."

He checked his watch. "I need to stop by Midtown." He hated being in the city.

Use your words.

"I'll stick around here," I replied, eager to explore the neighborhood. "I'd like to explore, and then I have to see Alisha later today." I told him the exact time when Reed said I could go meet Alisha.

"She said she's at some hotel near the office. Hotel Primrose?" I rambled at his expression going blank, nothing in his eyes. "I want a makeover. I don't want to always wear Selena's clothes. Most of them don't look the same on me."

He sighed in relief at that, and I felt a laugh emerge.

"I'm excited. Reed said she's good at things like this. Avani really loves her, and they're super close." And *prettier* than two people should be allowed to be.

He slowly blinked, and I saw emotion going through his eyes. "She's a good sister."

"I'm not trying to replace anyone. I just need women in my life, too."

"I know." Somewhere, he had gotten closer, and for some reason, I got emotional. "Come here, shortcake." I snuggled into him, inhaling the cologne he paid a fortune for.

Nobody smells like him.

"Thank you for everything," I said sincerely as he hugged me. "I'm surprised you agreed to all of this."

"Which reminds me." He held out a lily keychain. "You promised." I did. I took it, adding it to my new set of keys. "I'll drop you off and head to Midtown."

I blinked up at him. "You don't want to know when I'm back home?"

I was surprised, he usually did, and then his eyes drifted to my keys. Oh…that was good.

He smiled at my expression.

There was something in his eyes.

Something…like he wanted to say. I felt it in his demeanor.

"I think she's proud of both of us."

He knew *who* she was.

I saw his brow rise a centimeter as though he was surprised, and it wasn't always I got to surprise him.

"I did the bare minimum. You did the work. I'm happy Alisha is going to be there for you from now on." He squeezed me tightly. "I get to take a break."

I laughed easily.

From now on?

I knew Reed's crush was serious.

He'd spent years pining for her.

I was happy he was with her. I liked her so much.

A big sister. I was giddy.

"I'm not giving you a break," I teased. "I still need you," I said it like *Duh.* Gabriel rubbed my hair. His brow rose again. "Moving away doesn't mean I'm leaving you. I'll come visit all the time. *Annoy you* with cat videos…"

He grinned wide, looking up at the sky for patience at my laughter, holding me closer.

Thank you for taking care of me. You are home. I love you.

I felt like I saw Gabriel a little more clearly.

I realized I rarely did see him outside of our working life and the places we went to in Greenwich.

Thank you, sis. Thank you for finding the best man in the world.

I strolled through the neighborhood for an hour while Gabriel attended to whatever he had to do.

I settled into a cozy boba tea café nearby, discovering mochi donuts and looking at a few options for what to do in the neighborhood.

"We have art classes with animals," said one of the girls cleaning the table next to me. She looked over at me in her pink apron and easy smile. "If you're interested."

I smiled. "I'd love that."

I would love to try new things.

Deep down, I tried to tell myself that Luke wasn't the primary reason for this change.

Deep down, even I knew I was lying.

I wanted to call Luke. To tell him about my day. Invite him over. Feel him deep inside me.

I shook myself out of it.

I didn't know what to do with those emotions. I felt it in Gabriel's eyes when he said Alisha would be a good sister.

He was happy.

Sometimes, I wish I had Isobel. Everyone needed a big sister. A mom. A family. I had Gabriel and Reed, but they were my brother's.

What did you do? How did you make it?

She'd passed away at *my* age.

I knew why Gabriel was scared to let me go. But I needed to live. She had.

It had taken Lucas, maybe, to push me outside of my comfort zone.

He had always done that.

But it took me to take the first step. I had done that work.

Going to the convention alone, being brave enough to date him, being brave enough to open my heart to him, letting him into my life in little ways, and then opening myself up to new experiences? It had all been...part of living.

And I realized she had done that. She met Gabriel.

And he met me. But I wished I knew her better.

Isobel.

I wish I could talk to you sometimes.

Ask you for advice.

Isobel, am I making the right choices?

I walked down the halls, my eyes drifting up the grand home after my visit with Alisha.

This hurt.

The stairs, the massive columns, the intricate patterns, the space... this was home. This was Gabriel. And her.

Leaving a piece of myself at the manor was going to ache.

Letting go of Gabriel was going to hurt more. It already did.

CHAPTER 29
EVIE

GABRIEL HELPED ME SETTLE INTO MY APARTMENT.

Surrounded by the comforting scent of fresh paint and the vibrant green of plants on every surface, I felt a sense of accomplishment as I grinned at Gabriel.

He had shaken his head at the abundance of greenery, but I could see the happiness in his eyes.

He liked the place too. And it was safe according to him now.

But maybe he needs some space, too.

It was rare to see him in jeans and a hoodie outside the manor, but he'd seemed at ease, eating pizza on my new couch and watching TV, looking like a normal man.

Gabriel was on his phone with headphones in one ear as I watched TV, his eyes glazed over a little.

As I collapsed next to him, he put on a movie for me, the soft glow of the screen illuminating his features.

I fell asleep on his shoulder, and when I woke up, it was morning. I was tucked into my bed with no Gabriel in sight.

Slowly, things began to feel better.

I woke up that morning and dressed in a cute outfit Alisha had picked for me.

She said I should accentuate my legs because I was short, and she'd picked out dozens of mini A-line dresses.

I wore a simple one today, long-sleeved with leggings and thigh-

184

high boots. Alisha said it would be good for me, and it felt like a touch of Selena.

I think it would make Selena happy since you borrowed her clothes to see her influence on you, not just mine.

And that's why she was the best sister because she cared enough about everyone else's feelings.

Sometime during my date with Alisha, Kellan sat down with us at the mention of Selena.

Alisha had walked him through the different types of makeup and neckline cutouts, picking a high neckline for me with a shorter cut hemline, stating it would make me look taller.

It did.

Kellan and I lost our minds when she worked like a magician with her color wheels.

And he'd smiled at the "Selena boots" we started to call them.

I had seen Selena wearing a necklace to work lately, and she'd looked better in general.

I knew that was all Kellan.

Something had changed between them. I was happy for them. I asked Alisha if I could text her and come to her, and in turn, she also told me Avani was open to me reaching out.

And suddenly, I had two sisters.

I'm really happy Reed finally asked you. I watched him stare at you for three years through a screen.

She'd smiled as Kellan had distracted me with a question.

Today, dressed in my new Evie best, I had to pick up some items from Titan's Midtown office, the sleek black and high-tech surroundings that were Reed's dream come true.

My heart nearly skipped a beat at the sight of the tall, striking figure in a perfectly tailored navy suit.

The office was empty, the silence broken only by the soft hum of the air conditioning units cooling down the equipment Reed kept here.

That's why I had come by, seeking a moment alone with my thoughts to acquaint myself with my new workspace.

Could he be a new client?

"Excuse me, can I help—" The words died on my lips, my heart sputtering to a halt as my steps faltered.

The elevator dinged closed behind me, the sound echoing in the suddenly charged air. *"Luke."*

His head lifted, and true blue met mine, sending a jolt through me.

I felt my words trapped in my throat as it tightened, my chest hammering wildly.

Lucas Devereaux, in all his designer glory, stood before me. His ocean eyes flashing with a mix of exhaustion and something I couldn't quite decipher. Something I didn't know if I wanted.

A part of me *wanted* to know.

Another part of me just absorbed the impact of seeing him again. After weeks.

His usually chiseled features looked haggard. Those same eyes had once warmed when he moved inside me.

I exhaled shakily and shook my head, trying to clear the vivid sensations of his touch, his scent, the way he'd made me feel.

"Evie."

The man before me was a far cry from the Luke I had known, the one who wore casual pullovers and had a gentle smile that could melt my heart.

Now, I couldn't fathom how I had been so blind.

"How did you get here?" I felt my words trapped in my throat, true blue, and the scent of the ocean filled my body.

"You look different."

His eyes took in the shoes, the dress, and everything Alisha had done. It felt better. I felt...better.

I couldn't speak.

I shook as he looked...like himself.

Just like I felt like who I was on the inside...we both had come out in our true colors.

Somehow.

"Cherry, let me...just let me—it's been forever, doll."

In a few long strides, he closed the distance between us, his arms encircling my waist and lifting me with ease.

The heat of his body seared through the fabric of my dress, igniting my skin. Instinctively, I clung to the hard planes of his chest, fear and *desperate* longing warring within me at his touch, which reignited a fire I thought had been extinguished forever.

You, it's always going to be you.

"I miss you, I'm sorry, I'm so sorry, doll. Please let me explain—"

"No."

This isn't real. He isn't real.

Anger resurged in me at his audacity, a white-hot fury burning through the haze of desire and longing.

You lied throughout our entire relationship.

The reminder lanced through me with brutal precision, the pain *sharp and unrelenting.*

I wasn't *his* girl, his future—not after the lies and the betrayal that had shattered my trust, leaving jagged edges that cut deep. It was mine. Gabriel's.

I had a life outside of him.

"You lied to me," I whispered, my voice cracking under the weight of my emotions.

The words tasting bitter on my tongue.

Lucas's grip tightened, his forehead pressing against mine, the intimacy of the gesture causing my heart to ache. "Please...stop."

And just like that, I was set down.

"You should have told me...even if Gabriel hated you? I *would've*—"

Lucas's eyes widened, a flicker of pain crossing his chiseled features. The silence stretched on, the weight of my accusation pressing down on us both.

I wiped my eyes, trying to regain my composure, but I could feel his gaze on me, intense and searching.

"You would've what?"

"Please go," I choked out, every wall crumbling under the weight of his presence, the warmth of his body so close to mine.

"You would've what, Evie?"

I opened my mouth to respond, the truth spilling from my lips before I could stop it. "I would've stood by you. Regardless. I—"

I couldn't even look at him as the realization crashed into me like a tidal wave. I would have chosen him.

"You would have defended me?" he rasped, disbelief and something akin to hope mingling in his tone. Why was he stunned?

Did he not think I would?

"I would have," I whispered, my eyes fixed on the clean, gleaming tiles beneath my feet, unable to meet his piercing gaze. "Past tense. Please go. Someone will come find you here."

It was a lie. No one would come looking for him. But the threat of Reed showing up was better than the alternative of facing the truth that lay between us.

Lucas moved, his towering frame swallowing all the space around me, his presence overwhelming the confines of the office.

He dipped his head, his breath ghosting over my skin as he spoke.

"Cherry," he murmured. "Why would you pick me over your family?"

Use your words.

He was close, so close that I could feel the heat emanating from his body, the electricity crackling between us.

I couldn't push him away. I didn't want to.

Every fiber of my being yearned for his touch. When my eyes dared to look at him, I knew he knew my answer.

And I hated and loved it at the same time.

His lips brushed over mine, softly at first.

I couldn't tell who moved first, but suddenly, we were consumed by a ferocious, familiar hunger.

A muffled moan escaped my lips as my treacherous body instinctively arched into his hard lines, every cell alight with desire.

Hungrily, I devoured him, my tongue tangling with his as he groaned and thrust into my mouth.

As I sucked on his tongue, I felt tears prickling at the corners of my eyes.

I missed you.

His hands roamed possessively over my body, igniting a fire beneath my skin as he rained scorching kisses along my jaw and neck.

I couldn't hold back the moans that escaped my lips, my body betraying the desire I had tried so hard to suppress.

His touch was electric, sending shockwaves of pleasure through every nerve ending, awakening a hunger I thought had been laid to rest.

"Shh, Evie, I got you, I promise, I got you." I felt his arms tight around me.

The tension crackled in the air, thick and palpable, threatening to drown me in a sea of conflicting emotions.

Lucas pressed his forehead against mine, kissing everywhere he could, his fingers gently wiping away the hot tears that streamed down my face, the tenderness of his touch a stark contrast to the fiery passion.

A new voice interrupted us.

"Oh shit, Evie?"

I whipped my head around.

Busted.

"Reed?"

"What the fuck did he do to you?" Reed demanded, his fury palpable. He was on Lucas faster than I could move, ripping him off me.

"Reed, stop," I pleaded, my heart pounding. Tears stung my eyes as I grabbed at him for taking Lucas down.

But I couldn't stop him.

Reed was like a ravenous wolf.

"Why is she fucking crying?" He had Lucas by his throat, slamming him into the glass. It didn't shatter, but it cracked.

Oh, that's gotta hurt.

I screamed then, terrified of what Reed could do.

What I'd seen him do in the past against anything that came after Alisha. It wasn't a secret.

Reed was just as wild as Gabriel once unleashed.

No, not him.

"No, you son of a bitch, you look at me," Reed growled.

His fist slammed into Lucas's face. The shift was instantaneous. The predator emerged from beneath Lucas's suit.

"Reed, let him go!" I begged, desperate. *"Lucas, stop! He's my brother!"*

"What the fuck is going on with you two? How the fuck did he get in here?" Reed's questions came like hot bolts of rage.

Reed slammed him back; he had two inches on Lucas, but I watched Reed fight with Gabriel, and I knew those two were brutal.

Gabriel wasn't joking about it.

Keeping people on their toes was his thing.

"Is he the reason you were crying the other day?" Reed pressed, gaining the upper hand and slamming Lucas back.

Then his eyes widened with an ugly realization. *"How fucking long have you been sleeping with your brother's enemy?"*

"I didn't know who he was!" I cried more to Lucas than Reed, my voice breaking as I tugged Reed back.

Why wasn't he moving?

At that moment, I saw everything Reed had worked to hide about himself. The sheer similarity with Gabriel didn't escape me.

Lucas's eyes pleaded despite being pinned by Reed. He's just as big as Reed. *Why wasn't he fighting back?* "I'm sorry Evie, I knew if I told you—"

"That I would know my brother hates you!" I exploded, losing control. Raw pain seared through me.

"Yes," Lucas admitted. Shame filled his eyes.

He looked at Reed the same way. That's why he wasn't fighting back. Because deep down, inside, Lucas…thought he deserved it.

The admission was like a knife to my heart. Twisting and tearing at the fragile remnants of my love for him. Until it ached.

It ached so bad.

"What the fuck is going on?" Reed growled.

"Why don't you ask Lucas Devereaux, or should I say Luke Delaney!" I said, righteously angry.

Reed's eyes narrowed as he put the pieces together.

He glared at Lucas. "You knew she was his sister, and you..."

Fury contorted Reed's face.

"Gabriel isn't going to kill you. I am." His eyes locked on mine. *"He's the guy you've been seeing?"*

"Not anymore! I didn't know!"

"Doll, please," Lucas looked at me, his gaze imploring, begging me to understand. *"Evie, look at me—"*

"I'm not sleeping with him," I choked out, the words tasting like acid on my tongue.

Tears spilled down my cheeks, hot and bitter. I met Lucas's eyes, my heart breaking all over again.

"Do not call me Evie. Only the people I love call me Evie."

Lucas looked stunned. *Hurt.*

As if I had just ripped his heart out of his chest and stomped on it right in front of him.

Reed glowered at Lucas; his eyes filled with something I couldn't identify. *"You* need to leave."

"No need, I'm going home."

I had a new place. I locked eyes with Reed, desperation clawing at me like a wild animal. "Please do not tell Gabriel."

Reed gave me a weighted look. I knew what he was thinking. There was no way he could keep this from Gabriel. *"Evie."*

"I am begging you. No matter how much I dislike him right now..." I pointed at Lucas, my hand shaking with the force of my emotions. "I know what Gabriel is capable of. He will not stop until everything is burned to the ground."

My eyes found Lucas, drinking at the sight of him one last time.

He looked disheveled as he straightened his suit and ran a hand through his hair.

My heart squeezed painfully, a vice grip. "Gabriel will kill him."

I didn't hate Lucas *that* much.

Gabriel would stop at nothing to destroy Lucas, to make him pay for what he had done to me. I had seen his rage.

It was quiet fury but the kind that ruined empires.

"On one condition." Reed's voice was dark, cutting through the tension with the precision of a knife.

"Anything." I'd agree to anything to protect Lucas, even now. Even after everything he had done, I couldn't bear the thought of him coming to harm because of me.

"You never see him again. Ever. And he never shows his face around the Titans." Reed pointed at Lucas, who looked ready to throttle him. "I can't protect you from Gabriel if you do. It makes my job that much harder."

Because they were brothers, and I was already asking him for something awful. Not that Gabriel wouldn't forgive Reed. He forgave Reed for everything.

"Evie, please." Lucas's eyes blazed into mine, a desperate plea that tore at my heart. "Evie, I can take him. I can take Gabriel, Evie, don't—"

"You don't know why Gabriel hates him. But I do." Reed's gaze bored into me, a warning and a promise all in one. "Say the words, and I do not tell Gabriel—ever."

"Evie, I am begging you, I can protect you—" Lucas's voice cracked with emotion, the desperation in his tone almost enough to break me.

You lied to me, I whispered, my heart shattering into a million pieces. *"You knew who I was for so long. And you let me think you were someone else."*

I looked at Reed even as my soul screamed in protest.

"I didn't know who he was. I swear."

Reed tipped his head, understanding in his eyes.

Because he was my brother too.

I was still so naive.

So foolish.

"Evie—" Lucas tried once more, his voice breaking on my name.

I felt like I was breaking like I was being torn apart from the inside out. Reed was forcing my hand. I knew why. Lucas was a Devereaux.

The man who had lied to me betrayed me.

I couldn't go back. No matter what my heart wanted.

Some things fell apart...so I could be brought together.

Gabriel's grin flashed in my head, teasing me, and then there was an image of him when I first met him, blinking back emotion.

That man held me together.

This man broke me.

The choice was easy.

It shouldn't have hurt.

I tipped my chin at Reed, tears burning behind my eyes.

"Yes. I will never see Lucas Devereaux again."

But it did. It hurt.

CHAPTER 30
EVIE

THE WORST DAYS OF YOUR LIFE USUALLY DIDN'T HAPPEN WITH ANY consideration to your feelings. None at all.

So, a few days after I had that confrontation with Lucas and Reed, I was…displaced emotionally.

Sitting in my apartment on my computer reading over things Liam had sent me.

He was on a date tonight with Lara, and I was happy for him. For everyone.

I had my own path to be on, and I didn't recognize myself sometimes.

It was…strange being a person outside of the manor. Even my pajamas had changed thanks to Alisha. Now, I wore a short babydoll set.

And I felt…womanly.

And all of those emotions crashed to a halt one night.

I got a text from a number on a secure line.

Neptune. Where is Venus?

Nate thinks Selena is in danger?

Ice flooded my veins, chilling me to the core. I called Nate, my fingers flying across the keys as I pulled up the tracking systems.

"What was her last known address?" Nate relayed the details, and I waited with bated breath for the Oracle to load fully, my heart pounding in my chest.

Selena was one of the most hyper-competent people I knew. She would never just disappear like this. Something was wrong. Very wrong.

"Does Kellan know?" I asked, my voice strained.

"He knows, but he's with Alisha now, and he can't leave her," Nate explained gruffly. "She's been gone for the last twenty-four hours."

Finally, the street camera footage from Selena's last known coordinates popped up on my screen.

"I'm going to run scans for several days and see if I find anything with her biometrics," I told Nate, putting him on speaker as I worked.

Fear gripped me with icy fingers as I stared at the screen, searching for any sign of Selena.

"That's so weird," I murmured, rewinding the footage when the program failed to detect her unique gait patterns.

"I'm not finding her anywhere near that address." Confusion and frustration warred within me, mingling with the worry that gnawed at my gut.

A muffled commotion happened as Nate said something before an elegant voice cut in. "Evie, darling, might you have better luck if you start at her apartment instead?"

Who was that?

"Evie, meet Gemma," Nate huffed. "She thinks somewhere between Selena's apartment and White's place, is where something may have happened to her."

Nausea rolled through me at those ominous words, my stomach churning.

With shaking hands, I readjusted my search parameters and pulled footage from Selena's building.

Memories of Selena's larger-than-life smiles and how she held me as we salsa danced flashed through my mind, making my skin flush hot then cold.

Panic and helplessness warred within me as I searched block after block, finding no trace of her after Midtown.

My heart pounded with trepidation—Selena was one of the most competent people I knew.

Something happened between her and Kellan.

"Found her," I said, my voice tense as I watched Selena's figure hurry out onto the sidewalk and hail a cab on the video feed.

The rapid tapping of my fingers against the keyboard filled the room as I followed her route based on the location data.

"She looks rushed...I'm following her from here and..."

My words trailed off, as the video feed abruptly cut out. The tracking program lost Selena's trail as if she had ceased to exist.

I blinked, my eyes straining against the screen's glare as I tried to understand what I saw.

"The program doesn't have her anywhere. It's like she vanishes," I whispered, my voice slow and unsteady.

I re-watched the disjointed footage, my heart pounding in my ears as I watched Selena make it to the new neighborhood before vanishing entirely from the grid.

"It's like she never existed in the video after a certain point. This is insane..."

A shiver traced my spine, and I felt the hairs on the back of my neck stand on end at the overwhelming wrongness of the situation.

Fear and dread coiled in my stomach like a serpent, twisting and turning until I thought I might be sick.

The sudden sound of Nate's voice made me jump, my nerves frayed and on edge.

"Do what you can on your end," he said gruffly, his tone laced with the same worry that consumed me. "Reed is on his way. I'm filling him in."

"As soon as I find a trace, I'll call," I promised, my voice trembling slightly. I knew I couldn't rest until I discovered what had happened to my Selena.

She would never go missing.

The thought of Selena doing something reckless to prove a point to Kellen sent a fresh wave of anxiety coursing through me, my chest tightening as I ended the call.

My fingers were shaking.

In my imagination, in my room—covered in plants, warmth, and heat—Lucas appeared dressed in his pajama bottoms.

Breathe, doll. You can do this.

"I don't know if I can. Reed is better than me," I said to imaginary Lucas.

You said Liam was training you to be a Red Hat.

"I don't know if I can."

Yes, you can, doll. Breathe for me.

With a deep breath, I turned back to my computer, my fingers flying across the keyboard as I chipped away at enhanced filters and facial recognition software.

Good girl, let's find Selena.

The blue light from the screencast created an eerie glow across my face, highlighting the desperation and frustration that warred within me as I searched for anything to uncover the truth behind Selena's disappearance.

"Lucas, I'm not an operative."

You are now, doll. For you. For Selena.

I replayed the footage back until I caught it. A splice in the video. Something had—*someone*. This was *someone*. Someone...*Black Hat.*

Lucas, a Black Hat.

I don't need confirmation. I can tell. Nobody does this level of work—

"Someone erased that footage while she reached that neighborhood," I said, realization dawning on me, bringing a fresh wave of fear and confusion.

"But *why?*" I shook my head, struggling to make sense of the layers of manipulation at play. "How?"

Who would want to erase...Selena?

Frustration and desperation clawed at me, threatening to overwhelm me. Still, I pushed them down, focusing on the task at hand. I had to find Selena. Or the Black Hat.

At that moment, fear and stark uncertainty over what fresh hell we were facing slammed into me in full force.

Long moments passed before I received the text of my nightmares.

Everyone's nightmare.

All operatives were trained to obey these messages. Unless they had charges already, like Nate with Gemma.

Jupiter. DeltaCon. 13 Fulton Avenue House 4.

Something was horrifically wrong.

*That was a total recall of everyone, including...*alerting Killian O'Hara, who worked diligently for Gabriel.

"I'm not a field agent, Lucas."

Which means you have to be the best doll. Imaginary Lucas, right by my side, was nodding at me. *Keep going, doll. Do not give up. Selena is your sister, too.*

My eyes burned from staring at the screen, and my fingers ached from typing, but I didn't stop. I couldn't stop. *There had to be something there.*

"Oracle, this is Mercury, I need full control." *Come on.*

"Unfortunately, that part is locked at the foundation."

The foundation, the *core* programming of the AI, was inaccessible without higher permissions. But I had the highest ones.

Even Reed didn't work on Oracle, preferring to use his hands to dig rather than the AI.

I growled, frustration boiling over. "I've been trying to unlock the foundation *for so long!* What permissions do you need from me?" I hung my head, despair threatening to swallow me whole.

This was the first time I lost my mind about the program I worked so hard on. Anxiety formed in my throat. I hated this.

Hated. This.

"I cannot give you full control without permission from Miss Santos."

"I am Miss Santos," I growled, out of breath, feeling like a Reed.

Well, Monroe, but—

I looked up, feeling my heart stop for a moment.

Everything stopped but the soft hum of my humidifier for the plants.

What did she just say?

Wait a *minute.*

Wait a fucking minute.

I was Evie Monroe. How did she...Miss Santos?

"Oracle, *which* Miss Santos...?" I asked, my voice shaking as I dreaded her answer.

"Miss Isobel Santos," she continued, oblivious to the shock that sent my heart plummeting. "She is the founder of Oracle of Delphi. I cannot continue any further without her permission."

I was *reeling.*

Isobel was...memories flashed through my mind.

Gabriel said he wants you to work on this if you'd like.

Do you know who the voice for Oracle is? Gabriel, do you want to talk to her?

I'm good, shortcake.

How do I put emotions into you?

Reed, how does she work?

She only responds to call signs.

Except for the *founder...*Isobel designed an artificial intelligence bot? My sister was...a genius?

What did she need to unlock it?

Accessing Oracle's foundation was like opening a locked safe without a combination.

My hands trembled, the keys of my keyboard rattling softly beneath my fingertips as I took a shaking breath, reeling from the shock.

The air felt thick and heavy. The weight of the realization pressing down on me, choking me out with the knowledge of what I should've fucking guessed.

Gabriel *knew*; he had to have known this was Isobel's creation. He had taken it, but why?

"Oracle, this is Miss Isobel Santos, I need full control," I said, my voice shaking. "Password?"

"Gabriel." Wrong. "Monroe?" *Wrong.*

One more shot, and she would lock me out.

I could feel the opportunity slipping through my fingers like sand in an hourglass. I didn't know the combination of this digital safe, and it was critical that I did.

My eyes darted around my apartment, my new home, seeking inspiration amid the silence.

The walls seemed to close in on me as my mind reeled, the pressure mounting.

Gabriel and Reed were no doubt responding to the crisis. Everyone was.

I was alone. Just Evie.

If I messed up on this try? *Forget the foundation.* No Black Hat. No, Selena.

My eyes landed on a photo of Gabriel above my desk with the cats in his arms, his amused expression at the black one on his shoulder.

Isobel...*and Gabriel...*Reed's voice was in my head.

This program was named after the Oracle of Delphi.

The Oracle who gave messages to the Sun God, Apollo.

Apollo—Gabriel's call sign.

The realization hit me like a thunderbolt, my breath catching in my throat.

"The password is Apollo!" I exclaimed, my voice trembling with a mixture of excitement and trepidation.

"Welcome, Miss Isobel Santos, I am unlocking the foundation." Her voice had changed, warmer and more human. "What is your request?"

My eyes widened, my heart racing as I processed what had just happened.

The words left my lips in a breathless whisper. *"I just unlocked Oracle."*

A delighted scream left me. Something was in my memory that I couldn't remember right now about the threats over Selena.

Which meant Gabriel didn't know the password either. Isobel hadn't told anyone.

Gabriel was as good as Reed, but that didn't explain why he hadn't touched and kept this to himself? He could've, and I never would've known.

He wanted you to have a piece of her.

Reed's voice floated back to me.

He said you can work on it, but only if it's what you want.

Because Gabriel didn't have time to fix an artificial intelligence program. I did.

I knew him. He wouldn't even bother...but he was always interested in me fixing it. Fixing *her*. *Why?*

As I gazed at the screen, a new facet of the program revealed itself, the missing piece falling into place.

Gabriel had never told me that Isobel was so much like me and that we shared the same passion.

She was so much smarter than anyone.

We had walked the same path, chosen the same calling.

Reed's involvement had been fortunate, but Gabriel's pride in my work, his insistence on me taking on Oracle—it all clicked into place.

Why hadn't he told me? *Gabriel likes puzzles.*

And something told me, *so had my sister...*

My heart thudded in my chest as a smile tugged at my lips, tears welling up in my eyes.

I have had you this entire time...since college. You were her.

I wiped my eyes, my fingers shaking. I focused on the screen, the anomaly before me a beacon of possibilities.

Oracle, in this form, was unleashed and brimming with untapped potential. The program had blossomed.

I never needed to fix it...it had always been *there*...waiting to be discovered.

All these years, I had been gathering data, piecing together the puzzle, and the answer had been right in front of me, hidden in plain sight.

I wiped my eyes furiously. "Oracle, what anomaly am I staring at?"

"The section in the video you might be referring to looks copied. It was paused to show an empty street for approximately one minute."

"Is that how long it would take for someone to walk that street?" I asked, my mind racing with possibilities.

"Yes."

"Can you detect other cameras in the area?"

"No."

I frowned, my frustration growing.

"I found several anomalies that day in New York City, where footage was missing. This is the entire map. Shall I populate?"

"Yes, populate the entire grid map." I was on a roll.

You got this, doll. Keep going. Whoever it was, was hiding something. And they'd covered up Selena.

"Miss Santos, populating map of anomalies detected in the grid—"

"Put them in order of when it began," I instructed, my eyes scanning the screen intently. "It's not hiding Selena. It was following someone else. It *caught* Selena in it because she crossed paths with *someone* hiding."

Dread coiled heavily in the pit of my stomach as a new message flashed across my screen.

Apollo. DeltaCon. Gridlock.

Gabriel was issuing a gridlock. It usually meant all operatives were on standby for worse. *Why?*

Something had happened.

Something horrific. Outside my window, I heard sirens.

This is bigger than Selena.

Something was happening in the city. Something bad.

*Was Selena…*no. *She had to be okay.*

My fingers flew across the keyboard. *Where was Liam?* I had been brushing up on everything he had taught me. I had to find out who was hiding in the city.

"Oracle, expand to find similar anomalies on the East Coast," I said my voice firm. I was searching, trying to find the source.

I didn't care if I had to stay up all night. Someone was hacking into every single camera in the city.

That level of control and power?

Who the hell was I dealing with?

"Where is it *originating* from?" The map moved to…*Africa?*

"Miss Santos, the strongest detection of disturbances originates from West Africa. This is Cabo Verde, also known as *Cape* Verde. The anomaly begins here weeks earlier..."

As Oracle explained to me how the anomaly was tracked, I got to work.

"Oracle, I need full access to flight records from the day the anomaly started, street camera footage, and I need to know when they arrived in New York."

Because there was no way it was one person.

This was a *team*. And they had *power*.

What were they doing in the city? And why?

And Titan had gotten caught up in something bigger than I could've imagined. I needed to find out the source of the Black Hat.

Who it was. Cape Verde...I began there.

I wasn't a Red Hat now. *I don't recognize who I'm becoming anymore.*

This was unfamiliar.

I didn't know who to turn to. I was slipping into a Hat I didn't recognize.

With my sister. A chill ran down my spine...I could do it.

She died at my age.

Gabriel left me her legacy...he never pushed it on me. He just suggested it if I wanted it, and in turn?

I have to tell him when I get a chance.

As though he could read my mind, Gabriel texted me.

We found Selena.

Three simple words...and yet he didn't say if she was okay.

CHAPTER 31
LUCAS

As I stepped into the elevator of my sister's apartment building, my mind was preoccupied with thoughts of Lucy.

I hadn't seen her in forever.

The ding of the elevator interrupted my thoughts, and I glanced up to see an...enormous plant with legs rushing toward the closing doors. Leaves, countless leaves, invaded the space.

Was there a plant invasion happening in my building?

"Hold it!" The plant yelled, and I quickly pressed the button to keep the doors open, my reflexes honed by years of training.

My eyes widened as it entered, revealing a woman of diminutive size struggling to maneuver a massive planter filled with lush green leaves. *Who the fuck was this?*

"Sorry, I went to the store and got excited. They said they could deliver, but I couldn't wait."

My ears perked up.

I knew that voice...but what was she doing here?

"No problem. I've never seen anyone try to bring a jungle into an elevator before."

She laughed, the sound melodic and infectious.

That was the easy laugh that haunted my dreams.

I knew because making her laugh was one of my favorite pastimes.

I liked it almost as much as making her come.

I reached out to assist her with the planter, and our eyes met. For a moment, time seemed to stand still.

"Evie." I tried to stay calm, my heart racing in my chest.

It is her. I knew it.

"Luke?" she responded, equally taken aback, her eyes wide with surprise. I blinked in disbelief, my mind struggling to process the situation.

What were the odds of running into Evie, of all people, in my sister's apartment building?

But before I could gather my thoughts, she spoke again.

"Are you following me?" she asked a hint of suspicion in her voice.

I shook my head quickly, trying to dispel any misunderstandings. "No, my sister lives here. What are you doing here?"

Her brow furrowed in confusion, disbelief in her eyes. "I didn't know you had a sister. *I* live here—"

Realization dawned on me, and I felt a rush of embarrassment flood my cheeks, the heat rising to my face.

Of course, Evie lived in the same building as Lucy. Fate was a bitch.

"You moved out of your brother's house?"

When? Why? Because of me?

I hauled the planter into the elevator easily.

She got in, and I took in the dress she wore.

It hardly qualified as a shirt, but I mean—whatever women did nowadays was their choice.

Even if I knew if she bent over, I could see her—

"Could you hit number three?"

Right, I was closest to the buttons.

"How did you get this thing all the way here?"

I thought she wouldn't answer. Maybe she hated me too much to respond.

"Well, I had help from the store and then to the cab, but the cab driver refused to help me after I spilled so much soil in his car—"

I held back my laughter, imagining Evie scooping out the soil as she described, tossing it desperately out of the car with every turn.

And then I couldn't hold back my laughter as she described the leaves flapping in the wind and her wrapping her legs around it to hold it together.

"Oh God, stop—" I wiped my eyes, turning red with laughter, as the floors climbed. "You should've asked me for a hand, doll. I would've sent someone to help you."

And then I realized what I said as the floor dinged. Evie's own laughter had faded as she realized it. We both looked away as the doors opened. I felt my smile fade as I caught myself.

"Let me help you with that," I offered, eager to diffuse the awkwardness. "It's fucking huge."

I didn't know plants got this big outside of greenhouses.

A beat of silence passed as I walked to her apartment. It wasn't that bad for me, but I didn't know how Evie did it.

"His name is Harvey."

It was said in a quiet voice, but I looked over at her adorable blush.

"I named him after Harvey Kinkle...Sabrina Spellman's boyfriend."

"How could I forget? You used to watch it for breakfast..."

Evie stopped at her door, and as she opened it, I realized I hadn't been in there before.

I stepped in, and for a moment, the leaves made it hard to see, but when I set it down in the entryway where Evie motioned, I got to looking around.

I was *floored*.

"Holy hell, this place is gorgeous."

I hadn't actually ever been in Evie's space.

I didn't even *know* she had moved out of her brother's place.

I also didn't know she lived in a *fucking* garden. *Holy...*

Evie's botanical wonderland.

The large windows draped in gauzy white curtains let cool evening air into the place, and the soft breeze drifted toward the multitude of plants in the house.

Some were housed under lamps, some on top of her ottoman, vibrant shades of greens, from the emerald leaves of towering fiddle leaf fig to the delicate tendrils of ivy cascading down from hanging planters.

I looked up and followed the planters and feminine artwork along the walls. Warm lights everywhere.

"I had a lot of plants at home."

"Where is that sound coming from?"

Evie pointed to the trickling waterfall about two feet large in the corner. I was in awe; I didn't know where to look.

"I have more in the kitchen."

I followed the little green goddess into her retro-cozy kitchen, where I saw dozens of cascading pothos vines—all thriving under Evie's expert care.

Each corner of the room held a new discovery, from elegant orchids perched on windowsills to intricate terrariums filled with miniature landscapes.

"My brother got me these cool shapes and sizes..." She trailed off at the mention of Gabriel...

As I stood there, taking in the breathtaking sight before me, I couldn't help but feel a sense of awe and admiration for Evie, suddenly seeing her in a different light.

"You've got one hell of a green thumb, I should start calling you blossom."

She gave life. I looked at her. *God, she's pretty.*

Standing there, twirling her thumbs, a faint blush on her cheeks as I took her in. She was looking at me.

I realized it might've been one of the first times other than when she'd seen me when she promised Reed she'd never see me again—that I was in a suit.

Custom fitted and in navy—*could never go wrong.*

My mother had taught me that dressing well was a form of good manners.

Around Evie, I used to dress like a grad student, all hoodies, looking around twenty-five, so not too off from her twenty-three.

But now?

I looked my age; I had turned thirty without Evie, and I looked it.

Her hair was shorter, and if anything, lighter than the dark cherry I had seen her in, glossy and her eyes big as she took me in. In that. Fucking. *Dress.*

Barely covering her—

Focus.

Temptation. That's what she was.

Lush green mixed with something uniquely her. Her skin glowed in the soft light. Radiant.

I longed to touch it. Trail my fingers down her neck. I restrained myself. Admired from afar. Drank in her beauty.

Committed every detail to memory.

"These are lowlights, I thought warm lighting would make the place cozier, and that's my mushroom lamp..." She pointed to the mushroom wall plug.

"It's adorable, doll."

That was the thing about having subs who trusted you, they came and shared cute shit with you, and you relished it.

That she trusted you.

The way Evie…still did.

I didn't recognize my own voice. "Did you need anything else tonight, doll?" I didn't know what I was asking.

Please, need me.

"No, thank you for your help with the monstera."

The who?

I knew as much about plants as Evie knew about looking through ledgers.

"Harvey."

"Harvey."

Well, nobody ever said talking to your ex's wasn't awkward. Gemma and I just talked about work. I swallowed. Hard.

"Right, well, I should go—"

"Actually—"

"Yes?"

Stop it. Stop it. Stop. It.

I watched her avidly.

"I had a question."

Her eyes turned dark.

"Is our contract over?"

CHAPTER 32
EVIE

I REALLY SHOULDN'T HAVE ASKED THAT QUESTION.

But stumbling across my ex-boyfriend in the last place, I expected to find him—the curiosity had overwhelmed me before I could think better of it.

I had promised Reed I would never see him again after...*everything*.

But some deeply buried part of me still wondered about...what did that mean for me?

I told myself I simply needed that closure, that peace of mind.

But the moment the words left my lips, Luke's entire disposition transformed in the blink of an eye.

The softer, calmer version of him I had encountered vanished.

No, this was the Dom resurfacing—his powerful, unapologetic dominance radiating from every inch of his body. Overwhelming. Intoxicating.

Luke's velvet voice caressed the fragile air between us, laced with dark promise. "Did you need me?"

I hadn't been prepared for the rush of memories, of sensations his words would unleash. Heat.

Luke took a step closer, his intense gaze pinning me in place like a skittish doe. Instinctively, I stepped back, putting what little distance I could between us.

"Luke..." I began, then faltered, at a loss as my back hit the wall. My foot caught on the end of something, but before I slipped, he was there.

"I got you, I always got you. I missed that," he murmured, each rumbling syllable dripping with silken intent as he drank in my unguarded reaction. His head tipped backward ever so slightly.

The man before me was every inch the powerful, predatory Dom who had my love.

Except this time, I was the prey, frozen in his sight.

Something was different *about* him.

Something was different *in* me.

I felt so far away and so close at the same time.

My breath caught as he dipped his head, each heated sweep of his gaze across my body. Exuding quiet dominance with his restrained power lying in delicious wait. Power I had felt. Anticipation. Hunger. Both swirled in my abdomen.

How is anyone supposed to think with him this close? Lucas in casual clothes was one thing.

I was not prepared for *this* man.

"You what?" His deep voice caressed my skin, stopping just inches away so that I was enveloped in his familiar, intoxicating scent of his cologne. All his raw masculinity. "You want to renegotiate?"

My breath hitched at the bold insinuation. His eyes, the midnight depths of his eyes were dark. Darker than usual.

This was the game he excelled at—stoking arousal with just a few carefully spoken words.

Part of me was thrilled at the familiar heat unfurling low in my belly, at the anticipation only Luke could bring out in me.

But another part, the logical voice of reason muffled by pure want, knew diving in would not be—*I promised my brother.*

And myself.

"I can't think." I managed, proud that my voice didn't waver despite Luke's smoldering proximity.

"Use your words."

I inhaled and took a deep breath.

"No, I'm asking because things are different now."

Right. That was why.

"Are they?" One dark brow quirked upwards as he reached out, the backs of his fingers grazing a feather-light path along the back of my neck and down the column of my neck.

Gripping the back. Stopping at my pulse, his eyes centered there.

"I miss you, doll," he said with nothing in his eyes but the man I had met at the board game convention. My chest tightened, and I felt myself biting my cheek to keep from responding.

I ached. I wanted him.

Every fiber of my being screamed for his touch, his kiss, his possession. But I couldn't. I wouldn't.

Too much had happened.

I squeezed my thighs together at the spark of electricity his touch ignited as it dipped lower, cursing the instinctive fluttering of my pulse hammering treacherously beneath his fingertips.

Luke's lips curved into a devastatingly sensual smile, clearly sensing my body's visceral reaction to his nearness.

"Do you miss me?" he murmured, dipping his head until his lips brushed the sensitive shell of my ear. "I can feel you trembling. Do you still crave me, need me, late at night when you—"

I clapped my hand over his mouth. I was breathing hard. His eyes glittered.

He slowly pulled it down, capturing my wrist.

For a charged heartbeat, our heated breaths mingled in the scant space between us.

His eyes fell to my lips.

With a low sound of raw need, Luke's restraint finally snapped. His mouth slanted hotly, hungrily over mine. And I reacted. I was returning it. Every bit of it.

Just as needy.

Whimpers left my lips as I scrambled to latch onto him, feel him. Closer.

His hands were reaching for my clothes. At the first touch of his fingers against my bare skin, I gasped against the onslaught, only to melt helplessly into the familiar, dizzying heat as Luke's tongue delved past my lips to stake his claim.

Something had changed.

Within him.

Within me.

No, this was pure possession—Luke's large hands fisting in the hair at my nape to angle my head, our bodies crushed together from thigh to chest in a blaze of unadulterated hunger.

I clung to the solid planes of his back, instinctively arching into the hard planes of muscle, desperate. Hungry.

Luke growled his approval against my lips, the vibration of that predatory rumble moved straight to my core.

I wanted him. I wanted him. I wanted him.

The sound of fabric tearing and clothes being torn off was a relief.

He devoured me with the intensity of a man half-starved, cupping the back of my skull almost reverently as his tongue mated with mine, teasing, retreating only to surge forth once more in delirious conquest. I gasped into his mouth.

"Wrap your legs around me, doll."

I obeyed, never wanting to break contact with him. This...this was the annihilating passion I had craved for so long.

I want to be loved.

I want to be consumed.

I want to be more than myself.

I want to be with him.

He lifted me easily and pressed into me, groaning when he saw I had nothing but panties on. He rubbed a spot on my collar he hadn't noticed earlier, thanks to the dress.

Still in suit, I felt the power he always yielded over me coasting over me. I was still his.

Nothing had changed.

A noise left me.

"What is it?"

"Paint." He looked at my eyes, bemused. "I take classes."

Before he could say another word, I pulled him back to my mouth, the hard ridge of him pressing into my core.

The want, the yearning that had haunted my restless dreams.

Luke moved his mouth on mine with a low, tortured groan. "I can't fuck you until I know you want me the same way."

Something shimmered in those endless cerulean blues.

"I know you promised. I know you did. But I didn't. I made *no* such promise." Luke's thumb skimmed my lower lip.

"I can't let you go. I don't know how to—"

His tongue delved and retreated, stoking the smoldering desire inside of me. I clenched internally for him. My whimpers, soft, swallowed by the hot velvet of his tongue as he deepened the kiss with excruciating slowness.

And somewhere in those kisses, pressed against him, I felt the sting in my eyes. I felt it in his mouth.

The amount of desire that wasn't anything fake.

Luke pulled back just enough. "Tell me what you want. *Anything*, I'll give you anything."

The leashed power in his gravelly timbre sank into my womb. I remembered that voice, dark in my ears whenever he'd made love to me. *When* I trusted him.

When he had my heart. My submission.

And then he broke it.

"Please put me down."

I hurt him, too.

Slowly, he let me slide down his body. I felt every inch of him, how hard he was for me, and the resolve in him to not take me.

My brother was right about you.

Was he?

I looked at my new dress on the floor...I felt his jacket come around me.

I gratefully took it, the fabric swallowing me, and I buttoned the top of it to keep it from opening.

His face looked utterly enamored as he took me in his clothes. I had always worn his clothes.

They were comfier.

I bet this suit had cost a fortune. Because he was a *CEO*.

Not a student.

Not some normal guy.

He never had been.

Swallowing hard, I tore my gaze from the scorching heat of Luke's with a force of will I didn't realize I had. I wanted him. Of course, I wanted him.

But I had a place now.

One without Gabriel...

"I promised..." The words escaped my lips, and I felt...pain. It was aching through my heart. "*Gabriel*—" A long pause followed.

And then he said the most unexpected thing. "Evie, how much do you know about your sister's relationship with Gabriel?"

My head was spinning. "What?"

"I was going to wait to bring this up. My father was saying something..." And I heard him, but the conversation changed so abruptly I didn't understand why.

"He said something to me that I didn't know what to do with."

As he spoke, I felt like I was falling.

I know Gabriel didn't kill Isobel. She's your sister. She was his wife, wasn't she?

And all I heard was *Gabriel killed his wife.*

"*Gabriel?*" My lips were forming the words, but my feet shifted.

Lucas's eyes went wide. He said my name, and I felt myself unable to think. Unable to speak.

"No, he would *never. He would never hurt her.*" I had her project he'd given me. They were my family.

What happened to Isobel?

She couldn't make it.

I'm your next of kin.

Where is she now?

I'm sorry, sweetheart.

Your sister died weeks ago.

Why he never talked about her, why he never mentioned her, why he hated it. The floor shifted under me. I felt Lucas's catch me and hold me closer, I didn't even notice my body sliding from his grip.

"I'm sorry, Evie, I'm sorry. I know he didn't do anything to her. I'm just worried about you. I needed to tell you—I didn't know when."

Because he wasn't Luke Delaney.

"*No, he didn't kill her.*"

Gabriel would never. Not the man I knew. But Gabriel knew things I didn't. I hadn't even gotten a chance to tell him about Oracle.

And now?

Lucas's eyes held a wealth of sadness as he said the words.

"Evie, *where is Isobel buried?*"

CHAPTER 33
EVIE

I DIDN'T KNOW.

Gabriel never...we never went...we never went to see Mama in California.

Gabriel and I hated being surrounded by death...

"I think I need to be alone right now."

Lucas sat with me, letting me process what he had said with what I knew.

"I don't think that's a good idea," his voice was shaky. "I'm not saying he did. I'm only telling you what I think happened. I don't think he ever found her body." My heart clenched. "I think he's looking for her and who killed her."

What?

"Isobel died on an assignment with him. She's gone..."

Lucas nodded. "I know, I didn't know how to tell you at the time, but you brought him up and—" He had told me the truth, even if his timing was awful.

I couldn't even be angry sitting in his arms on my couch.

He had grabbed a blanket around me and cuddled me to him.

In his arms, though, I couldn't process the duality of the emotions running through me.

The difference between Lucas, the man who had lied but had been the truth in many ways, and Gabriel, my brother who had saved my life...and kept secrets.

I had faith in him, though.

"He would never. You don't know him like I do."

How much of him do I know?

"No," he agreed. "I don't, but I don't think you or anyone knows much about him. How much do you know about what he did for the government, where his money comes from, and who he is? Who he was before he...was Gabriel Monroe? What did you know about the Gabriel before you met him?"

I felt lost.

What did I know? In seven years, Gabriel had steered clear of personal conversations and anything too...well, if we weren't talking about me, we talked about work. And if not about work—he just talked about me.

I didn't need to be close to him because I already felt like I was.

I feel safe with Gabriel. He'd never given me a reason—

"He has her name on his chest..." He wouldn't do that and kill her.

I knew Gabriel...right? I know him.

I fell asleep on him all the time. He took me out when I was sad. He bandaged all my cuts and bruises. He took me in his arms like I was his whole life. I laughed with him. I knew what he liked on his pizza, how he took his coffee...

"I don't know what your father told you, but I know Gabriel." I knew him.

So why did I feel that niggle of doubt? Oracle would know...

"I just need to..." I needed to dig into this. "I'm not saying your father is wrong, but Gabriel hates your family. And I don't think your family knows the truth about what happened to Gabriel."

He has her name on his chest.

He adopted me.

This wasn't some elaborate scheme of his.

Gabriel loves puzzles.

"I don't want to leave you like this."

"I'm asking you to."

I needed to go and find my brother.

∼

MOMENTS AFTER LUCAS RELUCTANTLY LEFT, I FOUND MYSELF COMBING through every file and database I could access, searching for any trace of Gabriel's existence before we met.

I did it in Lucas's jacket, telling myself it was warmer than anything else I had.

It smelled like Lucas.

My head spun. There was nothing on Gabriel Monroe. It was like Gabriel had never existed.

But I know he did. He was my brother.

He married Isobel.

A long time ago, he had to have been real, right?

In our line of work, I knew people were nonexistent. Selena's identity was a secret because of her work overseas.

I knew she used a few aliases and could interchange them when she needed to. But she was somewhat real.

But everyone had been through so much with Selena in the hospital now recovering.

Alisha just waking up from her injuries. I couldn't bother Gabriel. I couldn't ask.

If only there was someone *else*...it struck me like lightning—*Liam*.

Liam and I work together all the time. He was Agency. I could talk to him.

I feel somewhat comfortable with him. And while I was excited to show him Oracle, a part of me felt like I was betraying Gabriel by telling Liam about Oracle first—so I didn't. I kept her to myself.

Instead, I called Liam, as late as it was, I knew...part of me felt the pull.

Liam talked like Gabriel, maybe they had been trained by the same person?

Which meant they were...they had to know.

Reed never allowed Liam near Gabriel, though.

Finally, after some shuffling, Liam answered. "Evie, I'll be right with you."

I waited, cautious, but also a little curious since I didn't know Liam *had* a personal life.

He was saying something about sequins on his face.

There was only one person I knew...*Lara*.

He laughed low. "You're fine...it's okay," he said, his voice uncharacteristically soft.

A pang of guilt hit me, realizing I might have interrupted *something*. "Sorry about that—"

"No, *I'm sorry* to have interrupted your night. I wouldn't have called unless—"

"It's important. At your service, shortcake."

This was the first time I heard just his voice and not his face, and it was really soothing. Calming. Strong.

"I was wondering if I could ask you something..." He made a noise of agreement as he drank something.

"Did you know Gabriel?" There was silence on the line. "You said you were Agency. You're one of the few people on the team that was. But Reed didn't work with Gabriel. Do you know anything..." I drifted hearing silence on the other line.

At his hesitation I knew he did. "Liam, please." I hated the vulnerability in my voice, but I needed him to understand how much this meant to me. "I need to know the truth." So much of it.

Liam let out a shaky breath. "Why are you asking me? He's *your* brother."

Emotions spilled out of me in a torrent. "He isn't. He adopted me." I could hear Liam sitting up. "And I just know you're the same age as Reed. You had to know, right? If not, do you know where I could look?"

Even Oracle found nothing on Gabriel.

Nobody knew? Liam might...There was silence.

"Evie, I've never worked with Monroe. I'm *sorry*, shortcake."

My heart collapsed.

"I know if you can't find him anywhere, and you've already looked, I *can't* look into him." Because Gabriel was *his* boss. He paused. "He adopted you..."

"He was married to my sister..." I trailed off feeling loss like never before...I needed to turn to Gabriel. I just felt like...something had been taken from me, and I didn't know what. "I was...looking for them both."

"Your sister...did she...?"

"She passed away, Isobel, I didn't know her...." Not like Gabriel did. And now they were both ghosts.

There was another pause, when Liam spoke, his voice was soft holding back emotion.

"I'm sorry, shortcake. I promise I won't tell a soul about this conversation since I can hear you worried, but I don't know either one of them. I'll do whatever it takes to make you the best in *your* own ways, just for you, Evie. Sounds good?"

He sounded...so human in that moment. His depth of empathy overwhelmed me.

I got the feeling, like the rest of the team, Liam hid behind his exterior, part of him wicked and wild former man-whore now dating Lara, but under? Liam was the *most* profoundly emotionally intelligent Titan.

He was still nurturing me despite not being able to give me anything. And he was willing to not tell anyone else.

"Yeah." I nodded. Liam was the last thing I had, and he said he never worked with Isobel or Gabriel...so where did I go?

I hung my head. I didn't want to tell him about Oracle yet. Not without telling Gabriel.

"I'm happy you finally asked Lara out."

His voice changed. "Oh, shortcake, you have no idea..."

I laughed softly at his dreamy sigh as he snapped back into his cover persona. And in that moment, I felt good I had a mentor in him.

"How's your man treating you? Need me to come and knock some sense into him?" Then, to my surprise he said. "I know what you look like when you cry, shortcake, I could tell you were upset, and nobody is sick for *that* long."

I flushed. I had looked upset the last time we spoke.

"I don't want to keep you," I said softly. "I'm happy you have someone in your life again."

"Me too. She's...*something*."

My shoulders shook. *He had it bad.* I let him go to enjoy his life. While I sat in my new one, I processed my emotions. Taking it in.

And even though I had discovered something...I also felt defeat in so many ways.

Isobel, what do I do?

CHAPTER 34
LUCAS

MY HEART WAS STILL IN KNOTS AFTER FINDING OUT EVIE WAS SO CLOSE and I couldn't have her.

The intensity of her holding onto me while I ate from her was a sensation I'd never forget. I chalked it up to the fact that I couldn't have her. I couldn't.

I shouldn't.

Oh, but how I craved it.

Evie had become my drug of choice—an addiction I couldn't shake.

Every fiber of my being yearned for her, and I ached to hold her close and never let go.

And then there was the mystery that my father had planted in my head. I fucking hated causing her to doubt her brother.

As much as it hurt, as much as it tore at my soul, I knew I had to honor her wishes. Forbidden fruit.

That's all this was.

Just me wanting something I couldn't have.

You wanted her even before you knew you couldn't have her.

As I walked to Lucy's apartment, the back of my neck prickled. Except I was in an empty hallway, and there were no windows in sight.

No windows.

My jacket was gone.

A perverse part of me loved Evie in it.

When my knocks went unanswered, I used the spare key I had made.

Lucy had chosen to live in a relatively affordable but secure building despite my insistence on providing her—with a far more upscale place.

Outside, it said her name, Luciana Delaney.

My big brother instincts drove me to know why Lucy maintained two separate apartments.

This one served as more of an office and workspace away from the other one she hadn't been to.

As soon as I stepped through the door, my well-honed survival instincts kicked into high gear.

The place was pristine.

My grip tightened on the doorknob as I slowly surveyed the room, eyes narrowing.

Lucy's meticulous organizational tendencies were something I had always teased her about, but now that orderly precision...made the hairs on the back of my neck prickle.

I caught a spill of items on her coffee table.

There were books everywhere.

And a small piece of paper on the coffee table caught my eye. It was a note written in Lucy's distinctive, precise handwriting.

Next to it, a card and a book about birds were open, and my fingers ran over them as if I were absorbing her clues.

She had a list.

Falcon. Raven. Sparrow. Dove.

Bluejay...

There were a dozen names of birds. But...Lucy worked in archaeology, not ornithology.

The name at the bottom made my blood run cold.

Reed.

The last time I had seen Reed, his fist had been connecting with my face. Hard.

The memory of that punch, the searing pain, and the coppery taste of blood came rushing back. But there was something else too. Guilt. Shame. I knew I deserved that punch. I had betrayed Evie, betrayed Reed's trust.

Reed and I had spoken privately after Evie had left looking as bad as I felt.

I knew Reed guessed a few things. I knew Gabriel had told him about the attempt on my life.

I asked about Lucy, and Reed said he didn't have anything from her.

But Lucy *did* work for Reed. I didn't know what Reed wanted with a pile of bones, but I didn't make it my business to ask that much; he looked uncomfortable, and then Alisha showed up, and he looked completely out of it.

He opened up about helping Lucy from a sticky situation in Colombia, and I didn't know how much he knew about Marcus Hagen, but I offered him that name.

I figured Gabriel would tell him everything anyway.

What does Lucy do for you?

Whatever I need—and no, not like that. Alisha is my girl.

He looked almost affronted. I would never think he'd do anything to hurt my sister. Which was comforting. I guess.

I couldn't relate.

I let Reed finally treat me with humanity despite him punching me and protecting Evie.

He was different from Gabriel.

The perfect foil to Gabriel. I could see why they were partners when he sat with me in Titan's Midtown office then for lunch.

And now, seeing his name here, in Lucy's apartment...it made my stomach twist.

Why would she leave a note with his name? The questions swirled in my mind, adding to the confusion and fear already churning inside me.

I ran a hand over my face, feeling the weariness settle deep in my bones. I knew what I had to do.

As much as I dreaded it, as much as it bothered me...I needed to call Reed. He was the only one who might have answers.

Where was she?

I pulled out my phone, my finger hovering over Reed's number that he'd given me in case of emergency. I took a deep breath, steeling myself. Then I pressed the call button.

It took several rings before Reed answered. "Lucas, this better be—"

"Your name is written on Lucy's coffee table. I haven't seen her and..." I told him everything in front of me. I looked over the book of birds with the word *Talon* circled...I frowned.

He let out a growl of frustration, and then I heard a shuffle and a feminine voice. *Oh, he was with his woman...*"Lish..."

It sounded like he was getting up.

"I'm going to throw both you and your sister into the Hudson. Tell me *everything*."

It sounded like he was closing a door and then moving. He was all business-like and efficient as I tersely outlined the situation.

"I knew she was hiding, but I didn't know it was that bad."

"What do you mean *hiding*? What the hell does an archaeologist have to hide from?"

Reed didn't answer and instead told me he'd be sending operatives to the apartment.

He didn't need me staying there any longer in case whoever it was might decide to come back.

"Not until you tell me where Lucy is." I should've kept someone on her. The silence on the other end was deafening.

Reed knew something, and he wasn't telling me.

My gut churned with a sickening mixture of fear and fury.

If something happened to little Lucy...

"No, but she isn't missing. I was the one who taught her how to hide after everything she's been through."

Everything she's been through?

"Why would you teach Lucy to hide?" Unless she was always in danger? Who...who was Lucy now?

Reed continued. "I think whatever mess your father is involved in might be a part of the shit she's involved in. It's not her fault. She's doing her job." He paused. "And so is Killian."

I stilled, running my fingers over the books.

"You knew about Killian."

Reed let out a breath. "I'm not the enemy."

No, he was just the keeper of keys. All of them.

"He's looking into everything you asked. Considering he cleaned up a bunch of messes for everyone a few days ago, I'd say you're in solid hands."

"If my sister is involved in this—"

"Lucy is not in the picture *right now*. The only person who is left is you—"

I stopped thinking.

"What do you mean *left*?"

Reed paused; he sighed as though letting out a breath. "I'm trying here. I really am. Let me talk to Killian and figure this out for you. I'm working as hard as I can, and I'm juggling my family."

I didn't know what he was talking about, but I had seen Alisha with her sister with him.

I ran a hand through my hair. Evie's scent on me. "Lucy is family."

"I'll send someone to you tomorrow." When he hung up, I had more questions than answers. I stood there in the midst of the chaos, my heart heavy.

Lucy was...gone.

Evie was off-limits.

Someone was trying to kill me...

I stilled.

My eyes landed on a black and gold card...the claw marks?

Why did Lucy have this card?

Does it get any worse?

CHAPTER 35
LUCAS

Turns out, it did.

"I'm staring at him," I said.

In the afternoon light, Killian O'Hara looked like he'd just rolled out of…bed in a car, his black hair tousled and falling rakishly.

One blue eye and one amber eye stared back at me, a contrast that only added to the unsettling presence.

His suit, well-tailored, did absolutely nothing to calm me or him down.

I sometimes forgot Killian existed because the other two O'Haras were so different.

Aidan had an enormous presence, but he was watchful and quiet.

I had met Kieran a few times, and his personality was warmer than the others while he was hiding what he liked in his personal life.

I knew he was close to Matteo.

It was hard to reconcile Killian with either one of his siblings. His energy was different. Barely contained.

Even Thierry had a better hold on his savagery.

Killian made no effort to hide it.

Being the second son, or chief, in a mafia family, the spare to the heir, couldn't have been easy.

Killian was looking at the black card with gold claw marks on my desk.

"I looked into the dead bodies of the board members in his father's old cabinet," Killian said quietly to his brother on speaker.

Killian turned to me, his expression serious. "You might want to consider getting a shadow, someone to guard you."

Like hell, I would.

I had every intention of getting Evie back in my life, one bird at a time, though. I didn't need a shadow. I just wanted Evie.

"Why do I need one?" I was almost afraid of the answer, even though I already knew what it was.

"Someone's killing your father's old associates," Killian continued, his brows furrowed in concentration as he pieced together the puzzle. "I asked around. I discovered a few inconsistencies. Marcus Hagen *died* months ago."

What the fuck?

"He double-crossed someone he shouldn't have." He paused, letting the weight of his words hang in the air. "Papa Devereaux, Charles, was familiar with Hagen. I have information on Charles calling his old associates and asking if anyone talked. We found some messages on one of their phones. It was cryptic. I need to talk to Reed."

Killian looked at me, his eyes filled with a sense of unease. He went on to say. "The reports of heart attack were false."

Excuse me? I sat up straighter. Someone was covering up...murder? *This was insanity.*

"My guys went and looked into them. We found kill shots to the head. Every single family was not allowed to see the bodies," he said grimly. "I *finesse*. It's what I deal with. It's the work of *professionals*. Professionals who turned up a few weeks ago, right after your sister showed up to the city."

He nodded at my expression. "Whoever's trying to kill you isn't trying to kill you just because of Lucy. Lucy had a *parcel*. But the other three? Had nothing. Which means..."

Two different motives? A package. And a lie. My mind raced with possibilities, each more confusing than the last.

"But why the fuck are they trying to kill me? I don't know shit," I said, frustration evident in my voice. Why? None of this made any sense, and as much as I trusted Killian, I was in over my head.

Killian shrugged, his own frustration mirroring mine. "I haven't figured that out. I'm still digging into the connection the three dead board members have besides your father."

"*That* is the connection," Aidan said softly. I almost forgot he was still listening. "I would bet money it's Charles. Question is, why is Charles focused on asking for the package, and not his colleagues dying…" His voice trailed off, leaving us with more questions than answers.

A silent message passed through the phone, and then I saw Killian straighten to his full six-three, rolling his powerful shoulders back.

"The parcel feels like a *distraction*…Charles either doesn't know, or he doesn't *care*. Charles says he's looking for a parcel, but it never came from Hagen. Now, his old board members are dying. Coincidence?"

Too fucking many. "Knowing my father, probably not." My brain was working. "Lucy is not in the picture anymore. My dad hasn't called."

"He might know *that*." Aidan sounded intrigued.

I looked at the phone and then at Killian.

I realized at that moment how close the brothers were. I couldn't comprehend their logic.

The gravity of the situation was starting to sink in, and I could feel the tension in the room growing thicker by the second.

"People are *still* dying…" Killian mused out loud. "So, what is the connection? That's what we are looking for—"

"Something tying Lucy, my father, me, and the dead cabinet members?"

"No." Killian shook his head. "My gut is never wrong. Something *is* off—"

Aidan finished. "And it has *nothing* to do with the fucking package."

"What the fuck did you two just figure out?" My brain wasn't working that fast. The pieces of the puzzle seemed to be scattered, and I couldn't quite put them together.

Killian turned to me, his eyes wilder, now his hands steepled.

"Your father called you about a parcel weeks ago. He said Lucy had it from Marcus Hagen. That isn't possible because Hagen was already dead prior to that. The timeline of Lucy getting it and coming to New York is after everyone says Hagen was dead."

My brain was on that. "Where—who did Lucy get the package from?" She came to New York. My father knew she had it. "*Someone* told my father, if Marcus Hagen was dead, how did my father know?"

"That's the part we are missing," Aidan huffed. "That, who is the team killing everyone, and why? If Lucy is gone, they should go after her. They haven't. As far as Reed is aware? Someone's still in New York."

Killian nodded. "When Lucy came to New York. I don't think your sister had any intention of meeting your father. Ever. The only person your sister spoke to was Reed. The entire time. Which means your father lied."

"*So,* who has the parcel?" I didn't know that. But that might be helpful with the whole "Someone's after my sister."

And then what about the—

"Is it related to the cards?"

Killian's face looked grim. "My guys found one copy of that card in every single house of the dead members. It's a kill card, and nobody fucking knows who it belongs to."

"I fucking hate all this mystery," Aidan grumbled. "What happened to the good old days when villains announced themselves."

Killian smirked. "Whoever's doing this shit loves a good fucking puzzle."

And it was getting on my nerves.

Something drifted in my memory, but I couldn't focus right now. Not when I was staring at wild eyes processing information lightning fast.

I put another piece together. "Lucy has no connection to the old board members." *What was going on?* My head hurt just by saying the words out loud.

Killian smiled then, and it was...a little scary. "Because it's two different killers."

"Two *different*..." My heart was thumping in my chest.

"Think about it," he said, turning to me. "Why did the attacks start after Lucy got to the city?"

Because of the parcel, and...

"There's a second reason none of us know. Someone told my father that someone is looking for something that has nothing to do with Lucy." I didn't understand how it was..."Are these black ops?"

Killian's eyes met mine. "Nobody I have spoken to has any fucking clue what they're even called. But so far? I have kill cards all over the city. No prints. No cameras. These are professionals. They've managed to kill another person. I just got the notification before I stepped into the office. Someone, something is *in* the city."

The office temperature plummeted.

Killian's energy was electric, giving me a glimpse of the mind under the suit. "Not to mention, what about the other bodies?"

Killian's rapid-fire words infiltrated my brain. "Why kill them? They didn't have *shit. It's two separate kill orders.* One for you. One for your sister. *That's* why Lucy is hiding. Reed said he assigned someone to work on her case. Because she dropped that package. And you still are on a kill list."

He held up the gold card. "See this? You're marked. You're next, or whatever order they're coming after you with."

"I think they already have."

I fucking knew it. That wasn't an ordinary card.

"Someone's been entering my office and leaving it—"

Oh Shit. My heart dropped to my stomach. "The security footage that's been missing." It all came out of me, the leaks, the bad press, the cameras. "They've been targeting me for a while. But—"

"If they killed everyone else? Why is Lucas *still* alive?" Aidan's voice echoed my thoughts. Killian looked uneasy for once.

"Unless they want more than me," I admitted. "If they take me out, it raises too many questions. What if they're coming after my company? Obliterate that."

"Or take it over…" Aidan said in a dark voice. "Killian, there's your second motive."

"Are they fucking with me?" Like playing with their food. Torture was agonizing if done right. "To steal my company and then kill me? Make it look like I offed myself?"

They would. That was the plan.

"No," Killian said firmly, his jaw set with determination. "I need to follow up on a hunch."

The intensity in his gaze made me uneasy, and I couldn't help but wonder what he suspected. Did he know more?

Killian turned to me, his expression softening slightly. "You need to find someone. I don't think you want the O'Hara name drawing suspicion to you."

He was right.

I didn't need my connections to the mafia made *public*.

The thought alone made my stomach churn with anxiety.

"I can ask someone," I said calmly, despite the chaos swirling in my mind. "What are you looking into?"

There were too many questions up in the air, but I was grateful for their honesty.

Killian looked ready for a fight with someone, his jaw clenched. "Just a suspicion."

But it was more.

He sounded like Reed, then.

He knows something more…he just doesn't know what…

"Aidan...you said Charles only knows you?"

"Yeah. He's currently on the coast of North Carolina. Don't tell me you're paying him a visit—"

"No." Killian looked at me. "Not quite." He tipped his head to me, telling his brother and me he would be back sooner than later. As he stepped out, I leaned in my seat.

I was going to die. Neither one of them said it outright.

Evie. I just wanted my girl. I just needed her.

I didn't want anything else in the world as my last wish.

Just my girl. I needed her like air.

Just wanted to be with her. Nothing else.

I knew they wouldn't come after her.

It turns out that only Mercury Group was the target.

I can smell trouble brewing.

Trouble was definitely here. And I had one more fucking call courtesy of Reed Whittaker.

CHAPTER 36
LUCAS

I ADJUSTED MY WEBCAM LONG MOMENTS AFTER KILLIAN LEFT.

When Liam Sullivan's face appeared on my screen, I immediately noticed his striking appearance.

He was leaning back in his chair, his jet-black hair and piercing green eyes commanding attention even through the screen.

"Reed filled me in on the situation," Liam said, his voice clear through my speakers. The mention of Lucy sent a pang through my chest. Again. It was fresh.

I understood the O'Haras were working from one angle.

Trying to find out why I was being targeted and my company. This was the man assigned to finding Lucy. *The other angle.*

Reed covered them all. I explained everything.

Explaining how interlaced the stories were.

Liam was only covering Lucy.

"Charles mentioned Marcus Hagen. Killian just said Hagen had been dead for a while. I don't know why Charles would bring him up—are you all right?"

Liam's green eyes had sharpened. He had the outside image of a man who looked like he couldn't care less, but he was taking in data, and something about that name had made him snap.

"I'm fine, please continue," he said, straightening in his chair.

I noticed he had something pink on one shoulder, which did little to quell the gnawing worry in my gut.

"I need to find her. Even if she is running from *someone*. I'm guessing Marcus Hagen was not a good man," I said.

Liam's gaze was hard. "Sometimes, people get caught up in things they never intended. I hope Lucy is good at staying hidden." I told him about Lucy and the parcel.

Liam stopped taking notes and asked. "Did Lucy take something from someone in Hagen's circle?"

I frowned. "I never thought about it like that. We didn't know who she took it from." If Hagen didn't give Lucy the parcel, then *who* could be *someone* else.

"Lucky guess," Liam replied, tipping his head back. "Did Charles say what Lucy stole?"

No, he hadn't.

"Whatever it was...it must've been *valuable*," Liam murmured softly as he wrote on his pad.

That's what I was worried about.

"Do you know how long your sister was working for Hagen?" Liam asked.

I paused. "I never said she was—"

His pen stopped at his lips. "*No one* gets into Hagen's inner circle. Was she working for Hagen or...was she working for someone else?"

I remembered the note. "You mean Reed?"

Liam's eyes widened with a small smile that reminded me of when Killian realized there were two killers. "Your sister was working for Reed..." he stated, not a question. He made a soft noise.

There was a slight chill in my room, and I couldn't place it if the AC was higher.

Something about Liam's assumption didn't sit right with me.

I felt the need to correct him and set the record straight.

"Reed said he never got anything from Lucy," I clarified, my mind racing with possibilities. "Wherever she is...I think she took it with her."

The words felt heavy on my tongue, weighed down by the uncertainty of what "it" could be.

Liam made another noise, his expression unreadable as he jotted down notes.

"Do you have a clue where she might be?" he asked quietly. "Someplace she felt safe?"

Some places came to mind, but nowhere concrete.

"No," I was ashamed. "Lucy and I...we aren't close at all. Things were different after our mother died. My father and I aren't close either." I bit back another biting comment when it came to my father. "Charles is…"

"Good at destroying things."

I looked at Liam, who was watching me. I nodded.

"Lucy and I are not remotely close. I never saw her in town. I'm sorry to say I haven't been the best brother to my sister. I loved her growing up; she was my best friend. But one day, I don't know what happened. I felt like I didn't keep *her…safe.* I hope you find her. Let me know when you do. I'd like a second chance to keep her by my side."

My chest tightened as I said. "I hope you don't judge me for that."

I couldn't keep Lucy safe. I'm a shit brother, and I hate myself for letting her down.

I let Evie down.

Images of a silly, grinning, chubby blond who followed me around with worship in her eyes made my chest tighten.

What happened to me? Her?

For some reason, a wealth of emotions went through Liam's face, and his head tipped as he tapped something.

"A second chance to keep her safe, I believe you," he said softly. "That's very noble of you, Mr. Devereaux—"

"You can call me Lucas." I waved a hand. "I'm not about formality."

One side of Liam's mouth tipped up, and his eyes gleamed. "I think your situation will work itself out. All of them. And for Lucy's sake, I'll do my best to find her. I would hate to piss them off, the people she stole it from."

Another chill went through my spine.

That made two of us.

I noticed Liam grimace slightly as he adjusted, and curiosity got the better of me.

"Were you in the military?" I asked.

"I wasn't."

But something was wrong with his legs.

I hesitated for a moment before sending him information via chat.

"There's this program, Pets for Vets. They match veterans with companion animals to help with PTSD and other challenges. I know you said you weren't in the service, but…it might be worth looking into."

Liam's eyes met mine through the screen, a flicker of surprise crossing his face.

I wasn't mistaking it—Liam *did* have sequins on his shirt and on his collar.

Behind him, hanging on a rack, was a pair of wings and a shimmering outfit.

It looked like something straight out of a costume shop or a theater production.

A woman's voice cut in, and the call was muted *so fast* I didn't see him move.

He held up a finger as he intently turned to whoever it was. It was her *costume*.

His smile slowly stretched into a genuine look of happiness.

It *was* a woman.

Even though I couldn't hear him, he looked younger.

Liam turned back to the camera, still smiling. He unmuted the call and said. "Sorry about that."

"Your wife?" I asked curiously

. I never took him for the type to…be *married*.

"I'm working on it," he said quietly, his grin wide, his eyes flickering to that general direction with mischief. "Where were we…"

There was something about him, unapologetic and raw, that was unsettling just enough to make me realize he made me uncomfortable because he was *unashamed* of himself.

Not when he interacted with me or *her*.

Quiet intelligence radiated even through the call.

His eyes took in everything as he toyed with a chain around his neck. He fiddled with it as he listened to me talk about my father and Lucy.

When my call was over, I didn't realize so much time had flown by.

He was easy to talk to, which for a Titan—I wondered if he knew his boss hated me, but I got the feeling it wouldn't stop Liam from doing his job.

"Lucas," his voice softened toward the end of our call. "When Lucy gets in touch with you, I'd like to take in some information from her."

When?

"You think she will?" I hope so. I failed once. I'd never fail her again.

Liam's eyes flickered to the other side of the room, and he smiled. "I'm betting on it."

I took a breath, my mind reeling from the events of the past few days. Lucy's disappearance, the first attack on me—it all felt like a nightmare I couldn't wake up from.

The note with Reed's name.

The suspicion added to the growing sense of unease in my gut.

And then there was Evie.

The way she had felt in my arms...it was like a dream come true, a moment of pure bliss amidst the chaos.

I needed her more than ever.

But I couldn't have her, couldn't ask her to break her promise, to risk everything for a man like me.

A man who was hated.

A man nobody wanted.

A man who couldn't function in public.

I knew my family's reputation, the dark shadow that hung over the Devereaux name like a persistent fog, obscuring any glimmer of goodness.

But since taking over the company, I had tried to change my family's reputation to steer us in a different direction.

It wasn't easy, undoing years of ingrained behavior and cutthroat tactics, but I was determined to make a difference.

I instituted shorter workdays and parental leave policies that were some of the best in the country, something that was almost unheard of in our industry.

I made sure that our employees had access to top-notch healthcare and mental health resources.

Gemma and I had launched a series of community outreach initiatives, partnering with local organizations to give back to the neighborhoods where we operated.

We sponsored internships, job training workshops, and free laptop initiatives at underprivileged schools.

As someone who had gone to private school, I knew what money could get you.

Gemma and I had talked about our upbringings and how sheltered we had been, never having to worry about our next meal.

She helped me set up Pets for Vets and everything else as well.

These were all things that I kept close to the vest, not wanting to draw too much attention to the changes I was making.

I knew that my father would disapprove, that he would see my efforts as a sign of weakness, a betrayal of the Devereaux way.

That was the fucking point.

But I didn't care.

I knew what I was doing was right and that it was the only way to erase what I hated. Who I was.

And yet, despite all of my efforts, I couldn't shake the feeling that it wasn't enough, that I would never be able to fully escape the sins of my family's past.

No matter how hard I tried, I would always be tainted by the Devereaux name, by the legacy of greed and corruption that had been passed down through the generations. And now? Someone was trying to kill me.

That's all Gabriel thought I was. Another Devereaux.

More scum on the Earth.

Not good *enough* for his sister.

He's not wrong. That's why I'm not getting a bodyguard.

If I ended up dead? Good riddance. Evie was the best part of me. I was scum.

I hated myself enough to know that someone was fucking with me. And I didn't give a shit anymore. If I went? I would go.

Fuck this.

Evie deserved someone who could nurture her growth and help her bloom and thrive. I wanted to be that person for her.

I closed my eyes, fighting back the memories that threatened to assault my head. By the end of the day, I was restless.

Before I knew it, my legs were moving, carrying me out of the building and into the cool evening air.

I walked without a clear destination, my feet moving on autopilot as my thoughts continued to churn.

I took a cab, muttering a destination I couldn't comprehend.

And then. *I was there.*

Standing outside Evie's door. My hand poised to knock.

My subconscious had led me here. Seeking *solace.* Something.

Anything but me.

I hesitated, my heart pounding in my chest. I knew I shouldn't be here. I had promised myself I would stay away. That I would let her go.

But the pull was too strong.

The need to see her, to be near her, overpowered everything else. I knocked, the sound echoing in the quiet hallway.

Seconds ticked by, each one feeling like an eternity.

Then, the door opened. A vision of soft green in another fucking dress that took my breath away.

This one hung from her slight frame, forming a swirl around her knees. She looked adorably edible. Her eyes widened in surprise.

A flicker of something—joy, relief, longing—danced across her face. But it was quickly replaced by a guarded expression.

A reminder of the distance between us.

"Lucas." My name fell from her lips. "What are you doing here?"

I swallowed hard, my mouth suddenly dry. I hadn't planned this far ahead. Hadn't thought about what I would say. How I would explain my presence.

"I..." I faltered, my words failing me. "I needed to see you."

It was the truth, plain and simple.

She studied me for a long moment, her eyes searching mine. Looking for answers. For reassurance. For something I wasn't sure I could give.

And then a masculine voice rang out. "Evie, who is it?"

My heart stopped. The world tilted on its axis.

I felt like I had been punched in the gut. A man. In Evie's apartment.

At *this* hour.

Jealousy flared, hot and fierce.

Possessiveness reared its ugly head.

I had no right. No claim.

But the thought of *another* man with Evie, touching her, holding her, fucking my girl…

"Who the fuck is that?"

CHAPTER 37
EVIE

I HALF CLOSED THE DOOR ON MY COFFEE DATE, MY HEART RACING IN MY chest.

I hadn't expected Lucas tonight. Or at all.

I'd gotten in touch with Avani after Alisha told her sister about me, and Avani had set up a coffee date.

Her temporary bodyguard, Kieran O'Hara, was the newest addition to Titan and her ever-present shadow.

After her kidnapping and Alisha's hospital stay, Reed wanted Kieran to accompany Avani around.

Kieran, with his chocolate hair and amber eyes on his charge, was protective of little Avani, who was *not so little.*

The gorgeous brunette was taller than me, and she hid under a black turtleneck and mini skirt with stockings.

I had started wearing stockings because of her and Alisha's love of them.

As we'd talked, one of her friends from school, Ben, bumped into us, setting Kieran on edge.

But Ben played *The Domain,* so I ended up talking to him.

Which was how I had ended up at home with him. Ben was actually a really cute grad student who did absolutely nothing for me.

But Lucas didn't know that.

"What are you doing here?"

And right now, Ben was standing up to him. "Who's this, Evie?"

"Don't call her *Evie*." Lucas glared at Ben, his eyes flashing with a possessive anger that made my stomach clench.

Indignation flared through me at his tone. Who was he to come here and ruin this for me? "Do not speak to him like that."

I looked back at Ben. "I'll be back in a second."

Lucas was glaring at him, looking furious, his jaw clenched tight.

"Seriously?" I couldn't believe he had the audacity to show up like this, unannounced and uninvited.

"Do you need help, Evie?" Ben stepped up and walked over, his face etched with concern. No, he was about to get caught up in Luke.

De-escalate the situation.

"No, Ben, I swear it's fine—"

"Don't call her Evie. And stay the fuck out of it—" Lucas snarled, his voice low and dangerous.

"*Luke*! You're *overstepping*—"

"Is this your ex-boyfriend?" Ben's tone was incredulous.

Lucas looked positively arctic. "*Ex?*" He swung his head to me, his expression twisted with pain and bitterness. "Already moved on?"

"*You* are out of line," I said firmly, my heart aching at the hurt in his eyes, even as anger simmered beneath the surface. This was insanity.

He couldn't just come in here and demand his way. And then Ben got in the way, his broad shoulders squared as he faced off against Lucas.

"I think you need to leave, bro."

Lucas looked ready to murder him, his eyes flashing with a deadly intensity.

His voice was dark. "I own this building. In fact, I own every single one on this entire strip. So, the only person who needs to leave is you."

"Stop it!" I pushed Ben back, knowing full well Lucas would—

"I don't give a fuck what you are, old man. You need to leave Evie and me alone."

A cruel smirk lit Lucas's face. He let out a breath and hung his head for all of a second. And then, I didn't even see the first hit.

I just gasped and scrambled back as Lucas's fist slammed into Ben's face.

A loud, sickening noise rent the air.

Ben let out a pained cry.

I saw the triumph in Lucas's eyes, a savage satisfaction that made my stomach turn.

I was unable to move, frozen in horror when Lucas lifted Ben up by the scruff of his collar like he was nothing more than a rag.

And *slammed* him into the wall by his throat.

Those calm blues burned hot, a fire I had never seen before.

Even when Reed had attacked him he never...

The thought made my heart ache, even as confusion and fear warred within me. I had never seen this side of Lucas. It wasn't the Dom.

"Lucas!"

This is something else.

Something that lurked under the designer suits and easy smiles.

Something that I hadn't sensed when he'd been Luke Delaney in his hoodies and sweats and light laughter.

"Here's what's going to happen, *Ben*. You're going to leave. You're going to pretend like you *never* saw my girl. You will never speak of her ever again. *Or so help me God, I will find out everything about you, and I'll come after you with everything I've got.*"

His voice was low, a velvet threat that made my blood run cold.

I blanched at that threat. That wasn't empty.

Lucas did have more power than he was sometimes willing to admit. I knew that much based off the research I'd done on him.

"And we both know you and I aren't remotely the same. Are we clear, *bro?*"

"You're fucking crazy," Ben spat. "I'll call the cops."

And if I thought Lucas was scary, he turned downright terrifying as he smiled dangerously. "I dare you. Do it."

His grip tightened.

I had enough. Somewhere in the middle of this, I realized just how much he was Gabriel.

I saw it in the unholy rage in his eyes.

The way he smiled at threats instead of balking at it.

"Let him go."

I saw his shoulders bunch.

How do I get him to listen?

"*Lily*. Now *let him go.*"

A nanosecond later, Ben fell out of Lucas's grip and dropped to the floor.

What was that feeling that went through me just then?

Only I could do that?

Ben's cheek was swelling, and his nose was bleeding. I didn't want to venture a guess, but it was probably broken.

A wave of sympathy washed over me, and I swallowed around it.

"Do you have somewhere he can go?" I didn't dare look at Lucas. I couldn't right now. I was so angry with him.

I was just so angry at everything that he'd done.

And even through the anger, I realized why he was here. What control I had over him.

"I do." His voice was gruff.

"Send him there."

"Don't bother." Ben stood holding his shirt to his face, and I saw his nose was bleeding. "I'll see myself out."

I watched, my heart tightening at how guilty and ashamed I felt.

Guilt for exposing Ben to Lucas's rage and ashamed for even allowing Lucas to get the upper hand in the situation.

As soon as the door closed, and I was alone in the room with him, I waited until I counted to ten to speak.

My anger simmered beneath the surface, a quiet fury that threatened to boil over at any moment.

"*What is wrong with yo*u?" I asked my voice tight.

"You."

I turned to look at him for once, and I saw the weary set of his eyes, the tightness on his face.

Normally, Lucas had always looked effortlessly put together, a little tired, no doubt, but I had thought it was from being a grad student.

Not the CEO of one of the world's most formidable real estate groups.

Not who he was. Now, looking at him, I took in his exhaustion, the dark circles under his eyes, the way he looked haunted.

My heart clenched at the sight, even as I fought to hold onto my anger.

"Having money doesn't mean you can go around threatening whoever you want."

"*Why not?*" He looked cruel. "Your brother does it all the time."

I felt that like a sledgehammer, the words hitting me with a force that nearly knocked the wind out of me.

"Reed did it. The moment he saw me. Hit first. Asked questions later. That's how your family handles business. It's different when I do it—"

"I *never* said that," I protested, my voice weak even to my own ears.

"You didn't have to."

I swallowed and exhaled hard, trying to regain my composure. "Am

I some sort of sick experiment to you? Fuck with Gabriel's sister and then—"

"*No.*" His growl cut through the tension, the sound sending a shiver down my spine. "It was *never* about that. I liked you the *moment* you showed up like a breath of fresh air, attracting the attention of every man around you wearing that...dress at a fucking nerd convention. I liked you then. *Before you* told me who you were, complimenting me. I liked you the *entire* time. It wasn't a game for me. Gabriel hates my entire family. I can imagine why, since I hate them just as much—knew you'd hate me if you knew who I was. So, I never told you."

My heart was hanging by a thin wire. On the edge of something. This man. I didn't recognize him.

And yet, if I took off the suit, the tie, he was...Luke Delaney. At his core. I knew that much. I didn't hate him.

Every time I asked Gabriel why he hated the Devereaux's he dodged the question.

I was torn between my loyalty to a brother who had given me everything in the past, and a man I had fallen for and saw a future with.

Once.

"It's bad enough you lied to me for weeks, you let me sleep with you —I did things with you that—"

I broke off unable to continue speaking to him, the memories of our time together flooding my mind, making my cheeks heat with a mixture of desire and shame.

"Is that what you're here for? To settle a score? To ask me why I want to move on from you?"

"No! I'm here because *my life is a fucking mess* without you in it, and I came here trying to make amends or something. Instead, I see you dating some frat boy—why was he in your house? How long have you—"

He broke off as though he was aware he had no right to ask me any of these questions. "I didn't lie to you without good reason."

"*You didn't give me a chance!*" I threw back, my voice rising with each word. "You didn't even give me an opportunity to get to know you. *You kept secrets, you lied,* and then you wanted me to trust you. To sign your contract!"

I was so angry right now. I had never hit anyone in my life. I had never wanted to. I did now. I stormed up to him and shoved at his chest.

He didn't even move. His eyes went wide as he took me in, and I felt hot tears in my eyes, now streaming down my face.

"Do you know how fucked that is?" I shoved him again, my frustration and hurt pouring out of me.

"You wanted me to open up to you. You lied to me. *Every. Single. Date.*"

I pushed him.

"You broke me!"

Shove.

"I trusted you! How could you!"

He didn't even budge, which frustrated me more.

He was an immovable wall, his expression tender.

And then slowly his hands came and gripped my arms, massive compared to my own slender ones, he could break them in half if he wanted to.

And he put them around his waist, pulling me in tight to him, tucking my head into his chest.

I stood frozen as he wrapped his arms around me, his hand on the back of my head, curving protectively, gently.

"I'm sorry." His voice came after long moments, the words soft and sincere. *"I'm sorry, Evie."*

"You should be," I whispered, my anger slowly giving way to a bone-deep weariness, my eyes burning.

"You can't come back into my life like this. You can't hurt people I care about."

His body stiffened at the mention of caring about Ben or anyone. I huffed out a breath, my heart already wavering beneath all the nerves and emotions I felt.

Being this close to him. Being pressed against him. It was already too much.

"Even if you came here to fix things, I have no idea how to trust you. To rebuild the trust..." I let him go and took a step back, wiping my eyes.

"I don't know how to let you in. I don't know where to start. You... *what is this?* You being a jealous protective ex-boyfriend or...?"

His eyes glittered as he looked at me, a mix of emotions swirling in their depths. "Why did you use your safe word to stop me?"

This man. "*That's* what you're thinking about?"

"Why did you do it?" His eyes dug into mine. Into my soul.

"I don't know. It just felt..." It had felt right. Like the truth.

I was his. Even if I wanted to date anyone else, it could never compare to Luke.

It all paled in comparison to the man standing in front of me right now in his suit and tie, looking worse for wear and desperately trying to keep me close to him.

I thought about it at that moment.

The way he had tried to come after me several times. Trying to get me to believe in him.

When he'd helped carry my plants and called me, saying he would've helped.

He would have.

I didn't know Lucas Devereaux the way I knew Luke Delaney.

It was hard to reconcile the two.

"Did it feel like I was yours?" His voice was soft despite the harsh lines of his face bracketed with tension, his hair in disarray, making him look more like the young man I'd met.

"Did you really like me?"

I felt my heart breaking, something was shifting between us. Something changed in the tension.

"Yeah. Just you..." he ground out.

My heart sputtered a little.

"I promised." I promised one brother to stay away and let the other one down.

"That you wouldn't see me."

A beat passed. I felt my nails digging into my palms.

"Not Luke Delaney." For the second time that night, he shocked me. At my expression, he continued. "Not Luke Delaney. You said you wouldn't see Lucas Devereaux."

I shook my head in disbelief. *"Why are you so—"*

"Obsessed with you? In love with you?"

In love with me?

"From the moment I met you—" He looked like he was struggling with himself. "Your laughter all over my apartment, you came up to me without caring about me and who I was—what my family *was*—complimenting on the parts of my life I didn't dare tell a soul about. I did that stuff as a hobby. And you liked and respected me. For the first time in my life, I felt..."

"Normal." The tension that had transformed became something else as his eyes met mine with relief.

"*Accepted.* That is how you made me feel. I have never met someone so disarmingly beautiful and someone who trusted me out of the goodness that she perceived me to be...Luke. *My entire life, I have been my father's son and my sister's brother, and for the first time in my entire life, I was just Evie's man. That's all I wanted to be."*

He took a step closer to me, and I didn't move.

"Every single thing you know about me was the truth. *It always has been.* I didn't tell you my name at the convention because I don't like using it. When you told me your last name, I knew I could *never* tell you."

Too caught in the stare that had ensnared me from day one. "I lied to you, pretending to be *just some normal man.* And in return, *that is what I became.* Just. Some. Guy. Not my father's son. I knew if you found out, you'd hate me. It's no secret a lot of people hate my family."

He continued like he hadn't just shattered my entire resolve.

"I just want to be Evie's. I want to wake up in the morning to you. I want you to call me in the afternoons when I've had shit days. I want to hear your voice in the evening when I come home. I want to massage your feet, take care of you after *your* long days, hold you while you sleep. Feed you. Protect you. Love you. *That's all I want."*

I just want to be Evie's. Just Evie's.

Love you. That's all I want.

My heart pounded in my chest as his words washed over me, all over they sank into my skin becoming a part of me.Seeping into me.

"Nobody is you, Evie Monroe. Not a single woman compares to your intelligence and wit. Nothing will ever be close. I've been chasing you around this city, trying to tell you that I fell for you so fucking hard. You got me in a chokehold. I can't lose you. Not to that frat boy. Not to anyone."

And then he stunned me, sinking to his knees in front of me, his hands on my waist as he bent his head before me.

I stood there, frozen, my breath catching in my throat as I looked down at him.

"You said you wouldn't see Lucas Devereaux. You never said you couldn't see Luke Delaney. I will come to your door every single day. I'll send you food and take care of *all* your plants."

He shook his head with a low, humorless laugh. "All one hundred of them. I don't care what you make me do. *Just make me do it.* I can't do this without you. Please don't let me."

I thought I'd stopped crying. I wiped my eyes. *Guess not.*

I was shaking, my entire body trembling with the weight of his words, the intensity of his emotions.

All other thoughts left my head as I looked down at his soft blond hair bent like I was his.

Begging me for *his...everything.*

The part of me that had been buried beneath the hurt and the betrayal, the anger and the confusion—it completely shattered.

My heart felt like it was cracking open. A part of me that still loved him, that still yearned for him, despite everything that had happened between us.

Every single thing was the truth.

You made me feel normal.

He made me feel like myself. Could I? Could I even?

He had chased me so much. I believe he didn't tell me because he didn't want to be judged for who he was. What his family was. And I had. Hadn't I? I had judged him. I hadn't listened. And suddenly, the guilt churned for a different reason.

Because I had confirmed his worst fears.

If he told me his name...I wouldn't see him.

And I had done him dirty.

He was still on his knees.

Luke Delaney.

Lucas *Devereaux.*

Halves of a whole, and as he pressed his head to my abdomen, my fingers laced into the golden locks in disarray.

I threaded my fingers through and could've sworn he sighed.

He was completely himself. He wasn't lying. Besides his name? I got the feeling now, that Luke Delaney *was* Lucas Devereaux.

All the best parts of him.

Was I lying to myself?

Was I using my loyalty to Gabriel to stop me from living? Like I had always done?

Was this where my journey led? I didn't know why Gabriel hated him or his family, but Gabriel had his reasons. And even if Gabriel saved my life? In so many ways?

I loved my brother. I saw Gabriel's laughter in my vision, his grins when he did something devious.

His love for me every time he indulged me while shopping, tried new pastries with me, grimaced at anything sour flavored, bandaging my hands after miserably attempting cooking, carrying my backpacks when they were too heavy. Helping me re-pot plants. Yelling at the team for exposing me to things I shouldn't have seen but I snuck in anyway.

I'm so sorry, Gabriel.

"Forty-seven."

His head looked up, and I saw his eyes glittering, hope and uncertainty warring in their depths.

Lean lines of his throat worked. "What?"

I wiped my eyes once more and sniffled, trying to regain some semblance of composure. "That's how many plants I have. Forty-seven."

He double-blinked, processing what I said. And then a small smile quirked his lips, a smile that made my heart skip a beat, that made my knees go weak and my heart to break at his hesitation. "Is that a yes?"

I nodded, a feeling of rightness, of inevitability, settling over me. "Yes."

I stopped him from standing, my hand on his chest, my eyes locking with his at this height. "But you have to promise you can't just threaten people like that ever again."

He thought about it, his brow furrowing, his expression pensive. "Are you still going to date if you're with me?"

"No." I huffed a breath, a small smile tugging at the corners of my mouth. "I don't want anyone else."

I couldn't believe what I was doing, my heart racing, my mind reeling—and yet *nothing* had felt more right, more true, more honest.

And while I wasn't one to throw caution to the wind, to leap before I looked, I recognized what was happening in front of me was the most real version of Lucas Devereaux I had ever seen.

And he was—is mine.

CHAPTER 38
LUCAS

My secretary knocked on my door a few days into my newfound relationship with Evie.

Now, my mornings were in her arms.

I had fewer nightmares; if anything, they stopped completely. I freaked out less. I still went to therapy, and I still continued the things I loved.

But I did them with her. I was going home to her, avoiding my own apartment.

I hadn't made love to her *once*.

I didn't touch her even when she squirmed against me. Because this was…this was about her trust.

I honored it. I'd never fuck up again.

And Evie clarified a lot about Gabriel to me, about *everything*.

It had made me slam back into reality to see Gabriel Monroe as more than an iceman, who was apparently haunted and burning hot for a woman who was no longer alive.

Even a part of me knew I had intentionally kept something from her. I had kept one lie from her.

And really, it was by omission.

I haven't told her about the attempt on my life.

I couldn't bring her to her knees like that.

Guilt trip my…woman into being with me?

It wouldn't matter if I died last night, she was mine.

I would never tell Evie that I was being targeted.

I couldn't put that burden on her shoulders, couldn't taint the fragile trust we had rebuilt with the *specter* of violence and danger.

"Mr. Devereaux, I have a question."

I looked up from the reports I was viewing.

I had a meeting at ten, and usually, she came in to remind me if she knew I was swamped.

Except she wasn't my usual, I had about two secretaries I switched out, and I didn't recognize her.

"Are you new?"

The stunningly beautiful woman with blond hair was swept back into a bun.

I don't know why the stark contrast against her peach skin looked pretty. But it did.

In a very eerie way. Her sharper features and bright eyes glowed in her business outfit.

This must be the woman Matteo was talking about.

Her eyes were the color of ice. Like Gabriels...she looked oddly familiar and yet *not* at the same time.

A shy smile graced her lips, and I could've sworn I knew her.

"Do I know you from somewhere?"

The soft accent was not what I was expecting. "I'm just covering for Jenny this morning. I work for Mr. O'Brian." I knew O'Brien. Solid guy.

Where was that accent from?

"Where's Ella?"

"She had a doctor's appointment this morning and her nephew to pick up, so I'm just covering until two o'clock."

That smile again got under my skin, but not in a bad way.

"I hope it's alright, I have everything you asked for today, your meetings organized, and your father called earlier when you stepped out. I told him I would pass you the message. I also have a list of questions, including your special requests. Would it be all right if I went ahead?" I could listen to this woman talk forever.

I couldn't resist. "Where are you from?"

I quickly realized my mistake, *foot meets mouth.* "I'm sorry, your accent is beautiful."

Evie's voice calmed me down with its soft grace.

But this was different.

She laughed at that, making her sound—I felt like I heard it before—I couldn't place it. "Brazil."

I motioned for her to go ahead, my mind still half on Evie, on the feel of her in my arms, the sound of her laugh, the scent of her hair.

"I contacted the store, and they just had a few questions about your request, so I wanted to go over it with you." She looked down at her notepad. "You said several small cacti, a few ferns, a five-foot fiddle leaf fig," I grinned at her struggling with the f's.

"And...a tree..." She looked up. "*Sorry*, my English is not the best, but—"

"Your English is *great*." I waved a hand. "I would never shame you for your accent. It's wonderful."

Her eyes widened as though she was surprised and turned a little pink.

I grinned. I thought flowers would be a nice thing to do for Evie until I saw her apartment and her green thumb.

I wanted to get her something for her, something that would make her eyes light up, that would bring that beautiful smile to her face.

"How big should the tree be?"

A question I never imagined answering. I thought about the ceilings, picturing the space and how the light would filter through the leaves. "Eight feet sounds good. This way, there's room to grow."

She blinked. Holding back the laughter that bubbled up in my chest like champagne bubbles, I bit my tongue. Light, airy, like my girl.

"Right away, sir. Eight feet. Got it." She paused, her eyes flickered. "One more thing."

"Yes?"

"I will make the arrangements to move all assets to her name, as you requested. And your will has been updated. I just need your signature. Could you spell her last name again?"

I thought I included it in the email. "Eva Monroe." Her head snapped up to me. *My friends call me Evie.* How long has it been since that day? "By the way, you said you work downstairs for O'Brien." I knew O'Brien's team.

Or I thought I did.

That smile lit her face up, and for a moment, I wanted to smile with her, Evie was rubbing off on me.

"I am new. O'Brien's on a warpath with the Walters and Jennings teams today, and I'm trying to avoid him. Guilty as charged," she quipped. "Monroe, I got it. I'll be moving everything today. Will there be anything else?"

I could imagine everyone trying to avoid O'Brien and how quick of her to get out of his way.

"Smart move. He should calm down by the time you get back. No, just make sure Evie—Eva's name is on everything I own. The trust and everything else—"

"Of course." Her eyes moved over me, and I wondered for a moment if she was checking me out. If so, she would know I was taken. And then the look flickered out. "I'll email you the confirmation of everything once it's done. Mr. Devereaux, do you love her?"

My head snapped up at the question, her eyes were unblinking, and for a moment—

I know this woman. But how?

In the past I would've denied it, would've pretended not to care, and asked her why she cared.

"I was just wondering if you'd like me to add that to the card with the seven-foot tree since you're sending your girlfriend, a jungle?"

"Eight feet," I said softly, looking back at my screen feeling the rush over me. "Yes, to both of those questions."

As she left, I felt strange...

Did I get her name?

My head felt unsteady.

Those lapses in memory eating at me now.

Before I could spiral, Evie's text lit up my phone, a snapshot from one of our earlier dates.

Evie texted me back green hearts to my question and photos of potting soil.

Evie would freak out when the tree came but with excitement. I would do my duties as her man and water all of them. Go home to her. Listen to her chatter as she cooked.

I was learning that I knew nothing about Evie, the homebody caring for her plants.

I tried new recipes that she often had with Gabriel, and grumbled about how nothing was built for short people.

In another life?

I'd get her a new apartment, a bigger one with an entire greenhouse attached. I thought about buying her a house to have after I was gone.

Nothing would stop me.

Not the secrets I kept, not the dangers that lurked in the shadows. But even as I basked in the warmth of our love, in knowing now?

There was no promise of our future together, a cold reality settled in the pit of my stomach.

One day, the attempts on my life would be successful.

One day, I *would* die. And there was something nice about knowing that.

I didn't give a shit if Gabriel killed me. Or who did.

I gave a shit about my legacy.

My end.

Evie.

It was a truth I had come to accept, a fate I had resigned myself to. But Evie...Evie didn't need to know.

I would never guilt trip Evie to being with me. No, she wanted me for me. As always, *my girl.*

She didn't need to bear that burden to live with that fear. But inside, I was terrified. Terrified of losing her. Terrified of leaving her alone in this world.

The knowledge that my time was limited, that every breath could be my last.

And I would love her with every beat of my heart.

She's mine. Fucking finally.

CHAPTER 39
EVIE

I HADN'T TOLD ANYONE ABOUT UNLOCKING ORACLE.

Not even Gabriel.

Not with Selena being injured, Alisha and Avani on his plate, and half of Titan operating all across the city.

Too much was happening.

With Reed helping Alisha, Liam had taken a lot off his plate; Garrett was aiding Selena and Kellan, and when he wasn't?

He operated the teams across the city while Gabriel ran around managing all of Titan.

I didn't even remember how much time had passed.

I didn't have the heart to talk to him right now. Especially not with taking Lucas back?

Where did I even start?

I padded out to my bedroom naked, slightly dripping water around my towel.

I hadn't washed my hair; it was too much, so I brushed it out.

Lucas hadn't made love to me since we'd gotten back together, and I felt like I was anticipating more so than usual. I knew he was trying to be patient.

Trying to date me for the first time again.

Building trust. I could throw that all out the window with how horny I was.

It was still early enough that he might still be at work, so I tossed my towel into the hamper and shook my hair out, walking into the living room and taking my speaker with me.

I set it down before I entered the room so I could move back and forth between the spaces and listen to my songs.

It switched to an upbeat one, and I ended up singing along, not paying attention to my space, and padding to the kitchen.

Avani had shown me pop music from Korea, and now I couldn't get enough. Gabriel would die if he heard me listening to this.

He barely tolerated the boy band music Selena played. But this was *my* freaking apartment.

And now I could walk around however I wanted.

I was so distracted I didn't even notice the slack-jawed mouth form of Lucas standing at the door holding takeout bags—and I *screamed*.

Immediately covering myself and rushing to turn off the speaker.

"You're supposed to be at work."

"I came home early since it's Friday!"

I ran into my room searching for a robe, unsure of why I was hiding from my boyfriend. *Was he that?*

I was so confused about where we were at the current state.

Lucas didn't even kiss me.

As soon as I found it, I wrapped it around myself, rushing back out to the living room where Lucas had walked into. He set the brown bag I recognized as a popular vegetarian restaurant around here in his hand.

"Do you always..." He motioned to the speakers. "You just *dance...* naked when I'm not home?"

A little burst of warmth fluttered through me as he called my apartment his home.

"Sometimes," I felt unsettled like he'd seen a part of me more vulnerable than I could've been during sex. "Sometimes, I just dance."

His eyes drifted over the tiny silk robe Alisha had picked out in a pretty emerald, heat evident in them. *Blatantly.*

Suddenly, I felt like I wasn't wearing anything at all.

I might as well be naked for all I knew. But it wasn't the same heat I had seen before, the kind that promised pleasure and passion and endless nights tangled in sheets.

No, this was something different, something deeper.

Lucas's confession had obliterated any notion I had of our previous relationship, but I didn't know how to start this one.

"I'd like you to do that more often...even when I am here." I turned beet red as he closed the distance between us, his eyes never leaving mine. "I'd like you to be you, all the time."

There went my heart, my throat was dry.

He stepped forward slowly, his hands cupping my face as he captured my lips in a soft kiss.

I melted into him, my own hands coming up to grip his shoulders as he poured every ounce of his pent-up emotion into the kiss.

He kissed me like he was trying to convey everything he couldn't say, like he was trying to brand himself onto my very being.

I kissed him back with equal fervor, equal desperation, equal love.

"The contract is still valid," his voice was gruff.

I was vibrating with excitement. "*Luke—*"

He tugged at his tie looking at me. "I've been holding back, doll. But watching your tits bounce when you come out like that, I think I have the image of you seared into my brain."

I swallowed. My hands shook. My nipples were pebbled. I still wanted this man. His tie came undone. "I want you, Evie."

I did. I wanted him like my next breath.

"I can't wait any longer."

And then as though he was seeking my permission?

I felt his fingers replace mine on the ties of the robe, as he slid the fabric off me, a groan leaving his throat when he saw my body.

For a moment neither one of us moved.

"You are so…" His breath caught. "I missed you, doll. I missed this."

I looped my hands around his neck, unable to look away, his eyes had always been warm blue.

I grew up near the beach, and sometimes I missed that, I missed the blue of the sky and the ocean merging into one beautiful shade that wasn't truly blue—yet it calmed my soul down.

Just like him.

"Why did you wait?"

His tongue darted out as he dipped his head. "I didn't want to scare you."

"You don't scare me." He smiled softly, I heard the sound of his belt and his zipper. "I feel safe with you."

"Still?"

Still?

"I never stopped feeling safe with you," I admitted. I turned to Harvey in the entryway. "I let you bring Harvey up."

His grin was breathless as his eyes gleamed with those blues.

"Evie." He turned back to me. "I need to fuck you." And then he turned me around, I heard the clink of his belt, as bent me over.

"You're fucking dripping for me." I was. I felt him parting my ass no doubt watching himself slide into me. The first stretch I let out a soft noise.

"And hungry," he growled. "Did you miss my cock?"

I had.

When I didn't answer, he yanked my hair and slid a few inches. I cried out. His dark chuckle filled the air as I felt my eyes water.

"You forgot how to take me." His hand snaked around to my clit, finding that little bud that wept for him. "That's all right, I can work that pussy to let me in, can't I? Practice every night if I wanted to now?"

I moaned as he rubbed my clit, sliding himself a few inches more. I arched my back to take him deeper.

"Such a perfect little thing, push back on me."

I sobbed, taking him deeper, feeling myself willingly stretched by impaling myself on him.

"That's it, that's my good girl taking my cock."

With the way he was working my clit, I didn't stop but I couldn't anymore.

"I know you can take a little more."

If he kept going I would come, gasping as he slid deeper, and bottomed out. I moaned as he nudged so deep that I felt him in my stomach. Only then did he stop working on my clit.

At the noise that left my lips he chuckled. "I know you needed it. But I just got you back after weeks. I'm not ready to let you come just yet."

I'd been afraid of that. I was already halfway there but I knew Lucas would drag it out. *And I'd let him.*

Because it was addicting. Because he was mine. Because I was still his. A sharp slap landed on my ass. I cried out.

"Am I boring you?"

"No." Sensations were sizzling along my body—I was going to *explode.* White hot pleasure formed patterns inside of me.

"I think I am." The first thrust made me scream. "Should I keep it interesting for you, pet?"

I screamed as he slammed into me repeatedly in vicious thrusts that left me unable to think.

There was a bite of pain to them, and it tethered me to my body while driving me insane.

Every drive pushed me closer, groaning and gasping at his length spearing into me. Over and *over*.

I couldn't breathe.

It was too rough.

Too much.

"I've had a rough day, Cherry, you gonna let me work it out?"

Oh God. Iloveroughdays.

"Y...yes."

He leaned back and continued his strokes, hitting that spot. "You're going to be a good girl aren't you, let your man fuck his frustrations into this tight little cunt?"

My eyes rolled back at how good that felt.

Dontstopdontstopdontstop.

"Don't stop—" He was driving into *that* spot— "*I'm—Luke!*"

He growled, fisting my hair in his hand.

"No." he tugged sharply, slowing down, and I cried out. "You aren't. I'm not done with you yet." I felt myself dragged from the precipice, and his lips grazed my ear.

"Spread your thighs *wider* for me." It was *brutal*, and Lucas was angry. I screamed his name as he fucked into me. I couldn't catch my breath. "Don't you dare come."

Tears streamed down my cheeks with the effort. I couldn't—*couldn't* —I needed. I must've made a noise.

Something to let him know.

As he left me then, a strangled noise left me, and I almost fell.

Lucas turned me around, and dimly, I registered I was completely naked while he was still in his suit—disheveled, buttons undone, and he never looked hotter.

I got a look at hot molten blue before he lifted me up into his arms.

Instinctively, I wrapped my legs around his, gasping as he slid me back down on his length easily.

An animal noise left me as he carried me to the bedroom, letting me catch my breath for a moment.

With every stride, I felt him, and I shook wildly as he laid me down in my bed, pumping into me with a ferocity that made me squeal.

I begged, tangling my hands in his hair, watching his lips part as incoherent noises left my lips as I fought it until tears streamed down my cheeks, and I was shaking. *Writhing.*

"*Luke!*"

I'm not going to make it.

His hands braced around my head as his eyes met mine.

"Come for me."

I shattered.

Pleasure crashed through me, wave after wave. I shook wildly as it raced down to where he was pumping into me, the look of triumph in his eyes before he closed his eyes.

I missed him.

Drawing out my orgasms like he always did after I crashed hard, Lucas captured my lips harder than before. He was close, I could feel him swelling.

I reached down and raked my nails down his back, lower, until I felt his powerful back gripping his ass and pulling deeper.

He gasped against my mouth. *"Evie."*

Hot jets of warmth flooded me. I was gasping for air, working my hips as he ground deep, pumping me full of his heat.

It felt so much better than it ever had.

He was panting. *"Shit, I forgot a condom."*

I mentally calculated what time of the month it was.

"It's all right. I don't think I can get pregnant now—" he was still semi-hard in me as I said it. "We'll just make sure we do it next time."

"Next time?"

"Mhm," I pulled him down again, needing to kiss him.

CHAPTER 40
EVIE

IT DIDN'T MATTER HOW MUCH OF HIM I HAD.

I wanted more.

I met him in his office one afternoon to surprise him.

Since he mentioned he'd been having bad days, I thought I'd cheer him up a little.

I knew Lucas didn't talk about the ins and outs of his day-to-day, but I could see something darker in his eyes.

Not knowing what to expect, I showed up in my coat and heels, his secretary Jenny eyed me up and down dubiously.

My palms were clammy as I stood before her, feeling like a six-year-old reporting for a meeting with the principal.

My chin barely reached the desk. I thought maybe this might be something nice to do.

Instead now, I felt *apprehension*. I was in an office building. Half naked. Sorta naked.

Okay, so I was pretty naked under the coat.

"Miss…"

"Evie." I nodded with a smile, hoping for it to be friendly and not like I didn't belong here. "I'm here to see Mr. Devereaux."

"Ma'am, I'm sorry his schedule is *completely* booked. Is this something—"

"I promise I'll be quick." I hoped.

"I'm sorry, Miss…"

"*Evie.*" I insisted. "If you call him he'll know."

But Jenny didn't look like she was willing to budge and I felt guilty for even thinking I could show up unannounced.

"Jenny, what is that?" The door to our right swung open, and Lucas stood dressed like a sun-warmed demi-god in his Italian wool and silk, his hair just a little disarrayed from when I'd kissed him this morning.

He double-blinked, molten hot blue, taking me in.

"*Doll?*" His lips spread into a soft smile.

I smiled, feeling shy all of a sudden. "I wanted to come see you."

"Sir, you have a meeting in twenty."

His features turned to granite lightning fast, and I didn't know this side of him existed…but it was *hot. This is Lucas Devereaux.*

He turned to her, fire in his eyes. "Next time she comes to your desk, do not make her wait out here. I don't care what I'm doing, is that clear?" I felt bad for the poor girl, but she blinked and nodded. "Evie, get inside."

He held the door open for me, and I passed her a sympathetic smile as I walked in.

I'll bring her flowers next time.

I didn't miss the way he took in my shoes.

Thanks, Alisha.

The moment the door closed, I would've apologized if he had not locked the door and cornered me in his arms, dipping his head.

"What's the matter? Are you hurt?" His eyes were full of concern.

How do I tell him I came here for him? Because I'd been craving him?

"No, I'm alright. I just—" I looked around his office. "You have a meeting. I'm sorry, I didn't think."

This was a stupid plan. I was trying to channel my inner Alisha. I suck.

I was already having second thoughts. I wasn't Selena, not some vixen or cool operative. I was just *Evie.*

He gripped my face in his hands. "I can see your anxiety, tell me what's wrong. You wouldn't have come here if nothing was wrong."

But something *was* wrong. And it was currently needing something from him.

I looked up at him, and if he saw the look in my eyes, he blinked, and then his expression changed. I licked my lips.

"I just missed you."

His head dipped lower as he looked down at my coat. "Please don't tell me you're naked under there."

"Not exactly."

I reached with shaking hands for the tie and the buttons as I shook it off, and the muscles in his jaw ticked as he watched the fabric drop, revealing the outfit I wore courtesy of Alisha.

Not only had I asked her for a makeover, I got a glimpse of why Reed loved her in person, and her lingerie advice was...*magical*.

She'd found a shimmery green set she thought would look good, and it was so cute.

A little bustier making my breasts look enormous, a tiny skirt that totally showed my butt, little garters for my thighs, and it was almost too cute to destroy.

But I saw what it did for Lucas.

His hand covered his mouth. "Tell me you took a car here."

I bit my lip, watching his eyes widen even more. "The jacket covered everything."

He ran a hand down his mouth as he stood to his full height and looked down at me. He swore, closing his eyes.

"I needed you," I whispered. "I couldn't wait. You said you had a long day today..." I squeaked, trailing off as he kept his eyes closed.

"Not a word out of you." *Was he angry?* "I want to see you in the light."

His office was a little dark. "But your *meeting*—"

"Fuck the meeting." He all but growled something about blueprints as he carried me closer to the windows that spanned the entire side of his office.

The place was huge, but I could still see him working out of this place.

"Let me *see* you." And then he sat me down near his desk.

He pulled his chair back, sitting down like a king on his throne.

And I felt like the woman he had hired to please him for the day.

"You look beautiful, doll."

There he was, despite his intensity, he was still...the sweet man with this...dominant who was about to destroy me.

Standing in front of him like his doll, his slave, his woman to do whatever he wanted with.

"Come to me."

I did. My hair was loose and flowing, and I felt like I was under his spell.

"Did you miss my cock?" He said gruffly against my lips as he tugged me even closer. "Did you come here to please me?"

"Yes." I ached for him to touch me. To do anything to me.

"Does this outfit come with panties?" I shook my head. His fingers tugged the skirt. But even calling it a skirt was generous.

"Evie, you couldn't have had better timing." He tugged at the bustier, tearing it in his hands, and I bit back a cry at the beautiful fabric. "I'll get you more. A hundred more."

I felt my throat work when he dragged his mouth down the center of my chest, down, and then he swirled it around my stomach. He breathed steadily. "You always smell like candy."

Probably all the caramel and perfume I keep on my desk.

I put my hand on his chest. "I wanted to come and make your day easier..." I bit down on my lower lip. "I've had this fantasy for a while."

His brow furrowed, and then his eyes went wide as I sank to my knees before him. I loved going down on him. I did. It made me feel powerful like I was holding *all* of him.

And then *after* Lucas was always more unhinged and uninhibited.

But here? In his office? My fingers were already on his belt.

"Evie—" I didn't think, I moved.

My fingers reached for his pants as I sank between his legs, his groan leaving as I pulled him completely out, the erect, long, and thick length of him, the mushroom tip that I circled my tongue over, once, twice. I loved this.

I moaned around him and struggled to fit him in my mouth.

He leaned back, watching me, eyes shuttered as he swore. "You came here to tend to your man, doll?"

I nodded, already feeling my lips stretching around his length as my fist gripped him.

He groaned, watching me moan around him. "Such a good hungry slut you are, look at you. We both know you can fit it more."

I *could*. And I did.

His groan was muffled in his fist as I did. I was so wet. I felt so wanton. There were people outside moving around, living their normal lives, and I was under my man's *desk*, sucking *him* off.

"You look beautiful."

I hummed in approval. My breasts felt heavy with need, my clit swollen, and my body wanting a thoroughly hard pounding after. He sat with me between his legs.

And I sucked obediently.

Lucas's hands gripped my hair, pulling me back. "I need you to be very quiet right now. Can you do that for me?"

I nodded, licking my lips. "Why?"

His eyes dropped to my tongue. *"We* have a meeting."

Oh. My. God.

I didn't say a word, but my expression was *right now?*

"They can't hear us. Or see me." He looked at the screen and then back at me. "Eventually, I'll have to say *something.* Do you want to stop, or should I give you something to do with your mouth while you wait?"

A wild sensation went through me at being so…uninhibited.

And then I took him in my mouth again.

It didn't even matter because Lucas hit some keys, and I heard the dull murmurs of voices, which made the moment even more erotic.

I fisted his cock in my hands. I licked. Sucked.

Slowly stroking my tongue over his length. Letting myself tease the tip and swirl my tongue around it before hollowing my cheeks out.

Oh God, this was filthy.

I hadn't ever dared to be so bold. I reveled in it.

I took him to the hilt, staying there, loving the way he sighed, and his hand came around to keep me there until I gasped for air. I moaned with pleasure at the feel of him deep inside my throat.

I didn't find a rhythm so much as play with him.

And considering he was in on his meeting, I didn't think he minded.

His muscles tightened under me, and I swallowed him whole, finding a rhythm finally and bobbing my head.

His grip in my hair felt delicious and painful while I moved my fingers to my clit.

Oh god, I was soaking wet.

"Damn, baby. Look at you." I moaned with pleasure. "Such a good little slut, taking my cock like that, is that turning you on?"

I nodded and circled my clit. One stroke. Two. I was so close.

I felt filthy.

And I loved it.

Whenever Luke had to unmute himself to say anything, I was depraved as I sped up, just using my mouth, loving the way he cleared his throat when someone asked him a follow-up question, and I bit back a grin, taking him so deep, his hand gripped my head *tight.* I saw his jaw work.

I was so *close.*

I was going to come. Just from that alone. I heard people chattering.

They don't know you're his personal whore.

Someone who comes over in nothing.

Sucks his cock under his desk.

I felt *nothing* but heat and pleasure.

I couldn't stop little noises, little whimpers and moans, and Lucas tugged at my hair. I drew back, feeling the mess on my chin and wiping my face.

He shook his head without looking at me, the promise of him utterly losing it in his darkened eyes.

Not a single sound.

I saw the warning in his eyes.

And grew bolder, wondering *what would happen if I did push him.*

I went back to his cock, feeling drugged with my arousal, moving his free hand not on muting the meeting to gripping my neck.

I miss him. All of him.

He licked his lip when I looked up at him, watching me through lidded eyes. I began playing with my nipples and hard, tugging on them the way I liked him too, soft sounds escaping either way.

I was so close just like this. So wet. So free. I was too gone. If he knew or understood where I was at, I felt him move.

He typed something, clicking, and looked down at me for a hot second.

I was panting as he undid his pants a little more, and then he was on me. Dragging me out from behind his desk, turning me around, my ass high in the air, my face pressed into the carpet. *Yesyesyes.*

The first thrust almost took my breath away.

His voice was dark and low. "I can't control myself around you and that's what you want isn't it?" I did. I loved him like this.

Dimly, I was aware of people talking. I bit down on my lip to keep from screaming when I did come.

They can't see me.

But if they could, they'd get an eyeful. Lucas was baring me down to the carpet.

Oh God, *right* there. I felt like a sex goddess, lying there tempting this man who I knew would ruin me after. I'd never felt him move as he did, angrily snapping his hips into me.

His hand clamped down over my mouth. It was a fast and brutal rhythm. Strangled screams muffled into his hand, and I felt my eyes roll back as he began fucking me wildly.

And all I could do was *take.*

This is what I wanted. The city before me in the high-rise office expanded, the sun was shining down on me, and I basked in the feeling of the spot he had hit so *deeply*. I was climbing fast.

"Does my little doll need to come?"

I nodded. *Yes, yes, yes.* I pushed back onto him fucking him back despite his violently hard thrusts.

"So *tight*," he growled. "That tiny little pussy's struggling, but you take it like a good girl, don't you?"

I felt my legs trembling as I sobbed my agreement into his hand. *I was. It was so good.* I felt myself grabbing the floor and scrambling to find a purchase, nearly dislodging him in the process.

"Don't ever," he growled, the most guttural sound from him as I struggled. "Try to keep this pussy away from me."

He'd lost it. "I own this pussy now. Use it when I need it. Keep you here to fuck out my day *every single fucking day*."

Yesyesyes.

He punctuated his filthy words with thrust after brutal thrust until I gave up and screamed my agreement into his palm over my mouth.

I sounded like an animal being taken in the wild. I wanted that, too. I imagined him chasing me through the woods, taking me out there naked, where we were no different from anything else.

"Would you like that, Cherry? Being my personal whore? Let everyone know who I'm owned by. *Who I own*."

His hips pumped into my pliant and shaking body, my legs spread open with his feet.

Yes.

"Be a good little whore, and come on your master's cock."

Oh fuuccck.

My orgasm slammed into me.

I repeated his name until it was a prayer on my lips, uttered over and over as he pounded my body until I swore I knew the shape of him existed in me. The pleasure was so intense I began to cry.

"I'm not going to stop until you're red all over."

I was sobbing my pleasure and agreement into his hand. *He could do anything to me.*

And then he said nothing as he gripped me tightly to him, working his hips until he emptied all of himself, the hot jets of his orgasm flooding me.

I loved him like this.

Loved him taking me like his life was dependent on it. I was gripping the carpet floors, shaking wildly, and trying to just—*breathe*.

"You okay, doll?" I felt his lips move over my tears. I made a quiet noise as he kissed my cheek. "I wasn't too rough, was I?"

No. He was *perfect*.

~

"HOW DOES IT FEEL?" HE GROANED, SHOVING MY FACE INTO THE PILLOWS as he absolutely demolished me. I was screaming and loving every bit of this.

He'd teased my ass to the point where I wanted it. I needed it. And I was letting him.

"It feels so good." It felt *incredible*. He'd brought me home, bent me over and proceeded to fuck me until I cried again.

He was buried deep, and the sensation was so…different.

And *then* he put the vibrator in my pussy while he was—

Oh God. I was all *animal*.

Lucas had growled at my reaction. "Squeeze it deep, Cherry."

I was. I was *so...full*.

And I loved it. I couldn't think or feel anything. At all. He didn't turn it on, he just filled me everywhere.

"If I thought you were tight before…"

I felt…impossibly full now.

Like the tiniest brush of movement and I'd come.

And then he settled back on his knees, helping me up and keeping me sitting back on his lap, one hand going between my legs working on the vibrator.

I gasped, sliding my thighs wider on my knees.

"Suck." He slid two fingers into my mouth, one hand working between my legs, and I obeyed—and I *came*.

Hard enough to shake and see stars at the sensation of being so decadent at being consumed, *filled*, completely.

Behind me, he groaned as I felt my eyes roll back. *"That's my girl, come for me."*

How would it feel to be filled in every part—?

Incredible.

I was shaking as I sucked and it was the most intense I had felt with him, it felt *magnified*.

"I fucking *knew* this would be good for you."

He rolled his hips, and I groaned at the sensation of him somewhere

I never imagined and the toy inside of that spot in me that made me come every time.

"Filled *everywhere*, by me, I told you Evie, I would never share you, but I can make you my whore every single night."

I trembled, sucking his fingers as he stopped moving the vibrator, keeping it in me while moving his fingers to my clit. I breathed hard, as I felt how hard he was.

*Oh God, he wasn't done—*I might *die* from the pleasure.

He slid his fingers out of my mouth and down to my nipples, his other hand playing with my clit.

Oh God, I was going to die.

It's too much. Not enough.

"Let me take care of you," he groaned, as he began to move, and I leaned back against him.

I was nothing but *white-hot* pleasure for long, endlessly long, *searing* moments through my body as he worked every part of me growling his praise into my ears. I couldn't think. Couldn't focus.

Everything left me then. I was just *his*.

His woman.

"*Yours,*" I whispered to whatever he asked me, I was *gone*. Lucas bent me over, his hand on the back of my neck as he fucked into me.

Endless sensation radiated through me as he stroked deeper than he ever had. I was lost. Put back together.

Held together with something more than me. I'd never be the same again.

"Next time I'm going to fuck you like this when you come see me."

I came so hard with that confession, he followed.

Lucas flattened me down to my stomach, pressing me down. Holding me steady while I shook with the intensity.

"I got you. *Sweet brave girl, I got you.*"

CHAPTER 41
LUCAS

As I entered my apartment tonight, foreboding washed over me.

Something was off.

The heavy air had an unnatural chill prickling my skin.

Danger lurked beyond—I couldn't shake that feeling. Evie was preoccupied but promised to join me later.

Without Evie's sunshine and laughter, my apartment felt cold and distant. It was freezing here.

Walking in, I knew who'd be at the kitchen counter—a whiskey bottle and an empty glass.

Only Gabriel Monroe would break in and help himself to my alcohol stash.

I remembered licking Evie's favorite lychee drink off her body.

Now, her brother, in his gray suit, sat on my island.

I anticipated this moment.

Here we fucking go…

Secrets couldn't stay buried from a former elite CIA operative like him. I was surprised it took him this long to confront me.

Undoubtedly, he meticulously researched the building owner where Evie resided—I owned several city properties. Or even the charity. I'd been playing it loose. And fast.

His eyes fixed on the cityscape beyond, twinkling lights hiding inner darkness. We were invisible amidst the urban sprawl, but his presence loomed, a reminder of lurking shadows.

"How did you know?"

He uncorked the whiskey. "Pets for Vets? Her apartment building? She's got a tracker on her keychain. It's the lily." Of course.

He poured himself a glass. He was here to finish the job he started.

I undid my suit, tossing my jacket on the floor along with the flowers I had gotten for her. His eyes landed momentarily on the white lilies.

"How about I offer you something better?"

He took a sip. "What's that?"

"I help you find your wife's killer."

The temperature in the room shifted so quickly, his pale eyes focused on me like an animal. *"That's* how you knew about her."

"I can help you."

His look was savage. "What makes you think I'd *want* your help."

"You don't, but it's been seven years, and you need all the help you can get. You haven't been able to find the motherfucker who did it." I worked in breaking ground. If there was anything to be found, I could. If not, once Lucy came out of her cave, we'd work together. I dug buildings, she dug graves.

It was one and the same.

The thought made me a little sick to be honest, even as a SEAL I'd seen some shit, but the gruesome image of any woman being treated like Isobel, made my stomach sour, and the fury in me rose.

"I would do anything for Evie. Let me do the same for her sister. I'm not your enemy. I don't give a shit what my father did. I'm not him." I sure as fuck tried my best not to be. "The only way you'll keep me from her is killing me." I met his gaze.

"Until then, I'll take you. I know why you protect her. She's the last thing that belongs to Isobel, isn't she? You don't want to let her go because you'd let Isobel down. I'm not going to hurt her. I love Evie." I took a breath. *Let's fucking go.*

"You need to stay away from her."

I stilled. Nothing mattered to him. Nothing I did.

I looked into his eyes and saw cold fury.

"You're not going to be enough for her. Ever. Trust me on this. You're going to hurt her. And when you do? It's going to break her."

"What the fuck is your problem?"

He stood and got up from the island, and I braced myself. I stayed steady.

I'm never going to have his blessing, his respect, his anything.

And suddenly? It didn't matter anymore. I didn't care if he was

Evie's brother. I was never going to be enough for him. I would always be shit.

I can take him.

I was her man.

"The only way to keep you away is to kill you." Iceman watched me, and for a moment he looked inhuman. "Bad enough you and...*with Evie,* but now you bring my wife into this?"

"You're insane. You know that?" I blocked the fist coming for me, ducking.

Only to get one to my side. I groaned and didn't fold.

Motherfucker.

Gabriel spoke; his voice was dark, ice, and cold. "After you're dead, I'm going to dismantle your entire empire, just like years ago."

Years ago?

As he advanced, though, I stopped breathing as a red dot appeared on his white shirt. I frowned, what the—*above his heart.*

I wouldn't let him—

I lunged for him, tackling him down with all my strength, watching his eyes widen at me as the window behind me exploded in glass.

"*Get down!*" I felt fire. Fire in my arm. I gasped, hitting the ground with him.

And then we were both scrambling for cover as I heard distant screams from down below.

I dragged him and groaned about my arm. I looked down. I was hit. His wide, shocked eyes bled out of rage. He couldn't believe I'd saved him.

My respect for this man overrode our conflict.

He is Evie's brother.

And I am not my father's son.

His eyes moved to my arm which felt like it was *on* fire. I looked at my shoulder, bleeding raw.

"You took the hit for me?" Incredulous was putting it lightly. Why was there so much blood? And why did it burn like that?

"*Stay down.*"

Another shot took out the glass on the island, and the glass outside my window shattered.

Gabriel was hauling me down the hallway. "*What the fuck is happening?*"

I was losing too much blood. My arm felt wet. My arm was soaking through.

"Gabriel—*Gabriel*—let her—let her bring me back."

Frantic words barely audible over chaos as another shot rang distant. We both ducked. I needed Evie.

She was my lifeline.

The adrenaline rushed through me as we hunkered in the hallway floor. Pain seared through me.

I gripped my arm, blood seeping between my fingers.

Gabriel had ripped his jacket off against my arm, his intense gaze searching my face, the rest of me, for anywhere else.

My body protested every agonizing movement. Scorching sun beating on burning skin.

"*Oh fuck, that hurts*—" I broke at the chunk of my arm it had to have taken off.

"*Lucas.*" Icy eyes furrowed as he grabbed his phone.

Struggling to cling to consciousness, the world spun as I was dragged to safety. Voices blended in. Filled with screams and gunfire.

And then I was out.

As consciousness slowly seeped back, Evie's voice reached me like a lifeline pulling me from darkness.

"Come on, wake up."

The scent of caramel wrapped around me, a comforting embrace that felt like...mine. She smelled like mine.

Blinking away the haze, I found her there, her eyes lush and wet, fixed on mine with concern and relief.

"Luke." Her brilliant smile warmed my soul. "You're all right. We have you."

Evie, get out. Get out.

"He's bleeding all over. Did we call Adam?" Gabriel's gruff voice came from the corner, but my eyes were locked on Evie's face.

"Luke, don't move—"

A wave of dizziness and nausea washed over me as reality sank in.

"Evie, you gotta go home. It's not safe here." My words slurred as if through molasses. "*Gabriel*—"

I needed to warn him, protect him still, but Evie pressed something cool to my lips. I drank. A soft laugh escaped her despite her tears.

"Slowly, it's all right. There's more." She turned to look over her shoulder. "Gabriel, can you grab more of these drinks from the fridge?"

269

A grumble, then the fridge opening. "I don't get lychee juice when I get shot."

Nestled in Evie's lap, swirling questions filled my muddled mind.

Why was it so dark? What happened?

As searing pain lanced through my arm, Evie's worried voice cut the tension.

Gabriel couldn't look at her, and I knew I had done a lot of damage. Living up to my name's sake.

Gabriel's scorn cut deep. "Evie, he's a SEAL, or former one anyway, even in his pansy-ass suits."

Evie's defiant expression speared him. "Don't be mean to him!"

Gabriel's cruel reminder of our rift came through. "I can't believe you lied about sleeping with him. You didn't think to tell me? Someone's trying to kill him. You just—"

"You hate him—"

"Not now," Reed's firm growl came through while trying to mediate paused the onslaught as Gabriel yielded, seething silently.

"Both of you, calm down or take it outside, I can't do this right now. He's bleeding faster than we can stop it, and I have no fucking clue what's lodged in his arm right now."

Agony lanced through my arm.

Evie paled at Reed's grimace.

Then, a nasty-looking knife sliced my silk shirt. Reed examined the wound.

Where the fuck did he carry that?

"Don't move." His bright, focused eyes held me still.

"That thing that hit his arm matches the one from the kitchen." Gabriel stalked over, eyeing my arm.

"Two shots is sloppy."

A young blond man in soft green scrubs arrived with a large case. "I have him, Reed. Let me help."

Reed moved aside as this man took over. I caught his badge.

Adam Whittaker? Reed had a brother?

"Shortcake, come here, Reed needs to work with Adam."

Gabriel's quiet words brought no argument as Evie looked ready to protest. She took his extended hand, looking angrier than she ever had.

"Mr. Devereaux, look at me." Adam's firm yet reassuring voice cut through the haze as he shone a light in my eyes.

Working quickly and quietly through my drifting consciousness.

Adam said. "We need to stop this bleeding. Reed, grab more towels. I need to get it cleaned. A bowl or something?"

"I got the other bullet." Gabriel had a hand in his pocket, the other holding Evie's tightly.

Adam said quickly. "I'm going to have to put him under—"

"I got him." Reed was steadfast.

Then, a pinprick in my arm as Evie's widened eyes were the last thing I saw before darkness took me again.

"I love you—" It left my lips before I blacked out.

CHAPTER 42
EVIE

I LOVE YOU, TOO.

I hated not saying it.

I hated that he blacked out when he did.

As I stood there, watching Lucas grimace in pain, I was grateful when Adam put him under.

I wanted to rush to him. I wanted to be by his side, but untrained, I could only watch uselessly.

A noise left my lips that had Gabriel bringing me closer to him.

Even upset at his bedside manner, I felt his warmth and heat suffuse my entire being.

He was still the pillar I had always known him to be.

Even if I was angry with him. Adam's hands moved efficiently, asking Reed back and forth for things.

Reed grimaced. "He moved out of the way just in time. Designed like a Nosler but arrowhead-shaped. If he got hit with it if it sank into his arm?"

He would be dead.

Adam didn't look up from where he was stitching Lucas up with efficiency.

Gabriel swore. "Arrowheads?" He took the bullet from Reed, covered in blood. "Sound familiar?"

He shared a look with Reed.

I couldn't even hear them watching Lucas.

I covered my mouth with my hands as Gabriel tucked me into his side.

"What does it do?" I looked at the nasty-looking bullet.

"It rips through on contact, shatters the bones to fragments at the point of contact, so they can't ever heal properly. When it lodges into the body, and you try to pull it out? The victim bleeds out faster the more you do. In the end, no matter what you do, you can't save them."

I paled at Gabriels' cold explanation, looking at Lucas.

"It grazed him, but even then, with how quickly he's bleeding out—" It took a nasty chunk. I saw that gash. "It's sophisticated for an assassination."

Assassination?

Adam interrupted, looking at Reed. "He's going to need blood. I have to call Perla."

Reed looked at Gabriel with a look. "He's lost a lot."

"He's B negative."

I was B-positive, and I knew everything I could about him now.

Reed and Gabriel shared another silent look.

"What?" I glanced between them. "What is it?"

Reed stared at Gabriel pointedly, who grimaced, cursing. "Don't say I didn't do anything for you." He began removing his suit jacket, and then his shirt.

Reed's eyes were hard as he took me in. He wasn't happy about me being here either. "He's AB negative."

Of course, Gabriel has the rarest type.

Reed kept going. "It's good it was his arm. Anywhere else, he'd be bleeding out a lot faster."

I held back sobs, heart clenching at Lucas's pale, gaunt appearance. Lucas had told me he loved me. I had to be calm for him.

Adam hooked up with Gabriel to take as much from him as he could. "Not ideal, nor pleasant. I trust your recent checkups are cleared?"

Gabriel gave a terse nod.

The sight was macabre—my brother and boyfriend tethered, one giving life, one taking.

In that surreal moment, I saw something in Gabriel's eyes.

Despite his recent upset toward me and the rift between us now, he still cared enough to willingly save the man I loved, who he despised.

If Gabriel didn't care, he'd have let Lucas die.

Yet he endured silently, exposing his hidden tattoo as Adam's eyes flickered over the ink briefly.

"Adam, oversee his recovery..." Reed gave Adam a set of orders after that.

"Yes, sir."

"How long has this been going on?" Gabriel's concerned voice cut the silence as Reed stepped out with Adam.

With a trembling breath, I answered softly. "Months."

Gabriel exhaled slowly, and I felt the weight of his stare boring into me. "And you didn't think to tell me."

Tears burned behind my eyes as I finally met his intense gaze.

"I knew how much you hate his family. But he does, too. I love him. I love him so much." My voice cracked as hot tears escaped down my cheek. "I didn't want to be forced to choose between you."

Something flickered in Gabriel's eyes—raw emotion quickly shuttered behind his stoic mask. "You think you'd have to *choose* between me or him?"

Something in my chest tightened at that.

What was he saying?

"You said I couldn't..."

"I would move mountains for you, *even* if it was for a Devereaux. Someone just tried to take him out. A professional. You don't think this changes things?"

I had never argued with him. Never gone toe-to toe with this man.

"No, I know you. If he told you someone was trying to kill him, you'd laugh and joke about target practice," I whispered, gently threading my fingers through Lucas's hair. "It was an accident."

I told him how I met Lucas at the board game convention, bringing a twitch to his lips.

I told him almost everything, leaving out the stuff I couldn't—probably best since Gabriel would lose it. Gabriel stayed silent for a long moment.

"Are you going to find out who did this?"

Another moment of silence passed before Gabriel nodded. "They ruined my suit."

A beat passed.

"I'm sorry, Gabriel."

He didn't say anything. And that hurt more.

CHAPTER 43
LUCAS

When I finally pried my eyes open again, I was in a dimly lit hospital room—the sterile antiseptic scent and rhythmic heart monitor beeping, telling me I'd been out awhile.

I blinked groggily, wincing at the dull throb pulsing through my injured arm.

The empty room held only machinery's faint hum and distant hospital bustle.

Evie?

Then, as my vision adjusted to the low light, I spotted a small, curled figure on the corner couch—Evie, wrapped in a faded blanket.

She was still here.

"*Evie...*" I moved. And the machines lost it.

Evie jolted awake, panicked, hurrying to my bedside with tousled hair and a rumpled dress.

Those fucking dresses are going to kill me before any assassin.

Who bought her those boots?

Seconds later, Reed appeared in the doorway, his expression grim and assessing.

Adam was on his heels, already moving toward the machines with practiced efficiency.

"He tried to get up," Evie explained tremulously, grasping my hand like a lifeline. I squeezed her fingers weakly, guilt twisting my gut at the fear, and exhaustion etched on her beautiful face.

"I'm sorry," I mumbled, wincing as Adam checked my vitals. "I just...I needed to see you."

Reed looked worse for wear, covered in some blood, but he'd changed into a plain white shirt.

An entire arm covered in tattoos was visible, and I don't know why I hadn't known he had it and kept it covered up.

He emanated the same energy as Gabriel without all his camouflage. Evie's grip tightened as her eyes met his, her lip trembling as she fought composure.

I hated her fear and vulnerability because of me—because of loving a man like me.

She'd promised Reed she wouldn't see me, so he'd protect her. She turned on them both. I sighed. I did this. I made her choose between her family and me.

Adam stepped back as Reed got closer, giving him some leeway.

"It was my fault. Don't blame her. I did this." I could take the heat.

"It is not." She looked at Reed fiercely. "If you're going to blame anyone, blame me. I have free will. Isn't that what you always said?"

Reed's expression was indecipherable. He let out a breath.

"It isn't that simple. Adam, do what you gotta do." I watched Adam slide his syringe back into my IV.

Adam's kinder brown eyes met my expression. "Get some rest. We'll be here when you wake up."

"I'm not going anywhere." Evie squeezed my hand.

As I passed out, Reed was softly saying something to Evie.

CHAPTER 44
LUCAS

THE MUFFLED SOUNDS OF AN ARGUMENT FILLED MY EARS. I KEPT MY EYES closed though.

"It's not safe." Evie's worried, frustrated tone cut through the fog. "We need to take him to the manor until we figure out who's behind this."

"He's got the money to take care of himself."

That was Gabriel, who I didn't think would ever forgive me for *shit*.

"I don't run a charity. If anyone comes after me and mine again, Killian, you have my blessing to end every single motherfucker in his family since they're clearly out for him. I don't care if he saved my life. I saved his. *We're even.*"

That *stung*.

But I didn't expect Gabriel to like me, let alone tolerate me.

Someone else made an uncomfortable noise. Someone else swore.

How many people were in my fucking room?

"Why do you hate him so much?" I hadn't heard Evie sound like that; I hadn't seen wild anger in her until I'd betrayed her. "He hasn't done anything to us. He almost died!"

"Evie, don't provoke him. Gabriel, I got this." Reed was firm.

Gabriel's growl sent a shiver down my spine. "I don't want him anywhere *near* her."

"He's my person!"

Use your words, doll.

A silken, deep voice sliced through the tension. "If I may interject

277

your family feud. Lucas is right there. He reached out to me weeks ago after the first shooting attempt. This was way more than that. He can stay with us in Chicago. It might make it easier."

"What first attempt?" Evie snapped, her anger palpable even through the medicated haze. "He was just shot last night."

Oh. Shit.

It had been an entire day?

Evie wasn't done. "This has happened *before*? Why am I just hearing about this now?" Silence hung heavy, the weight of their gazes pressing down on me even with my eyes closed.

I'm awake now.

My eyes fluttered open slowly, still under the haze of pain. That bullet was aimed from far enough with enough velocity to take enough of a slice of my bicep.

Even now, it was on a dull burn.

Aidan continued as Killian's eyes flickered over to me.

"He called me for help. His family has a long history with mine. He asked for discretion. I gave him my word."

Reed's resigned tone filled the room as he noticed I was awake.

"Lucas had informed Gabriel about the first attempt long before this. He thought maybe Gabriel was behind it, given their history."

"And you didn't think to tell me?" That was aimed at Gabriel.

That was my girl.

"I didn't know you were..." Gabriel let out a disgusted noise, and it was clear he had turned on Reed. "You and her, you knew for how long? Did you not think I'd find out eventually?"

"How did you find out?"

"The lily. She agreed."

"You can have that back," Evie snapped. "I *cannot* believe you'd be so heartless! *He was shot, Gabriel!*"

A growl came from Gabriel, who looked stunned at her. I had done that. Evie loved Gabriel. And I had come between them.

"Both of you—" Aidan growled.

"Cut it out—" Reed and Aidan were the two voices of reason in the room snapping on Gabriel, not Evie.

Gabriel looked furious. I had never seen this much emotion from him as he stared at Evie in disbelief.

"I had nothing to do with it," Gabriel bit out, fury barely restrained. "But clearly, someone wants him dead."

"He saved your life," Reed stated plainly. "We don't know which one of you the shooter was aiming for, if they mistook you or if they didn't care, and the two shots were for both of you. So, I suggest you behave. For now."

Reed's firm tone allowed no argument. "He'll come to the manor. End of."

Gabriel made a frustrated noise that grated my nerves. "We got him medical. He took enough of my blood that he's probably going to mutate into me. Why the fuck am I allowing...him and his fucked up family *near me and mine?*"

Evie lost it. "I *never* thought I'd get to the day I would be *so* angry with you!"

"You didn't tell me you were *dating him*. I asked you so many times to *let me in*." Gabriel was not pleased; his anger was like a cloud of smoke bomb around us.

"I'm going to throw you out the window," Aidan grumbled.

"That's because I knew you'd be like this."

I felt pride in her ability to stand up for herself now, especially to the man that mattered the most.

Her voice wavered as she said. *"He saved your life.* That should mean something to you."

"Gabriel." Reed's quiet reasoning was a balm after Gabriel's vitriol. "He's not his family. If anything, he's about to be yours. I've been watching him and Lucy—"

"Who is the thief," Gabriel interjected.

"Who works for *me*," Reed countered evenly.

"Does this lady work for *everyone?*" Killian's voice was edgy as he asked in a hard tone. "I thought she was a fucking *archaeologist.*"

"What the hell is going on?" Everyone but Killian and Reed looked at me.

"You shouldn't be moving," Evie fretted, rushing to my side, swiping her eyes angrily. She looked exhausted and worn out. "Why did you keep this from me?"

"I didn't want to sway you. You shouldn't have been with me because you felt guilty for me." I shook my head, glaring at Gabriel. "What do you know? And Lucy being a thief? I want answers."

Gabriel scoffed, undeterred. "What part of your sister's a thief did you need me to explain?"

He shot Reed a look to say, *see, he's an idiot.*

"You have the *worst* bedside manners." Reed looked more annoyed than anything, trying to diffuse the mounting tension.

Aidan's amber eyes were hard watching this unfold; he sat in his suit by the window, leaning in the corner, his dark hair and expression regal, looking like a dark king.

Next to him, the lean wolflike figure of Killian with his mismatched eyes sat guarded and ready to attack.

Both brothers looked at Gabriel with concern.

Why are they both out here? Shit had hit the fan.

Reed looked at Gabriel. "Considering the favor she did you? I'd say you owe him."

What favor? What was happening?

Gabriel glowered, his anger palpable, as he looked at Evie, and she glared back at him.

"Lucas is coming to Titan with us. And no—" Reed cut a sharp look at Gabriel. "This isn't your charity. It's my fucking call. End of it." His firm decisiveness allowed no argument. "Go to Selena."

Gabriel snapped. "Why can't Garrett do it?" For a moment, his dynamic with Reed shifted. Reed held all the patience in the world for him.

They sounded like a married couple...

"Because you almost broke his leg the other day." Reed speared him with a look.

Gabriel looked ready to argue, so Reed played his trump card.

"Or you can call Alisha and explain to her why I haven't been home for the last forty hours?" Gabriel paled at the mention of Alisha. Which was...interesting, considering it was him.

That did the job.

Gabriel walked out without a word, his eyes trailing over Evie, his shark-like menace scattering a cowering nurse in his wake.

Reed sighed. "Killian—"

"I know. Make sure he doesn't kill Adam."

Killian lupine blue and amber eyes raked over Evie in a manner that I wanted to confront right there if I wasn't hooked up to ninety machines. I was feeling better already after the blast of anger and jealousy. She glared at him, too. *Atta girl.*

Combined with the shock? It was a deadly cocktail flowing right through me.

As they left, Reed and Aidan, along with Evie and myself, were in the room.

Reed nodded his head to Aidan while leaning against the door. "You want to do this?"

"Figured we'd just tell them both together." Aidan straightened his tie, looking at Evie. "I've never seen Gabriel that upset. In all the years I've known him."

Aidan was *friends* with Gabriel?

I should've fucking known.

Evie looked between them, confusion furrowing her brow. "Both? What's going on?"

Together Reed and Aidan began filling Evie on some aspects that I already knew.

My father, Charles, and Aidan's father, Cormac, had worked together all over the country.

Reed began explaining. "Charles thought it would be a good idea to cut corners, costs, hire people who couldn't speak English properly, and he made sure to pay them shit. So, when people started getting sick? Long hours, hard work, toxic chemical exposure, they couldn't fight back."

I felt my stomach rolling, empty, and pumped full of medication that wasn't doing its job.

Reed's eyes met mine. "Because he's a bully even to his kids."

Evie's eyes cut to me, and she squeezed my hand.

That he was. Reed's gaze met Aidan's, and the larger man leaned forward, his presence a looming storm front. Amber eyes bored into me as the first sickening drops began to fall.

"Eventually, when people started threatening them because of the numbers, Cormac helped keep it under wraps. A fact I remembered after we spoke when Killian and I wondered what the connection was. Those board members who were killed? That group was the last of the ones who knew what Charles was doing."

Aidan looked at me. "I thought some of those names sounded familiar. I remember—" He looked at Reed, who shook his head and moved his hand in a *not-yet* motion.

Aidan looked at me again. "When you told me someone was after you, I didn't know until Killian confirmed it when he started digging."

Next to me Evie squeezed my hand shaking and I wanted to hold her closer, but I forced myself to listen.

Reed and Aidan exchanged glances as though checking each other, and I didn't know they worked that well together. "When those people started getting sick, dying of cancer and illnesses...your father buried the truth. Paid off families, silenced witnesses, the whole thing."

"He used Cormac because originally the O'Hara's ran New York, but interests changed." Reed's tattooed arm stretched out over the couch. "Are you both still good?"

Evie nodded.

"My dad made sure he killed off anyone who opposed him?"

Aidan looked at me with some semblance of remorse. "When we tried finding the connection to just your case? That is the one common between you and everyone else. We are not even looking at Lucy's case, just yours. Hers is a different story entirely."

I shook my head numbly, denial's last futile grasp slipping through my fingers. "I had no fucking clue."

"How?" Evie's soft query cut through the fog swirling around me. "You took over as CEO?"

Reed leaned forward. "Sometimes, kid, new leaders are left blind by the old guard silencing whistleblowers," Reed stated. "When Lucas took over after his PTSD and deployments, his dad made him an unwitting patsy. He didn't know—"

"Because no one would tell him, even if they did know," Evie finished, her realization a blade twisting in my gut. "They were too afraid. Your father silenced everyone."

"All but five. Four are dead." Aidan held up one finger, the damning count searing itself behind my eyelids.

I already knew the answer, but I asked anyway, mouth dry with dread. "And I'm the last one."

"Kinda." Reed looked irritated.

Aidan shared another loaded look with Reed before dropping the final anvil. "You...and your father."

What?

The world tilted violently as nausea surged. "*I just found out—*"

"Nobody would believe you." Aidan's words were ice picks lobbed directly at the fragile remaining shards of my identity. "I couldn't understand until I talked to Reed. I had a suspicion, but Reed and I both agree. Someone's out to kill you for what happened to their family member."

Evie's shaking voice grounded me, if only momentarily. "Someone out there is trying to kill Lucas now because they're trying to get revenge?"

"Someone has already been running around New York murdering four out of five of the individuals responsible in this city for what happened." Reed's voice was steady as he watched Evie. "Two nights ago was a test run. It'll happen again."

282

He looked at Aidan. "I need to change my clothes before it does."

Aidan smirked.

"Liam is cross-referencing someone's family member who might've died recently with the attacks on his life. He's trying to find a connection between Lucas and the attacks."

"But Killian said whoever it was, was a professional hitman. Not some random—" I stopped. "It's a relative."

Of course, my father would kill someone's family who was related to a professional hitman.

The sins of my father.

I was forgetting something, though. But this was just about me and the other board members someone felt were guilty of not getting *justice.*

"Is there anything else I need to know before we go to the manor?"

"Just one—" Aidan broke off as he looked at Evie. "Sorry, little Monroe, you're up."

Evie? "What does Evie have to do with my family?"

Reed looked sorry as he took her in. "Evie, do you want me to talk to you like you're my sister or you're my operative?"

"Operative."

He nodded, and his face shifted. "I hope you forgive him for this."

Evie frowned, puzzled by his words. And I was too.

Aidan didn't mince words, his gravelly tone laced with a terrible finality. "Devereaux doesn't just have real estate on the East Coast."

"No, they have properties all over the globe," she said calmly but confused.

Aidan nodded. "Including the West Coast. There was a line of hotels owned by Mercury Group. All over California. It was a line known for having a series of issues. Safety violations. All of them were torn to the ground by Lucas when he took over. He thought it was due to asbestos." Aidan pointed at me. "But it wasn't."

I knew what he was talking about.

What did that have to do with Evie?

"Your mom worked for the Devereaux's. She was hired for all the reasons we just said earlier." Reed was level.

He pointedly watched Evie. "Until she got sick. Stage 4 lung cancer. A bunch of the workers died the same way. Shortly after, Charles Devereaux buried the entire thing. Got a super-powered PR firm to make it go away. Make the victims look like they had chain-smoked or worked elsewhere or *worse*—painted them as criminals."

I felt Evie's hand slip from mine.

Her mouth opened and closed as her eyes welled.

Reed's eyes were steady as he held up a hand to Aidan to pause.

"Gabriel found you, and when he found out? He stepped in and tore everything apart. He got Aidan to take over the O'Hara's syndicate from his father. Together, Gabriel and I went after Charles. We were busy that month. We took out everything, and Gabriel put Lucas in charge. We went after Charles."

Reed looked at me. "It might explain why your father hates Gabriel. And Gabriel hates your entire family. Charles tried to fight back. But we had more dirt on him. Plus, Aidan was discreet, and he didn't give a shit about..." Reed trailed and shook his head as Aidan smiled in a way that looked awfully like his brothers.

Reed shot Aidan a look. "Gabriel threatened Charles. Forced his hand. When Lucas took over, I had Aidan keep an eye on him without anyone ever knowing, and Lucy worked for me after she got into trouble several times. Between Lucas running a company, he couldn't handle a sister running amok. So, I did. Aidan made sure he stayed close to Lucas. Enemies and friends...all that shit. We wanted to make sure we had full control. Gabriel doesn't tolerate a lot. Neither do we." He motioned to Aidan, who nodded.

Evie went utterly still beside me—a statue carved from ice. I saw the tears falling, and I could do *nothing* for her.

"Gabriel *never* would've told you," Reed said softly. "He didn't want you to know your mother was a victim. He wanted you to think it was a natural way to go. And he never would have told you—*but then you two*—" Reed pointed at us.

Then understanding bloomed in those beautiful caramel eyes, raw and terrible as a physical wound.

Aidan spoke up. "We won't bother explaining the rest."

I watched, paralyzed in horror, as the light drained from her face.

This was why Gabriel hated me. My family.

Fat droplets streamed down her cheek, the memories crashing over her in ruthless waves of comprehension flashing on her face.

Her mother. Her cancer.

Cruel twists of fate that I had never imagined could be tied to the depravity of my father's legacy. In that instant, everything became crystal clear.

Gabriel's seething hatred for me, the violence simmering ever-present beneath his restraint. Reed's grudging tolerance left me ever the outsider.

All rooted in the truth.

"That's why Gabriel never said a word," Evie whispered, her voice quivering. "All this time, he knew."

And in that moment, I knew with every anguished fiber of my being that I would never be worthy of Evie's love...not after this.

"*He knew,*" she repeated.

Aidan was the one who said. "Gabriel knew, and he never wanted to break you."

No, but I had.

He had known this entire time.

My father had killed Evie's mom.

CHAPTER 45
EVIE

I WAS MOVING, VISION BLURRED BY A HAZE OF ANGUISH. I COULDN'T SEE. I called him heartless.

I called Gabriel heartless.

Come here, shortcake.

Just you and me, family.

There will be no one else.

Nothing else mattered. No one else.

Cut deep, I stumbled.

"I need to see him." I couldn't be in the room anymore.

I felt everyone watching me, and I wanted to shatter. And the only thing my body knew was…home. *He is my home.*

I had screamed at him. *Gabriel.*

Reed stood as I walked to the door in a trance. I felt on the verge of shattering. I couldn't see anyone else.

Fate's cruel joke crushed me under its immense weight.

The pain in my chest was all-consuming, making me feel violently ill.

I drifted without direction, Gabriel's private clinic a dizzying, disorientating maze. I walked slowly as if the very air around me had thickened to a viscous pool, dragging at my limbs.

Tears blurred my vision as I gasped for deep, steadying breaths that would not come.

"Evie?" A blurred, indistinct figure swam into view ahead. *Adam.* His hands bracing me.

"Gabriel," I whispered, his familiar presence, the only anchor in this roiling sea of turmoil. "Where is he?" Something inexplicable yet powerful tugged me toward my brother.

I stumbled blindly with Adam, who put his arm around me. He knocked on a door, and I couldn't see.

Gabriel's gray suit filled my narrowing tunnel of sight.

I couldn't look at him. He closed the distance in a long stride, hauling me into his chest.

I made no sound, feeling as if the slightest parting of my lips might unleash a scream to shake the foundations of the earth itself.

So, instead, I allowed myself to be pulled into his solid form, cradled and carried as if I were a kid.

The same kid he met in a similar world.

I had come with the intent to *rage* at him for keeping secrets.

For lying to me by omission over something so visceral, so tragically life-shattering.

But he hadn't lied—not really.

He had simply done what he always did: protect me, shield me from the harsh realities he knew would bring me low. I felt it sink into my skin, and I gasped.

It's why he worked so tirelessly to keep me away from the legacy of the Devereaux's.

I had *never* known a pain so utterly annihilating as this.

A white-hot anguish that seared through my very essence, the devastation of learning that Luke's family had been responsible for robbing me of Mama.

I wanted to unleash a scream; it built up immense pressure behind my eyes, and I wanted to cry out until my voice was gone.

But the words caught in my ravaged throat like shards of broken glass.

Gabriel murmured something, the vibrations of his rumbling baritone a small comfort against the void surrounding me.

Adam asked if we required anything at all, then excused himself to go watch over Selena as the door closed, allowing us our tiny sanctuary away from prying eyes.

Only then, cocooned in the protective circle of Gabriel's arms, did I allow the dam to burst.

Great, racking sobs tore from the deepest pits of my shattered soul, each one wracked with the entire cumulative weight of my grief—of almost losing Lucas.

Of watching him almost die, of discovering the deranged force sought to snuff out his life, and *finally*...the cruel revelation that the Devereaux's themselves had decimated my world once before by taking Mama from me.

I was that lost, hollowed fifteen-year-old once more.

"I have you, shortcake," Gabriel soothed, his solid warmth and strength the sole tether anchoring me to this reality. "It's all right."

Long moments passed as I sobbed into his arms.

But it *wasn't*, and some small lucid part of me knew it wouldn't be all right for a long, long time to come. Not at all.

That kernel of truth was what Reed had spoken of indirectly—the need for me to find some way, *any way*, to forgive Lucas.

For things he hadn't done.

For the things he paid for daily.

"You knew."

"I knew you'd get like this," he replied, devoid of accusation or heat —just a simple statement of fact laid bare.

"But yeah, I always did, I didn't know how to say it." *No, he usually never did.* "Every time I look at him, I see you, crying over your mom's body, and it makes me angry to think that if I had been a second late—"

I wouldn't have him. Or anybody.

I wouldn't have the life I do now.

I could see why Gabriel's hatred ran deep for him. His calloused hands brushed soothingly through my hair as he cuddled me closer.

"I wasn't expecting him. When I found out about him, I tried keeping him away from you."

He paused, seeming to weigh his words carefully. "I think Reed did his best to help when he realized Lucas wasn't like the rest of his twisted family. But every time I see him...hear his name...I think of—"

Every time Gabriel laid eyes upon Lucas, he was reminded of my pain, of Mama. But it wasn't his fault. Even I recognized it.

I can't imagine why Gabriel hates my family, but I can imagine several reasons why.

And at that moment, as Gabriel simply held me with the grounding warmth, I was reminded of one thing—I was no longer that fifteen-year-old girl.

She had grown up. And she had choices to make. She could live in the past.

Or. She had a choice.

"I like him." *No, I love him.*

His voice was wry. "I gathered that."

"Is it because of who he is, or is it because he's a man?"

Gabriel answered with zero hesitation. "Both." He paused. "I realize I probably won't ever be okay with you dating. Men are awful."

"You're a man."

"Exactly."

A breathless laugh, despite my anguish, left me. Only Gabriel could. His lips quirked.

"Are you upset with what his father did, or are you upset you feel like Lucas has had to pay for it?"

I took a breath. "I don't blame Lucas. It just *hurt*. I felt like I was in the hospital again, and Mama was right there. And I *knew* how and why she got so sick."

I wiped my eyes again, looking at Gabriel's own soft, pale ones. "I think about how much she suffered, and how hard she worked, and how dirty she was done. It really hurt.

But I know Lucas never did it. *He didn't even know.* And now someone's trying to come after him and his family over the same thing I went through with Mama."

He wiped my cheeks with his thumb. "I tried to give you the best because she would've wanted that. It's the least I could've done for your family."

I told him in Spanish that Mama would be so proud of him. She would've thought he was handsome for Isobel, and she would've loved his appetite.

I rarely spoke Spanish with Gabriel. But I knew he was fluent and sounded like a native.

When I did, he said he liked it more than when we spoke English.

His eyes, a mesmerizing shade of pale blue, held a softness that made my heart flutter. I knew I had to ask him the question that had been nagging in my mind.

"Can I ask you something?" The words tumbled out, a sense of urgency in my voice. It was now or never at this moment.

"Always," he replied, his voice soft.

As he helped me off his lap, he gently wiped my eyes and cheeks, and I gathered my courage.

"Why didn't you tell me Oracle was Isobel?"

The moment the question left my lips, I watched as his entire demeanor shifted. Even in his arms, I could feel the depth of emotion I had stirred within him.

His gaze intensified, locking onto mine. "I didn't want to pressure you to follow in her footsteps. If you want to work on the program she left behind, it would be yours out of choice. Not guilt."

His words carried a weight of understanding. He knew how much I loved working on Oracle and how it had become a passion project for me.

I nodded, appreciating his thoughtfulness.

"She did it as her passion, but...it wasn't what she always wanted to do."

"What did she want to do?" I asked, my voice trembling slightly as I wiped away the remaining tears. The energy in the room shifted, an almost palpable change whenever Isobel was mentioned.

Gabriel became still, like a statue carved from marble. His eyes darkened, a hint of sorrow swirling in their depths. "She just wanted to be normal."

The words were simple, but the ache in his voice made my chest tighten.

I found myself opening up to him, sharing the challenges I had faced with Oracle, the breakthroughs I had made, and the full potential I had unlocked. I even confessed about the Red Hat training, knowing he wouldn't judge me for Liam's involvement.

As I delved into the anomalies I had traced back to Cape Verde, Gabriel's eyes flickered with interest.

A small smile played on his lips as he listened intently.

"The Black Hat sits in Cape Verde?" he asked his eyebrow arching, impressed by my findings.

There was a look in his eyes I had rarely seen.

He did it when he was focusing on his prey. The Black Hat.

"Possibly," I explained how, between Selena and everything else happening in Titan, I wouldn't have said a word.

That had been nearly two weeks ago.

Alisha and everyone else were recovering, and my boyfriend ended up with a target on his back. Gabriel's eyes sharpened, but his smile remained. I explained to him that Selena had been caught in the crosshairs on the same street as the team.

"And you didn't tell anyone, did you?"

I confirmed that I wouldn't make a move without his input.

"Keep it that way," he instructed, a pleased glint in his eye. "I want you to find the Black Hat." I agreed without hesitation.

As we sat there, the weight of my emotions pressing against my chest, I found myself opening up to Gabriel.

I confided in him about the sense of loss that had been consuming me lately and how I longed to talk to Isobel, even though I knew it could never be the same.

The words about my conversation with Lucas lingered on the tip of my tongue, but I held them back. I could never bring myself to accuse Gabriel of hurting Isobel.

Instead, I approached the subject gently, expressing my desire to know more about her and maybe, someday, *visit her* resting place. I already figured out he was a ghost for the same reason Selena was, no doubt.

His gaze met mine, steady and unwavering. "She's buried next to your mother," he said, his words carrying a sense of finality. Deep down, I knew there was a reason for everything, and I trusted that Gabriel had never caused her harm.

"I'd like to ask you for a favor, shortcake," he said, his voice softening.

"Anything," I replied without hesitation. For him, I would do *anything*.

The next words that left his lips felt like a blow to my very soul.

"I don't want to talk about her anymore."

The impact of his statement hit me like a physical force, stealing the air from my lungs.

"I'm ready to start moving on," he continued, his voice quiet yet resolute like he didn't just take the air from lungs. "The last few weeks changed my perspective on a lot. It's time I start moving forward."

It was like a sledgehammer *shattering* my chest, the pieces of my heart shattering with each word.

As I looked into his eyes, I saw a part of him that seemed to have vanished, leaving behind a void that I couldn't quite comprehend.

Gabriel leaned forward, pressing his lips gently against my forehead.

"I will always love you, nothing will ever change that, no one will take me away from you," he whispered, his breath warm against my skin.

Tears streamed down my face, my vision blurring as I struggled to form words.

"But w…what a…ab…bout—" My voice broke. *"Stories?"*

A sad, beautiful smile curved his lips.

"I'll still tell you stories," he assured me, his voice laced with a bittersweet tenderness. "I just don't want to talk to you about the worst moments of my life. I'll tell you the best, yeah?"

I nodded shakily. I imagine it was like me repeating about how Mama died over and over again.

It did hurt even now.

The soft light cast a gentle glow on his features, highlighted and strikingly beautiful despite not sleeping properly.

For me, for Lucas. He and Reed never got a break. And Reed had almost lost his family. *No wonder he's fighting so hard for me and Lucas.*

"One time, I took her out, and I thought I was taking her to a place she had never been to," he began, a soft smile playing on his lips. "Turns out your sister was a regular there. After the waitress who worked there told your sister and her best friend a sob story about how someone stole her dog, an ex-boyfriend or something."

Gabriel paused as his eyes opened, full of an emotion I only recognized when he talked about her.

"Your sister decided it would be a great idea to steal the dog *back*."

Even Selena wouldn't do that. My mouth dropped open. *Isobel?*

He went on. "She distracted the ex-boyfriend while her best friend snuck in and grabbed the dog. In return, the waitress let them *both* eat for free. I had no idea. I found out *weeks* later. *After* the bill came back at zero—" He paused, his cheeks flushing slightly, that smile on his lips.

My sister was a rebel.

I gaped at him, taken aback by the sudden shift in the conversation.

It took me a moment to realize what he was doing—he was trying to show me what he meant, to give me a glimpse into the memories he cherished.

He liked that part of her.

Gabriel, always the sphinx, was telling me *what* he meant.

That familiar smile returned, lighting up his face. He leaned his head back, his eyes drifting shut as if savoring the memory.

Understanding washed over me like a gentle wave.

It seemed easier for him to talk about Isobel now, to share the moments that brought him joy.

Perhaps, in his own way, he was finally letting her go, allowing himself to move forward while still holding onto the love they shared.

"You'll tell me more stories," I said softly, a statement rather than a question.

"I can do that. But be warned, she made Selena and Nate look tame."

A bubble of surprised laughter escaped my lips, mixing with the tears that still clung to my lashes.

In that moment, I saw a different side of him—a man who had loved deeply, who had suffered immensely, but...he deserved to move on...it felt so painful to hear him say that, and I didn't know why.

Something twisted in my chest.

"So that's why you didn't tell me," I teased, a playful glint in my eye. "You were afraid I'd get ideas."

His nod was accompanied by a low laugh, the sound filling the room with a lightness that had been absent before.

"How did you not go crazy?" I teased.

That smile remained as he admitted softly. "I did."

My own smile faltered, the weight of his words settling in my chest.

"You keep crying like that shortcake, and you can water your plants just by sitting here," he teased gently, his chuckle mixing with my embarrassed laughter. "Come here, sweetheart."

I didn't hesitate, wrapping my arms around him tightly, his lips on my temple, my cheeks. *I love this man so much.*

"I love you," I whispered, pouring every ounce of my heart into those three words. It was a love that had taken root years ago, growing stronger with each passing day. *"I love you so much."*

"Do you remember what I told you years ago? My love will *never* be conditional." I nodded through my blurry vision. "Even if you are with him." He grumbled about something about him not deserving me, and I laughed low.

Nobody would deserve me, according to Gabriel.

Long moments passed before we finally stepped outside the room. Gabriel rubbed his chest right over his tattoo, his gaze sweeping the hallway.

It was empty, save for a nurse stationed at the end of the hall, right in front of Luke's door, her head was down looking at a clipboard.

The nurse's blond, almost silver, hair was swept back, and her hourglass build was visible even from a distance, the way her top tucked into her waist.

Gabriel's eyes lingered on the nurse for a long moment, an unreadable expression on his face.

"You're wrong," I said.

His gaze flickered to me, amused. "About?"

"You being awful." I would've smiled at his expression had I not been teasing him. "No way you got my sister to fall for you with that attitude."

I grabbed his hand. "Come on, let's go get you food."

I felt light laughter leave me as he muttered about rabbit food.

CHAPTER 46
LUCAS

I SAT ALONE IN A ROOM CALLED THE LION'S DEN AT GABRIEL'S MASSIVE estate, where everyone was currently staying for the night.

In the corner, I spotted a letterman jacket and women's boots looking similar to Evie's minus the heels on these, belongings of whoever had occupied this room before me.

Killian had mentioned that both of them had moved out.

My mind was reeling from the bombshells that had been dropped on me.

The realization that my dad was a murderer hit me like a ton of bricks, shattering any sense of normalcy I had left.

And then there was my sister—a *thief*.

But the hardest blow of all?

The truth about Evie's mother.

My father had murdered her, unknowingly...

While Gabriel had rescued Evie from foster care?

How many lives had my family ruined to get to where I was?

If Gabriel hadn't intervened, what the fuck would have happened to Evie?

I hung my head, the weight of it all threatening to crush me. I felt lost and alone, desperately needing a moment to process the harsh truths that had been laid bare before me. Laid in front of me like a dead body waiting for me to view. I felt sick.

Reed had brought me to the manor, mentioning something about Gabriel taking Evie home while he texted Alisha.

Evie hates me.

Reed didn't say a word, but I noticed the dark circles under his eyes and my blood still staining his clothes.

He seemed to be fading out, still on the phone with Alisha despite the late hour. Texting. Calling his girlfriend.

Reed had assured me that he would handle Lucy and the fact that he was working my case with Liam.

Adam, who I now *knew* was Reed's brother, had provided me with bandages and other supplies to clean my wound, which was already healing better with sleep and medication.

The brothers had exchanged a look of exhaustion with each other, and Adam was instructed to come to the manor in the afternoon to check on me.

Even though the wicked-looking bullet had cut my bicep, all I wanted was to sleep like the dead.

I wasn't sure how much time had passed, but I felt like I could sleep forever.

As the car approached the gates, I couldn't help but marvel at the Titan headquarters. This was the Greenwich manor. Evie's home. Her life was here. Not with me.

Reed had gestured for Killian to accompany me to a room at the manor.

Killian led me down winding hallways and through rooms larger than I could have imagined, even with my wealth.

This is Evie's home.

"Call if you need us," Killian said quietly. "As someone who comes from a family as fucked up as yours, you are not your father's son. None of us are."

Of course, he knew.

He had filled in Aidan, who had delivered the blows.

As the surprise rocked through me, Killian's lips tipped into a hint of a smile before he left the room.

WHEN I GOT OUT OF THE SHOWER, I WAS BONE-DEEP TIRED.

I want to sleep forever.

My apartment's wrecked. My family sucks. My sister is missing.

My company is under attack.

And someone's trying to kill me.

I crawled into the bed, towel dropping on the floor, feeling like shit. I was safe at the manor—but I knew they were coming.

I didn't know why Reed thought this estate would stop them.

I sighed, and the moment my head hit the pillow, I was out like a light.

In my dreams, I dreamed of my mom.

Wondering if she was at peace. Wondering if I ever made her proud. Lucy, *wherever* she was.

If she was safe, I'd get a second chance with her.

Be a better brother.

And Evie.

I dreamt of Evie. Making love to her, her weight against my good arm, sliding over my body, her lips on mine.

I love you, Luke. I love you so much.

Love you too, doll.

I did not expect my body to have dreams about Evie, this *graphic*.

This real.

But I wasn't about to wake up when I felt my dick stir, and I recognized the feel of her mouth trailing kisses down my body, her hands pressing into me. I memorized that sensation.

I knew it was a dream.

But damned if I didn't love this fucking woman.

Love you, doll. Love you.

She echoed the sentiment as I gasped awake the moment she took me in her mouth.

Holy. Shit.

"*Evie.*" And then I threw my head back with a ragged groan as she swallowed me, all of me.

Evie wasn't a dream.

She was here, in my bed. Why?

I gripped the sheets tightly as she took me the way she knew I fucking loved. The back of her throat worked, swallowing me, and I groaned.

"Come up here—*no, fuck*, not like that." Oh *shiiiitt*. I needed her now. I couldn't fucking think. "*Evie—*"

She popped me out of her mouth, moving to straddle me. I didn't even breathe as she pressed me into her, a whimper leaving her lips.

I swore. "Evie, lean forward on me...good girl, come here, give me your mouth." I kissed her hungrily. "Sweet, brave girl, trying to sneak into my bed."

I smiled at her soft, shy smile. "Push back."

I met her halfway, loving her gasp. I could feel it in the sheer dedication she had trying to fit me inside of her. I groaned as I slid in deeper.

"*Condom*—" I gasped, a last-ditch attempt at responsibility.

"I don't care—" She kissed me wildly. I groaned as she worked her hips until she took all of me.

"*Evie*—" I held her face in my hands, searching her eyes.

"*I don't want to talk*—" she whispered, her pussy fluttering around my throbbing dick, making it hard to form words. "I just want you."

And then she kissed me again. I pushed her away a fraction.

Her eyes bore into me. I processed then, as she didn't move, what she was asking me.

"*I can't do that to you*—" I started, my voice hoarse with desire and conflict.

"*Yes, you can. You can terminate the contract*—" Her words were urgent, pleading.

"*Evie*—" I tried to interrupt, to make her see reason.

"*Luke*—" She pressed her hands down on my chest as if that could hold me down. Her touch burned through me. "I am *asking* you for whatever I want. *I want you to make love to me.*"

I knew what she was asking me. I knew neither one of us could say it outright. She was afraid. I was *afraid*.

She forgives you.

She's begging you to have your fucking kid. Even after everything.

And fear made people do stupid shit.

I knew my fate.

I stared at her for long seconds, long moments of absorbing her bright eyes, taking me in the same way she had when she told me she loved me, the way she forgave me for everything.

The way she held my face.

The way she sat on my fucking dick. *I knew. She knew.*

Understanding passed between us, silent but profound.

Something shifted in me at that moment, a seismic change that rocked me to my core.

I brought her mouth down to me.

Keeping my mouth on hers, I snapped my hips up to her body.

I kept my body close to hers, pumping my hips back in long, easy strokes that weren't as violent as I'd demolished her in the past.

This was different.

This was making love. Her eyes searched mine, gasping against my lips.

"I wanna make it last. Want to fill you all night. Don't wanna make you sore."

I couldn't form sentences properly, overwhelmed by sensation and emotion.

Just feel her.

I confessed, the words torn from my throat. "You were the only thing that made me feel like I was a better man—"

I didn't know who was crying.

She wiped my eyes and hers, the tender gesture nearly undoing me.

"Just love me for tonight," she whispered. *"Please."*

Anything you say. I tucked her head into my neck, fucking into her. My *girl.*

Her whimpers and squeals in my neck felt like music to my ears, and I promised I'd love her forever.

As long as I could. Evie worked herself down in tandem with my hips, and I was groaning, losing myself in her.

"P...please, come inside me, Luke."

Oh. Fuck. Me.

I lifted my knees just a little, the leverage allowing me to hit her— *right there*—over and over again.

I was fucking into her like a man possessed. With the need to fill. The need was pulsing through me.

Plant my seed so deep it would finally grow. A better Devereaux. A softer one. With Evie's heart and her eyes, not mine. *Not me.*

Evie screamed into the pillow as she came, and I followed her, lost in a haze of pleasure and love. I put my hand over her mouth.

"I don't want them to think I'm hurting you."

She moaned against my hand. It was always so intense with her. Even more, knowing I was trying for something with her—a fucking baby. When I finally kissed her, I couldn't stop.

"Stay like this," she gasped. "Don't move."

"I'm not going anywhere." I wasn't going to move. For a long moment, I stayed with her. And my mind worked. "I'm guessing this helps...?"

I was trying to have a baby.

"Yes." She looked adorable, smiling all shy like that, and I felt my heart crack open. "I looked it up before coming to your room."

I raised a brow, and she turned so pink I was fighting the urge to throw her down and fuck her harder again. "But the best positions are from the back."

I smiled softly at her through low-lidded eyes. "And we both know you don't like that."

"It's not *that*." I loved when she got all shy like I wasn't balls deep in that pussy. "Oh, don't smile at me like that, I like looking into your eyes when you…"

Yeah, she did.

"We could do it in front of the mirror." I looked at the wall behind her. "It might help you."

I felt her tighten around me.

My sweet, brave girl. I love you.

CHAPTER 47
EVIE

I MISSED FALLING ASLEEP WITH HIS HEAD ON MY CHEST.

My fingers threaded through his hair.

My heart had calmed down hours later as he finally passed out after fucking me standing up. My legs were like Jell-o. Throat a little sore from screaming. And my heart?

Didn't know what to feel.

I was processing what my last few days were like.

Everyone else at Titan must've had *years* like this. Parts of me shifted tonight.

The last forty-eight hours. I was...something was happening to me. I felt different from the whirlwind of events, finding out about Mama, Lucas, Isobel...

It was too much.

I laid there feeling like sex was just taking part of it off.

This is why everyone had an outlet. And I had never needed one.

I didn't know what was happening to me. Lucas' head on my chest felt like it kept the emotions like smoke tendrils from escaping me.

He'd almost died. He'd *saved* Gabriel. He *never* hit Reed.

I don't want to be my father's son.

He wasn't.

You're a good man, Luke Delaney.

My eyes no longer watered; instead, the smoke tendrils were shifting inside of me, transforming, forming a wall of resolve, rebuilding me as someone I didn't recognize. *Was I becoming a Gray Hat? A different version of Evie?*

Even now, the new me refused to fall asleep. I wanted to safeguard this man despite not sleeping for a few hours. In the corner of my eye, a shadow *moved*.

I turned my head slowly.

Someone was *outside* the window. *In the yard*. My heart rate sped up, but I was calm. With Lucas over me, his soft exhales, I was...alert.

"Luke?" I murmured, but he remained deep in slumber, oblivious to the danger lurking outside our window.

A sense of unease settled over me as I saw the shadow.

From the second floor, I could see the backyard.

Why hadn't I closed the curtains?

Because we'd made love in the moonlight. I need to wake him up. *Move.* He'd been shot. He was *exhausted.*

"*Luke,*" I shook him gently, trying to rouse him without alerting whoever was outside.

And then, I saw it—it was *moving* in the backyard. My breath caught in my throat as I froze, praying he would wake up. *Who was that?*

The shadow was far away but sending shivers down my spine. Terror gripped my heart as I stared out the window, my eyes fixated on the eerie *woman* in the backyard.

The blond hair flared in the moonlight, a stark contrast against the darkness that surrounded her.

She stood there, unmoving, her gaze locked on the manor. Her face was covered. She moved...like she was under a trance. "*Luke.*"

The intensity of her sent shivers down my spine, making my skin crawl with an inexplicable sense of dread.

My heart raced, pounding against my ribcage like a trapped bird desperate to escape. The woman's presence was far away, yet it felt as if she was right there, her aura suffocating me with an overwhelming sense of terror.

"Luke!" I couldn't hold back the scream.

Lucas jolted awake, his eyes wide with alarm as he followed my line of vision. In the backyard, two dark figures moved swiftly, chasing after the woman as she fled.

She took off faster than them. Into the woods beyond the manor.

"Who the fuck is that?" Lucas asked.

"I don't know." My heart was pounding in my chest. "Killian?"

Nobody else was here, and the figures were too lean to be Reed or Gabriel.

Gabriel would never leave me unattended, not after everything. Suddenly, the door slammed open, causing both Lucas and me to flinch.

Lucas moved instinctively to cover me, a groan escaping his lips as he did so.

"Evie, are you decent?" Reed was in the room.

Oh God. Did the horror never end?

"She's not," Luke groaned. Reed handed me a robe without looking at me.

"Did she try to shoot?" My mind raced, trying to process the events that had just unfolded.

The eerie woman in the backyard, the dark figures chasing after her, and now the possibility that she had attempted to shoot.

"No."

Fear gripped my heart, squeezing the air from my lungs.

I clung to Lucas, seeking comfort in his presence, as the realization of the danger we were in settled over me like a suffocating blanket.

"No." *She hadn't done anything.* "Is that Killian outside?"

"With Alexei. He decided to stop by." Reed walked to the window, watching the duo move in the shadows.

Lucas hung his head over me. "Is there ever *not* chaos in this house?" he muttered, frustration evident in his voice.

Reed looked amused as a resigned expression crossing his face as he looked at me finally.

"Welcome to my world," he remarked wryly.

Reed left the room, motioning for us to follow, muttering about how he was never going home at this rate.

"That woman—"

"She didn't have a gun..." I looked at Luke. "She didn't have anything." *Why didn't she have anything?*

That was even more frightening.

CHAPTER 48
LUCAS

"Was that the third attempt?" Evie voiced the question that lingered around me. "She didn't have a gun. She just stared at the manor like she saw a ghost."

Except, she had been the ghost.

It looked like Reed and Aidan led us. I got the feeling Gabriel couldn't work with Evie and me without getting his feelings involved, and Reed stepped in often.

"She's fucking fast," Reed said to everyone in the room. "Alexei said she's trained to move like that. He doesn't know how."

When the fuck did anyone sleep?

I mean, I knew I had a hard time sleeping—but this was insanity. I was on edge—my nerves frayed.

Gabriel was nowhere to be found. I wondered if he'd taken off after the woman.

Alexei was doing rounds for security since he was Aidan's Enforcer.

The blond with the mask up to his nose had appeared like a wraith next to Killian. Aidan sat with Reed in front of me and Evie. The four of us were in a conference room with no windows and downstairs in a basement Reed brought me to.

"I need to figure out how she got through—" Reed broke off as his fingers flew over his phone. "I'm looking it up, Aidan—" He broke off.

Why was Aidan here? He had a syndicate to run? Why was he so invested in me?

Evie spoke up first, despite looking shaken up and so young in her pale blue cloud pajama set she dug up from her old room. A pang of guilt twisted in my chest at the sight of her looking like that.

Reed never looked up. "She won't come back tonight. Alexei is outside with Killian now."

He didn't say where Gabriel was. Gabriel hadn't appeared all night. Was he just avoiding me now since I was in his house?

"Do I want to know why you have so much confidence in Alexei?"

Just who the fuck was Alexei?

Aidan grinned wide at that question. I realized, Aidan O'Hara, while a handsome motherfucker with his hair combed back and whiskey eyes, I *never* wanted to see him look like *that*. He looked as dangerous as Gabriel, and I saw why they got along then.

"Alexei is my head, Enforcer," Aidan smiled easily. "He's my shadow. He's good."

He was the head Enforcer of the O'Hara syndicate.

Why...why would the top three heads of the mob come out? This was bigger than me. Something big is coming for us.

Evie blinked a little at him. "Alexei gets me cupcakes whenever he visits." She blinked up at me. "He is good."

I got the feeling Aidan's version of Alexei's *good* didn't involve cupcakes. Aidan smiled at Evie, softening just a fraction. He leaned back in his chair. I knew for Aidan to be out here, something was *wrong*. I didn't know why, but I got the feeling that whatever was out in New York was threatening them, too.

Because he doesn't know who this threat was. And it's tied to his business.

Reed looked at Evie. "It's a woman."

Why did that strike something in me?

"She was wearing a uniform," Evie said. "Maybe five-four, five? Blond hair. Her face was covered like Alexei's. She moved like...she was *fluid*." Evie's eyes were haunted. "She didn't shoot. *She just stood there...*" She trailed off, unable to find the words to describe the eerie encounter. "I can't get her out of my head."

A sudden realization hit me, and I turned to Reed, my voice laced with suspicion.

"How did you know to come into our room that fast?" I asked, my eyes narrowing. "You knew they'd come after me here." *He had.*

"Because Gabriel saw her at the hospital," Reed said; his voice was calm, not looking up from his phone. His fingers were still texting.

Evie turned to me, her voice still trembling slightly as she looked at Reed and me. "Gabriel and I saw *someone* outside your door at the hospital. She had blond hair, and I thought she was a new nurse." I had been so close to my would-be killer without even realizing it. The thought made my stomach churn.

Reed's voice was soft, his gaze fixed on Evie. "I thought she was new too. She didn't come into the room. Gabriel knows everyone in that ward. He didn't recognize her. He suspected she would try again."

I felt my hands shake at the idea of an assassin being so close to me and not trying anything. I hadn't noticed her.

I did think she was a nurse.

Aidan looked exhausted. "The first two attempts on your life failed. I don't know how. The first one was sloppy. The second was not. They missed it because you saw the sniper. *Someone* fucked up. That woman outside tonight, that was not someone who was going to fail. But for some reason, she didn't—"

He looked at me. "I have no doubt even if Alexei and Killian weren't here? She turned back. It's *too* suspicious. We're trying to figure out what's going on. But—*none* of this has ever made sense." He looked at Reed. "Any luck?"

Evie was alert as she looked at Reed. "Do you know who it is?"

Reed looked up at her. "No, I have no clue what or who these guys are. But Gabriel is actively looking. He thinks this is the group tied to your anomalies."

Evie whipped to me, then her eyes wide. "You are the reason for them?"

What?

"What are you—" And then Evie explained how she'd been tracking strange occurrences in New York, and I was one of them. She told me about the missing footage.

"The missing footage Evie found matches the locations of the kills we talked about," Aidan said.

I racked my brain as I talked, trying to piece together the fragments of information, but my memory wasn't what it used to be.

The shots and car bombs I had lived through had taken their toll, and sometimes, my mind would space out, leaving me struggling to keep track of everything.

Evie was talking. "It makes sense, but I didn't realize they were after *you*."

"Not just him, Evie," Aidan said. "His entire company. They're going to save Lucas for last to send a message. Someone double-crossed someone. The only thing I can suspect is something big happened, like a seismic shift. Something's happening in the underworld."

That's why the O'Hara's got involved.

A seismic shift that even he has no clue what it brings. War.

He looked at me. "You never figured out who kept attacking your company?"

I shook my head. I hastily explained to Evie the conversations between me and the O'Hara without bringing Lucy into it. Liam was working on Lucy, and Evie didn't need that shit tonight.

Having to explain to your girlfriend, who was trying to have your baby, that your sister was a jewel thief, and she might be the reason why you had a hit over your head?

That was not the way I wanted this to go down. *Lucy could wait.*

Evie nodded, taking the lead as she began to explain what she knew.

I sat there, feeling a bit lost, realizing that I had no idea about the details she was sharing. Reed's eyes were fixed on her, his gaze searching as if trying to piece together the puzzle in his mind.

"I *knew* they were here for a *reason*, but I never guessed the reason would be Lucas. *They've been here for weeks!*" She turned to me. "*Weeks!* You've kept this from me even when we were dating? *Why?*"

Here it fucking goes.

"Because I didn't want you to date me for anything other than me. I just wanted to be with you. I didn't want to guilt-trip you. I never even told you the truth. I loved you then, and I love you now—" I lowered my voice even though both Aidan and Reed stopped what they were doing to watch me.

Evie's endless string of brothers.

I wasn't a fool to not know Aidan was Gabriel's replacement in a quiet version. One who would hang me from the FDR bridge if Evie was his sister.

"I lied about my name—"

Aidan blinked twice looking between Reed and me.

I just focused on Evie's face as she gaped at me. "When the first attack happened, I told Gabriel—"

Don't tell her. She doesn't need to know he tried to kill you—

"I thought it was him. It wasn't. But that was right before *the* dinner at the Italian place, with the pesto—" She gasped.

"You lied to me *that* night!" She slapped my good arm. "No wonder you were like *that* before dinner—" She broke off, turning pink as she looked at Aidan avidly watching us. "Do you mind?"

"Not at all." Aidan leaned back and motioned for her to *go on.*

Shameless. He was thoroughly enjoying this. I fucking knew he'd tell Gabriel. Evie gaped at Aidan for a second.

"You are worse than Gabriel," she said with zero animosity. I realized that…Aidan O'Hara actually might be Evie's older brother, too. I bit back the urge to groan.

Endless. Brothers.

If he hit me, though, I didn't know what the fuck to do.

"I'm invested." He shrugged, looking normal for once without the pressure of an empire at his shoulders. "Killian mentioned he saw you two together, but it's not his business who others choose to fuck."

Killian knew? *Of course, he fucking did.*

"I, on the other hand, find this much more interesting than Kieran's cat videos. Besides, if you were *my* sister, I'd have him beheaded before he stepped foot in the manor." Aidan said it like he was reading off a menu at a diner.

One order of beheading, coming right up.

Evie blinked as she looked at Reed. *"This is why I moved out."* Reed's grin was wide, his tongue darting between his teeth in a way I recognized in Adam.

"I told you I loved you." She was spitting mad as she turned back to me. "I cannot believe you would keep assassination *attempts* from me. This is *worse* than you not telling me your real name."

Aidan gaped. "You *lied* to Monroe's little sister?"

He looked at Reed in awe. "How is he still *breathing?*"

I had never seen Aidan O'Hara like this. I never imagined he was *human.* But judging by the way Reed smirked, he was.

Aidan got along with both of his brothers. *This is the other side of him. He's nothing like his father.*

Because I knew Aidan O'Hara was capable of violence.

When he'd taken over, I knew of the bloodbath that he'd ripped through his father's old ranks. Completely changing it up.

He just doesn't have to be that person all the time. He turns it on and off.

Why can't I do the same? I'm trying so hard to not be my father's son.

I'm not being myself.

"Don't worry," I said without thinking at Aidan. "Gabriel already tried to shoot me—"

Evie gasped, and I realized I should've said nothing.

Foot meet mouth.

"Evie, please—"

"I hit him too," Reed admitted. "But he made her cry, so I didn't give a shit."

She looked at Aidan. "You are not allowed to behead him. *At all.* I'm not your sister." Aidan shrugged like he would consider it, tucking it away like a piece of news. "Oh, for fucks sake, there's an assassin who showed up, and you two are acting like this isn't a big deal."

They were too calm. *They know something.* Because Aidan and Reed didn't leave the hospital room with me. And I knew Adam had taken Evie to Gabriel. They hadn't left either one of us alone. Killian had said he was staying up. All roads led back to...

"That's because they know something," I said, looking at Aidan and Reed. For some reason, Reed was holding cards close to his chest. Ice moved down my spine when I realized something.

Gabriel was nowhere to be found. Reed had never said a word.

They know something.

Aidan held up a hand. "I want to hear the end of the story." He motioned for me to continue.

These two fuckers.

I started. "Fuck you guys." Aidan and Reed shared a quick grin.

Aidan glanced at Reed, his eyes darker. "Did you find the ghost?"

Reed nodded. "They have a Black Hat." He looked at Evie. "That's all you."

Evie stepped in, her voice firm. "I'm working on finding the Black Hat. And I'm close." Aidan looked at her, surprised and impressed.

Reed's smile grew wider as he looked at her with admiration. "Gabriel said so."

I gaped at Evie, stunned by the revelation. I had no idea she was working on this on her own. She turned to me, a gentle smile on her face.

"It didn't come up with *everything*..." She shrugged apologetically. "We were focused on not getting you killed. I didn't know the anomalies I was tracking related to the movements for your—" She couldn't say it. *"But you didn't tell me you were being attacked."*

I held up my hands in surrender. My eyes softened as I looked at her, a wave of pride washing over me.

"I'm proud of you, doll," I said, my voice soft. "I didn't want you to be with me because you felt guilty. You've got the biggest heart."

I continued to be aware Aidan was shamelessly watching me like a jaguar in a forest watching its prey.

I'll be texting Kieran to send this man more cat videos.

"That's why I tried so hard," I admitted, continuing despite his curious stare. "Because you knew none of this, and you still wanted to be with me."

Evie beamed at me, her eyes shining with love as she took my hand in hers.

She turned back to the two men, Reed, who was smiling at me with pride. That was a little discomforting.

"The anomalies I found correspond with movements made by our silver friend outside and another person. There's no way she moves that fast. Which means there's a hacker, two assassins, and something tells me there's more in the city.It's a *team*. "

Aidan leaned back in his chair, watching Reed. "And she got in through your security?"

Reed was annoyed. "She got in through a *loophole*. She never should've been able to. That Black Hat is working to disable little points letting them slip in and out. I need to figure out how." He let out a breath. "The good news is, anyone else in the house where the four were murdered were alive. One of them, his family, found him. They don't target innocents. It's like they operate like samurai…"

Reed looked at Aidan. "Which one is the one that says you won't kill anyone—"

Aidan's voice was soft as he spoke. "*Bushido*. She will operate ethically and make decisions based on what is right. Her movements, as Evie said, *were* fluid. I've never seen that style, save for—" He paused, hesitating for a moment before continuing. "Save for very few fighters."

Reed said it first. "She's scoping out her kill."

Evie's face grew even paler, the gravity of the situation weighing heavily on both of us.

My mind raced, trying to process the new information. A hacker. An assassin. A name drifted through my thoughts, just out of reach, taunting me with its familiarity.

"When she does, we'll be ready," Reed said quietly. "You two should stay out of sight. She won't break into the manor."

"Because it involves us—" Evie whispered. "She's going to try and lure Lucas out?" Reed nodded.

"How?" I would hate to find out.

Reed looked at me then. "The only ammunition she had against you is currently in hiding."

Lucy.

"Well, almost—" He looked at Evie. Something was in the back of my mind.

Do you love her?

I gasped, my hand reaching for my injured arm. Both Evie and Reed moved toward me, and my head was reeling.

"The *blond* woman. She was...*she was in my office*. She's...*I've seen her*," I looked at Reed, who had moved to my right, and Evie to my left, her arms around me and my arm in case I was in pain. "Her eyes, they're blue. I know her. I saw her face."

"*Reed.*" I looked into his stormy eyes and his grim expression. "She's been in my company for a while now," I told him everything. About the will. About Evie, who was shaking in my arms. The trees I ordered and her question.

"She knows. She knows about Evie." Because there was one way for her to draw me out, and I was holding her in my arms.

Reed looked at Aidan, who swore.

"She wasn't here for Lucas—" Aidan said.

Reed shook his head. "She was here for Evie."

CHAPTER 49
EVIE

I STOOD IN MY CLOUD PAJAMAS, FEELING A SENSE OF FEAR, UNLIKE anything I had ever experienced.

It wasn't the fear of losing Mama and the unknown, Gabriel spiraling out of control, or even the fear of losing Lucas.

No, this was a different kind of fear altogether—the fear of being everyone's weakness.

As Reed pulled me aside to talk while Aidan spoke with Lucas in another room, all I wanted was to stay together with Lucas.

The thought of being separated from him only amplified my anxiety.

"Can you figure out who the Black Hat is?" Reed asked quietly. "I need to handle some things upstairs."

I nodded, understanding that there was still so much going on. Why couldn't we just be a lazy family for once?

"I can't believe the team in New York is tied to Lucas," I said, my voice trembling slightly. "All this time..."

Reed, who looked like he hadn't slept in days, shook his head. It dawned on me that he had probably stayed awake, working tirelessly to keep us safe.

"Killian told me the locations, and when you told Gabriel about Oracle, he put two and two together," he explained.

Suddenly, a thought occurred to me.

"Where is he?" I asked, referring to Gabriel. Reed's throat worked as he hesitated for a moment.

"He's working on something," he finally said. He looked at me quietly. I moved without thinking into his arms, finding comfort in his familiar scent of sea and spice.

I squeezed him back hard as if holding on for dear life.

"I'm going to ask you what I always do," Reed said, drawing back to look at me. "Just trust me, okay?"

I nodded, a little upset that he had machinations and plans he wasn't telling me about. I knew *that* look all too well.

"If I'm going to be an operative, I want to know what you're planning," I insisted, my voice growing stronger. "You keep secrets from me, I know—"

"We wanted to confirm," Reed interrupted, his honesty evident in his eyes. "Gabriel was waiting for them to get cocky. And she did." He paused, taking a deep breath. "I haven't been home in days, working for you. I'm trying to figure out the best foot forward. I would do anything to keep us safe."

And I knew he would. He always had.

"You never told Gabriel," I said, realization dawning on me. Reed shook his head. "Why?"

"Because Lucas looks at you like you're his world. I knew that day at Titan when he apologized to you. *He isn't his father's son.* And you aren't just Evie Monroe to him. I knew then he wouldn't stay away from you. He couldn't. It was inevitable." Reed's words sank into my skin.

He looked rueful, a hint of a smile tugging at the corners of his mouth. "I wasn't expecting an assassination attempt, though; I thought at max I'd have to hold Gabriel back from shooting him."

I felt a chill run down my spine at the mention of the assassination attempt. "He almost did—" I started, but Reed nodded, cutting me off.

"Life came at me fast when I wasn't looking," I said, still trying to process everything that had happened. It felt like my world had been turned upside down in a matter of days.

"Don't I know it?" Reed chuckled, shaking his head. "I don't know how Alisha tolerates me."

It had been almost three days since Lucas had been shot, and Reed had only gotten Alisha back maybe three weeks ago? Time had become a blur, the days bleeding into one another.

As I stood there in my cloud pajamas, I couldn't help but notice how exhausted Reed looked.

The dawn light filtering through the windows only served to highlight the dark circles under his eyes, the weariness etched into every line of his face.

And now this?

Reed watched me with those stormy eyes of his, and I knew that look all too well.

"You said you want me to talk to you like an operative?" he asked, his voice low and serious. "Someone's been trying to fuck into our network. I can see the markers that don't belong to our guys."

Invisible tracks, he called them.

"Just like the hacks all around New York. Oracle picks up on that stuff, and I don't think their hacker knows we use Oracle. I know I don't use it often, but that hacker can't get into Titan's network. Gabriel *knew* she was on the property; he was watching her the entire time. She only appeared for a moment, but he had eyes on her the entire time, back at the hospital, here."

My eyes went wide, my heart pounding in my chest. *"He knew she was here?"* I gasped.

He nodded. "I feel like everyone forgets he's just as good as me, he was up late watching her for a bit. I noticed the moment she appeared, our network began to bug out, like wherever she goes, the Black Hat knows to follow her. It's definitely a team. They didn't erase the footage from the night prior, but they're trying."

My vision remembered the blond from last night. Reed and Gabriel's domain was a fortress.

"There are streaks of them and signs they are trying to get in my network. They're fucking with us." Reed smiled without humor. "Professionals. They're trying to cover her, the Blond, and tonight." He showed me the last thing on his phone.

Footage...

My eyes widened as I realized what I was seeing.

Gabriel had taken Lucas to his hospital, where Reed monitored him. And *then* the manor.

"The blond woman! You got her on tape both times. Reed, that's the first time anyone's..." I trailed off, unable to finish my sentence as the magnitude of what he had accomplished sank in.

Suddenly, everything clicked into place.

"That's why the hacker is scrambling. The Black Hat can't *hack our network* to get any of this footage."

"You didn't just bring Lucas to the hospital and manor to protect him," I said slowly, realization dawning on me. "You brought him here to set a trap. Because you knew they would come. And when they did, she was in *your* trap."

That's why Gabriel let her go.

Because he had her either way.

Gabriel and Reed had known all along had anticipated *every* move their enemy would make.

The entire thing had been a trap, a carefully orchestrated dance designed to lure the black hat and their team out into the open.

Gabriel loves puzzles.

"You don't just want the Black Hat. You want the entire team?" I asked, although I already knew the answer. Reed's smile widened, a predatory glint in his eyes.

"Remember when Gabriel said they were discreet? Not only are they bouncing IPs, but we can't find anything on the Blond. But it's clear, the Blond and the Black Hat are two different people."

And neither were traceable.

"There's a whole darker world out there, Evie. I don't think Gabriel wants you messed up in this part of Titan." But Titan was already messed up in it.

"*This* is what Gabriel does." All those times I had wondered why he and Reed split tasks the way they did, all those long hours Gabriel spent locked away in his office. "This is what he does in his office, in the dungeon, with the O'Haras?"

Reed nodded, his expression grim. It was a side of Gabriel I had never seen.

Two halves of a whole.

Reed and Gabriel.

I feel like I hadn't known the extent of the darkness he lived in if Gabriel was handling this.

I had seen Reed's face, he was familiar with all this.

"You have to understand. He's seen much worse than you have. He's comfortable with this, but Evie, *he doesn't want you to be.* I try to protect Alisha from this stuff; sometimes, when I tell her things, I know it bothers her; I feel like she listens, so I don't lose my shit."

Who listened to Gabriel?

And suddenly, some of who he was made sense.

"Trust me now?" My head bobbed, but my head was swirling.

Reed's hand gripped my shoulder, a firm, steadying presence that anchored me to the moment.

"You didn't know until now that it was my mom, did you?" I hesitantly asked him.

He shook his head. "I thought Gabriel was trying to get back at someone. But I didn't know how deep it ran." And Reed would do anything for Gabriel.

"I'm going to get some coffee," he said, his voice low. "I need you to be an operative while you're at the manor from this point on. When I say jump, you jump. You don't ask how high. And when you need to know, I will tell you."

This is Reed, team lead.

I was so worried about Reed not telling me anything I didn't realize he was already letting me in. He leaned back.

Reed leaned back, his eyes boring into mine with an intensity that left me breathless. *"Do you copy, Eva?"*

"Yes, sir."

Reed's lips brushed over my forehead, a gentle reminder that despite the gravity of the situation, he still loved me, but he was choosing to be a mentor.

Something Gabriel couldn't do.

"I'm proud of you, Eva Santos."

CHAPTER 50
LUCAS

I DIDN'T IMAGINE IT WAS EASY TO SLEEP KNOWING THAT PEOPLE WERE OUT to kill you. But somehow, Evie and I collapsed into each other's arms.

Adam would be here eventually to change out my bandages, but if he was moving on Reed's order, then Reed would let us sleep.

I needed some semblance of normal.

I was surprised at how quickly life at the Titan manor reacclimatized.

And my mind was swirling while I slept.

I dreamed of the blond lady who had shown up to my office, my brain desperately trying to remember how she looked. Her eyes had been bright and vibrant.

She hadn't looked like an assassin.

She seemed *friendly*.

But that was the point, right?

Assassins weren't dicks.

How else would they kill me?

My brain churned with what Aidan had pulled me aside for.

I knew Reed was talking to Evie.

And Gabriel was nowhere to be found still.

Both he and Reed scrambled last night, no doubt. Working tirelessly with Killian and Alexei to figure out how to fucking fix this problem.

When I woke up, it was late in the afternoon. I had never slept this late. Evie was passed out in my arms. I wasn't an idiot. We got sleep because nobody else did. As much as I hated it, I got out of bed. We were downstairs with low windows.

I didn't even want to know why there were rooms down here. Or who bothered to stay here.

The house was quiet, with the sunlight streaming in as I padded to the kitchen upstairs. I got lost twice, but I followed the scent of coffee.

I found Reed, shirtless, stirring coffee. He had hickeys on his neck, which he hadn't had the night prior. His sleeve of tattoos stretched to his shoulder.

"Aidan talked to you," he didn't look at me.

"Yeah. He did." I didn't bother repeating it. I didn't need to. Gabriel had been the one who wanted to do it.

"I'm going to make coffee for Gabriel and take some food to Lish, and I'll be back," he replied, turning away.

Alisha was here? When had she come?

And then fucking finally, Gabriel walked in, dressed to the nines in his usual gray suit, looking sharper than I had previously seen him. "Reed, there are kids in the house."

Reed smirked. "Don't even fucking start."

Evie had joked about them being a married couple.

Gabriel grumbled as he went to get coffee, muttering about being a work-wife. Meanwhile, I wore Killian's clothes.

"Never thought you two would be a couple."

"Tell me about it," a soft and husky feminine voice chimed in, and we all turned to see Alisha standing in the doorway, her dark hair cascading down her back, longer now and waving wildly.

Her hazel eyes were strikingly bright as she took in Reed, lips curled into a soft smile at the sight of him.

"Lish." Reed's eyes heated at the sight of her.

"I know you said you'd get food, but I felt weird staying in bed," Alisha said, stepping into the room.

She wore a short black robe, and her cheeks were pink from Reed's stubble.

He paused, making coffee, and walked over to her, tucking her into his arms. I saw the subtle look they exchanged while Gabriel's gaze remained on making his coffee.

"Angel, I'll go back with you in a second."

She looked uneasy. "There's something wrong in the house."

Did she know about the occurrence last night, or could she just feel it?

"*Someone* was trying to get in the house." Gabriel's eyes drifted to the backyard.

"Gabe, maybe you should Palo Santo the house," Alisha suggested, as though discussing ghost assassins was a normal conversation. "It may help remove the negative energy."

Gabriel seemed to consider it coming from her.

Reed chimed in. "While we're at it, can we Palo Santo Gabriel?"

Alisha pressed her lips together, giving Reed a look when Gabriel gave Reed the finger. Alisha sent Gabriel an apologetic smile.

"Reed, be nice to your wife," Alisha teased, and my eyes widened as Gabriel turned pink.

She teases him? Both of them?

Alisha's eyes focused on something on the table. "What's this? This is beautiful."

Reed and Gabriel exchanged a look as Alisha's eyes landed on the card. "Have I seen this before?"

Reed paled. "Lish—"

"It's so shiny." She smiled at Gabriel. "Is this yours?"

Before either man could say anything, Alisha said. "When I was a little girl, my mum would hate the word claw because these are bird claw marks, so she called them talons."

Gabriel and Reed both double blinked. "*Talons?*"

Had I heard that before?

Why did it sound so familiar?

She nodded, smiling, unaware of the shift in the room. "A bird talon, singular. *Talon.*"

She pointed at Reed. "My accent is *not*—darling, will you—"

A bird talon? Why was I forgetting something important?

"Talon," Reed said in his Northeastern accent. He cast a sardonic look at Gabe. "*The Gold Claw?*"

Gabriel shrugged, looking embarrassed. "I was just guessing. Now that Alisha said Talon, it sounds better."

"What are you two talking about?" Alisha looked bemused between them. Reed let out a breath as he looked at her, leaning against the kitchen counter.

Gabriel moved then, sitting in front of her. "Have you seen that card before?"

I straightened. I knew what he was asking her. If she had, whoever got the card was marked.

Not Alisha...

319

She nodded. "I think so…"

Reed swallowed, looking at Gabriel with an expression I felt in my gut. Both men laser-focused on Alisha.

"I just can't remember where I saw it, but I'd remember the design." She looked at them. "I…I can't remember."

She frowned. "That's so strange; it's like the thought was right there."

As she spoke, Reed looked at her and his eyes. I saw something in them I rarely saw in him, discomfort.

Something *had* happened.

Gabriel was quicker than Reed. "Let it go. It'll come back."

She looked embarrassed at him. "Drat, is that what Perla warned me would happen?"

Reed was pale and looked like he could carry her out there. *Memory issues?*

"I've even blown up enough times to not have any memories either. I usually wake up in the hospital," I volunteered. "My brain is shot."

Alisha's eyes started. "That's horrible. Can you not remember your time in the military?" She knew when I had dated Gemma.

I shook my head. "I have fragments of memories, but the core events are missing."

She nodded. "I feel more forgetful." She looked at Reed. "The other day, I forgot how to get home. I was walking like I was in a fog. I knew *where* I was going, but I didn't know *what* it was. Kieran was there."

Gabriel shifted as she said the words, his head tipping a little. Reed looked at Alisha with softness in his eyes, sitting beside her and all but taking her into his lap.

Gabriel's eyes took her in. "I've been looking into hiring some specialists who deal with brain injuries and memory loss. It might be worth considering."

I blinked in surprise, not knowing that Gabriel had been investing in medical research.

The man had his hands in everything, and apparently, that included the clinic where I had been treated.

Alisha's lips curled impishly. "I'm guessing you're picking me up for our dates instead of Kieran?"

And the look on Gabriel's face was genuine warmth, a stark contrast from the man I knew. "As long as it's not a fucking vegan place."

Musical laughter from Alisha lit up the kitchen, and Gabriel—the man who despised me all of days ago was now just having his coffee in the morning—flashed a quick grin at Reed.

Reed observed the two of them with amusement.

Alisha looked at me, eyes bright and cheeks flushed, and I marveled a little at her being with both of them and handling them deftly. There was no way they *weren't* together. I'd never even seen this type of relationship.

She glanced at me while Reed went back to finish up whatever he was doing.

Her voice dropped, her accent low. "It's good to see you. Reed filled me in. I'm happy for Evie and you. You look much happier."

I wasn't miserable with Gemma, but we had about as much chemistry as sardines on pizza. I knew Alisha from my brief time with her friend Gemma, and I knew she was tactful enough not to bring it up.

Gabriel's gaze never left Alisha as she spoke to me. "What are you two whispering about?" A hint of something in his voice.

"Jealous?" Alisha raised a brow. I didn't miss his smirk.

"What's it like sharing them?" I didn't think as I asked the question to Alisha considering the company I kept.

Gabriel's eyes darted to me, his smile dropping from his face.

"It's not that hard." she smiled softly. I didn't understand the look on Gabriel's face. "I want to come up more to see them both."

She smiled at Gabriel, who hadn't looked away from me, his eyes eerily sharp right then. Reed had paused making coffee.

I didn't understand Gabriel's expression.

"Do you guys go to *De Nuit?*"

Through Kieran. That made sense.

Alisha looked at me, her smile polite. "I beg your pardon?"

Was she playing dumb? *Why?*

Granted, I don't have many friends, but I didn't think I was off the mark here. They were fucking.

"I fucking knew you were an idiot," Gabriel turned on me, his expression savage with anger as he turned to me. "Who's the third DuPont?"

I blinked, caught off guard by the sudden change in topic.

"*Wait, what?*"

Reed turned with an expression in his eyes that told me he absolutely understood. "Why is he a fucking ghost?"

Reed was on me. Both of them were in attack mode.

I backed up a little in my chair.

Foot meet mouth. Because you just insulted them.

I opened and closed my mouth. I swallowed as Alisha looked horrified.

"Did you just presume I was sleeping with *both of them?*" Alisha reacted finally. The three of us whipped our heads to her with equal expressions of horror.

What the fuck was happening right now?

Alisha's eyes flashed with anger as she held out her hand to Gabriel, who wordlessly grabbed the first thing he saw, a *ladle* from behind him.

I didn't understand.

Before I could react in shock, she moved in, whacking me with it, standing up to her full five foot three inches.

Reed blinked, a little stunned at Gabriel standing to look around the drawer behind him.

What was happening to me?

Two women wanted me dead now?

I covered my head, trying to protect myself from her onslaught. "How could you be so daft? You arsehole! *He is my friend—*"

Alisha punctuated each rapid fire insult with a whack of the ladle.

I winced, feeling the sting of her anger which to be fair felt like nothing. But I sensed it would only piss her off more if she saw that.

"I'm sorry!"

Reed's head tilted in wide-eyed amusement when Gabriel finally pulled out a rolling pin from a drawer.

My eyes and mouth widened in disbelief as he walked over to her. Mid whack, he switched it out with the rolling pin. I gaped as she pointed the rolling pin at me. Reed advanced on my other side, looking impressed.

My God, they're a team.

Gabriel leaned against the table with his hands in his pockets, right behind Alisha, a smirk playing on his lips as he looked at me. As if to say, *Well?*

"Answer Reed's questions." Alisha always seemed so sweet.

I underestimated her. I swallowed hard, knowing I had to face the consequences.

Sorry, Teo.

"She's scarier than both of you." The words slipped from my lips before I could stop it. Alisha's eyes softened, a small smile playing on her lips.

322

"Thank you, *that felt good,*" she said softly, a hint of satisfaction in her voice.

Her expression quickly shifted back to a frown as she pointed the rolling pin at me, her delicate features a little sharper now.

She's like an angry fairy.

I took a deep breath, knowing I had no choice but to come clean.

"The DuPonts are my oldest friends." I looked at Reed, resigned. "I don't know why Thierry is a ghost, but...I don't know his last name. He never took DuPont..." I began, spilling what I could remember about the DuPonts and the rest of the tangled web I had found myself in.

Reed's eyes were filled with understanding of what I was doing.

"Andrei is one of my good friends, and Teo is like a little brother to me. I don't want to hurt them. They've never done me or anyone I know wrong." I admitted.

I explained Matteo as the one who told me to come clean to Evie and his principles.

Reed exchanged a look with Gabriel.

And then he turned to me. "Why would I ever be invested in DuPont's—" I motioned to Alisha. She blinked at Reed, a silent question.

"Lish, I'll explain this clusterfuck to you at home." She nodded understandingly. She didn't even say a word.

Reed asked me. "*Where* did Thierry come from?"

I shook my head. "I don't know. I just know Andrei and Teo protect him. Tremendously. I don't want to hurt either one of them." I couldn't remember *shit* now. I looked at Alisha, who frowned at me. Gabriel right behind her backing her up.

It was like seeing two different sides to all three of them.

Gabriel would hand her a knife if I stepped a toe out of line. I didn't realize he was *friends* with her. *The company you keep.* Evie's words rang out to me.

The company I kept...mafia and a billionaire playboy. I never left my home.

No wonder I felt my life wasn't satisfying and shit.

I stumbled over my own words half of the time when it came time to have normal conversations.

Unless you're with Evie.

I thought about it and told Reed anything else I knew.

All the money in the world didn't buy you this. Evie has this. *These people in her corner.*

"That's all you know?" Reed asked, his eyes taking me in with a serious expression. I nodded.

Alisha cleared her throat. *Right*, I almost forgot. I turned to both of the guys, grinning at me.

"*My apologies*, I shouldn't have assumed—" I broke off at the look on her face. "Right, just friends. You're in a relationship with Reed, though," I thought to address the only person in the room who had the most power. "Not—"

I looked at Gabriel, who was watching me over her head, his eyes flat and predatory.

He's good friends with her.

I had been interrogated before by the two of them, but this was different.

This was disarming for a reason I couldn't identify.

Her eyes were warmer as she looked at me, less angry. "I *do* have a relationship with Gabriel. He's my *friend*."

Reed watched the exchange silently; he looked at me and motioned to Alisha. *Right.* "I'm sorry, Alisha."

"Pardon me for asking, but since you so crassly implied what you did, I must ask, have you not any female friends?" she asked, her eyes big, taking me in.

Even when angry, her accent was thicker, making her sound proper. *Articulate.*

I considered that. "Gemma works with—"

Alisha shook her head.

I caught Gabriel's quick grin behind her, his eyes delighted. I didn't even know he had—*he was married.*

She didn't sound mean when she said in that voice of hers. "Do you have *any* good friends?"

Who was this woman? Both men exchanged a knowing look.

I shook my head. "I don't leave my apartment." *Just with Evie. Only her.*

"Matteo doesn't count." Reed looked at his girlfriend with amusement.

Alisha softened, lowering her rolling pin. "That's awful. Is it because of your PTSD?"

She's holding a rolling pin. Do not lie to the woman.

I nodded, watching her eyes warm completely.

"We can be your friends. You're dating Evie, after all." She held up the pin. "But not another word against them."

She pointed at the two towering men in the room, who both wore different expressions of delight.

They needed her to defend them…why did they let her?

Gabriel has tried to murder me before…

Because they love and respect her.

Just like Evie.

"Was I just…*adopted?*" I looked at Reed, who wore an easy smile on his face as he took her in and then me with a nod.

Gabriel blinked slowly and tipped his head as he looked at Alisha. "He's not coming to brunch."

"No," Alisha looked up at Gabriel over her shoulder, her eyes soft. "That's just you and me."

Gabriel's expression shifted, a pleased smile on his lips as he leaned against the table.

Reed, who had gone back to typing on his phone, shook his head, a knowing smile on his face.

He's fully aware of them. He trusts them.

I suddenly realized I didn't know how to talk because I didn't know how to be.

I fought so much within myself, I punished myself for things outside of my control.

Everyone in Titan went with it. That's how they *adapted.*

All of them.

My family had been lacking, in so many ways, my relationships with people.

This is family. Not the toxic sludge I've had my entire life. I had a family now. Thanks to Evie.

Reed's head snapped to the door before the figure at it could knock.

"Am I interrupting something?" Adam asked in his soft green scrubs, his dark blond hair styled and warm brown eyes taking us in, his brow furrowed with concern.

Alisha smiled with warmth. "Not at all."

She handed the rolling pin to Gabriel, who took it. I noticed the way Reed's jaw tightened.

He didn't have a problem with Gabriel, but he has a problem with his brother?

Adam motioned me to another room to change my bandages.

"I'm taking you home." Alisha went up to Reed and pulled his head to her shoulder.

Reed held her tight as Gabriel finished his coffee.

I wasn't dumb enough to comment this time.

CHAPTER 51
EVIE

LUCAS TOLD ME WHAT HE'D DONE IN THE KITCHEN WHEN I'D WOKEN UP.

I explained to him what had happened three weeks ago. When Alisha had been *kidnapped.*

With Avani and Selena.

He'd been shocked, to say the least.

I also realized he hadn't met Kellan and Selena, and then there was what I knew about Nate and his charge, Gemma.

Or the four of them.

That was a headache I didn't want to figure out since Gabriel had stated *that nobody* had been allowed to visit Selena until she healed.

Not even Kellan.

I asked Reed, and he said Kellan had been removed as per Gabriel's request. That piece had dug into me.

Kellan wasn't allowed to see Selena? What had he done?

Kellan now belonged under Gabriel, which was a scary thought. I didn't think Gabriel hated Kellan.

No, it was the same idea of pushing and pulling until he got the operative he needed.

Gabriel always said, *good enough gets people killed.*

And since I hadn't seen him?

I couldn't imagine what Gabriel had him do. Despite all the chaos, Reed had hired someone new privately, and that newbie was training with Kellan.

Gabriel had made it clear that except for Selena's nurse, Nisha

Graham, who had been thoroughly vetted by Adam, Garrett had been the *only* one allowed to stay around Selena. And nobody disobeyed.

I miss Selena. But I had also been juggling someone trying to murder my boyfriend.

I told myself I would go see her when there wasn't an assassin over my head. Or his.

Lucas had *no idea* how complicated it could be having all these relationships.

I would have to teach him to navigate since I , too, accidentally spilled the beans on Reed installing cameras in Alisha's old apartment. Assuming Alisha had already known. She didn't.

That hadn't gone well since it somehow led to a fight between Reed and Gabriel long ago. Neither spoke about it. But they'd moved on since then.

For a man who lost his mother and then his sister, *sorta?* I could see why Lucas might assume things, especially when he explained his friends.

Kieran had *not* been the likely candidate for a sex club.

No, but then again, I felt like I just met a different version of Aidan O'Hara—and I realized I didn't know any of the three brothers. Killian and Alexei, who had vanished the night prior. I saw everyone differently now.

I mentioned a few things to Lucas.

By contrast, Gabriel was the friendliest with Alisha.

Gabriel's close with them both.

I sat on the edge of the bed, my heart heavy as I watched Lucas pack a duffel in the room.

"Aidan said you have to leave with him?"

Lucas nodded. "He needs to get back to Chicago. It doesn't matter what we don't know. Splitting us up is the best thing to do."

It all made sense—keeping Lucas away from the Titans, leveraging Aidan's connections with the Devereaux's, and protecting Lucas.

I need you to be an operative.

But being one didn't make it any easier to accept. Being an operative meant making tough choices, ones that tore at your soul, no matter how much logic was on their side. I knew that better than anyone.

Lucas stopped pacing and knelt before me, his hands resting gently on my hips as he gazed up at me with those piercing eyes. "You can't go with me, Evie," he said softly.

His words cut through me like a knife. Of course, I couldn't go with him. Gabriel wanted Lucas gone, out of the picture, while he schemed and planned who knows what. It made sense. But it hurt. It hurt so badly I could barely breathe.

Tears pricked at my eyes as I cupped Lucas's face. "I know," I whispered, my voice cracking. "I hate this. Every part of it. But I understand."

Understanding didn't lessen the pain.

It didn't fill the aching chasm growing in my chest at the thought of being separated from him, of not being by his side to keep him safe. But I didn't have a choice.

This was the path before us, and we had to walk it, no matter how much it broke my heart.

I leaned down, resting my forehead against his as a tear slipped free.

"Just promise me you'll stay safe," I breathed. "Promise me you'll come back to me."

"*Always*," he murmured. "I will always come back to you, Evie. No matter what it takes."

"When do you leave?"

Lucas pulled away slightly, his hands still resting on my hips.

"I'll let you know when. Aidan wants to review some things with me, and Adam wants to check in and make sure I'm good. Chicago isn't too far. I'll be back home to you before you know it."

He smiled, his eyes shining with hope and love. "I love you, Evie."

"Why does it feel like I haven't told you I love you enough?"

His grin was heartbreaking. "I think you said it in other ways." His fingers brushed over my stomach.

I leaned in, capturing his lips with mine. When we finally parted, Lucas gently brushed a strand of hair from my face.

"Reed mentioned your old setup is still in the solarium. If you want to do something with your time. Keep your head occupied."

Reed had left the manor and gone home with Alisha, who was apparently cleaning out some old boxes Gabriel had.

From what I understood, we were changing hands to Gabriel and Reed wanted Alisha out of the way.

Right. The Black Hat.

A short…interlude.

For a moment.

Before the ghosts returned to finish their job.

CHAPTER 52
EVIE

As I sat in the solarium, surrounded by the lush greenery and the gentle rustling of leaves, I delved deeper into the mystery of the Black Hat.

The sunlight filtered through the glass ceiling, casting a warm glow on my face as I focused on the computer screen before me.

I could feel the tension in my shoulders as I watched the Black Hat's attempts to breach our network, their desperation to erase the footage we had captured.

After attacking cameras all throughout the city, they wanted ours.

"You can't get into my system," I muttered. Ever since I knew, I set up little safeguards in place. The earthy scent of the potted plants filled my nostrils, grounding me as I traced the origins of the attacks.

Cape Verde? *No, they moved.*

The Black Hat *left*. I opened Oracle and began. "Oracle, retrace and populate the origins of the camera anomalies across the city."

When it did, I paused again.

No way, the signals are stronger in the city?

The Black Hat was *in* the city? *They left Cape Verde? Why...Lucas.* We had footage. If they didn't get it one way...

My mind raced as I considered the possibilities. Everyone had mentioned the likelihood of a family member's involvement. I wondered if I could uncover any connections to Cape Verde. I dug deeper, and my search yielded nothing substantial except for one crucial piece of information: Aidan had mentioned that only *two* people remained as targets—Lucas *and his father.*

But his father hadn't said a word. In the midst of the chaos?

Nobody had mentioned his father…I dug into Charles Devereaux.

I knew Lucas hated him, and I didn't truly understand my relationships with Reed and Gabriel being so different.

In the same way, Lucas didn't understand good relationships besides me and his brothers.

I asked Oracle to run the four names of the deceased Killian found, according to Lucas.

Lucas's father had spoken to these people some way before their deaths. *Was I looking at the puzzle wrong? Isobel, what do I do?*

This entire time I unlocked Oracle, I had been focused on the wrong perspective.

If I change my perspective, would that unlock this?

Aidan said this looks like a double cross…why? Who double-crossed—

"What if I entertained the idea that Lucas's father was the one who double-crossed someone? *It's in his nature.* He did it to his *entire* family." I was talking out loud at this point to my plants.

But how?

Something is missing.

I recalled Reed's teachings about people's motivations: *Love, Object, Revenge.*

What if the attacks *were* driven by revenge…*but by the wrong family member?*

Gabriel and I took Charles down.

We put Lucas into power.

We were so busy looking externally…we didn't look *internally…we missed one.*

I paused, a bead of sweat trickling down my temple as my fingers shook.

"Oracle, is there any connection between Charles Devereaux going to Cape Verde?" I was looking at this wrong.

I was looking at it like a White Hat or a Red Hat.

I needed a new one to go into it.

"I have found a few connections between Charles Devereaux and Cape Verde," Oracle responded, her voice mixing with the gentle hum of the ventilation system. I swallowed hard.

"When was the most recent one?"

"I have a call on a secure line made by an anonymous source to Charles Devereaux. Shall I play it for you?"

An audio file appeared on the screen. A call.

I clicked play instead, and a man's deep voice, presumably Charles, filled the solarium. **"What do you want, Hagen?"**

Marcus Hagen.

What was Charles Devereaux doing with him? I had been filled in.

"Your daughter has something of ours."

I sat up straight, and a mechanical voice responded.

How cliche...but *that was the Black Hat.*

My gut told me it was.

"You have instructions to return it to us."

Lucy Devereaux had an object?

This revelation sent a chill down my spine despite the warmth of the solarium.

As the conversation unfolded, I listened in horror as Charles negotiated the lives of four people, including his own son, in exchange for the object Lucy had stolen.

The pieces fell into place.

People had died because of Lucy stealing something, but Charles had told the Black Hat in exchange for getting the artifact back to them?

He wanted...everything.

Charles had thrown *everyone* under the bus for his own gain.

The mechanical voice came again.

"Marcus Hagen is dead. You do your best to remember that."

Hagen had died prior to Lucy stealing the artifact.

Lucas's father is pissed.

"I don't know what you're talking about. I don't have *anything*. Lucy—that bitch I don't know who she would go to. I can give you names, but if I give it to you, I want something in exchange."

I was already repulsed by Charles Devereaux.

He sounded callous, and someone threatened his life, and he was simply negotiating. Because he did this often.

He killed people and buried things.

Mama died because of this man.

He had a lot of secrets he didn't want getting out.

Gabriel took his company from him.

A company he couldn't afford to lose.

"Give us the object Lucy has. In exchange, we will give you what

you want." The mechanical voice was searching for the object Lucy had?

They would kill everyone for this artifact?

What was it?

Charles told the Black Hat that Lucy *might* deliver the parcel to those people.

And one by one, they had gotten offed them, but Aidan had said that those people *were the only people also connected to Charles' crimes.*

"Oh my God!" I paused the audio. "Did he just...he used the Black Hat to kill the only people *who knew the truth.* In exchange for an object his daughter had. So where was—" I broke off.

"Oracle, look up Lucy Devereaux."

As she did, I listened to the rest of the audio, and my blood turned to ice when he listed his own son.

Charles was a bully.

"Lucas would for sure have the package. He cares so much about that fucking company he stole from me with Monroe. He thinks I don't know—"

And then I listened to my boyfriend's *father* tell the Black Hat that he didn't care if they did go after his own son.

People started dying after Lucy came to New York. As collateral damage for something she stole.

Something so valuable someone had sent teams of people for it.

My Luke was under *threat.*

Lucas's father threw everyone under the bridge as a grab for his company back.

I cracked the case.

And it didn't feel satisfying at all. Instead, my heart broke.

For Lucas. For a sister who didn't care.

For a father who sold his kids and his friends for power. Lucas's father wanted his old company back.

And all this? It was a power grab. A calculated power grab with the object as a distraction.

Black Hat gets their object.

Lucas's father gets his company back.

Oh my God.

"Oracle, do you have any information relating to Lucy Devereaux?"

"Yes, miss, I have her on the K2 servers. Jupiter backed this up—" She populated the images of Lucy leaving K2 weeks ago.

With a gym bag?

"*Where* did she go after this?"

I followed Lucy through the city. I watched her walk into a building looking a little rundown.

And not exit out. Any of the exits.

"Oracle, can you scan her entire body and see if she populates anywhere else in the city?"

She did not.

That was so strange.

But she also didn't leave the country? That was almost impossible to do without training. But one thing was for certain.

"Lucy Devereaux never left the city."

Oracle never glitched.

She could find anyone.

That had been the initial design of the program. Reed's words came back to me.

The Oracle of Delphi's schematics show that it was an intelligence created to find missing people. It's designed to find anybody. Anywhere. It just needs data points.

It can find anybody?

Anybody.

I could find Lucy.

Somehow. I just need the information.

She never left.

And the Black Hat was *in* the city...

But *how* did the Black Hat know Lucy *never* left?

Unless they figured out where Lucy is before me.

How is that even possible?

Do they have something like Oracle?

The Black Hat's team was *swarming.*

The anomalies were growing erratic in the center of the city.

They were *hunting.* Because they weren't after Lucas. I saw an erratic glitch in the cameras near *our* town.

She was coming. The ghost from last night.

"I have to find Gabriel!"

I took off running.

CHAPTER 53
EVIE

I WAS RACING THROUGH THE HOUSE.

Gabriel! He was upstairs.

He had to be. *He wouldn't leave.*

I haven't seen him since I got home.

The entire manor was so cold. As I raced through the halls, I caught a flash of movement in the yard.

I hadn't missed Lucas yet; the sun was going down since we had been up in the afternoon, and he'd leave later in the night.

Aidan wanted to remove themselves without anyone knowing.

The sun was going down as I saw his outline. *I knew him—*

"Luke?"

I stopped running right before I hit the foyer when I caught sight of Lucas in the backyard.

Why is he—?

I opened my mouth, wondering why he was *outside* when his life was in danger, and a loud crack went off in the twilight. I saw Lucas—*my Luke—hit with a shock.*

Everything in me froze.

My heart lurched in my chest to see Lucas, a look of pain and shock etched across his face.

Before I could react, someone—*Adam*—appeared out of nowhere, grabbing me from behind and hauling me to the ground.

"No, Evie, don't!" Adam urged, his voice filled with urgency as he restrained me from rushing to Lucas's side.

My world *shattered* as I watched Lucas crumple to the ground, his blood blooming like a crimson flower across his chest.

A guttural scream tore from the depths of my soul, raw and primal, as I fought against Adam's restraining arms.

"*Luke!*" I cried, my voice breaking with anguish.

My eyes widened in horror as I watched Lucas falter, his body collapsing to the ground in a heap.

Blood blossomed all over his chest, the red stain spreading rapidly.

A wild cry escaped my lips, torn from the depths of my soul, as I struggled against Adam's hold. He was dragging me away as I watched in horror at my *baby*—my Luke.

He lay there, bleeding, and *nobody came to help him.*

Gabriel! Where are you!

The sight of him *alone* made me *scream* harder, my desperation reaching new heights.

Adam dragged me back into the halls in his arms, my screams echoing through the space until we were out of sight. I was making an animal noise.

The dread that had settled in the pit of my stomach intensified as the realization of what had happened sank in. *Luke.*

Luke!

I hadn't been there for him in his final moments.

My vision blurred with tears, each ragged breath feeling like shards of glass tearing at my lungs.

This couldn't be happening. Not him.

Not my Luke. When, not if.

When I'm gone.

Time seemed to fracture, each agonizing second stretching into eternity as I wept, my heart shattering into a million pieces.

"*Let me go, Adam!*" I pleaded, my voice cracking as I struggled.

"I'm sorry, Evie," he murmured, his voice laced with sympathy, but he didn't even budge.

Tears blurred my vision as I fought against his restraint.

He carried me up through the halls, my heart aching with the need to be with Lucas and touch him one last time.

"*Please,*" I begged, my voice raw with anguish. "*I need to be with him. He's alone, please.*"

I didn't realize Adam Whittaker was ever that strong as he held me.

Suddenly, something went off in Adam's pocket.

He answered, holding me in his arms, his resemblance to Reed striking in that moment.

Whatever they said, he nodded, hugging me close.

"Yeah, I got her. Yes, sir."

Reed.

When he hung up, he brought me into his arms, tightly shaking his head.

He was...gone.

CHAPTER 54
LUCAS
A FEW HOURS EARLIER

"Are you sure this is how you want to do it?" I asked Gabriel, who finally appeared after Reed and Alisha had left.

They'd gone to his office for something, and Reed had left with some boxes.

Gabriel took me into the basement to fully tell me what Aidan had started telling me.

Things I never told Evie.

Not because she wouldn't understand, but the sheer drastic measures Gabriel had been plotting all fucking night were too... macabre to even start explaining.

How did I tell my girlfriend her psycho brother wanted to fake my death.

Evie had been asleep still. Aidan and Killian had been a part of this.

Alexei would take the shot since he was a professional killer. In the background, Killian watched over me, and Gabriel would stand by to oversee.

Aidan would extract the confession.

Because it was Charles behind it all.

Gabriel explained all this to me while assembling a sniper rifle.

He's fucking proficient. Gabriel methodically assembled the M200 rifle, his hands moving with a fluid grace that spoke of years of experience.

Despite the gravity of our conversation, he seemed to find solace in the familiar task.

I remembered Evie telling me how a happy Gabriel was worse than an angry one. Because when that man was happy, he was positively frightening.

"What about Marcus Hagen dying set off my father?" I asked, my thoughts turning to Aidan's father.

Gabriel didn't glance up from the rifle. "It didn't. Hagen was taken out by one of his own, power struggles and war are common in Aidan's world. Your father was shaken up already. Lucy stole something from someone close to Hagen, shaking it up even more. I doubt she even knew what she was doing. She just did her job because she's a good soldier. Lucy lives in this city with you, it was only about time before it landed on your door. Figured if he took out all his guilty sins, he'd be a free man with a company. Plus, this isn't the first time I heard he wanted his company back."

Because Mercury Group was international.

Which meant power. I knew I had power.

I had never used it.

I never stepped into being my own man.

I spend my time running from who I am.

Was the object Lucy took valuable enough for a unit to be sent to New York?

Gabriel slid the bolt into place with a satisfying click.

I shook my head in disbelief. "Charles hired a fucking mercenary group to get rid of me. Did he trick the group into thinking I had the object?" I muttered, watching as Gabriel expertly attached the scope to the rifle.

Gabriel was running this op.

I'd never seen him dressed in anything other than his usual gray suits, but now, in all black, he looked...striking and unleashed.

"Charles made that group think everyone had the possibility of getting it. They moved through people efficiently," Gabriel adjusted the rifle in his hand.

"Do you know what she took?" I asked, my curiosity getting the better of me.

Gabriel's expression remained steady as he fine-tuned the scope's alignment, an odd glint was in his eyes. "Did your father say who it belonged to?

I couldn't remember. "He didn't say."

"It doesn't *belong* to Hagen," Gabriel replied softly, ice in his eyes.

I heard him mutter something about his stupid key under his breath.

"This group threatened your father. He used the opportunity to lie to them that all the people he colluded with years ago would have the object. Reed told you they operate off a code of ethics? He knows that based on how they kill. No families. No innocents. No disruptions."

Gabriel paused. "They aren't stupid, honorable maybe, but not fools. They know by now that you probably don't have it."

But we had to do this to find the person who had wanted me dead.

"Do you notice how nobody else is dead? These aren't black widow killers. They're precise, deliberate, exact," Gabriel went on. "If your father came back to power after your death? Nobody else would know his secrets. Nobody would even question it."

Not me.

He shrugged. "Either way, they won't get the fucking object. It's inevitable. Your father will be their last kill." He looked at me. "They won't take it easy on him."

My eyes narrowed as I began to understand the implications.

"And that's where the blond lady comes in," I said, my voice tight.

Gabriel nodded grimly, attaching the magazine well to the rifle. It was empty, but for show, he did it.

"She didn't just want you dead. She had no gun. Alexei said he saw weapons. My guess is knives. Aidan thought she might be here for Evie. But Reed and I believe she only has eyes for you. She was at the hospital. She could've killed anybody. She chose not to."

"Because they don't kill innocents."

He nodded. His eyes were on the rifle. "Your father wants power. He doesn't like being a little scumbag, *nobody* in the middle of nowhere. Sitting at Mercury Group was the highlight of his shit life. He wants it back. When they contacted him, he used it as an opportunity to take it from you. From everybody."

Because Gabriel had wiped all the people out in the past. Removed the old guard members and put me in power.

"This was a power grab." Gabriel nodded. "Happens all the time."

"All this for what? One team after an artifact, someone else after me?"

I heard Gabriel say something under his breath about his soul. There it was again. *That look.*

"How did you know about Charles being behind it?" I shook my head.

Gabriel shrugged, his demeanor still calm and composed, but the coldness in his eyes never wavered. "He killed enough people with a smile on his face. I figured it might make sense he'd off his own son."

That wasn't a hunch. It was too elaborate. Somehow, Gabriel had found out.

Gabriel is just as good as Reed, he just hides it better.

A heavy silence settled between us as I absorbed the information. "You and Reed know what the object is," I said, looking directly at Gabriel. "Why can't you tell me?"

When Gabriel turned to look me in the eyes, he was steady and unwavering. "I don't know what Lucy stole. The only one who knows is her." He stood up, the fully assembled M200 in one hand.

"Why did you build that?" I asked him. "Alexei is the one taking the shot."

He didn't say a word as his eyes met mine. "Why do you think?"

Because he doesn't trust anyone else to do it.

He was taking care of me. In his own way. I saw why everyone was afraid of him.

His eyes burned with a feral intensity.

It was as if a switch had been flipped, unleashing a side of him that had been carefully contained in those suits of his until now.

He leaned leaner and meaner, his body different, this was...him.

The slight curl of his lips, a ghost of a smile that held no warmth, only a cruel anticipation, made my blood run cold.

"You ready?"

Alexei is trained. Alexei does this all the time for Aidan.

But Alexei kills people for real.

The energy in the room was of raw power and unbridled ruthlessness, between a force of nature that would stop at nothing to achieve his goals, and *me*, his sister's man who he didn't like weeks ago.

Dressed in a white shirt that hid enough of what I had borrowed courtesy of Killian, and dark slacks, I nodded.

I watched him, the rifle in his hands like an extension of his very being.

"You're enjoying this, aren't you?"

"You made my sister cry." His smile was dangerous. "What do you think?"

I shook my head in disbelief.

This was Evie's brother.

I thought about how months ago I felt nothing but dread at the thought.

Now, I felt nothing but respect.

CHAPTER 55
LUCAS

I GROANED, THE SOUND OF EVIE'S DISTANT SCREAMS PIERCING MY EARS.

"I need to see her," I urged as Killian's professional gaze swept over my body, his hands methodically assessing the damage.

Alexei had taken the shot, and now Aidan and Gabriel were waiting for me.

"*Later*," Killian grabbed me, his hands steady, telling me he was no stranger to this shit.

While I was rubbing my stomach, Killian explained he had been Alexei's test dummy all day.

The bullet-proof vest and the convincing illusion created by the exploding bags of blood.

"You could pursue a career in acting," Killian remarked dryly as he helped me remove the vest.

The O'Haras were known for their ability to snap into work mode. I didn't recognize him or Aidan anymore. Darkness settled over Killian's eyes as he worked so fast I didn't even follow.

It had taken every ounce of my willpower not to move.

As I sat there, wiping my chest and quietly donning the borrowed clothes. I made a mental note that I owed him a new wardrobe at this point.

This was it.

Reed, who had been monitoring the footage from home, sent the video to Aidan and my father. He checked in with Adam about Evie, making sure they both stayed out of the way.

343

"What can I do for you, Captain?" my father's gruff voice crackled through the speaker.

Aidan? I didn't understand the rank structure of how he and Killian worked.

"I was just notified Lucas is dead?" Aidan asked him. That was the angle. That Aidan knew everything.

My father's response sent a chill down my spine, causing goosebumps to erupt across my skin. "Why are you telling me this?"

He's not surprised. It was him.

Aidan's voice remained unwavering, with a coldness to it that I hardly recognized. "Because I know you're the one who pulled the hit on him. You think I wouldn't find out? I run the Underworld."

The long pause that followed made me know Gabriel was right.

When my father's sigh crackled through the phone, I felt my heart sink, my stomach twisting into knots. "How much fucking money do you want?"

I collapsed into a nearby chair, my legs suddenly weak, unable to support my weight. Killian's eyes had turned hard and angry as he listened to his older brother on the phone.

As Aidan named a sum that could buy a small country, my father agreed without hesitation, his voice devoid of any emotion. "You're sure Lucas is dead?"

Aidan's tone matching my father's, empty and cold. "I had my guys grab his body."

Realization dawned on me.

That's why Killian had asked if Charles knew him in my office.

I turned to Killian, my eyes wide with shock, but he refused to meet my gaze.

My father's next words cut through me like a blade, the pain of his betrayal searing my heart. "I don't want this coming back to me." Anger and disbelief surged through my veins, and I felt Killian's hand tighten on my shoulder, a silent reminder to stay composed.

Aidan laughed without humor, sounding colder than I had ever heard. "Power grab, old man? You could've just asked. I would've offed him for free. How much did you pay them?"

"Monroe and his fucking right hand cut me off at the knees. You don't think I would take the shot?" There was a pause. "I didn't pay shit. Talon offered, and I took it."

There was a chill in the room as I watched Gabriel straighten.

Talon offered?

The betrayal shouldn't have cut so deep, shouldn't have hurt at all, but it did somehow, sinking deep into my gut, into my bones, into my blood.

My blood. Memories of not wanting to be his son. Not wanting to ruin Evie.

Not deserving of shit. Alone in my apartment and isolated. He was worse than Matteo's father.

Aidan's jaw clenched, his eyes flickering with barely contained rage, but his voice remained deceptively calm and cold. "Did you want me to clean up your girl?"

My heart skipped a beat, a wave of dread washing over me. Gabriel sat back, his arms crossed and his expression unreadable, while I slowly rose to my feet.

Killian held me back, his eyes locking with mine as he stood in front of me, a silent warning not to say a fucking word.

"Lucy is a pain in my fucking ass. Just like her fucking mother—" He broke off and Aidan's eyes sharpened and then he smiled. That fucking smile. When I asked him why Alexei was good.

I knew Killian would punch me if I ruined this. We were taking a gamble.

Over the years, Aidan's relationship with everyone had always been under the table. On paper, Aidan worked in real estate.

Nobody knew Aidan O'Hara and Gabriel Monroe were partners.

Aidan's eyes were molten, the fury barely contained within them.

I was shaking again, my hands trembling as I gripped the edge of my seat.

I understood now why Killian hadn't budged from my side.

My father's voice took on a different tone, one I hardly recognized.

It was cold, detached, and filled with contempt.

"Where's Lucy, Charles?"

"How the fuck should I know? *That stupid bitch stole from Talon.* They killed Hagen for double-crossing *one* of them. I don't fucking know." My father sounded inhuman. "Now, Talon is breathing down my neck! You think I'm not going to throw everyone under a bus like they did with me with that sonofabitch Monroe?"

He laughed, a sound that sent chills down my spine.

"Listen, O'Hara, you're cut from the same cloth as your father. Do the job, and you keep your empire. I'll get mine back."

Aidan's jaw tightened, and he exchanged a look with Gabriel.

Gabriel was deep in thought.

Talon.

Anger surged through my veins, intertwining with the nausea that threatened to consume me. The way he spoke about Lucy? I was... shaking.

"You sold both of your kids to Talon for your company?" Aidan's voice was cold and calculating. My heart was losing it. I was trying to hold it together.

My father's response was laced with contempt. "When I'm back in my seat, I'll make sure Lucas never did shit. I knew he was working with Monroe."

A realization struck me then. Aidan had been working with Gabriel and Reed from the shadows, and my father had no idea.

That's why they had used Aidan. That's why Aidan had stuck around.

To do the job right.

Killian was shoving at me gently.

A wave of nausea washed over me, and I felt ice flood my veins.

Killian's eyes never left mine, his gaze intense and unwavering. Aidan's voice was laced with an unnerving calm as Gabriel nodded his head.

With a fierceness that I couldn't quite comprehend, Aidan turned to Gabriel and asked. "Charles...I remember something as a kid. Your wife, didn't she off herself?"

I froze, my breath catching in my throat. Killian began pushing me out of the room, his actions spurred by whatever he saw in my eyes.

My father's voice sent another wave of nausea crashing through my body, his words dripping with a sickening smugness. "What about it?"

"Bullet to the brain at that angle is oddly suspect..." Aidan said the words, and I bit back the bile in my throat.

At that moment, Killian shoved me out the door, his urgency palpable. I stumbled outside, gasping for air, my mind reeling from the revelation of my father's cruelty.

I didn't even hear what he said. I didn't need to. Not anymore. I was gasping.

My mind reeled, struggling to process the magnitude of the revelation. I couldn't see. I couldn't breathe. I clenched my fingers into my chest.

"I got him," a quiet voice spoke from behind Killian, who hung back silently before returning to Aidan's side.

Gabriel's voice was steady and resolute as he explained, I felt his hand drop down on my shoulder. I couldn't look at him.

He was right.

"Reed cleaned out your father's accounts. The feds will raid Charles' house in the next two hours. If Talon doesn't kill him before that."

I didn't want to know how the fuck Monroe figured this shit out.

I couldn't breathe. The realization that my father had killed Mom and would have killed Lucy had she not run hit me like a ton of bricks.

My eyes burned, and my throat constricted. My world was spinning. I clutched my chest.

Memories of my life flashing in front of me.

I hung my head in my hands, overwhelmed by the weight of it all. I was breathing hard. I couldn't see straight.

Gabriel's words pierced through the haze of my thoughts.

"You aren't his son, no matter what you think. You had every chance to be." He paused. "You inherently chose to be good."

You inherently chose to be good.

I hung my head, wiping my face. Gabriel's hand never left my shoulder.

A few days ago, he hated me.

Sorta. It was…a dichotomy.

The man who had tried to kill me saved my life now.

I wiped my face, feeling a profound sense of something lifted off my shoulders and relief for the man standing behind me.

"You do shit like this often, don't you?"

He didn't answer.

As the initial shock subsided, I realized that I didn't feel as awful, just shock, processing all my thoughts.

My hands shook as I stood there with Gabriel silently behind me.

"I have to protect Lucy from now on." It was the first words I could muster. "She's family." *I have to keep her safe.*

"She didn't even turn to me."

"Reed had her," Gabriel said. "Reed's kept his eyes on her for a long time."

And I had been dumb enough to think he ever wanted anything romantic with her after I saw him and Alisha.

"I'm an idiot."

A soft laugh came from behind me. "I won't argue that. You got a lot to learn."

He was a year older than me.

Right now, I felt twenty years apart from him.

"Who taught you?"

Was it Isobel? I didn't know much about Evie's older sister. But from the looks of it? Gabriel was who he was because of her. Evie said that much.

He had been married once.

Just like Evie taught me.

The thought of Evie hurt, but I needed to ask him something.

"What are you going to do about Talon?" I asked, but Gabriel didn't answer.

I pressed further. "They're looking for the object Lucy brought to New York."

Not even Lucy.

Just what they thought she had. I turned over my shoulder to look at him,

Gabriel's gaze drifted to the yard. He didn't know yet.

"When Talon gets their hands on your father..." He left the sentence unfinished, but the implication was clear.

A sudden thought struck me.

"I'm cleared, aren't I?" I was safe.

Evie was safe. Because they didn't kill innocents.

Gabriel nodded. "That show was for your father only. Talon has figured it out since they're all over the city."

He turned to me, his eyes flat. "If you see or hear anything about them, call me." *Forget you have this number.*

I nodded.

"Alexei didn't see our blond friend even though she's still around town." He said it with a weight in his voice.

"She's not coming back..." But I saw it on his face.

"You're wondering why she's still here?" He nodded. "But they don't kill innocents."

He was staring at where she stood the night prior. I was cleared. I was safe.

Evie was safe.

Lucy was *not*.

As I stood there, trying to process the gravity of the situation, Gabriel's words cut through my thoughts like a sharp blade. "If they're so good, how did they miss twice?"

"Did they?" Gabriel met my gaze, his expression serious. "You don't know how they operate. Killian thinks they did *everything* on purpose.

If we backed your father into a corner, they were backing you into one. They just weren't expecting this corner. So, you'd be brought closer to Lucy. Eventually, you'd start asking—"

"And lead them to *what* they're looking for," I finished, the realization hitting me like a ton of bricks. Whatever the fuck it was, it better be worth it.

Gabriel nodded, confirming my suspicions. "But that never happened since nobody has what Lucy had."

"So where is it?" I asked, my mind racing. "What the fuck is it?"

He shrugged lightly, his demeanor calm, and his gaze was steady on me. "No clue."

Gabriel's eyes bore into mine. "The O'Hara's need to get back to their positions. They won't say a word about this. You can tell Evie, but I recommend you keep this to yourself."

"Lucy—" I started, but Gabriel cut me off.

"I have a hunch," he continued, his voice laced with a mixture of something with determination. "I have to look into Talon. And what the fuck they want..." He shook his head in disbelief.

I realized that this was the version of him Evie had spoken about— the one who had stood by her, stood by me.

Your family is scum.

I am not my father's son.

My mom died when I was eleven; she was distant from me.

Gabriel? He's actually super sweet.

And he wasn't the only one on my side.

Evie's screams echoed in my mind, a haunting reminder of the pain and devastation my father's actions had caused. To my family. To Evie's. To Gabriel's.

"I want to be better than my family," I said, my voice sounding foreign to my own ears.

He had been a statue of resolve during the call, almost bored. But beneath his stoic exterior, I could sense the undercurrent of anger and disgust at my father's actions. He tipped his head in understanding. "You are."

And from Gabriel, that was the fucking compliment of the year.

"So is Lucy. This is not her fault. She did her job. Too fucking well." He shook his head a little, looking slightly wild.

"Thank you," I managed to say, my voice hoarse and raw with emotion.

Gabriel nodded, his expression softening ever so slightly. "You didn't spazz out."

I blinked, realizing that I hadn't freaked out. Normally, my PTSD would have lost its shit.

But *this* time, something had changed within me.

"You were afraid of your own emotions instead of the situation," he said quietly. "Mastery over self and all that *crap*."

I didn't fully grasp his meaning, but I understood the essence of it.

"I need to see her," I said, my heart aching at the thought of Evie suffering. He knew who I was talking about. "She needs to know."

Gabriel's eyes met mine, a flicker of understanding passing between us. "She's with Adam, probably in her old room." He paused. "You're the reason why she moved out."

I wondered if Gabriel knew I owned the building.

He fucking knows.

Taking a deep breath, I gathered my courage. "I want to ask her to marry me."

Telling your girlfriend's psychopathic brother you were going to marry her after he'd fake killed you was not something I had on my bingo card for the year.

To my surprise, Gabriel leaned back, his hands in his pockets and eyes calm. "Are you asking?"

I didn't think people always caught him by surprise, but this time, I did.

"Not just you," I replied, my voice steady despite the nerves fluttering in my stomach. His brow rose.

"Evie knows she is *who* she is, not just because of *you*," I softened my voice, although he'd already seen me break. "But because of your wife. Would *she* have liked me?"

I wasn't a complete idiot to believe Gabriel was who he was, without Isobel's influence.

Gabriel had raised Evie with everything he had. I could tell how Evie spoke about him. He'd given Evie the *world*.

Evie once told me he could move mountains. For *her*. The wife whose name he still couldn't say.

I wasn't a *complete* moron.

My father had never looked at my mother the way Gabriel did, even when *mentioning* Isobel.

I continued. "I know that Evie wouldn't be the woman she is without—I'm asking for *both*. She was yours. You know her answer."

Because he knew what I was asking. Gabriel was silent for a long moment, staring at the backyard.

"She's your everything," he said softly.

"She is."

I know she was yours.

"I promise to love her."

More than you.

Just let me love her, please.

Finally, he tipped his head, closing his eyes.

I felt a smile spread over my lips, my heart beating so fast it felt erratic.

I won't let you down.

CHAPTER 56
EVIE

I couldn't stop crying.

Adam hadn't left my side carrying me to my room.

Where was *everyone*?

Adam pressed his lips to my hair, holding me on the bench near my bed.

His presence was steady and strong as he held his hand around my head, holding me to his chest. I hated him and still was grateful he was there.

Keeping me from falling apart completely.

Lucas was gone, ripped away from me in a single, horrifying moment.

The image of his lifeless body, the blood blooming across his chest, was seared into my mind, a nightmare from which I couldn't escape.

I couldn't breathe, couldn't think, couldn't do anything but weep for the man I *loved*, the man who had become my *everything*.

Suddenly, a familiar voice cut through the haze of my despair. *"Evie…"*

My head snapped up, my eyes widening in disbelief as I saw Lucas standing in the doorway of my bedroom.

Alive? Was he…alive?

A noise left my lips.

"H…how?" *Was this a dream?* *"L…luke?"*

He smiled, his eyes rimmed in red as he walked up to us. "Hey, Cherry."

I cried out, ripping myself out of Adam's hold and *scrambling*.

I couldn't get to him fast enough, my legs trembling as I threw myself into his arms, clutching him tightly as if he might disappear at any moment.

Lucas lifted me up, holding me close, my tears soaking his shirt.

"*Evie*," he whispered, his voice soft and soothing. "You're breaking my heart. I'm okay. I'm okay, baby. *Look at me*."

I couldn't look at him, couldn't stop the sobs that tore through me. Lucas just held me, whispering reassurances into my hair as I cried.

His arms holding me against his chest felt like a home I could never get anywhere else in the world.

I couldn't stop touching him, my lips pressing against his face, his neck, any part of him I could reach.

Desperately, I kissed him, needing to feel the warmth of his skin, the beat of his heart, the realness of his presence.

He's alive. He's alive. He's alive.

Lucas returned my kisses with equal fervor, his hands roaming over my back as he held me close.

Vaguely, I was aware of Adam leaving the room, giving us some privacy, but I couldn't focus on anything but Lucas.

I needed him, I needed to reassure myself that he was really here, that this wasn't some cruel trick of my mind.

My fingers fumbled with his shirt, ripping it open further in my desperation to feel his skin against mine.

I couldn't get close enough to him, couldn't erase the memory of his lifeless body from my mind, and he did the same to my clothes—tearing them under his hands until I was blissfully naked.

I was lifted. The first thrust felt like heaven. I held him as close as possible as he swallowed my screams.

"*Harder*."

A vicious growl left him as he carried me to the bed, dropping down, and pounded into me.

Life.

That's all I wanted.

CHAPTER 57
LUCAS

LONG MOMENTS LATER, I LAY WITH HER IN MY ARMS, SILENTLY CRYING, feeling my own eyes wet as I explained everything to her.

Lying in Evie's bedroom in the manor she used to call me from was surreal.

I never wanted to leave.

When she held me to her chest, threading her fingers through my hair, I let go.

I don't know how long I stayed with her, only coming up to feed and take care of her. I ravaged her body.

Taking Evie with a ferocity that imprinted every part of me onto her soul. I couldn't let her go.

Call it almost dying for *real* or finding out my entire life had been a lie, save for the one woman who saved my soul...

I wanted to give her *everything*.

We stayed in Evie's old bedroom for days.

Every time I was inside of her, I possessed her thoroughly, marking that exquisite body—with my teeth, fingers, cum—everywhere until she felt me *everywhere*.

She was *my* Evie.

Utterly, irrevocably mine in a way that transcended pretty words and empty vows.

I wedded us in the most primal sense, lashing us together with brutal need and blistering want until separating where she ended and I began was impossible.

With her, I wasn't anyone's son or brother.

This was the woman who disarmed me completely.

It was easy to talk to her, to be with her, her understanding, her compassion, her heart—the family she introduced me to.

The family that had saved me—kept Lucy safe and hopefully hidden.

I was *hers*.

I didn't leave. I couldn't.

And she didn't want me to. I just texted my secretaries to figure it out and tell them family emergencies had occurred. I took time off, and we stayed in her manor wing.

"I don't ever want to leave this place," I admitted, feeling utterly broken apart and healed by her.

I popped a bubble in the water, the scent of flowers around us, and Evie in my arms as she leaned back into me.

I'd drawn us both a bath. But Evie had gotten in with me, and I wasn't complaining.

"I felt the same when I got here," she whispered. "I don't know what it is."

I did. Like the damn place was built on a lot of love—it was seeping through it.

I couldn't believe I had ever thought Gabriel was a cold bastard.

In the brief time we'd been here, the housekeepers had turned up to clean up the room and brought us food.

We didn't leave this wing. I hadn't wanted to leave.

Probably because I knew when I did, there would be work to do. And my father had, no doubt, been arrested or *worse*.

Talon.

I told Evie briefly about them.

I leaned my head back onto the tub.

"Do you think…" I drifted. "We could move in together?"

We would do more than that.

I just needed to get a ring, clean up my company, and make sure this shit never happened again to anyone's family.

I was returning for sure.

This time with a fucking vengeance. I was done running from myself, and everything was going to turn on its head when I got back to Mercury Group.

"You want to make an honest woman out of me?" she teased.

"I mean, if you want." I laughed as I eyed her finger. Dainty and small like her. "I was actually thinking we could stay at your place."

Since I didn't have a home anymore and well..."Your landlord is pretty generous, I hear."

"Is he?" Once Evie knew I owned the building, I cut her rent back to her.

"He can be persuaded. He just needs to clean up some messes first. Which reminds me..."

I explained my plan to her, and she nodded, her eyes huge.

"I'd love to," she said in awe. "You really want me to do that?"

I nodded. "If you don't have more work between Reed and Liam? I'd love it if you took over for a bit and showed those idiots in my IT department how to actually do their jobs."

I liked that look on her face.

"I would love that." She beamed in my arms, settling into my chest.

"Evie." I watched her, her caramel eyes meeting mine, the color of candy and warmth and promise. "You saved my life. What am I going to do with you?"

She smiled shyly. "What you said..."

My heart was full when I kissed her.

CHAPTER 58
EVIE

LUCAS AND I TALKED FOR HOURS.

I showed him around my manor wing, the solarium, and my room. He looked over all the photos of the team in my room, grinning at the silly ones.

It felt unreal to be able to show him this aspect of my life.

And I realized this was the most honest we had ever been with each other, and we relayed the news.

Lucas explained to me about his sister Lucy, who while I was still mad, recognized Lucy as just another pawn.

There was a *bigger* game.

And there was one person who might be familiar with it. Lucas had gone off to his office, not to work, but to get some things ready for what was coming for his life.

The last few days had been a whirlwind, and the weight of almost losing Lucas still hung heavy in my heart.

I needed to talk to Gabriel. I left my room finally, walking up to Gabriel's floor. The sensations were familiar, but the house was different.

Colder.

Empty.

But as I stepped into Gabriel's office, the space where he had always been, my stomach twisted with a sense of unease.

He wasn't here?

Reed's stormy eyes looked up at me with warmth.

"Reed? Where's Gabriel?" I asked, my voice trembling slightly despite my efforts to keep it steady. The worry that had been building inside me seeped into every word, and I couldn't shake the feeling that something was amiss. Gabriel's absence was like a gaping hole in the fabric of the manor, a void that couldn't be filled.

But I wanted to talk to him.

"He's taking a break, Evie. I don't think he has in ages," Reed said, his words measured and calm as if trying to soothe my frayed nerves. "The last few days were a lot for everyone. Even him."

I had thought about that.

For a moment, just a moment, it occurred to me that when I saw Lucas die, or what I thought was him dying, the agony ripped through my chest like wildfire.

And I knew for that moment Gabriel had felt the same. For years.

My Luke came back.

Isobel was never coming back.

"He isn't in his room?"

"He's not at the manor."

What?

"He needs his time, too," Reed said, a hint of something in his voice as he looked down.

What is Reed protecting Gabriel from? Was he—

"Lucas told me about Talon, is Gabriel investigating them?"

Reed's eyes shuttered. "Right now, he's not doing anything. He just needs a break. I think everyone does."

The realization crashed over me like a tidal wave, leaving me reeling. More than three weeks ago, Selena had been attacked, Alisha and Avani were just settling again, and then this happened.

Even for Titan, it was intense for Reed and Gabriel. I recognized when Alisha had been injured, Gabriel had run ops for a long time—something he didn't usually do. And so, I knew, right now, Reed was trading places.

But Gabriel wasn't in the manor. And the thought made my heart constrict painfully in my chest.

"Anything I can do for you, Evie?"

I swallowed hard, pushing down the lump in my throat.

"I wanted to thank him." I whispered. "I'm not angry. I know why he didn't tell me. Or you. I know we both figured it out."

Gabriel had figured it out...I didn't know how without Oracle. But I didn't know a lot, even if I thought I did.

Selena had once explained to me a long time ago that as an operative, everyone had a role. I was never a field agent.

There was nothing I could do in the field, so Reed had given me my strengths. Finding the Black Hat. Which was something only I could do.

I realized even though they had never told me the plan, they also relied on me to fulfill my piece of the bigger picture. And I was drawing up as much on the Black Hat as possible.

I'm the one that can.

The entire thing was an elaborate test.

Me, going on my own helping the team how I could.

How none of the others could. And the field agents working to support themselves—I couldn't do everything. I ached.

But I understood.

This is why Reed asked me to be an operative. It meant watching and making those calls.

"Is Talon off our backs?"

Reed nodded, a flicker of something unreadable in his eyes.

"Something like that," he replied.

He motioned for me to sit, and I did, a sense of dread settling over me like a heavy blanket.

"I was going to wait for Lucas, but I know he left. It's all right, I'll talk to him at some point. I might as well tell you now," Reed began, his tone serious and somber.

"Lucas's father was murdered a few hours after he confessed. In the same style as the other kills. The black marker was left in his house."

Shock and disbelief coursed through me.

"The assassin in the city has a partner. Gabriel thought Charles double-crossed them," Reed said. "The Black Hat stopped hacking our network because they don't care. These guys, Talon, want the bigger prize. All of them are in New York. Liam and I worked together to figure out that there might be five critical players. It's too big of a map to be two people. We think it's one hacker, three others based off the data we have right now. One person is still unaccounted for."

He smiled softly. "I decided to give you a break while I did my part."

Reed and I talked more about Lucy as he filled me in.

"I want you to understand *very* carefully, Lucy Devereaux is not the bad guy. She was under orders," he explained. "That being said, I already told Lucas, and so did Gabriel, everything we know on the object Lucy stole. I'd like you to do what Gabriel asked and find the

Black Hat. That is your mission as an operative. Disable them. Leave Lucy to Liam and me."

"Yes, sir." I was not a field agent, but I was valuable in my own ways.

Reed's smile was wide and genuine as he asked. "What are you going to do now that you're in the clear, both of you?"

I told him about Lucas's plans, my voice filled with a mix of pride and disbelief.

"No shit, he wants you to lead his cyber department? That's great!" Reed exclaimed, walking around his desk to stand closer to me. "Look at you, all grown up."

I moved to let him pick me up into his arms, and I squeezed him back, feeling tears in my eyes. I dropped my chin on his shoulders.

"Reed," I whispered. "I hate being a grown-up," I admitted, my voice tinged with a wistful longing as I realized I had...in such a short burst.

"I know, kid." I felt his breath in my hair. "You have me and Alisha. She suggested doing sleepovers at the manor with the girls would be fun."

I laughed despite my eyes welling up. "I'm sure Gabriel would love screaming women, bubble guns, and tiaras in his home."

"You'd be surprised." Reed chuckled. "Garrett and a few of the new hires are staying here. I asked Garrett, and he said he didn't mind being here."

So Gabriel wouldn't be alone in his mausoleum.

And that made me cry a little harder.

There was a time where I'd run into Gabriel's arms and pester him to make dinner, and I'd sit with him in the kitchen making food for us.

Now, Gabriel wasn't even at the manor. It felt like a lifetime ago, a distant memory of a girl I barely recognized.

"I miss home so much sometimes, but I know I can't turn back."

Reed pressed his lips to my temple.

"Alisha misses her old apartment sometimes. She misses the home she had with her parents. She says it's normal to want the good things in your past, but it's important to not let them stop you from living in the present." He held me tight to him. "And no matter where you end up or what happens, we will always be here for you. You're still family."

I nodded. As Reed set me down, I brushed my eyes. "I think after all this, I want to go and see Selena. I can't wait to—" I didn't like the look on his face. "Reed?"

"Evie, you might want to sit down for this."

As Reed sat me down similar to Gabriel a long time ago, he spoke, and my head spun.

"What do you mean *Selena is no longer a Titan?*" I asked, my voice trembling.

Leaning forward, Reed explained. "Selena left New York. It's been a little over three weeks since she was attacked. Selena is no longer on the team. We have a new hire Kellan's been training—"

"What do you mean Selena is no longer on the team?"

Selena is the team. First Nate, and now her?

"Kellan," I interrupted, my heart sinking. *"He's going to be devastated—"*

"He already knows," Reed said, holding up a hand. "He's leaving soon for an assignment for the next month. He isn't in the city either."

Kellan was working this entire time?

And what about Selena? My mind raced with questions.

"Selena is no longer a Titan..." I mumbled, the words feeling foreign on my tongue.

It was as if saying them out loud made the situation more real, more painful.

"But I never got a chance to say goodbye."

My vision blurred as tears welled up in my eyes, threatening to spill over.

Reed's arms wrapped around me again. "I hate being the baby Titan."

A low, gentle laugh escaped Reed's lips. "There's nothing wrong with you being a baby," he reassured me, his tone filled with warmth. "You're always going to be Gabriel's sister and mine. I just want you to accept that your strengths are your own, in their own ways. You don't have to be me. Or your brother."

I shook my head, my emotions threatening to overwhelm me.

"C...can I still talk to her? Can I call her?" I asked, my voice trembling. Selena was more than just a teammate; she was a sister to me.

The thought of her leaving without a word of goodbye felt like a knife twisting in my heart.

"Is it because I didn't go see her—"

"No, Evie, come here—" Reed interrupted. "I think Gabriel gave her an out. And she took it."

"Which was?" I asked, my curiosity piqued despite the ache in my chest.

Reed's expression softened, a mix of understanding and melancholy in his eyes.

"To be *normal*," he said softly, his words carrying the weight of a profound truth. "Selena was your age when we brought her in. She never wanted this life. I think her accident weeks ago really hit her hard. Don't you think she just wanted to be a normal girl sometimes, like you?"

His words struck a chord within me, resonating with a deep-seated longing I had often felt myself. The desire to be ordinary.

To live a life without Titan.

But Selena always looked like she loved it.

Selena Tavares was...the best.

Reed held me tighter, his embrace, a silent acknowledgment of the pain and confusion I was experiencing. "Gabriel gave her life back. The normal one."

As I processed his words, a bittersweet realization dawned on me. I was growing...so was she...my heart was pounding.

Selena had been given a chance at a different life—one she had always yearned for.

While the pain of her absence was still raw, I couldn't help but feel a flicker of happiness for her. She got to live.

She was free, free to pursue the normalcy she had always *craved*.

I had gotten that. She should too.

I nodded in understanding. "I'm going to miss her."

"What about Kellan?"

In my mind, they had always been intertwined—two halves of a whole.

All the moments she spent pretending to be irritated at his goofy gorgeous grins. *Now just gone...*

Reed's silence was deafening, confirming my fears without a single word.

Hot tears streamed down my face, the saltiness stinging my cheeks as I struggled to process the overwhelming changes.

My heart ached with a dull, throbbing pain that seemed to pulse through my entire body.

The familiar scent of Gabriel's office, usually a source of comfort, now felt painful.

Everything was different now.

I had grown up, but Gabriel was moving on, Selena was off the team, and Kellan was gone too.

I missed *the* family.

I clutched onto Reed's shirt, desperate for something solid to anchor myself to.

THREE WEEKS LATER

LUCAS

"As you know, recent events have shed light on the incidents that transpired before I took over. I wanted to address it all…"

I continued, ignoring the looks of shock and nerves from some of the old guards who were shaken by my words. "If you don't like the new policies, the door is right there."

A murmur went through the room, and I didn't give a shit. I felt different.

Luke Delaney had merged with Devereaux, and he had come out better.

Over time, I realized who I was becoming instead of running away and avoiding being my father's son.

I had never stepped into who *Lucas* was.

I smiled dangerously.

"While I express profound sorrow that comes with losing a parent at my father's untimely death, I am also acutely aware of the pain and suffering that his actions, and those of the old guard, have inflicted upon countless families…"

My grip tightened on the podium as I continued. "I want to make it clear that I am committed to ensuring that none of the families affected do not have to suffer. To that end, I have set up a dedicated team to handle the matter directly, headed by our cybersecurity liaison at Titan Security, Evie De—Eva Whittaker."

I paused, catching sight of the bomber jacket in the back of the room, standing next to a petite figure dressed in a dress that was still too short, and I loved it.

I bit back my emotions, realizing I had almost called her by my name.

Not yet.

I always thought it was Eva Monroe. Evie had *never* used Reed's last name, but Reed had warned me that if I was going to use her name *publicly*, it would have to be with his last name, not Gabriel's. Which didn't make any sense. And yet, I could never find anything on Gabriel. Which meant Reed was protecting them both.

I stopped trying to make sense of what Titan did. I just went with it.

"All of the assistance is provided to the families as a joint project with the Poppy Project, Titan Security, and Mercury Group. I know most people say this, but I truly mean it when I say please reach out to me directly. I put my email on the slide behind me, much to my secretary's dismay, so if you have anything to say, please contact me directly. There is *no more* chain of command when it comes to bringing forward issues."

I didn't give a fuck. The chain of command was the old guard's way of keeping people silent. So, I didn't know shit.

Never again.

I promised myself that. It would never happen under my watch. I was going to turn into a fucking O'Hara if anyone pissed me off again.

A breathless laugh escaped me as a chorus of. *"Thank fucks"* went up in the crowd. And people sighed and clapped. I bit back a wider grin.

I wasn't the only one fed up with the old guard.

I paused, gathering my thoughts.

"And if you haven't all met him, Duke and his friends in the building…" I looked down at the golden retriever and therapy dog Jenny and Ella picked out for the company. "Will be a constant, so please warn Jenny and Ella if you're allergic."

A light ripple of laughter went up, and although I wasn't expecting any applause given the circumstances when it came, I found myself blinking back my emotion.

I went into all the new things the company was going to do, as well as the several new locations we were expanding to, some of which Reed was interested in, including a few luxury villas in Bali.

Evie was leaning against Reed in the back and a tall, dark-haired gentleman I didn't recognize, but I took as a new hire to Titan.

Reed had shown up more often as he was running Titan for the time being while Gabriel had vanished. He was working on Talon. I knew that.

That's my girl.

I continued with regular therapy sessions and hit the gym harder than ever, much to my girl's delight.

With several brothers ready to keep me in check and a *fucking Godfather*, I also focused on improving my fighting.

Not that I'd ever strike them.

I headed to my office, where I found Evie waiting.

The moment I entered, I saw her expectant look, dressed in a short blue dress; the color of my eyes and everything else faded away.

In a few long strides, I was on her before the door even had a chance to close.

As soon as her mouth was on mine, I was distracted.

"I missed you, Cherry." I held her face in my hands, kissing her the way I dreamed of. "I love you."

"I'm so proud of you," she whispered. "I got the surprise you left with your secretary."

"Did you?" I pulled back with a smile. "Besides the flowers?"

She frowned. "Just flowers. Was there more?" I grinned, walking her over to my desk. I had worked on it sparingly, but I had finished it when I lost Evie those few days.

"I submitted it to the creators of The Domain recently, and they approved it." I handed it to her, loving how big her eyes grew. I grinned as warmth went through it.

Leaning back against my desk, I laughed as she squealed and hugged me.

"You made a new card?"

"Actually, they asked me to design a new game. I was going to theme it after Spies." I grinned down at her glee.

The new Goddess card, complete with a sniper rifle, was something I had halfway started as just a goddess, but I modified it after my near-death experience.

The creators wanted to make it a limited edition one with how popular the hype for the new game was for next year.

I had given the first one to Evie.

To add to our board game nights. Which frequently ended with both of us all over each other.

We were still living together, and I hadn't proposed yet. Both of us just wanted to enjoy the calm.

I wanted to take a break and actually do it right. Take her to Ha Long Bay. Somewhere nice.

But with my sister still currently on the run, and *well...everything* else happening at Titan Evie had filled me in on, it didn't feel right.

I found out about Evie's friend and sister, Selena Tavares, not being a part of Titan and how Evie often missed her but how she hoped Selena was happier.

I knew it was a huge step to letting go of a lot.

I was proud of her.

But I privately checked up with Reed since Gabriel had gone dark for a long time after things had calmed down since they'd asked me for a few favors for Selena and someone named Kellan Watts.

And Evie had mentioned they might be together.

Reed had said Selena's situation had calmed down, and he told me to just take care of Evie.

They knew something.

I didn't tell Evie what I knew. Not yet. Since Reed and Talon were closing in on Lucy's location? I asked Killian to look out for her. He had already been on it.

I didn't know how Lucy had successfully managed to avoid so many people. I only knew whenever I got her back, I'd be a better brother.

I also knew I had told Titan about Thierry, and eventually, someone would find out whatever secrets the DuPonts held.

And I wanted to be around better and different people, too. I wanted to grow up and not live in my past, as Evie told me.

Gemma took me on lunch dates where she helped me as a friend, not just a work partner, and her bodyguard, Nate Wyatt, accompanied us, completely invested in everything she said.

I pretended not to notice how close he sat or how his arm rested on the back of her chair, and she ignored him the entire time. Evie was right.

There were a lot of things I didn't understand.

I stepped into my role as CEO with a vengeance, though, shedding my insecurities and becoming the man I knew I could be.

Evie helped revolutionize my IT department, hiring dozens of people to work in organized clusters. Everyone praised the newfound efficiency.

Evie did have a lot to bring to the table. In so many ways.

And as a thank you to my future brother-in-law for raising Evie, I'd sent Gabriel dozens of small trees to fill his manor with.

Reed thought it had been a practical joke as he watched people unload it all.

The housekeepers were utterly gleeful at the amount of work they had to do.

Gabriel now had cherry blossoms and lemon trees, and parts of the manor were covered in just foliage, and he'd texted her.

What the fuck?

Meanwhile, I'd made myself a home in Evie's home.

I kept my word and watered all her plants. Loved her. Made my home. Learned to be a better man every single day.

We're both growing together.

"None of what happened with Talon is over..." she said one day quietly in pajamas.

"Are you worried?" I faced her still in my clothes from work, not having the energy to change out of them.

"A little," she whispered. "It involves your family—"

I nodded. She didn't forget about Lucy, which I appreciated.

Evie had said it might be nice to have a sister...even if she was a professional thief. Which I thought was open-minded since she took the news better than I did.

"I know Reed said not to look for her..." she admitted. "But I can't help it. She feels like family, too." I *loved* that about Evie. "I'm still trying to figure out how someone walks into a building but never walks out."

We had considered tunnels, but she'd never been found again in the system.

Lucy was still alive because Reed and Gabriel spoke about her like they knew something. I had told Evie that.

"And then there's the thing she stole," Evie whispered. "What was it? I feel like I'm asking all the wrong questions."

I felt that. But I was also a soldier. And I didn't ask questions because...

"When I put my trust in Gabriel, it all worked out. I don't want to be that person, but I got the feeling there's something happening they might not want us to know about just yet."

"That's what scares me."

"Speaking of family—" I rolled over onto her. "I've been thinking—" I rushed to explain myself. "I don't care if you're pregnant or not. I love you. I'd like to enjoy just us for now. When you are...*if* you still want that, it'll be because it's good for both of us. And not because someone's out to kill me."

My heart swelled with emotion. "What I'm saying is, if you want to think about it. You don't have to answer now or do *anything*—"

Her smile grew as I talked. "You're giving me a choice."

"Yes." I let out a breath of air. "You have always, always been the one in charge. Evie, I would never—"

She kissed me. And then she rolled me over.

I laid there in awe watching her rise above me taking off that pajama set she called a baby-doll top.

"I don't need to think about it," she whispered, and I swallowed as she worked my tie. "I already know what I want."

And then she kissed me again.

"Good to know."

DEBRIEF PART I

Congratulations...

You've successfully completed your second assignment at Titan Security.

Your third assignment awaits. And it isn't what it seems. Revisit the past to uncover another key piece of the mystery that awaits.

But to do so, you're going to be leaving New York.

Details for your new destination will be disclosed in the following files.

Your next assignment awaits in…

YOUR MISSION CONTINUES

Stroke of Lust
Titan Security Book 3

Pre-Order Stroke of Lust

STROKE OF LUCK

TITAN SECURITY BOOK I

If you liked Evie and Lucas's story and you missed Reed and Alisha's, check it below.

He's the the last man I ever saw coming...

Sexy. Seductive. Sinful.

I had no room in my carefully planned life for romance.

Especially not one dangerous man hellbent on proving he's the right man for me.
But Reed Whittaker has always had a way of tearing down every wall I built with precision.

So when I find myself trapped with nowhere to turn, he becomes my only hope for survival.
The only man who can protect me.
The one man who would burn the world down to keep me safe.
He's a man known for being ruthless and dangerous.

Now? He's mine.

Except I don't know if his luck will run out before he can save me.
Or if the secrets of his world will consume us both.

But I know one thing.
Reed will stop at nothing to make me his.

His woman.
His life.
His love.

And I'm helpless to resist.

Get Stroke of Luck

STROKE OF LUCK EXCERPT

I WAS GOING TO THROW MY DRINK AT THE SLEAZY SUIT AND TIE WITH A cocky smirk, his wedding ring glinting under the club lights.

"Let me take you home tonight."

Biting back a comment, I tried not to let it grate on my nerves that it was because of men like Suit and Tie over here that I was bringing in my twenty-fifth birthday today, a virgin.

Instead of blaming it on life, a tiny dating pool filled with arseholes, and the responsibilities that consumed me?

My frustrations were on this idiot.

I had come to Teasers, one of New York's premier burlesque clubs, intending to escape.

Around me, the 1920's style decor, with floating multi-colored parasol umbrellas and lush, warm lighting, created a wonderland for seduction.

Scantily-clad performers in colorful wings, lingerie meant to be torn off with guests, and feather boas wrapped around their necks—I would have been in girl heaven.

The scent of white sage and flowers from the live plants mingled in the air, usually a comfort—now tainted by Suit and Tie's cheap cologne. Fidgeting with the vines dangling near my shoulder, I leaned back against the plush velvet barstool, trying to maintain distance.

"No, thank you," I replied firmly, but his eyes only widened, his smirk growing.

"Goddamn, your accent is sexy," he was undeterred.

"I'm waiting for someone." *Anyone. But you.*

As he reached out, I scooted further back, but before I could react, a figure in black obstructed my view.

The unmistakable scent of sea and spice filled my senses, and for a moment, I shifted in my seat, my heart pounding.

Reed Whittaker, CEO of Titan Security and the source of all my sexual frustration for the last three years, blocked my view. Broad shoulders. Chocolate hair.

The kind of look that made a woman think twice about her late-night decisions.

"Not gonna happen," Reed rumbled, his rich, velvety baritone laced with quiet menace.

The Suit and Tie sounded offended, his bravado deflating. "Who the fuck are you?"

"Don't even think about it," Reed said in a voice I heard over the music. "Turn around, go back to your friends."

Reed cut an intimidatingly rugged figure even among the common masses, exuding an undercurrent of raw power usually reserved for archangels strolling among humans.

The aura of intensity radiated from him.

Reed liked to make the occasional unannounced visit to Teasers, and by some stroke of luck, I seemed to be there on those nights.

His focus remained fixed on me the nights he was here, ensuring my safety even when I hadn't realized I needed protection.

But I figured that was his job. I told myself it wasn't a big deal. He'd usher me into cabs, steadying me with those large, calloused hands.

Except for that one night months ago when a friend's early departure prompted my exit shortly after.

As I approached the entrance, Reed materialized from the shadows.

Is everything all right? Is there anyone taking you home?...I can.

Why? I can catch a cab...

I just want to make sure you get home safe. Can I do that?

Sure...

Reed walked me to my doorstep, remaining in the hall until I was safely inside.

The entire interaction burned itself into my consciousness. Just a man ensuring a woman's safe passage home. Even though I hadn't so much as touched a drop at the club that night, the memory alone intoxicated me for weeks afterward.

He wanted to make sure I was safe. Without touching me. He never pushed for more.

Almost like he waited until I was comfortable.

A warm heat blossomed within me that had nothing to do with filling any empty space. Just his mere existence was enough to set me alight.

Because I wanted Reed. Lara confided that she trusted him implicitly to protect everyone.

Reed took that responsibility seriously.

I didn't hear what Suit and Tie said to Reed.

He was sputtering before Reed, and even surrounded by the dancers, every eye around me in the club seemed inexplicably drawn to this. Suit and Tie grumbled something under his breath.

The taut line of Reed's shoulders tensed like he was physically restraining himself.

"I'm not going to repeat myself. Get out. Or you can get kicked out."

"Yeah, and who the fuck are you?"

Find Out What Happens
In Stroke of Luck

Book I of Titan Security Series

AUTHORS NOTE

Thank you so much for getting to Stroke of Fate.

If you loved it, please leave a review.

Reviews are great for authors in general.

If you liked this story, you'd love Reed and Alisha in Stroke of Luck, released prior to this book.

You can also subscribe to my newsletter below.

Lots of Love,
Lilah

Subscribe to Lilah's Newsletter

ABOUT THE AUTHOR

Lilah Lance writes romance for all the girls who dream of being seen, being *accepted*, and being loved for *who they are*.

Get exclusive content and giveaways by signing up for Lilah's newsletter on http://lilahlance.com where you can get sneak peeks and news before anyone else.